Elizabeth Jeffrey was born in Wivenhoe, a small water-front town near Colchester, and has lived there all her life. She began writing short stories over thirty years ago, in between bringing up her three children and caring for an elderly parent. More than 100 of her stories went on to be published or broadcast; in 1976 she won a national short story competition and her success led her onto write full-length novels for both adults and children.

Elizabeth JEFFREY

Dowland's Mill

piatkus

PIATKUS

First published in Great Britain in 1998 by Judy Piatkus Publishers Ltd
This paperback edition published in 2012 by Piatkus

A CIP catalogue record for this book
is available from the British Library.

ISBN 978-0-7499-5793-3

Printed and bound by Clays Ltd, St Ives plc

Papers used by Piatkus are from well-managed forests
and other responsible sources.

MIX
Paper from
responsible sources
FSC® C104740

Piatkus
An imprint of
Little, Brown Book Group
100 Victoria Embankment
London EC4Y 0DY

An Hachette UK Company
www.hachette.co.uk

www.piatkus.co.uk

Chapter One

It was a beautiful evening in early April in the year 1910. The sun was just beginning to dip behind the trees on the far side of the River Rowell, sending a shimmering red gold shaft of light across the water towards a heron, standing still at the edge of the incoming tide. Rose Bentley paused for a minute to savour the warm, salty air before resuming her dawdling pace. It was ridiculous of her mother to forbid her and her sisters to walk home from Granny's along the sea wall. It was far prettier than going by the dusty road, even though it was a bit further. Anyway, tonight she was in no hurry, with any luck by the time she reached home the milking would all be done.

A fishing boat came chugging up the river, accompanied by the usual complement of screaming gulls and she stood and watched it pass, waving back to the man on deck. Then she wandered on, stopping now and then to examine a flower or watch the solitary heron. She came to a tiny shingle beach and went to the water's edge to pick up a smooth pebble and skim it over the water. She smiled to herself as the pebble bounced over the water four, five, six times. She hadn't done that since she was a child and she glanced round to make sure no one had seen her, a grown woman of twenty-two, playing ducks and drakes. Satisfied there was nobody about she selected another stone and did it again.

Then she continued happily on her way, busy with her thoughts. Granny was making over a costume of Aunt Madge's for her and she had been for a fitting. Granny was very clever with her needle and Aunt Madge always had nice things so Rose was delighted with the costume, especially as it was

1

green, which suited her colouring. She had a pale, creamy complexion with the faintest dusting of freckles on her nose, deep brown eyes and hair that was long and thick and the colour of ripe chestnuts. The costume would look nice with a high-necked cream blouse, she mused. And she would need a hat, too. Perhaps her mother would let her have some of the egg money to buy one or the other. Probably the blouse. She could always trim up her black hat ...

She had been so intent on mentally refurbishing her wardrobe that she hadn't noticed the gathering dusk. Now, quite suddenly she realised that the sun had gone and that the light was fading fast. In the growing darkness the river bank began to take on an eerie emptiness, there was not a soul in sight now, it was nearly ten minutes since she had passed a man going the other way walking his dog. To her right the river stretched, grey and uninviting now that the sun had set and to her left the saltings, criss-crossed by the cracks and fissures worn into them by tide and weather till they resembled a giant ill-fitting jigsaw puzzle, looked suddenly hostile and menacing in the damp mist that was beginning to rise. The cry of a lone curlew only served to emphasise the emptiness and desolation.

Rose began to hurry. Now she understood the wisdom of her mother's warning and she remembered with a shudder of fear all the ghostly tales of strange lights and shadowy figures on the marshes that she and her sisters loved to frighten each other with as they all sat together in the warm comforting circle of lamplight in the big farm kitchen.

She looked over her shoulder in the forlorn hope that the man walking his dog might be returning, but there was not a soul in sight. The river bank and the marsh were empty as far as the eye could see, except for a few gulls pacing around in the mud and a cormorant sitting on a broken spar. She was completely alone in the falling darkness and there was still nearly a mile to go before she reached the road. She quickened her pace, then, as a gull wheeled close by making her start, she picked up her skirts and began to run.

She ran on and on, holding on to her hat, until at last the stitch in her side forced her to stop. Then, taking stock, she noticed that the path she was on followed the river in a wide curve, and she realised that she would reach the road much more quickly if she were to leave it and cut straight across the marshes. She was desperate now to get back to some kind of civilisation, away from the same river bank that only a short time ago she had seen as such a haven of beauty and solitude. She veered off the path and began to run across the saltings, jumping over the gaps and gullies that were gradually filling as the tide rose, giving a cry of fear when a gull rose white and ghostly from near her feet. She began to run faster, lost her footing and slid into the soft, wet mud of a shallow gully. Her hat fell off as she clambered out but she didn't stop to retrieve it; her one thought was to get to the road before it became too dark to find it and she had nightmare visions of being trapped on the marsh all night, going round in circles because she couldn't see which way to go. The curlew gave its eerie cry and the humps and mounds of marsh grass took on ghostly shapes in the rising mist. A sob rose in her throat and she tried to run faster still, but she was hampered by her skirts clinging wetly round her legs, muddied when she fell. It was rapidly getting darker now and she had to tread carefully so that she didn't fall again; some of the holes were quite deep and she was terrified she might get stuck in the mud. She hurried on as fast as she dared until she came to a long wide gully, more like the bed of a stream. She hesitated for a second, then gathered her skirts and took a desperate flying leap, landing heavily on the uneven ground on the other side to sprawl full length as a searing pain struck her ankle.

She lay where she had fallen for several minutes, sobbing with a mixture of pain and relief. She had hurt her foot, but at least she had cleared the gully! She sat up, shivering and began to rub her ankle, trying to regain her self control. It was stupid to panic like that, she told herself sternly, there was nobody else on the marsh so there was nothing to fear. All she had to do was to keep the river behind her and she would eventually reach the road. Pulling herself together she got up and tried to walk, but it was no use, the injured foot wouldn't bear her weight.

'Help!' she called, her voice rising in desperation, but the only sound that came back was the chugging of a boat on the river, muffled by the mist and too far away to hear her. She stood shivering with cold and fright in the damp evening air, balancing on one leg and trying to think clearly, to decide what she should do.

The nearest house was Dowlands' Mill at the head of Stavely Creek. It couldn't be very far away, in fact as she peered through the mist and gloom she was sure she could see the dim outline of the white weatherboarded mill in the distance. She knew that the Dowland family were known to be strange people who kept themselves to themselves and only communicated with the outside world as it was necessary for their business, but surely they would help her if only she could get to them. Slowly, painfully, she began to make her way towards the pale outline, hopping on one foot until she couldn't hop any further and then getting down on all fours and crawling. Twice she tried the injured foot on the ground but the pain was so bad that the second time she nearly fainted, so thought it best not to try again.

Her progress was agonisingly slow, especially as now she could no longer jump the rills and gullies but had to make a detour until they were narrow enough to manage. The tide was rising fast now, snaking through the gullies over the mud and flotsam left from previous tides, turning bits of wood or old cans into grotesque shapes in the dim light. Rose remembered that sometimes, at very high tides, the whole of the marsh flooded and she prayed that tonight's tide wouldn't be such a one. She didn't want to drown. Oh, please God, she prayed, don't let me drown. She came to a particularly deep gully and was about to turn away to find a way round it when she saw a strange muddy shape in the water. It looked just like a man lying there, she could even see the shape of an outstretched hand. It was a body! A dead body, half covered in mud!

She screamed and began to crawl away as fast as she could, whimpering with terror and not knowing which way she was going except that it was away from that awful *thing* she had seen. Somehow, she never knew how, she reached the safety of the sea wall bordering Stavely Creek and began to crawl along it in the direction of Dowlands' Mill. If only she could get there this nightmare would be over. She vowed that she would never, ever again set foot on this accursed sea wall.

'Bloody hell! What the devil's going on here?' Suddenly, a man's voice cut into the silence. 'Good God, it's a woman!'

Rose cringed away, petrified with fright. She had been so intent on getting to safety that she hadn't noticed him approaching.

'Oh, it's all right. You needn't be afraid. I shan't hurt you,' he said impatiently, 'But what in tarnation's name are you doing, crawling along on your hands and knees at this time of night? You lost something? It's a sure thing you won't find it here in the dark.'

'No. I haven't lost anything ...' She sank into a heap and began to cry, managing to say between huge sobs, 'But I've seen ... Out there, in the mud ... a body ... a dead body ...'

'A dead body! Of course you haven't seen a dead body. Oh, my God, whatever next!' His voice was rough with irritation.

'I tell you I did. I saw it lying there. In the ditch.'

'Don't be so bloody daft, you silly little bitch. I never heard such a load of clap-trap in all my life.'

'But I did, I tell you. It was in a gully, lying there with its hand stretched out.' She shuddered. 'It was horrible.'

'Listen. The river washes all manner of muck up into those gullies,' he said more kindly. 'When you're scared your imagination can play tricks on you. And I can see you're frightened half to death.' He got down on his hunkers and Rose recognised that the man was Michael Dowland, one of the three brothers who ran the mill. 'But what were you doing out here in the first place? That's what I'd like to know.'

She took a deep breath and said unsteadily, 'I was on my way home to Stavely village. I live at Crick's Farm. I'd been to see my granny out at Bramfield and I thought I'd go home along by the river because it was such a lovely evening. But then it began to get dark so I cut across the marshes and I fell and hurt my ankle so I couldn't walk and had to crawl on my hands and knees. And I got more and more frightened when the mist came down and then I saw ... *it*, back there in one of the gullies.' She shuddered again at the memory.

He gave a gasp of exasperation. 'You mean you imagined you did.'

'No, I did. I really did. It was *horrible*.'

He stood up and helped her to her feet. 'I think you'd better

5

come home with me. Might get some sense into you there.' He stared at her. 'Good God, you're in a mess. Look at you, you're covered in mud.'

'I know. I fell in one of the gullies. I was so frightened ...' She tried to stand alone and nearly fell.

He caught her and said more gently, 'Well, you're all right now. You don't need to worry any more, I'll look after you. Hold tight, I'm going to pick you up and carry you. And don't go screaming or making a fuss else I shall leave you here to fend for yourself.' As he spoke he swung her up in strong arms and strode sure-footedly back along the sea wall in the direction of Dowlands' Mill.

With her ordeal on the marsh behind her and the comfort of Michael Dowland's arms round her, Rose had an almost uncontrollable urge to giggle at the thought of being carried through the gloom in the arms of this tall, dark man whom she hardly knew and when she stole a glance up at his shadowy profile and saw the stern, set jaw she began to shake with hysterical laughter that was in fact very near to tears.

'There's no need to be frightened. I told you, you're quite safe now,' he said soothingly, misinterpreting the cause of her trembling, and she felt his arms tighten comfortingly round her.

She rested her head on his shoulder, calmer now. 'I don't know what I'd hev done if you hadn't come along,' she said in a small voice. 'It looked that real ... I was quite sure ...'

'Well, don't think about it any more,' he said, talking to her as if she were a child. 'It's all over now. Look, we're nearly there.'

The moon was up by the time they reached the mill and she could see the big water wheel outlined blackly against the end of the white weatherboarded building and the faint gleam of water on the mill pool to the left of it. But Michael Dowland strode on, over the bridge that spanned the mill stream and across the mill yard, never slackening his pace, to the dark, square bulk of the mill house. Ignoring the front door set between large bay windows he went round to the back of the house, where a shaft of light shone from the window across a cobbled yard and kicked open the door.

Rose blinked, immediately conscious of light and warmth as he carried her across the big kitchen and laid her carefully on the cushioned settle that stood adjacent to the big range.

A small, dainty-looking woman with an old-fashioned lace cap perched on her grey hair was sitting at the long refectory table which took up most of the space in the middle of the room. She put down the intricate embroidery she was doing by the light of the oil lamp and looked up over her *pince nez*.

'Good gracious, Michael, who have you got there?' she asked, pinching them off as she got up from her chair. 'And why are you both covered in mud? Just look at my cushions!'

'She's one of the girls from Crick's Farm, but I dunno what her name is, I never thought to ask,' he said over his shoulder as he straightened up. 'I was too surprised at finding her crawling across the wall on her hands and knees. Look, she's hurt her foot.' He smiled down at Rose. 'You'll be all right now, Miss. My mother will look after you. I'll see you later.' He turned back to the door. 'I must go and see to ...'

'Not until you've cleaned yourself up a bit and had your meal,' the little woman, clearly his mother, said sharply. 'It'll spoil if you don't eat it because Lissa's kept it hot over a saucepan for you.'

'I really haven't got time now. I'll eat when I get back.' He was clearly impatient to be gone.

'Then you must make time. It's all ready.' She turned to a girl sitting at the other end of the table where the light of the lamp didn't quite reach. Rose could see that she was a thin, pale girl, rather plain, with fair hair that was scragged back and tied with a rag. 'Lissa, dear, get Michael's dinner for him.'

The girl immediately put down the sock she was darning and fetched a knife and fork from a drawer in the dresser behind her then scurried to the stove for the plate of meat and vegetables keeping hot there. Then she sat down and resumed her darning.

With an exasperated sigh Michael went over to the sink and washed his hands. 'You've forgotten the salt and pepper,' he said as he dried them and sat down. 'And I'll have a drop o' beer, too, while you're about it.'

Lissa put down her darning again and hurried to get him what he had asked for.

The older woman had watched all this without speaking. When she was satisfied that Lissa had supplied her son with everything he needed she turned to Rose. 'Now, my dear,' she said with a smile, 'let's have a look at this ankle of yours.' She came over to the settle. 'My goodness, you *are* in a mess,' she said with a frown. 'Lissa, dear, get some hot water and wash some of this mud away,' she called over her shoulder. 'Quickly, now.' Then in a softer voice, 'Whatever have you been doing, my dear?'

Rose told her story whilst Lissa cleaned her up as best she could and bathed her foot, which was now badly swollen.

'I see. So you're Rose Bentley from Crick's Farm,' Mrs Dowland said when she had finished, nodding her head. 'Ah, yes, we have dealings with your father from time to time.' Her expression conveyed that those dealings were not always satisfactory as far as she was concerned. She leaned forward and prodded the foot, which made Rose wince. 'I don't much like the look of this. I think we should call Dr Holmes.'

'Oh, no. I don't want that! I think I oughta go home. Me mum'll be worried. I oughta been home hours ago,' Rose said anxiously, very conscious of her Suffolk drawl, very much at odds with Mrs Dowland's clear, precise way of speaking.

Mrs Dowland took no notice. She turned to her son. 'Have you finished your meal, Michael? Then perhaps you'll be good enough to get on your bicycle and go and fetch Dr Holmes. And you'd better call in at Crick's Farm on the way and tell the girl's parents that she's safe.' She turned back and gave Rose's ankle another painful prod. 'Tell them she'll be staying here overnight.'

'Why can't Lissa go? I've got to shut the chickens up and finish off over at the mill. We're short-handed with George and Dan both away.' Michael pushed his empty plate away as he spoke.

'You know very well Lissa can't go,' Mrs Dowland said with a trace of impatience. 'It shouldn't take you long. You can be there and back while you're arguing about it.'

'Oh, all right.' Michael shrugged his coat on again and went off, slamming the door behind him. Mrs Dowland replaced her *pince nez* and picked up her embroidery again, whilst Lissa made Rose a cup of tea and then went to make up the spare bed and put a hot brick in it.

Rose drank the tea and leaned drowsily against the cushions of the settle. She was very comfortable except for the throbbing of her ankle, and even that was more bearable now that her shoe was off and it was resting on a pillow. Looking round she noticed that the big kitchen was well furnished. The long refectory table on which the lamp stood was scrubbed white and a tall oak dresser reached along the whole length of one wall. There was not a thing out of place in the kitchen. The dresser held a whole dinner service in white, with an ivy-leaf decoration round the rim, and shining copper jelly moulds on the top shelf reflected the light from the lamp, as did the copper saucepans hanging graded for size on the wall by the stove. Everything shone, even the black-leaded range and the stone flagged floor was well scrubbed. Conscious of her own muddy appearance, Rose couldn't help contrasting this kitchen with the one at home at Crick's Farm, which was just as big as this but always cluttered and untidy, the floor filthy from the muddy yard and the table usually strewn with crockery that nobody had had time to wash up after the last meal – or the one before it.

'You have brothers and sisters?' Mrs Dowland's voice roused Rose from her reverie.

'Three sisters. One older than me and two younger.' Rose yawned, the warmth of the kitchen making her sleepy. 'I'm sorry. It's the warmth ...'

'And I daresay you're hungry, too.' She turned to the girl at the table. 'Lissa, dear, cut some bread and butter for our guest.'

Lissa put down her darning once again and scuttled to the bread crock where she took out the remains of a loaf. The bread and butter she gave to Rose was wafer thin and spread with real butter, not the margarine she was used to at home. And it was neatly and carefully laid out on the plate; obviously Mrs Dowland had taught her little servant well. Rose ate with relish, she hadn't realised that she was so hungry. Indeed, she could have eaten twice as much, but didn't like to say so.

After she had eaten she dozed off to sleep. She dreamed she

was back on the marsh again and that the body in the gully sat up as she got to it. She woke with a scream.

Mrs Dowland was at her side immediately, soothing her and asking her what was wrong.

'It was that body. That body I saw on the marsh.' She was shaking uncontrollably.

'Body? What body? Whatever are you talking about, child?' Mrs Dowland asked, puzzled.

Rose told her, finishing, 'That man ... your son ... he said it was my imagination. He said all sorts of funny things get washed up into them gullies. But I was certain sure ... I saw its hand,' she whispered.

Mrs Dowland looked at her suspiciously. 'But I thought you said it was dark,' she said.

'It was dark. Leastways it was nearly dark.' Rose put her head in her hands. 'Oh, I dunno whether it was dark or not. But I know I saw something horrible and it looked like ... what I said,' she shuddered.

Mrs Dowland patted her shoulder. 'Well, try not to think about it any more now. I'm quite sure you must have been mistaken, but it might be as well to investigate the matter. When Michael gets back we'll send him out with a lantern.' She glanced up at the clock. 'He seems to have been gone a very long time. I don't know what should have taken him so long. Ah, this must be him now.'

There was a clatter of horse's hooves on the cobbles and then the door was flung open and Dr Holmes strode in, followed by Michael, who looked dishevelled and distinctly put out.

'You were gone a very long time, Michael,' his mother said, while the doctor was examining Rose's ankle.

'So would you have been if you'd had to walk best part of the way,' he snapped. 'I got a b... a puncture before I was at the end of the lane. And Crick's Farm is right at the other end of the village. I'd still be walking if the doctor hadn't given me a lift in his trap.'

'But you told my mum I was all right, didn't you?' Rose said anxiously. 'And you never told her where you found me?'

'Yes, I did. I told her the truth, that you'd fallen on the marsh and hurt your foot and that you'd be staying here the night.'

'Oh, dear, she won't half be cross. I wasn't supposed to come that way.'

'Well, I could hardly lie to her now, could I?' Michael shrugged his shoulders and picked up his cap. 'Anyway, your father is bringing a cart to fetch you tomorrow.'

'That's good.' Mrs Dowland nodded approvingly. Then she frowned at her son. 'But where are you going now, Michael?'

'I told you before, Mother, I've got things to do. With George and Dan both being away we can't expect poor old Jacob to do it all.'

'Well, before you go anywhere else I really think you should take a look on the marsh. If this young lady did see a corpse ...'

Dr Holmes straightened up, suddenly losing interest in Rose's foot. 'A corpse? Where?'

'Of course she didn't see a corpse,' Michael said impatiently. 'It was her imagination. You know what it's like out there when the light fades. You can imagine all manner of things.'

'All the same, I agree with your mother, Dowland. I think we should take a look,' the doctor said, rubbing his hands together with what in other circumstances might have looked like glee. 'You never know, it could be a body washed up from the wreck of that coal barge. You know, the one that sank in the estuary. One of those bodies never was found.'

'Oh, I hardly think so,' Mrs Dowland said doubtfully. 'That storm was a couple of months ago.'

'Ah, but these things take time to get washed ashore, what with wind and tide,' the doctor said sagely.

'It'd need more than wind and tide to wash a body into Stavely Creek from that wreck,' Michael said. 'The way the tides run round here it'd more likely fetch up round Shotley Point.' He nodded. 'All the same, I expect you're right. We'd better take a look, if only to set the young lady's mind at rest. I'll have a word with Jacob and then I'll fetch a lantern.'

The doctor shrugged back into his overcoat. 'The ankle will be all right,' he said as he buttoned it across his ample stomach. 'It's just a bad sprain. Rest it for a few days and it'll be as good as new.' There were obviously more pressing matters on his mind now.

The two men were gone a very long time. They came back filthy and dishevelled and the doctor was not in the best of humours. 'That bloody marsh is a place not fit to turn a dog out on,' he said, then remembering Mrs Dowland, nodded in her direction, 'Begging your pardon, Ma'am.'

She inclined her head. 'No offence taken Doctor. But did you find anything?'

'Look at me, mud up to my knees where I fell in,' he went on as if she hadn't spoken. 'Where's the brandy you promised me, Dowland? I think I deserve something to warm these old bones before I get on my way home.'

Michael produced a small cask of brandy and two tumblers. 'No, of course we didn't find anything,' he said in answer to his mother's question. 'Never thought we would. And we combed that marsh, didn't we, Sir?'

'We certainly did.' The doctor took the brandy and drank it with relish. 'The only thing we found that could possibly have been mistaken for a body was a bundle of old rags that had been caught up in a branch in one of the gullies. I guess to anybody with an over-active imagination it might have looked a bit like a body.'

Rose let out a sigh of relief. 'Oh, thank goodness for that. I must admit I never stopped to look too hard at it. I was too scared. All I wanted was to get away.'

The doctor held his glass out for more brandy. 'Yes, it can be a bit eerie out there when the light begins to fade. But no doubt that's what it was that frightened you, my dear.' He downed the second glass. 'That was a drop of good stuff, Dowland. A keg of that would grace my cellar.' He tapped the side of his nose. 'Is there more where that came from?'

Michael raised his eyebrows and nodded. 'Could be, Doctor. Could be.'

'Good.' He turned to Mrs Dowland. 'I must be on my way. What the young lady needs is a couple of aspirin to calm her down and help her sleep. She'll feel better in the morning.'

After the doctor had gone Michael turned to Rose. 'Well, there you are,' he said, and she wasn't quite sure whether or not he was laughing at her, 'are you satisfied now?'

'Yes,' she said sheepishly. 'you must think I was daft to make sech a fuss. I'm sorry.'

'It's understandable,' Mrs Dowland said gently. 'You had a very bad fright, my dear. But as the doctor said, you'll feel better after a good night's rest, I'm sure. Now let me see. You'll need some sort of a crutch or you'll never manage to get up the stairs. Ah, the broom.' She snapped her fingers. 'Fetch the broom, Lissa, dear.'

'That's all right. She doesn't need the broom. I'll carry her.' Michael came across and swung her up into his arms as if she were no weight at all. 'I reckon if I managed to carry you home from the marsh I can manage a few stairs, don't you?' he said, smiling down at her. As she smiled back at him she noticed how dark, almost velvet black, his eyes were and her heart gave a little skip.

Chapter Two

Lissa came and helped Rose to undress and put on the snowy white cotton night-gown that she had already laid out for her. Then she left Rose in the warm, comfortable feather bed to savour her surroundings by the light of the candle on the table beside the bed.

For Rose, it was the height of luxury to have a bed all to herself, let alone a bedroom. And a feather bed, at that. At home she shared a lumpy flock mattress with her sister Grace, who was two years older, whilst Millie and Babs, their two younger sisters shared a bed at the other end of the room. She turned her head on the soft, down pillow and gazed around. The bedroom suite was heavy and dark, with a huge mirrored wardrobe and a matching dressing table on which stood little rose-patterned china jars and dishes that matched the basin and ewer on the wash stand. Everything gleamed and there was even a carpet on the floor. Rose had never known such luxury.

She leaned over and blew out the candle, noticing that the china candlestick was also rose-patterned, and snuggled down into the soft warmth. Thinking about it now, in the safety and warmth of a comfortable bed, she realised how stupid she'd been to panic and imagine she'd seen a body out there on the marsh tonight. She felt a pang of guilt at the thought of Dr Holmes and Michael Dowland combing the marsh in the dark, knowing they wouldn't find anything. Tomorrow she must be sure and apologise to Michael. He had been very nice to her, considering the trouble she had caused him. She felt a sudden warm glow as she remembered the way he had looked at her and the feel of his arms round her as he had carried her up to bed. He must be very strong, she thought admiringly, being able to carry her like that without even getting out of breath. And he was *very* handsome with those deep set dark eyes and firm jaw. A masterful man, she decided. She sighed. It was a pity she had to go home tomorrow.

She slept soundly and didn't wake until Lissa tapped on her door, bringing her a cup of tea and a jug of water for her toilet. She also had Rose's skirt over her arm.

'I cleaned it as best as I could, Miss,' she said. 'And dried it off in front of the kitchen fire. I took the liberty of washing your stockings, too, and cleaning your shoes. They're still downstairs, stuffed with newspaper so they don't lose their shape.'

'Oh, thank you,' Rose said, surprised. 'But you shouldn't hev bothered. I'm not used to people waiting on me, you know.' She got up on one elbow, surprised at the girl's softly modulated voice and watched as Lissa drew back the heavy velvet curtains. She was very small and thin, and couldn't have been more than sixteen or seventeen, yet she moved with a kind of grace. 'What's the time, please?'

'Just gone seven, Miss. Will there be anything else? Oh, is your ankle better?'

Rose wiggled her toes. 'Thass not too painful at the moment. I dunno whether I shall be able to walk on it, though.'

'I'll bring the broom up in case you need it as a crutch.' She gave a little half smile, 'I'm afraid Michael isn't here to carry you this morning.'

Rose flushed. 'I'll manage all right with the broom.'

Lissa went to the door. 'I reckon Dan will be home today,' she said shyly. 'He's been gone nearly a week so I hope he will. Sometimes when he goes away he brings me home a ribbon for my hair.'

'Who's Dan? Is he Michael's brother?' Rose asked, sitting up in bed and drinking her tea.

Lissa nodded. 'That's right. And George is the other one. Dan's gone to Ipswich to fetch George back.'

Rose frowned. 'Why?'

Lissa frowned too, but her frown was one of concentration. 'Because he's been away too long, I think. He does stay away too long sometimes and then Dan has to go and fetch him back.' Her face cleared and she smiled. 'Dan's nice. He helps me get the coals in.'

Rose smiled back. Lissa was obviously not very bright. 'What about Michael?' she couldn't help asking.

Lissa hesitated. 'Michael's different.'

'Lissa, dear!' Mrs Dowland called from the foot of the stairs, her voice surprisingly shrill and piercing coming from such a small frame.

Lissa hunched her shoulders as if the very words were like a blow. 'I'm coming,' she called and hurried from the room. A few minutes later she was back with a tray on which was a bowl of creamy porridge. 'I'm to tell you that you're to stay in bed as long as ever you like,' she said. 'But I mustn't stay and talk or I'll get all behind with my work.' She gave Rose the little half smile again and hurried from the room.

Slowly, Rose ate her porridge. This was a life of real luxury she thought, smoothing the snowy linen sheet. And Mrs Dowland was so kind, such a gentle lady. She finished her porridge and put the bowl on the table beside her. It was funny the way she called her little maid 'Lissa-dear' as if it was all one word, although occasionally, Rose noticed, she had been rather sharp in the way she said it. Then there was Michael ... Michael who had rescued her like a knight in shining armour. She stretched lazily, wondering whether she would see him this morning. She hoped she would. She swung her legs over the side of the bed. Her feet touched the warmth of the carpet. It was sheer bliss.

When she was dressed she made her way carefully down the stairs to the kitchen, gratefully using the broom as a crutch. On the way she took note of her surroundings, the thick turkey stair carpet and the brass-faced grandfather clock that stood in the hall, its polished weights and pendulum gleaming through the glass bulls-eye in the door. Through an open door at the foot of the stairs she glimpsed a room furnished with deep buttoned armchairs and sofas in red velvet, with red velvet curtains at the deep bay windows. There was a large round table in the middle of the room and a chiffonier standing against the wall and several nice pictures. She would like to have investigated further but she knew it would be rude to stop so she carried on down the hall to the kitchen. Nevertheless, she had seen enough to realise that the Dowland family were well off, everything she had seen reeked of wealth. It didn't strike Rose as in any way strange that in spite of this the family lived in the kitchen.

It was a hive of activity this morning. Mrs Dowland, in a voluminous white overall, was standing at one end of the table kneading dough on a big scrubbed pastry board. The other end was covered with a white cloth and a breakfast place had been set for one. Lissa was busy frying bacon and eggs at the stove, whilst washing his hands at the sink in the corner was a tall, broad-shouldered man in brown corduroy trousers and a checked shirt. Rose noticed that his hair was very fair and curled into the nape of his neck. He turned from the sink for the towel to dry his hands and Rose could see that he was Michael's brother, although he was fuller in the face than Michael, with a fresh complexion and a pleasant, open expression. Not nearly so handsome, though, Rose thought smugly.

Lissa turned and smiled at Rose, a smile that said, 'See I told you he'd be home!' and she fingered the red ribbon that had replaced last night's rag. So this was Dan, Rose decided. She wondered where George was. She slid quietly to a seat on the settle where she hoped she wouldn't be in the way and waited for him to appear.

'Why is George not ready to come home, then, Daniel?' Mrs Dowland's gentle voice had a hard edge to it. 'Surely, he must realise he's needed here?'

'He was doing a spot of decorating for Granny Dowland and he hadn't quite finished it. He said he'd be home in a day or two.' Dan sat down and poured himself a mug of tea while he waited for his breakfast.

'That old woman always manages to find something to keep him longer than he intended to stay,' Mrs Dowland said impatiently. 'Doesn't she realise he's got a mill to run?'

'He doesn't run it single-handed,' Dan reminded her mildly. 'Mike and I do our share. And more besides,' he added under his breath.

'Oh, I know that,' Mrs Dowland snapped. She banged the dough into shape. 'You should have brought him home with you,' she said, her mind only on George.

'Mother! He's my eldest brother. Do you think he's going to take any notice of me? As far as George is concerned I'm still only a whipper snapper. Anyway, Granny Dowland wasn't all that well when I saw her. Her rheumatism was playing her up.'

'She'd say that just to keep you there,' Eve Dowland said. It was quite obvious there was no love lost between her and her mother-in-law.

'Maybe it would have been better if Michael had gone,' Dan said, taking a gulp of tea.

'You know Michael can't bear towns,' Eve set the dough in front of the range to prove. 'He's only happy when he's out on the marsh watching his beloved birds.'

'Here's your breakfast, Dan,' Lissa put a great plate of rashers and eggs on the table. 'I 'spect you're hungry, coming all the way from Ipswich.'

Dan sat down and smiled up at the girl. 'Oh, Lissy, Ipswich isn't all that far. It's only about twenty miles away. But you're quite right, I am hungry. I was up at the crack of dawn and caught the paper train out because I knew we were expecting the grain barge on the morning tide and Mike would need a hand. But I walked back from the station along by the river. It's the best time, the early morning, everywhere's so sparkling fresh. It certainly sharpened my appetite.' He rubbed his hands together. 'Ah, this looks good.' He ate in silence for several minutes before looking up and noticing Rose. 'Hullo. Oh, I'm sorry. Nobody told me we'd got a visitor.' He pushed his chair back and went over to where Rose was sitting.

'Daniel Dowland.' He held out his hand. 'I'm very pleased to meet you. We seldom have visitors to stay at Dowlands' Mill.'

Rose smiled up at him but before she could speak Eve Dowland said, 'She's Miss Bentley, from Crick's Farm. She hurt her ankle on the marsh last night and Michael found her and brought her home. She was rather frightened so we thought it best to keep her here for the night. Her father will be coming for her this morning.' She smiled at Rose as she spoke.

'Miss Bentley thought she saw a dead body on the marsh,' Lissa said importantly, pouring more tea for Dan.

'A dead body? Really?' He cocked a quizzical eyebrow at Rose.

She blushed. 'It was nearly dark. It was very silly of me. I'm afraid I caused a terrible fuss and palaver.'

'Not at all. Is your ankle improved this morning, my dear?' Eve Dowland smoothly changed the subject.

'Yes, thank you. But I still can't bear much weight on it, I'm afraid.'

'Never mind I suggest you rest there until your father comes for you. Are you quite comfortable? Would you like another cushion?'

'No, I'm quite all right, thank you.' Rose smiled gratefully at Mrs Dowland.

'Good.' Mrs Dowland turned to Lissa. 'You can clear the bread-making things away now, Lissa-dear. And pour me a cup of tea. No, I don't want a mug. You know I don't like my tea in a mug. I don't know how many times I have to tell you I like a cup and saucer. No doubt Rose would like another cup, too.' She sat down in the rocking chair opposite Rose and waited for her tea.

Rose studied Mrs Dowland with unconcealed admiration. Although she had been busy with her bread making she still managed to look immaculate. Her overall looked as crisp as newly fallen snow and she was also wearing white detachable sleeves to protect her dress, which she now proceeded to remove and fold carefully. She still adopted the slightly old-fashioned habit of wearing a lacy cap, although this morning it was more in the shape of a mob cap, covering a good part of her grey hair. Her features were sharp and her skin pink and smooth; Rose could imagine that she had once been a very pretty woman. Pretty rather than beautiful. The sudden thought struck her that Eve Dowland looked far too dainty to have given birth to three hulking sons.

Daniel finished his breakfast and stood up. 'That was a real treat, Lissy.' To Rose's surprise he laid an arm carelessly round the shoulders of the little servant girl, who blushed and dropped the potato she was peeling on the draining board. Lissy was like a little bird, Rose mused – or perhaps more like a little field mouse, scuttling about doing her work and shrinking away if too much attention was paid to her. Yet there was something about her that was not unattractive, her shy smile could light up her face and her features were fine and even.

19

And she was obviously willing and eager to please her mistress.

It must be nice to be part of such a happy household, Rose thought with a sigh, and with a pang of guilt she realised that she really didn't want to go home to the mess and muddle that was Crick's Farm.

The mill yard was full of activity by the time Chad Bentley fetched his daughter. The grain barge was tied up at the little jetty and the grain sacks were being unloaded and taken up into the mill by the big sack hoist attached to the gantry that projected from the red-tiled roof. Rose looked for Michael. She wanted to thank him again for rescuing her the previous night but when she saw him he was in mid-air, riding up on the pulley chain with a grain sack, which looked extremely dangerous to her. However, he seemed quite at ease and he waved to her from his vantage point. Disappointed at not being able to speak to him she had to content herself with waving back and then with some reluctance and her father's help climbed up on to the cart.

Her father had climbed up beside her and they were about to drive away when Michael came running over. 'Miss Bentley,' he said a trifle breathlessly, 'I didn't think you'd be going quite so soon. I was going to come indoors shortly to see how you were. Have you quite got over last night's little adventure?'

She smiled down at him as he stood with one hand on the cart looking up at her in a way that made her heart turn over. 'Oh, yes, thank you, except my ankle is still a bit sore.' She turned to her father. 'Did Mr Dowland tell you how silly I was, Dad, getting all frightened out on the marsh in the dark and thinking I saw a dead body?'

Chad Bentley roared with laughter. 'Oh, my goodness, whatever next! No, he didn't tell us that. He just said he'd found you there and that you were frightened. Oh, Rose, my dear, you'll have to learn to curb your imagination.' He turned to Michael. 'This comes from all the ghost stories she and her sisters scare each other with at night by the light of the lamp.' He shook his head, still laughing.

'Never mind,' Michael said, laughing with him. 'I hope your ankle will soon be better, Miss Bentley.' He watched them drive off, waving his hand. When they reached the lane and Rose turned round he was still standing there and he waved again. She waved back. She was sorry to leave the mill, and especially sorry to say goodbye to Michael Dowland. She wondered if she would see him again. She hoped so.

She turned her attention to where she was sitting and with some irritation pulled her skirts more closely round her. The cart was caked with mud and worse because it hadn't been cleaned since it was used to transport the manure from the pig sties, but her father, dressed in old corduroys tied under the knee and a jacket with both elbows out, appeared quite oblivious to the smell.

'I do hope you won't be discommoded for long, Rose,' he remarked as they clattered along. Chad Bentley preferred books to farming and would have liked to have been a school master, spending his life in a book-lined study into which students would only rarely intrude. 'You know it's most inconvenient, with all the lambs ... and the piglets ... and your mother has just procured another sitting of eggs ...'

'It's inconvenient for me too, Dad,' Rose replied. 'And painful.'

He nodded vaguely. 'Yes. I daresay.' He brightened visibly. 'But it will be a good opportunity for you to get the accounts up to date. I believe there may be one or two bills outstanding ...' His voice trailed off.

Rose sighed. Her father should never have been a farmer, but he had inherited Crick's Farm twenty years ago when his own father died. Joshua Bentley had loved farming and had prospered. His one regret in life had been that Chad, his only child, didn't share his enthusiasm, but preferred to sit indoors with a book. Nevertheless, he did his best to enthuse the boy and to teach him all he knew, knowing that after his death the running of the farm would be Chad's responsibility. She looked sideways at him as he held the reins and let old Socrates amble his way home. He had been a handsome man in his time, but now his thick wiry hair was grey and his face weather-beaten and lined with worry through trying to keep up with seasons that moved too quickly for his leisurely pace. And who but her father would name a cart horse Socrates! She slipped her hand affectionately through his arm and squeezed it.

'I'll soon get the accounts back into shape for you, Dad, don't worry,' she said.

He sighed and patted her hand. 'I knew I could rely on you, Rose!'

When she got home the farm seemed even worse than usual because now Rose compared everything with what she had seen and experienced at Dowlands' Mill. The farm kitchen was in its usual pickle, with muddy boots left where they were kicked off, last night's supper dishes strewn among the morning's breakfast things on the table, books that Chad had been reading piled in a heap in the corner and at least one article of clothing on every available chair.

Rose hopped in, leaning on her father's arm and he swept a pile of laundry waiting to be ironed on to the floor so that she could sit down.

'Oh, Dad, now look what you've done, thass all gone in the cat's milk,' Rose said, trying to rescue what she could.

'I didn't notice the cat's milk was there,' he said, all apologetic.

'The cat's milk is *always* there. But never mind, the milk's caked solid anyway and it was only your shirt that went into it.'

'That's all right then.' He beamed at her. 'I'll go over to the office and fetch the books.'

'Oh, hold on a minute, Dad. Let me get my foot inside the door. I'll come over there later on. I've got to face Mum first.'

'That's true,' he nodded. 'Ah, here she comes. I must go. I've got things to do.'

Rose smiled to herself as he hurried away. It wasn't that her father was afraid of his wife, it was rather that she was always pressing him to do things he had no taste for, like hoeing turnips, or sowing the spring wheat, or doing the unpleasant things that had to be done to sheep, or bringing in the cows to be milked. Chad was quite willing to watch the wheat grow, he could stand and do that for hours on end, provided somebody else had actually ploughed the land and sown it in the first place.

Emma Bentley came up the yard, scattering the chickens that were pecking for scraps in all directions. She was a tall, gaunt woman, wearing a man's cap on back to front, a stained and patched black skirt that was stiff with mud round the hem and a jumper full of holes that had stretched completely out of shape. She was trudging along in boots two sizes too big and carrying a bucket of swill, which she deposited outside the back door. Then she washed her hands at the pump before coming in and kicking off the boots.

'So you thought you'd come home then,' she said sternly, eyeing Rose up and down.

'I'm sorry, Mum. I know I shouldn't have come home along by the river and I never will again, I promise. Oh, I was that frightened!'

'Well, all I can say is, it serves you right. Next time perhaps you'll listen to what I say.' Emma's expression softened. 'Let's have a look at your foot, then. Is it very painful?'

Rose held it out. 'Not so very. Not now. But I can't walk on it without it hurting.'

Emma poked it gently, then straightened up. 'Well, there's plenty you can do sitting on your backside. That pile of ironing, for a start. And then you can peel the vegetables ready for dinner. I must go down to the field to help the girls mend the hedge.' As she spoke she was rescuing the ironing blanket from under a chair and putting two flat irons on the stove to heat.

'We oughta hev a man in to do jobs like that,' Rose remarked.

'Do you think I don't know that? But where do you think the money's gonna come from to pay him? If only your father ... Oh, what's the use of talking.' Emma shrugged impatiently and stood back with her hands on her hips to survey the pile of ironing on the table. 'There, I think you can reach everything.'

Rose inched her chair nearer the table. 'It's all right, I'll be able to get what I need, as long as I've got something to hold on to, Mum.' She smiled up at her mother.

Emma smiled back and her stern face was transformed, giving a hint of the attractive girl Chad Bentley had swept off her feet twenty five years ago. The girl who had grown into a disillusioned wife who now viewed her feckless, dreamy husband with a mixture of love and exasperation in equal measures.

After her mother had gone Rose tested the flat iron by

spitting on it and holding it to her cheek. Then she rubbed it on a piece of brown paper to make sure it was clean before pulling the first garment towards her. Ironing was a pleasant little task, even when like today the pile was so high that you couldn't see over the top of it, she thought contentedly. It gave you time to think. And to dream. To dream of Michael Dowland and the slow smile that seemed to transform his features, and to dream that Crick's Farm was as clean and well run as Dowlands' Mill, to imagine the kitchen smelling of wax polish instead of something unnameable but vaguely unpleasant, to think of carpets on the floor and feather beds to sink into at night. She sighed. It wasn't that her mother and sisters didn't work hard because they did, but there was so much to do that they could never catch up, however hard they tried. Rose knew, because she had to share in the daily grind of feeding the animals, mucking them out, milking the cows, collecting the eggs, as well as working in the fields. Her father worked, too, but he was a dreamer and never finished one thing before going on to the next, and so he left a trail of half-finished jobs, and tools that had been forgotten and left out in the rain to rust.

She worked her way through the pile of ironing, seeing Michael Dowland's dark eyes and slow smile in place of the patched shirts and torn skirts. When she was hungry she had some bread and cheese, her mother and sisters would have taken theirs with them and her father never knew when it was time to eat anyway. The ironing finished and the vegetables prepared for the evening meal, she hopped about the kitchen, trying to restore some kind of order out of the perpetual chaos they lived in, a chaos she had never before noticed, having lived with it all her life, until her visit to Dowlands' Mill.

By the time her mother and sisters came in from the milking the kitchen was unrecognisable. Even the floor had been scrubbed. But they didn't even notice. And as they shed their muddy boots and peeled off grubby clothes, too hungry and tired to worry where they put them, the room was soon as bad as it had been before. But they were all so pleased to see her that Rose hadn't the heart to scold them.

It wasn't until they were in bed that night that Grace and the two younger girls, Millie and Babs, had the chance to bombard Rose with questions about her brief stay at Dowlands' Mill.

'Wass the house like? Is it very big?'

'Is it true Mrs Dowland's a dragon? I hev heard ...'

'If she is, she ain't a very big one. She ain't no bigger than Granny Robins.' Robins had been their mother's maiden name. 'She's as dainty as a china doll.'

'Tell us about the house again,' Babs insisted.

'Oh, thass real bootiful,' Rose breathed. 'Better'n than this pig sty any day.' She wriggled irritably on the old flock mattress. 'And the bed was a sight more comfortable, too.'

'I knew there were three brothers,' Millie mused. 'But I've only seen one of them. Are they all handsome?'

'I only saw Michael and Dan. George was away in Ipswich.'

'Well, that's one each for you, me and Grace,' Millie ticked off her fingers.

'I don't want any of them. I've got my Albert.' Grace had been engaged for the past two years to Albert Giles, a farm worker on the next farm.

'But you can't marry. Not while his mother is alive, you've said so yourself,' Babs pointed out.

'Mrs Giles ain't gonna live for ever, is she?' Grace said primly. 'Then me and Albert will be able to hev the cottage to ourselves.'

'Hmph. You might as well marry someone else while you're waiting,' Babs said tactlessly.

'Well, I don't want to, so there. And you can mind your own business, Miss Bossy Boots.'

'Oh, all right. I'll marry one of them myself, then,' Babs said with a toss of her head.

'You're only sixteen. You can't marry for years,' eighteen-year-old Millie told her.

'And then you've got to find someone who'll hev you,' Rose said with a grin. 'And that won't be easy. Now, you two, go and get into your own bed. I'm worn out. And we've all got to be up early in the morning.'

The two younger girls went over to their own bed. 'Tell us about coming home along the sea wall again,' Babs said as she pulled the covers up. 'Did you really see a body?'

'Yes, I did. It was all horrible and bloated ...' Rose blew the candle out, pitching the room into darkness, 'And it reared up ...'

25

Babs screamed and Millie cried, 'Oh, stop it, Rose, do. You'll frighten the wits out of us.'

'Good! Now for goodness sake go to sleep, both of you.' She turned over and put her arm round Grace, who, in spite of the noise was already more than half asleep.

But it was a long time before Rose slept. She thought about Mrs Dowland, such a kind, gentle lady, and about Lissa, her simple-minded little scrap of a maid of all work, who between them kept that lovely house so spotless and shining. But most of all she thought about the two brothers she had met so briefly; Michael, as dark as his brother was fair, and Daniel, as open and friendly as his brother was mysterious. But it was Michael she found attractive and exciting, and it was Michael who had run across to say goodbye to her this morning so perhaps he had found her attractive too. She felt an unfamiliar tingling as she recalled her journey across the dark marsh in his strong arms, and the smell of him, a warm, masculine smell mingled with the smell of salt sea and bran from the mill. It was a smell she savoured, a smell she didn't think she would ever forget.

Chapter Three

The days at Click's Farm resumed their usual pattern of trying to keep abreast of things. Too few people with too much to do made for a messy, demoralised existence and having seen what it was like to live in a house where everything was neat and clean and ran like clockwork Rose found it more and more irksome. But she knew she could do nothing until her ankle was better, so she had to exercise patience and she passed her time trying to restore some kind of order into her father's book keeping, which when left to him consisted of recording money that came in and ignoring the bills, thus keeping up the pretence of solvency.

So each day she hobbled across the muddy yard to what Chad Bentley was pleased to call his office. This was a partitioned-off corner of the barn where he kept an old desk and a comfortable chair, to which he would retreat when life got too complicated. She worked methodically through the untidy mound of papers and on the third morning, when she was congratulating herself on the fact that she could now actually see the desk top, to her amazement Michael Dowland walked in, ducking his head under the low lintel as he came. He was carrying a bunch of daffodils.

'Your father said I'd find you here,' he said, obviously feeling a little awkward. 'I was surprised. I didn't expect to find you at work! I thought I was coming to visit the sick. That's why I brought these.' He thrust them at her.

She buried her face in them to cover her delight at seeing him. 'Oh, aren't they lovely! And such big heads!'

'Oh, they grow well in our garden,' he said carelessly. 'I

expect it's being so near the water. I picked them for you early this morning, while the dew was still on them. They're supposed to be at their best then.' He frowned at her. 'But shouldn't you be resting that foot?'

'I am resting it. Sort of. This is something I can do sitting down, that's why I'm here instead of down in the field with the others.' She made a face. 'In spite of the muddle here I think I've got the best of the bargain!'

He began to prowl round the office as if he didn't want to go but didn't quite know what to say next.

She bit her lip. She didn't want him to go either, but if she were to offer him a cup of tea she would have to take him into the house and conditions in the kitchen were, to say the least, squalid. But as she hesitated he said, 'Well, I suppose I'd better be on my way. I've got to make some deliveries. I'm glad to see you're making good progress.' It was his turn to hesitate now. He went to the door, then turned back and said in a rush, 'When your foot is better you must come to the mill again. If you'd like to, that is.'

'Oh, I would,' she said eagerly. 'I was intending to come back to see you all and thank you for your kindness, as soon as I could walk properly again.'

'Oh, that was nothing.' He waved his hand dismissively. 'We'll look forward to seeing you, then.' He touched his cap and was gone.

Rose sat back in her chair and tapped her teeth with her pencil. He'd come to see her. Michael Dowland had taken the trouble to come and see her. And after all the trouble she'd caused him, too. Her heart felt as if it was bursting and she could dance on air.

Then sanity prevailed and she realised he was probably only being polite. She returned to the depressing work in hand.

But the next day he was back again. This time with an invitation to tea from his mother.

'Tomorrow!' Rose said, dismayed. 'Of course I'd love to come, but I couldn't possibly walk that far yet. My foot is still quite sore and it's nearly two miles.'

'I could take time off from the mill and fetch you in the trap,' he said eagerly. 'Will three o'clock suit you?'

'Yes, but ...'

'That's settled then. I'll be here at three.'

'Yes, I mean no. I couldn't possibly put you to all that trouble, Mr Dowland.' She was so flustered she hardly knew what she was saying.

'Oh, don't worry yourself about that, Miss Bentley. Believe me, I'll be only too pleased to come and collect you.' He smiled at her and his dark eyes seemed to twinkle. 'My name's Michael. Remember?'

She nodded, blushing. 'And mine's Rose.'

'I know. It suits you.' He touched her hand and said softly, 'A real English rose. I'll see you tomorrow, Rose.'

She dressed very carefully for the visit, wearing for the first time the green costume her grandmother had been making over for her on the night she fell on the marsh. Grace had picked it up the previous evening when she went to visit her Albert, who lived with his mother next door to Granny in Bramfield. The costume fitted perfectly, and with her chestnut hair piled into a soft bun on to which her best black hat was precariously pinned Rose felt she looked smart enough to visit the Queen, let alone Mrs Eve Dowland.

She got Babs to pick her a large bunch of primroses from the copse on the edge of the farm and waited for Michael. Her mother approved of the visit. After all, Mrs Dowland had been so kind that she deserved a visit of thanks. Rose had to be very tactful in refusing to take dust-laden jars of jam with mouldy tops as a thank-you gift.

'The mould'll scrape off easy, Rosie. It's my best plum jam from two years ago,' Emma said, hurt when Rose refused it.

'It'll be coals to Newcastle, Mum. Mrs Dowland's got a cupboard full of jams and preserves.' Rose was sure this must be true, although she hadn't actually seen them.

'Oh, all right, then. But what about some eggs? I reckon she'd like some eggs from my speckledy hen.'

Rose recalled the fat, healthy-looking hens that scratched round the mill yard and the ducks that swam on the mill pond. 'Oh, very well. I'll take half a dozen.' She could always leave them in the trap and say she forgot to deliver them.

Michael arrived at three o'clock on the dot and she could see the admiration in his eyes as he helped her up into the trap, putting a clean sack for her to sit on by his side.

'I'm afraid I've got to get back to work,' he said. 'We have to work according to the tides, you see.'

'Oh, I'm sorry. I didn't want to be a trouble,' she said anxiously. 'You must think I'm an awful nuisance.'

'You know I don't think anything of the kind, Rose.' He turned and smiled at her in a way that made her heart do funny things. He went on, 'It's me who's sorry to think I can't spend more time with you. But I'll be finished by the time you're ready to go home.'

When they arrived at the mill yard it was empty apart from the chickens contentedly scratching around. But she could hear the rush of water and the creak of the big mill wheel turning and there was a dull thud of machinery from inside the building.

Michael helped her down and they stood together for a moment drinking in the scene. The mill was a pretty building, the white weatherboarding contrasting with the red tiles of the mansard roof and it presented a picturesque scene as it stood reflected in the mill pond against a background of drooping weeping willows. Rose could see the last of the daffodils making a splash of yellow in the grass under the trees. To the left of the mill the tide was ebbing from the creek and a red sailed barge was making use of the ebb to leave the little jetty, its cargo of grain delivered.

'It's really bootiful here,' she said, not quite managing to conceal her Suffolk drawl. 'If I was an artist I'd paint this scene.'

'Can you paint?' he asked.

She shrugged. 'I dunno. I've never had time to try.'

'Perhaps one day you will.'

'Pigs might fly.'

She waited, content simply to stand in the sunshine with this darkly handsome man whilst the chickens scratched and clucked happily round their feet. She glanced up at him and blushed as their eyes met.

He shifted his feet awkwardly and cleared his throat. 'I'd better take you across to the house. My mother will be waiting for you.' He fell into step beside her.

'Mike! Can you come? I need a hand with this ... Oh, I didn't realise ...' Daniel had come to the door of the mill. As fair as his brother was dark, he was dressed in white overalls, and when he saw Rose he came over to them. 'I beg your pardon, Miss Bentley, I didn't realise you were still standing there or I wouldn't have shouted. But you see, we're still a bit pushed with George not being here.'

She raised her eyebrows. 'You mean your brother still hasn't come back?' she said, surprised. 'Oh, dear. I hope that doesn't mean your grandmother is worse.'

The two men exchanged amused glances. 'Oh, no, she was perfectly all right when I saw her the other day. She's as tough as old boots,' Dan said.

She looked from one to the other, frowning. 'Then what's keeping him there?' She clapped her hand over her mouth. 'Oh, I'm sorry. Thass none of my business.'

'Oh, we know right enough what's keeping brother George in Ipswich,' Michael said with a trace of sarcasm. 'And I can tell you this. It isn't Granny Dowland.'

Rose frowned. 'But I thought that's where he'd gone, to visit his ... your grandmother?'

Dan gave a funny little grin. 'We'll let you into a secret, shall we? That's what we always say when George goes off on one of his benders – drinking sprees to you – that he's gone to see Granny Dowland,' he said.

'Yes, we know it's safe to say that because the Matriarch, that's our name for our mother, isn't even on speaking terms with her, so she's never likely to find out that he never goes near the poor old girl,' Michael explained.

Rose's eyes widened. 'Your brother's a drunkard?'

'Not all the time,' Dan said quickly, 'only now and again, when things get on top of him.'

She looked from one brother to the other. 'But why?'

Michael shrugged. 'Why does the sun shine? That's just the way he is, I suppose. It's his way of escape because he doesn't much like milling. Not that he hurts himself when he is here,' he added under his breath.

'Oh, it doesn't happen all that often,' Dan said. 'When it does, he takes himself off to Ipswich and meets his cronies.'

'And your mother doesn't know about it?'

Michael laughed. 'No, she just gets furious to think he goes to visit Granny Dowland, because she can't stand the poor old

31

dear. But she'd be even more furious if she knew the truth, I reckon.'

Rose frowned. 'But aren't you both worried because he isn't back yet? Or is George usually away as long as this?'

Michael and Dan exchanged glances, then Dan said with a sigh, 'No, he isn't usually away this long. And it is a bit worrying, although we've got a good idea what he's up to. You see, when I was in Ipswich I saw him leaving the Cock and Pye in the company of a woman. I've seen him with her before and anyone can see with half an eye – anyone except George, that is – that she's the kind of woman who won't let him go until she's run through all his money. And if I know my brother George he'll have taken plenty with him.' He gave a sigh. 'But that must have been nearly a fortnight ago because after I'd seen him I went to see Granny, quite thinking he'd be home by the time I got back.' He shrugged. 'I was surprised he wasn't. But no doubt he'll turn up, like the proverbial bad penny, when he's spent out.'

'Oh, yes, he'll be back,' Michael said with a trace of bitterness. 'He always comes back when his money's gone, just like the prodigal son, and just like the prodigal son he'll get the fatted calf killed when he returns, because he's the firstborn and can twist Mother round his little finger.' He stopped. 'But I really don't know why we're telling you all this, Rose. I'm sure you're not interested in our wayward brother.' He shrugged. 'Anyway, most of the time we get along all right with him.'

'And when he's sober and puts his mind to it he can charm a bird off a tree,' Dan added, 'as you'll no doubt find out when you eventually meet him.' He gave a cheeky grin. 'He's nearly as charming as Mike and me, and that's saying something.'

'Don't tease the young lady, Dan,' Mike said with a laugh. He put his hand under Rose's elbow. 'Come along, Rose, you don't want to listen to any more of my brother's back chat. I'll take you indoors.'

Dan raised his eyebrows very slightly but made no comment on Michael's use of her Christian name, contenting himself with saying as he walked away, 'Well, don't be too long. Don't forget I need help with that shaft that's been giving us trouble.'

They reached the back door and Michael opened it for her.

'I've brought the young lady to see you, Mother,' he called. Then, more quietly, 'I'd better get back to the mill, but I'll see you later, Rose.'

Rose nodded eagerly. 'I'll look forward to that,' and she smiled at him as she stepped past him into the big kitchen.

It was just as she remembered it, clean and shining with not a thing out of place. Eve Dowland was sitting in the rocking chair by the fire with lace-making bobbins today. The fire was necessary because even on such a warm April day the north-facing room had a chill to it. She was wearing a dark blue afternoon frock with white collar and cuffs and a white embroidered apron. A white lace cap was pinned to her hair. As always she looked neat and prim. Lissa was at the table cleaning knives, a sacking apron protecting the white one underneath and her straggly hair escaping from the red ribbon that was supposed to tie it back.

Rose hobbled across and gave Eve the primroses. 'Just a little thank-you for your kindness the other night,' she said, kissing her cheek.

'It was nothing, my dear. Nothing at all. Sit down, there on the settle.' She shook her head. 'Oh, dear, I can see your foot is still painful, you should have waited until it was better before coming, my dear.'

'But ...' Rose frowned. Why should Mrs Dowland say that when it was she that had issued the invitation?

'Never mind, you're here now. Michael said you were anxious to come and it was really kind of you to bring me primroses,' Eve buried her face in them. 'I've always loved primroses, they really *smell* like spring, don't they?' Her voice changed. 'Lissa-dear will you find a vase for these?' she called. 'The copper one on top of the dresser, I think. Come along now, child, take them before they drip on my lace.'

Lissa scuttled over and took the flowers. 'I was just putting the cups and saucers on the tray,' she said, 'but I'll do the flowers first.'

'No, put these on the draining board until you've made the tea,' Eve said with exaggerated patience. 'You can do them later. And take that sacking apron off, Lissa. You know very well you only wear that when you're doing dirty work. Make the tea first. I'm sure Rose – such a pretty name, you don't mind if I use it, do you? – is ready for a cup of tea.' She turned to Rose, 'Isn't that right, my dear?'

Rose nodded and smiled. 'There's no hurry. I wouldn't want to put Lissa to any trouble.'

'Oh, you don't have to worry about *Lissa*,' Eve said with a little laugh and a wave of her hand. 'She likes to be kept busy, don't you, Lissa-dear?'

Rose looked over Eve's head to where Lissa, still holding the flowers, was pouring milk into the cups 'Oh, yes, I'm always busy,' she said flatly, without looking up.

Rose stared at her. There was something in the girl's tone that gave the impression that she wasn't happy, although why that should be, living in this lovely house and with such a kind mistress, Rose couldn't think. She pursed her lips. If Lissa were to visit Crick's Farm she would soon realise which side her bread was buttered, she thought grimly.

Lissa brought over the tray daintily set with two cups and saucers and a plate of little biscuits and placed them on a stool near Mrs Dowland.

'Do have one of my biscuits, Rose,' Eve said, ignoring the girl. 'They're fresh. I only made them this morning.'

Rose bit into one. 'Mm, delicious. And you made them yourself, Mrs Dowland? How clever of you. You must enjoy baking.'

Eve gave a shrug. 'I don't. Not really. But I've no choice. Someone's got to do it.' She leaned towards Rose and there was a faint waft of lavender. 'Lissa can't cook at all,' she whispered conspiratorially. 'She's too heavy handed to make pastry, her cakes always sink and heaven knows what she does with her bread! It's hardly fit to give to the animals.' She half turned as Lissa went out of the door with two steaming half pint mugs of tea for Michael and Dan, then went on, 'She's not the brightest of creatures, you understand. Oh, she can manage the cleaning, preparing vegetables and such, but I couldn't trust her with anything that needed too much intelligence.'

Rose nodded. 'I see.' It was in keeping with such a kind lady as Mrs Dowland that she would give employment to a simpleton. She sipped her tea. 'Well, Lissa makes a good cup of tea, whatever else she can't do. Has she been with you long?'

Eve Dowland looked at her over the rim of her cup. She

took several sips before replying. 'Oh, yes,' she said at last. She leaned forward and picked up the plate. 'Another biscuit?'

Rose took one. 'She's very lucky to live in such a beautiful house, too,' she breathed, gazing admiringly round the kitchen.

'Yes, it's a very nice house. It belonged to my father-in-law.' Eve nibbled a biscuit. 'But you live in a farmhouse, don't you? I've always thought how nice it must be to live on a farm.' She gave a faint sigh. 'Of course we've got chickens and ducks and a few cows, but it's not the same, is it?'

Rose gave a most unladylike grunt. 'Living on Crick's Farm isn't very nice,' she said gloomily. 'Me and my sisters have to work from morn till night every day, looking after the animals, working in the fields ... '

Eve raised her eyebrows. 'You and your sisters? But that's not women's work. What about the men?'

'There ain't any. Oh, we did hev an old man working for us until a few years ago, but he upped and died and me dad can't afford to employ anyone else, so now we have to do everything ourselves, me and me sisters.' The words came tumbling out so fast that she forgot to be careful of the way she spoke. 'And Mum, o' course. She works harder'n anybody. Oh, I can't tell you how much I hate it. I hate the mud and mess, I hate the muddle we live in because nobody's got the time to clear it away. I hate always heving to wear dirty old clothes and boots because the work is so filthy; I hate the fact that we never seem to ketch up even though we work from dawn till dusk; I hate it because there's never enough money ... ' She paused and with a horrified look put her hand over her mouth. 'Oh, I'm sorry, Mrs Dowland,' she said, trying to refine her voice a little. 'I shouldn't have run on like that. Whatever must you think of me?'

Eve patted her hand. 'It's quite all right, my dear. It's probably done you good to talk about it. We all have our troubles, don't we?' She smiled again. 'Although I must say that to look at you today nobody would ever know you had to work so hard. Look at your hands. They're beautifully soft and white.'

'They won't be, this time next week when my ankle's better and I get back to doing my proper share.'

'You look quite charming in that green costume. It suits you,'

Eve interrupted. She put out her hand and touched Rose's hair. 'And such lovely hair. I've always admired that chestnut colour, its so unusual. You really are a very attractive girl, Rose.' She put her head on one side. 'It won't make you conceited, my saying that, will it? No, of course it won't.' She leaned over and poured more tea. 'Now let's talk of other things. Tell me about your family. How many sisters did you say you have?'

Half an hour and two cups of tea later, when Rose had told her new friend practically everything there was to tell about her family, Eve got to her feet and Rose realised it was time to leave.

'I hope you'll come and see me another day, Rose,' Eve said, offering her cheek again. 'I don't often leave the mill except on Sundays when I go to church – my arthritis, you know – so you can come and see me anytime. You'll always be welcome.' She turned and saw the knives and cleaning materials strewn across the table where Lissa had left them when she made the tea. 'Tch. Tch. Where's that girl got to! She'll find any excuse she can to get out of the house!'

'I saw her take Dan and Michael a mug of tea each,' Rose volunteered as the door opened and Lissa came back.

'I had to stay and help Dan with something,' she said breathlessly, as if she'd run across the yard. 'I'll finish the knives now. It won't take me long.' She tied the sack apron back on, picked up the cloth and began polishing as if her life depended on it. Suddenly, she looked up. 'Oh, I nearly forgot. Mike says he's ready when you are.'

'Then you can run across and tell him Rose is ready now.'

'She's only got to . . . '

'*Now*, Lissa.'

'All right.' Lissa threw down her polishing cloth and went off.

Eve watched her for a minute or two, then shook her head. 'She can be quite difficult, sometimes,' she said. She turned and smiled sweetly at Rose. 'Now, don't forget. Come and see me whenever you like, Rose my dear. You'll always be welcome at Dowlands' Mill.'

'Did you have a pleasant afternoon?' Michael said as he helped her up into the trap.

'Yes. Very.' Rose gave him a sidelong glance. 'But you told me your mother had invited me.'

'What do you mean?' he asked innocently.

'Well, your mother seemed to think I'd asked to come today. She didn't say anything about inviting me.'

'Ah. Well ...' A smile spread across his face.

'It was *your* idea, Michael, wasn't it?' she said, understanding dawning. 'You arranged it all, didn't you?'

He nodded. 'That's right. I had to think of some excuse to keep seeing you and that seemed as good as any.' He turned and looked at her. 'You don't mind, do you, Rose?'

She shook her head, unable to speak for a minute because her insides all seemed to be turning to jelly. 'No, I don't mind at all,' she whispered at last.

'Good.' He smiled at her. 'Then we don't need to be in any hurry to get you home, do we?'

'I dunno. I really ought to be home to help with the milking,' she said doubtfully.

He grinned. 'You can't do milking with a bad foot.'

'I don't milk with my feet, silly.' She burst out laughing.

He looked at her thoughtfully. 'It's nice to hear you laugh, Rose. Do you laugh a lot?'

She hunched her shoulders. 'I dunno, really. Only when there's something to laugh at, I suppose. Or when I'm happy.'

'And are you happy right now? This minute?'

She tucked her arm into his. 'Oh, yes. Very happy.'

That evening she waited impatiently for bedtime. That was the only time the four girls had the opportunity to share confidences because there was precious little time for talking during the busy working day.

But when they all got to bed that night Grace was far too full of her own news to listen to what Rose or anybody else had to say.

She had already told them briefly over supper that the head cowman on the farm where her Albert worked had died and the farmer had offered Albert his cottage but now she expanded on it until Rose felt she knew the ins and outs of old Darby's cottage as well as she knew her own home.

'But what about Albert's mum?' Rose asked when she could get a word in. 'I thought you said he couldn't never marry, not while she was alive.'

'Well, that was what we thought. Because we knew we could

37

never afford to rent a place, not with him heving to pay his mother's rent as well. But this cottage is rent free, Mr Bowcher – that's the farmer – said, that'll make all the difference. Albert is going to talk to his mum tonight. See what she's got to say.'

'He shouldn't oughta do that,' Millie said from the other bed. 'He should tell her straight out that you and him are to be wed.'

'Oh, he couldn't do that, not with her bad heart.' Grace was appalled.

'If you ask me, her heart's only as bad as she wants it to be,' Millie said. 'You never hear her complain when she wants to go apple picking, do you? Granny says ... '

'Never you mind what Granny says,' Rose said sternly, 'You know right well how Granny and Mrs Giles argue over the fence. They're never happy unless they're rowing with each other.' She cuddled her elder sister. 'I do hope it all works out for you, Gracie. You've been walking out with Albert these last five years so thass high time you were married and settled in your own house. And it'll be so much better than living with Albert's mother. She's nice enough, but Millie's right, you know, she doesn't half play on having a bad heart when things don't go her way.' She sighed. 'Oh, it must be nice to be married.' As she spoke a picture of Michael Dowland rose before her and she felt herself blushing into the darkness.

Chapter Four

Two days later, whilst Rose was continuing her battle to restore some order into her father's finances, Chad came into the office rubbing his hands and looking extremely pleased with himself.

She looked up. 'I dunno what you've got to look so happy about, Dad,' she said reproachfully. 'I've jest found a whole stack of unpaid bills tucked into the back of this ledger. Did you know they were there?'

'Of course I knew they were there. I'm not entirely disorganised,' Chad said cheerfully. 'That's my filing system. That's where I put the bills as they come in.'

'But do you know how many there are here? Do you know what they all amount to?'

He nodded sagely. 'I could make a rough guestimate, yes. Anyway, there aren't as many as there were. I paid one last week.'

'Which one?'

'Oh, I don't remember. To the farrier, I think. I know it was for ten and sixpence.'

Rose sighed. 'Oh, Dad, thass a drop in the ocean! Don't you realise these bills total well over a hundred pounds?'

He dropped a kiss on the top of her head. 'You worry too much, Rose dear. We shall be selling lambs at the market in a week or two. Then there'll be haymaking. Soon we shall have enough money to pay all the silly bills.'

'Except that more will have come in by that time. Plus the fact that we shall need to buy . . .'

'First things first, Rose dear. Let's sell the lambs and make the hay, then we'll worry about what to do with the money. Something will turn up, dear, it always does.' He leaned over and took the ledger from her, closing it firmly. 'Anyway, I've got something much more important to talk about than finances. What do you think?'

'I can't imagine, Dad,' she said, with more than a touch of exasperation. 'Tell me.' She leaned back in her chair.

'Well, I've been to Dowlands' Mill this afternoon to fetch bran for the animal feed ...'

Rose felt a flush spreading over her face but she counteracted it by saying briskly, 'Did you pay for it?'

'You know I never pay at the time. I have an account with them.'

'And when was it last paid?'

'Oh, I don't remember.' He made an impatient gesture. 'Don't prevaricate, Rose. As I said, I've been to Dowlands' Mill and I saw young Dowland – you know, the dark one, the one who's been to see you several times.'

She nodded, feeling her colour rise even further. 'You mean Michael.'

He sat down on the corner of the desk and picked at the torn sleeve of his jacket. 'What do you think of him? Michael Dowland?'

'He's all right,' she said in a masterpiece of understatement. She riffled through some papers to cover her sudden embarrassment. 'Why do you ask?'

'Because he's asked me if he can walk out with you.' He paused. 'With a view to marriage.'

Her head shot up in surprise and her heart missed several beats. She knew Michael liked her but she hadn't dared to hope ... and so soon ...! Somehow she managed to keep her voice level. 'And what did you say to that?' she asked, trying to sound as if she'd known all along.

'I said that I had no objections to you walking out, but I did feel it was a little soon to talk of marriage. After all, you hardly know each other. What is it? A fortnight? Three weeks since you hurt your foot? It can't be more than that. And you didn't know much about him before then, did you?' He rubbed his chin. 'At the same time, you're twenty-two now. Old enough to know your own mind. I wouldn't want you to have

40

to eat your heart out for five years like poor Grace and Albert, so when – if – it comes to it I'd be happy with a fairly short engagement.'

She stood up and flung her arms round his neck. 'Oh, thank you, Dad.'

He caught her arms and held them. 'You're fond of him, then?' he asked, his eyes searching her face. 'You're sure this is what you want?'

She nodded. 'Oh, yes,' she said firmly, 'I've never been more sure of anything in my life.' Suddenly she felt as if she was dancing on air and for the rest of the day she had to add up every column four or five times and even then they wouldn't come right.

Her mother was less euphoric when she heard the news.

'What about this Michael Dowland then, Chad?' she asked as she and her husband lay in the big bed they had shared all their married life. It was the only place where they could talk without fear of interruption, although most nights they were too tired for much conversation. But this was important. 'Is he good enough for our Rose?'

Chad didn't answer for several minutes and she thought he'd fallen asleep, so she nudged him. 'I was thinking, dear,' he said slowly, 'and insofar as anybody is good enough for our Rose, yes, I think he is. He's well-spoken and polite and he comes from what I believe to be a good family.'

'You don't sound very sure, Chad. What do you mean, what you *believe* to be a good family?'

'Well, to tell you the truth, Emma, although I've been dealing with the Dowlands practically all my life I could never really say I know all that much about them, except that the oldest son – what's his name? George, I think – is a bit of an oddity. I've never been quite sure whether he drinks too much or whether he's ninepence in the shilling.' He paused briefly and then went on, 'I would hazard a guess that as a family they're quite well-off, millers are not generally renowned for being paupers and the mill is well kept and in a good state of repair, but as they've always kept themselves to themselves and never been people to mix much in the village I wouldn't know anything about their personal finances.'

'No,' Emma mused, 'they've never been people to mix much.'

'Then again, neither have we, so I couldn't hold that against them,' Chad reminded her, determined to be fair.

'We're always too busy for much of a social life,' Emma said with a sigh. Then she added, 'Of course, as you say, millers are always prosperous,' in a tone that conveyed it was a pity Chad's family hadn't been millers. She screwed up her face in the darkness. 'It's just that I don't understand why the man should want to court Rose after such a short acquaintance. After all, they hardly know each other.

Chad put his arm round his wife and pulled her towards him. 'I hardly knew you when I decided I wanted to marry you, Emma. I saw you on that merry-go-round at the Fair with your sister Madge and I thought, "That's the girl I'd like to marry", and six months later I did.' He pulled her to him and kissed her. 'I've never regretted it. Have you?'

'No, I've never regretted marrying you, Chad. But I wish you'd been able to do what you wanted and become a school master, instead of being trapped here on the farm. You're no farmer, lad, although you try hard enough.'

'I know it.' It was his turn to sigh.

'It's a pity we don't know a bit more about them,' Emma went on, pursuing her former train of thought. 'We know more about Albert Giles and his family than we do about the Dowlands. And the Giles' live in the next village.'

'Oh, be reasonable, Emma. That's hardly surprising. The Giles family have lived next door to your mother since long enough before we were married.' Chad shifted his position and the bed springs gave a protesting groan. After several minutes he said thoughtfully, 'Of course, the Dowland boys didn't go to school in Stavely, did they? They were sent into Ipswich for their education.'

'Ah, yes, that's right. So the family can't be short of a copper. And that would account for them being so well-spoken, too.'

'Yes. And also for them not mixing much in the village. Except in the line of business. And in that I must say I've always found them fair. And reasonable,' he added, remembering that they never pressed him to pay his account in full.

'Like their father before them. He was a decent man, as I remember. But he's been dead these ten years and more. Ha, wait a minute. Wasn't there a daughter, too?'

Emma frowned into the darkness. 'I don't remember seeing a girl, Chad. But there, I've never seen much of the boys, either.'

'I believe there was a girl, Emma. Yes, that's right, she often used to be about with her father. He doted on her, as I remember. Used to call her his little Nelly, or Melly – some such name. I never knew what became of her after he died.'

'I expect she's married and moved away now.'

'Yes, I reckon that's about it. Well, anyway, I think Rose could do a lot worse than marry young Michael Dowland. He seems a hard-working, upright kind of man and she'll be marrying into a good family. They'll make a handsome couple.'

Emma yawned. She'd had a long, hard day, as usual. 'Well, as long as you're happy about it, Chad, I'm satisfied.'

'Yes, I am. To my mind it was a blessing in disguise, young Rose getting herself in such a state on the marsh that night,' Chad said firmly. 'Because if it hadn't been for that I don't suppose they would ever have met.'

Rose was blissfully happy to be walking out with such a tall, handsome man as Michael Dowland and she held his arm proudly as they walked along Stavely village street on Sunday afternoons, knowing full well that a good many eyes were watching their progress from behind lace curtains. It was not often that Michael Dowland was seen in the village, and never on foot, so there was a good deal of speculation about this new relationship. But no one could deny that they made a handsome couple, he in his blue serge suit and bowler hat, and carrying a gold-topped cane; she in her green costume and cream, lace-trimmed blouse, with her newly-trimmed black hat perched at a jaunty angle on her chestnut hair.

They met whenever Michael could get away from the mill and Rose could be spared from the farm. He showered her with presents, a brooch, a tortoiseshell comb for her hair, a watch to hang from her lapel. He even bought her a bicycle so that they could visit the beauty spots of the district and picnic

43

in the fields. It seemed as if he couldn't do enough for her and Rose knew that her younger sisters often looked enviously at her when she came home with yet another trinket.

But not Grace. Grace refused to be impressed, saying, 'Me and Albert've got better things to spend our money on than fol-de-rols now we're to be wed.' Their wedding was fixed for the second week in June and she was busy preparing for it.

Rose didn't care what Grace thought. She was happy and loved nothing better than to walk hand-in-hand with Michael along by the river whilst he named the plants and grasses that grew there and pointed out to her the places where different sea birds nested.

One day as they were sitting side by side on the river bank watching the barges and fishing smacks plying the river she put her head on his shoulder and sighed contentedly.

'It's funny, isn't it?' she said – she tried never to say 'ain't' in his presence now and was always careful of the way she spoke. 'I thought I'd never want to see this marsh again after that dreadful night when I hurt my ankle.' She moved even closer to him. 'But I don't mind a bit when I'm with you.' She smiled up at him and squeezed his arm. 'Oh, Michael, you must have thought I was a silly little goose that night, crawling along on all fours and gabbling about having seen a dead body.' She began to laugh.

He didn't share her laughter. 'I think you should try to forget all about that night, Rosie, my love,' he said seriously, putting his hand over hers. 'It's all in the past now and I wouldn't want the memory of it to turn you against the marsh. Because to me this is a beautiful place, so quiet and peaceful, and there's so much to see.'

'It won't, I promise you. But I'll bet there aren't many couples who can say they met over a corpse that didn't exist.' She gave another little giggle. 'See, I can even joke about it now.'

He turned and looked into her eyes, his expression sombre. 'But we did meet. That's the important thing,' he said softly and leaned over and kissed her cheek.

She put her hand up to where his lips had been. He didn't often kiss her, which she felt was only proper, although she had to admit that she liked it when he did. But in her innocence she considered that it would be quite wrong to show too much affection before they were married.

Therefore she was quite horrified to discover that her sister Grace had no such inhibitions.

They were moving bales of straw one day when Grace said, 'If you do this instead of me, Rose, I'll do your milking for a whole week.'

Rose straightened up and stared at her sister. 'Why? Whass wrong with you? Turned weak all of a sudden?'

'Well, thass a bit heavy. It hurts my back.' Grace didn't meet her eyes as she spoke.

'You've never complained before. And I've seen you do heavier work than this. Come on, if we both get at it it'll soon be done.'

'No. I can't. I'll hurt meself.'

Rose frowned and leaned on the side of the cart. 'Whass the matter with you, Grace? Are you ill?' She studied her sister. 'Come to think of it, you do look a bit peaky.'

Grace lifted her chin. 'No, I'm not ill.' She hesitated for a moment and then said in a rush, 'All right. If you must know, I'm heving a baby.'

'You're *what*?' Rose dropped the bale of straw and almost screamed the words at her sister.

'I'm heving a baby.' Grace looked her straight in the eye as she said it.

'But you don't get married till next month! How can you be heving a baby?'

'Well, things jest got a bit outa hand, thass all,' Grace said with an unrepentant shrug. 'You know how it is. You know how when you get kissing and cuddling you get hot for each other ...' Wide-eyed, Rose shook her head in disbelief, but Grace didn't notice and went on, 'Well, one night ... like I said, things got a bit outa hand and we went too far, and after that, well, we'd done it once so we couldn't help doing it again.' She looked up at Rose. 'You must know how it is. You and Michael ...'

'Me and Michael don't do things like that,' Rose said primly. 'We're waiting till we're married.'

'Well, all I can say is, if you have to wait as long as Albert and me have had to, you might change your tune,' Grace said, with a trace of bitterness. 'And we wouldn't be getting wed now if his mother had her way.'

'Does she know? About the baby, I mean?' Rose asked, nodding toward's Grace's flat stomach.

'No. Nobody knows, except you, so don't you let on. I only jest know meself, so with any luck when it's born people will think it's come a bit early, thass all.'

'I wonder what Albert's mother will say. Is she still trying to stop Albert leaving home?'

'Yes. But she won't. Especially not now we've set the date. If she kicks up too much fuss Albert will tell her straight out that he's got me in the family way so he'll have to marry me. She can't argue with that, can she!'

'What a good thing you've got that cottage to go to.'

Grace gave a little secret smile. 'P'raps thass what did it. We were so excited we forgot ourselves. He was all over me and, well ...' she gave a little shrug, 'men are all alike, aren't they?'

'No. Michael isn't at all like that, I'm pleased to say,' Rose lifted her chin as she spoke.

Grace sniffed. 'There must be suthin wrong with him, then.'

'No there's not. He respects me, that's all.' Michael went up several more notches in Rose's estimation.

Grace married her Albert on the second Saturday in June. It was a quiet wedding. She wore her best dress and a pretty hat she had borrowed from Aunt Madge because there was no money to spare for finery. After the wedding breakfast, which Emma and the girls had prepared, the happy couple went off in a shower of rice to begin life together in the little cottage on the outskirts of Bowcher's Farm. Albert's mother didn't see this. She had managed to get to the wedding but had been so upset at losing her only son that she had had to be taken home in a tumbrel as soon as she had eaten her fill.

A week later, Michael took Rose to Ipswich on the train.

'Why?' she asked as they sat together in the otherwise empty compartment. 'Why Ipswich?'

'You'll see,' he said mysteriously. 'But I'm glad you've put that nice green costume on. I like you in it. It suits you.'

She didn't tell him she'd had no choice because it was all

she had to wear. Instead she tucked her hand into his arm and smiled up at him expectantly. Ever since her conversation with Grace she had felt differently towards Michael. Instead of being glad that he hardly ever put his arm round her and almost never kissed her, now she wished that he would, and she gave him every opportunity. She guessed he held back because he was shy.

'Is your brother George still in Ipswich?' she asked, as the train rattled along.

'Goodness knows where he is,' he answered. 'The Matriarch got into such a state that I came to look for him again only last week, but although I went to all his old haunts I couldn't find him.'

'Hasn't he even written?'

'No. I reckon he's too ashamed of what he's done. The fact is, we've since found out that he took more money with him than he was entitled to and by the time he'd spent out I reckon he didn't dare come back and face the music. Of course, it'll get worse and worse because the longer he stays away the harder he'll find it to come back.'

'But he ought to have written, didn't he? Thass – that's the least he could have done. I know how your mother frets about him.'

'Yes. And of course we've had to tell her the truth, that he never goes near Granny Dowland.' He shrugged. 'That didn't go down too well, I can tell you. But even though she knows now that he's a drunken sot she still thinks her blue-eyed boy will come back. And when he does, you'll see, all will be forgiven,' he added with a trace of bitterness.

'You think he will come back, then? Eventually?'

'He always has, although he's never been away for as long as this before. But who can say? I tell you this, though, if and when he does come back he'll have to alter his ways, Dan and me'll see to that. He won't be able to idle and drink his time away while we cover up for him. Not any more.' His mouth closed in a thin, hard line.

'Perhaps he realises that. Perhaps that's why he's not in any hurry.'

'Yes. Perhaps it is.' His mood changed and he smiled at her and squeezed her arm. 'But we don't want to spoil the day

47

thinking about George, do we? Come on, this is where we get off.' As the train drew to a halt he opened the carriage door and got out, then turned and helped her down.

'Why are we here? Where are we going?' she asked, her eyes bright with excitement. She had never been to Ipswich before.

'You'll see when we get there, Miss Nosy,' he said mysteriously, putting a finger on her nose and smiling again.

They walked up the long road to the Butter Market. Rose hung on to his arm because she was a little frightened of the big buildings and the traffic. She had never seen so many motor cars before in her whole life and the trolley buses clanking by made her jump.

'No. I don't like towns much, either,' Michael said, putting his hand reassuringly over hers.

'Then what did you bring me here for?' she said with a laugh. She was beginning to find it all quite exciting now she was getting used to the noise.

'Well, it's like this,' he began slowly. 'Now your sister Grace is married I thought it was time we made our engagement official and you can't buy engagement rings in the village, so I thought we'd better come here.' He glanced at her, his eyes dancing. 'Is that all right by you?'

'All right by me!' Her voice was almost a squeal she was so excited. 'Oh, Michael, I think it's a wonderful idea! But why didn't you tell me thass what we were coming for?'

'I wanted to surprise you.'

'Well, you've certainly done that. You've quite taken my breath away!' She put her hand over her heart. 'Oh, mercy me, I'm all of a fluster.' She took a deep breath. 'I don't know what to say.'

He laughed aloud. 'You don't have to say anything, Rosie. It was worth springing it on you like that just to see your face!' They walked on a little way, then he said, 'I've already seen the ring I want you to have, Rosie. It's got a blue stone in it.' He nodded encouragingly. 'It's very pretty.'

'Oh, Michael Dowland! I'm sure it is! I can't wait to see it. Why, if we weren't in the middle of the street I'd kiss you here and now.' She looked up at him adoringly.

'So what do you say to getting married a month from now?'

he asked eagerly. 'Your father said he favoured a short engagement and so do I.' He put his head on one side. 'Will a month give you time to do the things girls have to do before they get wed?'

'You're in a mighty hurry, aren't you?' In her excitement she didn't know whether she was laughing or crying.

He smiled at her again. 'Yes, you're right, Rosie. I'm in a mighty hurry. I want to make you my wife.' He slid his arm round her waist. 'But first, come on, I want to buy you this ring.'

Rose never told anyone but the ring wasn't *quite* what she would have chosen herself. It was a tiny blue sapphire, with an even smaller diamond either side, set into a plain gold band. Privately, she compared it with the ring Albert Giles had laboriously saved up out of his farm-worker's wages to buy her sister Grace. Hers had five stones in it, all bigger than these. But she said nothing, because Michael seemed so delighted with his choice and he kissed her on the lips, right there in the shop in front of the jeweller, as he slipped it on her finger, making her blush bright red.

Afterwards they went to a little tea shop at the corner of the Butter Market where they sat in the window and celebrated with tea and cream cakes and discussed their forthcoming marriage.

'You won't mind living at the mill, will you, Rose?' Michael asked anxiously. 'Only it would be difficult for me to live anywhere else on account of the way we work. With the tides and everything, you understand. Sometimes we have to do a night shift.' He took a large bite out of a chocolate eclair.

'I think the Mill House is the loveliest house I've ever seen, and I'll be very happy to live there,' Rose answered warmly. In truth there was nowhere in the world she would rather live, but she didn't tell him that. 'But what about your mother? How will she feel, having me there?'

'She likes you. She says she'll be glad of your company. She'll like to have another woman about the place.' He waved his hand. 'You can't count Lissa, and Mrs Slaughter is only there in the mornings to do the rough work.'

'You mean you've already spoken to your mother?' Rose frowned. She was a bit put out to think she wasn't the first to know about the engagement.

'But of course. Why not?'

'Because you should have told me first. I'm the one it concerns, yet it seems I've been the last to know,' she said a trifle huffily, spearing a cream puff with her pastry fork. 'I might have said no, after all.'

'I didn't think you would.' He took her hand and stroked it. 'Can't you understand? I wanted to get everything sorted out before I said anything to you, dear.' He gave her the special smile that always melted her heart. 'Now, pour me another cup of tea. We don't want to start our engagement off with a squabble, do we?' He gave her hand a squeeze before releasing it.

Obediently, she busied herself with the teacups, hardly able to take her eyes off the little ring on her finger long enough to pour the tea safely. The stones might not be very big but it was a *very* pretty ring and she was the happiest girl in the world.

Chapter Five

She was still admiring her ring when suddenly, Michael got to
his feet, craning his neck to see something out in the road and
nearly spilling the tea she had just poured. 'Well, I'll be b... I
shan't be a minute, Rose.' He threw his napkin down and
rushed out of the tea shop.

She stood up and craned her neck, trying to see what it was
that had attracted his attention. He was pushing his way
through the crowds thronging the pavement as if he was
chasing someone, but she couldn't see who. Soon he had
disappeared round the corner.

She continued drinking her tea and tried not to look
concerned. Wherever he had gone he would be back soon and
then she was sure he would tell her all about it. That was
something she would insist on when they were married, there
must be no secrets between them.

She ate two more cream cakes and drank two more cups of
tea, which left her feeling slightly sick, and alternately studied
her ring and watched the people going by. The last eclair
sitting on the tall cake stand didn't tempt her in the least and
she hoped he would come back soon and eat it, especially
when the waitress rather pointedly began to hover so that she
was forced to order another pot of tea.

Eventually, after nearly twenty minutes, he reappeared. He
sat down and ate the eclair without a word.

'Well, what was all that about?' she asked, a slight edge to
her voice. 'Surely I'm entitled to an explanation. You can't jest
go off and leave me for twenty minutes and then come back as
if nothing had happened, Michael.'

He passed his hand across his eyes. 'No, of course not. I'm sorry, Rose. I'm a little upset, that's all.'

'Oh, sweetheart, I'm sorry,' she said, immediately contrite. 'Why? What is it?'

'I've just been talking to my brother George,' he said without looking up. 'It was him I saw going by when I looked out of the window.' He lifted his head. 'I'm sorry, Rosie. I didn't have time to tell you because I was afraid he'd be gone before I could catch him.'

Rose poured him a fresh cup of tea before she spoke again. 'Well, what did he say? Aren't you going to tell me about it?' she asked, handing it to him. 'After all, we're engaged, so there should be no secrets between us now.'

He took several gulps of the scalding tea and then nodded. 'Yes, of course I'll tell you. But it was a bit of a shock, that's all. He says he's married, Rose! I can't believe it! And to think, if I hadn't seen him in the street today we might never have known! But he's married and settled in Ipswich – well, near Ipswich, he didn't say exactly where.'

'Was his wife with him?'

'Oh, yes, she was there, hanging on to his arm like grim death. She's well and truly caught him, if you ask me.'

'So isn't he coming back to the mill? Ever?'

'No. He says not. He says he's taken a pub just outside Ipswich and he's happier than he's ever been, so he's never coming back.'

'Whatever will your mother say?'

'Goodness knows. She won't like it, I can tell you that. George has always been her favourite so she'll be pretty cut up, I reckon.' He drank some more of his tea. 'I told him he should at least have written and told her, instead of leaving all of us wondering and worrying all these weeks with never a word from him.'

'What did he say to that?'

'Nothing. Just shrugged his shoulders.'

She patted his hand. 'Well, it was a good thing you chanced to see him today, then. At least your mother will know he's still alive and well.'

He drained the last of his tea and took his watch out of his pocket and looked at it. 'Yes. At least she'll know that.' He put his watch back. 'We must go, we've got a train to catch. If we don't get a move on we'll miss it and there's not another one for two hours.'

He paid the bill and hurried her out of the tea shop. It was quite a distance to the railway station and he seemed preoccupied, walking so fast that Rose had to run to keep up with him. His mood seemed to have changed since seeing his brother George, but she had no breath to question him about it.

They reached the station and had to wait nearly ten minutes for the train.

'See? You needn't have made me run like that. We're in plenty of time,' she said when she got her breath back.

'The train must be late,' he snapped.

She put her hand on his arm. 'Michael, dear, I know you're upset about seeing your brother,' she said, 'but please don't let it spoil our engagement day. We were so happy until you saw him ...'

He looked down at her and put his hand over hers. 'Yes, you're quite right, Rosie, my love. We shouldn't let my stupid elder brother spoil our day. It's just that, well, it was a bit of a shock, seeing him like that. I reckon my mother will be pretty upset when I tell her.'

'So he isn't even going to bring his wife to visit her?'

'Seems not. Anyway, the Matriarch wouldn't like her. She looked common to me. Not like you, my love, pretty as a picture.' He bent and kissed her cheek, making her blush. 'Ah, here's the train at last.'

They climbed aboard and found a carriage that was empty except for an elderly man snoring in the corner. Rose snuggled up to Michael and held his arm with both hers. She felt she could allow herself to be a little more forward now that they were engaged. And he clearly felt the same because he stole several kisses on the journey home and she had to straighten her hat and compose herself before she could get out of the train when they reached Bramfield.

'Shall we walk back to Stavely by the river?' Michael asked as they left the station.

'Oh, yes, let's. It's such a lovely evening. And it's appropriate, too, isn't it, because that's where we first met.' She gave a little giggle. 'Only today the sun is shining and I'm with you, so I shan't be afraid of seeing dead bodies on the marsh.'

'You and your dead bodies! You are a silly little goose, aren't you!' He put his arm round her and gave her a squeeze.

'Michael!' she said, both shocked and delighted. 'Don't forget there are people about.'

'Well, what matter? We're engaged, aren't we?' And he took off his hat and kissed her, right there and then, outside the railway station.

She had never seen him so carefree and happy and had never loved him so much.

'You do love me, don't you, Michael?' she said as they wandered along with their arms round each other.

'What a question! Would I have spent all that money on a ring if I didn't?' he teased.

She held her hand out and looked at it, turning it this way and that so that it caught the sun. 'Well, a girl likes to be told from time to time,' she said.

'All right, I'll tell you.' Laughing, he caught her round the waist and swung her round and round. 'I love you, I love you, I love you. There, will that do?' He pulled her to him and held her close for several seconds before lowering his head and kissing her in a way he never had before. When he released her they were both a little breathless. 'Now do you believe me?' he whispered in her ear.

She could only nod in reply because the feelings he had aroused in her were new and slightly troubling, and she couldn't trust herself to speak.

For the rest of the way her feet didn't seem to touch the ground. They didn't talk much, they just walked with their arms entwined, delighting in simply being together. Even the river, at full flood, seemed to sparkle in celebration.

As they approached the mill Michael said, 'I think it'll be best if we don't say anything about me seeing George today, Rosie. I believe my mother and Lissa are making a special tea for us so we don't want to put a damper on things. I'll tell them all about it later.'

'A special tea? Oh, Michael, I don't believe I could eat a thing after all those cream cakes.'

'You will. You'll see. My mother will be offended if you don't,' he warned.

He was right. The long table in the kitchen was covered with a white cloth and places were laid for five. There was ham and cheese to go with Eve's home-made bread and two kinds of jelly surrounded an enormous blancmange. In the middle of the table there was a large sponge cake with their names in pink icing.

Michael's mother was so pleased at the engagement and had taken so much trouble to provide this special tea that Rose forgot to be annoyed that she had had prior knowledge of it. Especially when Eve came up to her and kissed her.

'I hope you'll both be very happy,' she said warmly. 'And I'm sure you will. Now do come and sit down. I've put the two of you together on that side, with Dan opposite and I'll sit at this end.' She turned her heard. 'Lissa-dear, pour the tea, then you can sit at the other end of the table.'

It was a very happy tea party and Rose thought it was a nice touch that Lissa was allowed to join in, although she did have to keep getting up to fetch things and wasn't included in the conversation much, except by Dan, who Rose had noticed was always kind to her.

After they had eaten – and again Michael had been right, Rose did full justice to the spread in spite of the cream cakes she had already eaten – Eve said, 'Now, I want you to come upstairs with me, Rose. I've something rather special to show you.'

Mystified, Rose followed her up the wide staircase to the big bedroom at the front of the house. On the bed, lying in a nest of tissue paper was the most beautiful cream lace wedding gown Rose had ever seen.

'It's mine,' Eve said proudly. 'I wore it on my wedding day over thirty years ago and I've kept it upstairs in the attic ever since in the hope that ...' Her voice trailed off. Then she brightened. 'But never mind that, now. Do you like it, Rose, dear? I hope you do, because I'd like you to wear it on your wedding day. Will you try it on now? I'm anxious to know if it will fit.' She looked anxiously at Rose.

With something approaching reverence Rose tried on the dress. It fitted perfectly, although because she was slightly taller than Eve it only reached to her ankles instead of sweeping the floor. But it was such a fairytale dress that it didn't seem to matter, and Rose felt like a queen, especially when Eve placed the gossamer-like veil on her head. 'Oh, it's perfect,' she breathed, feeling exactly like Cinderella with her fairy godmother.

'You like it?' Eve was obviously delighted.

'Oh, yes, I do!' She bit her lip. 'But—'

'But what?' Eve looked at her expectantly.

She shook her head and stooped to kiss her future mother-in-law. 'Nothing. The dress is lovely.'

'Then you'll wear it on your wedding day?'

'I'll be honoured to.'

She wriggled carefully out of the dress. How could she tell Eve that she was worried about upstaging her elder sister, married such a short time ago in her rather shabby best dress because that was all she could afford? And another thing. A fairytale dress like this demanded bridesmaids in pretty dresses. But Babs and Millie didn't have pretty dresses. Their best clothes were either serviceable navy and green, that didn't show the dirt, or check gingham, faded through many washings.

As Eve carefully laid the tissue paper back between the folds of the fairytale dress and got it ready to put back in its chest, Rose tried to put these thoughts from her mind by gazing round the room. It was large and bay-windowed, situated directly above the parlour, and it reflected Eve's lavender and lace appearance to the extent that everything possible was delicately draped with muslin and tied with a blue ribbon bow; the lace curtains at the window, the drapes on the big four-poster bed, even the kidney-shaped dressing table was draped with muslin. Yet the room, being large, didn't look over-fussy because the carpet was a plain blue and the wallpaper was blue with cream stripes, colours picked up by the hand-stitched patchwork quilt on the bed and the patchwork cushion on the blue velvet chaise longue under the window. In spite of the large bed it was definitely a lady's room and Rose couldn't imagine the dainty Eve ever sharing it with a husband. In fact, she couldn't imagine Eve ever having had a husband, let alone three strapping sons. And to think that they must have been conceived in this very bed. Her imagination balked at the thought and she blushed at the way her mind was working.

To cover her embarrassment she went over to the window and looked down into the courtyard, where Michael and Dan were on their way over to the mill. As if he was aware he was being watched Michael turned and waved and Dan did the same. The brothers were quite alike from this distance, but dark-haired, serious Michael was the one she loved and to whom she would soon be married. She gave a contented sigh at the thought and turned back to follow Eve from the room and down the stairs.

As she walked she ran her hand over the highly polished banister and just as she reached the hall the grandfather clock at the foot of the stairs chimed seven o'clock. She looked up into its brass face and listened to the steady tick as the pendulum swung rhythmically to and fro, to and fro, its sound gently muted by the thick carpets. Soon I shall be a part of all this, she whispered to herself, putting out a hand to trace the prettily marked walnut grain of the clock case and savouring the smell of wax polish and something else – she could only describe it as 'quality'. Yet quality couldn't be smelled, could it? Or could it? Because the house at Dowlands' Mill had an aroma that reeked of something that she could find no other word for. An aroma that was very different from any that emanated from Crick's Farm.

Rose's family were as delighted as the Dowlands with the engagement and if Emma had reservations she kept them to herself. Not that she could have explained her feelings, had she been asked. Perhaps it was the speed with which the courtship was progressing – the marriage date was already set at the third week in July, perhaps it was the lack of any demonstrations of affection between the engaged couple – although that could easily be put down to reticence or shyness, after all who knew what went on between them in private? The shock of learning that Grace was already pregnant on her wedding day was proof enough of that! Michael Dowland was undoubtedly a well set-up and handsome young man, a man any girl would be proud to be seen with. And Rose was a very pretty girl and carried herself well. Together they made a handsome couple. Yet the feelings of unease persisted and try as she might Emma couldn't shake them off.

Rose seemed preoccupied, too, as she went about her work.

Emma watched her, saying nothing, but she was not surprised one day when the two of them were alone in the dairy together and Rose paused in the act of churning the butter and blurted out, 'I'm that worried, Mum, I don't know what to do.'

Emma kept her face impassive. 'Well, you'd better tell me about it. A trouble shared is a trouble halved.' Rose wouldn't be the first girl to have had second thoughts. The whole affair had been a bit of a whirlwind after all, hardly giving the girl time to catch her breath.

Rose sat down on a milking stool and poured out her misgivings. 'And what poor Grace'll say when she sees me in that dress I can't think,' she finished up, nearly in tears. 'I'm afraid she'll think I'm trying to go one better than her and it isn't that at all. It's just that I don't know how to tell Michael's mother I won't wear it. And what about bridesmaids? What can Millie and Babs wear? We can't afford ...' She gave a great sigh. 'Mind you, Mum, it is the most beautiful dress I've ever seen.'

Emma folded her arms and leaned back against the bench. This was not at all what she had been expecting and in truth she didn't know whether to be sorry or pleased that her suspicions had been ill-founded.

'I think you should go and see Grace,' she said after a minute. 'Tell her what you've just told me. You haven't been to see her in her little cottage yet, have you?'

'No. I haven't had time. After all, she hasn't been wed much more than a week. Anyway, Michael and me ...'

'That's no excuse. You should have been to see her. You might know she's bursting to show everybody her new home. You'd better go and see her tonight.' Emma gave a little chuckle. 'Although, if I know Grace, what you wear at your wedding won't worry her a bit, as long as she's been told.' She pinched her lip between her thumb and forefinger. 'As to the business about bridesmaids, I could always go and have a word with my sister Madge. It's time I went to see her and Mum.'

'Aunt Madge's clothes won't fit Millie or Babs. And anyway, she won't have anything suitable for bridesmaids dresses,' Rose said gloomily.

Emma tapped the side of her nose. 'Your Aunt Madge can sometimes get material cheap from the Co-op where she works. If it's a bit faded, or the colour's not right. And if she can get something suitable there's still time for Granny Robbins to run up a couple of bridesmaid's dresses. She'd enjoy doing that. And I expect Madge'll be able to find them a hat each and one for me. I've never known such a one for hats as my sister Madge.'

'Oh, Mum. I feel better already.' Rose went over and kissed her mother.

'Well, it'd be a pity not to wear such a pretty dress on your wedding day, wouldn't it?' Emma said gently. 'And you don't want to start off your married life by upsetting your future mother-in-law, do you?'

Rose raced through the rest of her chores so that she could visit Grace that evening. It was true, she hadn't visited her elder sister since her marriage and that only compounded her feelings of guilt towards her.

As her mother had predicted, she needn't have worried. Rose had never seen Grace looking so happy and blooming.

'Oh, Rose, I've been dying for you to come and see the cottage,' Grace said, kissing her. 'Ain't it jest a treat? Yes, come and see the bedroom. We ain't got much in there yet, only the bed and a chest of drawers, but Albert's going to make me a dressing table when he's got time. He made me the rocking chair in the kitchen for a wedding present. It's ever so comfortable and it'll be jest right for me to sit and rock the baby in. He's going to make a cradle, too. He's ever so clever with his hands, you know. Oh, I must stop talking. Wait a minute, I'll put the kettle on and we'll hev a cuppa tea. Or would you rather have a glass of Albert's dandelion wine? It's very good. But you mustn't drink too much or you'll fall off your bike on the way home.' She laughed delightedly and without waiting for Rose to speak got down two wine glasses from the cupboard beside the chimney breast. 'You must hev one of my little short cakes, too. This stove cooks a treat as long as you get the dampers right.' She motioned Rose to sit down while she poured the wine and fetched the tin of cakes and then sat down herself. 'Well, now, what about you? You hevn't hardly said a word yet.'

'You haven't given me much chance!' Rose laughed.

Grace laughed with her. 'No, I hevn't, hev I? Oh dear, I always let my tongue run away with me when I'm excited.

Well, go on. Tell me, then. What hev you been doing with yourself?'

Rose blushed. 'Michael and me are engaged and we're to be married next month, on the twenty-first.' She held out her hand for Grace to admire the ring.

'Oh, Rosie, how lovely!' Grace clapped her hands as she leaned forward to look at Rose's ring. 'Now ain't that jest pretty!' She got up and kissed her sister. 'But thass a bit sudden, ain't it? Are you ...?' She put her head on one side and pointed to her own waistline, just beginning to thicken.

'No, indeed I'm not!' Rose said indignantly.

'All right, Miss High and Mighty,' Grace said mildly. 'I only asked.'

'Sorry, Gracie. It's just – well, it's just that Michael wants us to be wed soon, that's all. And there's no reason why we shouldn't be.'

'Where are you going to live?'

'At the mill, of course. That's where Michael's work is.'

'What about his mother? I couldn't live with Albert's mum, not was it ever so, the miserable old hag.'

'Oh, Eve – she likes me to call her that – is really nice. I'm sure we shall get on well together. She's looking forward to me going there to live, she's said so.' Rose hesitated. 'Eve wants me to wear her wedding dress when we get married. It's the most beautiful dress you ever saw, all cream lace, with a veil and everything.' She put her head on one side and looked uncertainly at her sister. 'I hope you won't mind, Gracie.'

Grace frowned. 'Mind? What difference will it make to me?' she asked, puzzled.

'Well,' Rose hunched her shoulders. 'You didn't have a white wedding with bridesmaids and everything. I wouldn't want you to think ...' her voice trailed off uncomfortably.

'Think what?' Grace was still puzzled.

'I wouldn't want you to think I was trying to go one better than you,' Rose said in a rush.

'Oh, that! Don't be daft. It doesn't worry me what sort of a wedding you have, Rose.' Grace waved her hand dismissively. Then she smiled. 'I've got my Albert and my little house and I couldn't be happier if I lived in a palace. Oh, and I didn't tell you, did I? Mr Bowcher says there's work for me in the dairy here if I want it. It's not heavy work so I'll be able to carry on nearly till the baby's born. Albert says I'm to put the money I earn away to buy things for the baby. He says he earns enough to keep us, as long as we're careful, of course.' Her eyes took on a dreamy look. 'Oh, he's a lovely man. So good to me.'

As Rose cycled home she reflected that it hadn't taken much to make Grace happy. Her Albert was a nice enough young man, not nearly as good-looking as Michael of course, but hard working and very fond of her. But the cottage itself was tiny. Two rooms up and two down and hardly room to swing a cat in any of them. Even so, they hadn't managed to furnish more than the kitchen and one bedroom and the lino must have been left there when old Darby died because the pattern was all faded and there was only a single rag rug at the hearth to cover it. Her thoughts went to Mill House, the big rooms, the sweeping staircase, the thick carpets and good solid, highly-polished furniture, and she realised just how lucky she was to be marrying into a family like the Dowlands.

Chapter Six

The days leading up to the wedding were spent in feverish activity. As Emma had predicted, Aunt Madge, who worked in the drapery department at the Co-op in Ipswich, had managed to get a bale of mauve shantung cheaply because it had proved an unpopular colour and Granny Robins burned the midnight oil night after night to get the bridesmaid's dresses made for Millie and Babs. This meant frequent trips to Bramfield for fittings, which in turn meant that work on the farm got neglected unless Chad did it himself. Emma borrowed a dress from Madge, which only needed taking in at the sides because Emma was thinner than her sister. And Madge had enough hats in her wardrobe for them all to have one each, which she trimmed to match the dresses.

But Rose soon discovered that as one problem was solved another took its place. Because Emma insisted that the wedding breakfast should be held at Crick's Farm.

'But, Mum, Mrs Dowland has already offered for it to be at Mill House,' Rose said, filled with dread at the thought of her new mother-in-law seeing how she and her family lived. 'And there's much more room there.'

'It's very kind of her, I'm sure, but as parents of the bride it's up to your father and me to provide the wedding breakfast, and provide it we shall,' Emma said firmly. 'Don't worry, child. We shall manage. You'll see.'

Nevertheless, Rose spent sleepless nights worrying about it and she was sure she would go to her bridegroom haggard through lack of sleep and this set her off worrying again.

Her fears proved groundless. A week of feverish cleaning

and polishing before the wedding transformed the farmhouse, although it couldn't hide the shabbiness of the place, the peeling paint, the worn linoleum and the sagging furniture, which looked even worse than usual, to Rose's critical eye. And Emma revived the skills learned when she was undercook at Tattingstone Hall and with her daughters carefully obeying her instructions she provided a feast that would have done credit to royalty. Even Rose was satisfied when she saw the spread all laid out in the front parlour.

It was intended to be a quiet wedding, but on the 21st of July 1910 the whole village turned out to see the girl from the run-down Crick's Farm marry wealthy Widow Dowland's middle son and the churchyard was lined with both well-wishers and the frankly curious as Rose Bentley walked into church on her father's arm in a cloud of lace and tulle, followed by her two sisters in identical dresses of mauve shantung and all carrying bouquets of rosebuds. After the ceremony a great cheer went up and Mr and Mrs Michael Dowland emerged into the sunshine and everybody remarked what a handsome pair they made. Rose felt she would burst with happiness.

Back at the farm the atmosphere was jovial, helped along by the liberal amount of beer Chad had provided, although Rose's relatives far outnumbered Michael's. The Dowlands appeared to have no relatives at all except for Granny Dowland, who professed herself too ill to attend, and of course George, who still hadn't put in an appearance. But Daniel was a very affable best man – even more so than the bridegroom, who seemed a little shy. Eve Dowland had brought Lissa with her, which Rose thought very considerate, and had even bought her a new dress to wear. Lissa, for her part, stayed close to her mistress, anticipating her every need. It was clear that she was not used to being in company, and she tended to shy away if anyone spoke to her.

Rose observed all this from her seat beside her new husband and, ever watchful, noticed Eve casting a critical eye around the table, but later she was gratified to hear her new mother-in-law complimenting her mother on the spread she had provided, and even asking for the recipe for Emma's carrot cake.

Nevertheless, Rose was relieved when it was time to leave.

She didn't want to be there when things got too relaxed and Granny Robins took her dentures out – as she always did, and Uncle Tom from Bury St Edmunds started telling his awful jokes and flirting with Aunt Madge. Families were all very well, but they could be an embarrassment and she was glad to be marrying into a family with no skeletons to rattle when they came together at rites of passage such as weddings and funerals.

As old Jacob drove them to Bramfield station to catch the train to Clacton in the Dowlands's trap, specially decorated for the occasion, Rose put her head on her new husband's shoulder and smiled contentedly up at him. Michael smiled back and bent his head and kissed her, himself gently pleased with life viewed now through a slight alcoholic haze.

Rose had never been to the seaside before and she loved the long expanse of golden sands. The hotel room overlooked the sea and she loved to watch its changing moods; at low tide little gentle wavelets lapped the shore way out in the distance, whilst when the tide was high big, noisy waves lashed the beach. Everything was new and exciting, and the sun shone nearly all the time and they were able to go for long walks along the sands.

Yet deep down inside Rose found her honeymoon a little disappointing, because Michael wasn't quite the lover she had expected from the penny novels she and Grace used to read under the bedclothes when they were both at home. Oh, she didn't doubt that he loved her. He demonstrated it nightly, although in a way that left her bruised and breathless and totally unsatisfied, leaving her to stare up into the darkness, unfulfilled, remembering her sister Grace's words, 'Well, you get hot for each other, don't you, and then, well, you know what I mean ...' while he snored beside her. And she was too shy to tell him his love-making disappointed her, she just hoped things would improve as they got to know each other better. Because when she thought about it, less than four months ago she'd hardly known Michael Dowland at all and now here she was, married and lying beside him in bed and listening to the roar of the waves. She could hardly believe her luck.

The day before they were due to go home it rained.

'Oh, dear. We can't walk on the beach today, Michael,' Rose said as she pulled back the curtains, 'It's much too wet. What shall we do?'

'I'll take you into Colchester on the train. I've been wanting to do that ever since we've been here but it's been too hot,' he said sitting up in bed. 'Would you like that?'

'Oh, yes, I would.' She went and sat on the bed beside him. 'I do love you, Michael,' she said. 'You do love me, don't you?'

'Of course I do, you little goose.' He put his arm round her and pulled her down to him. 'I married you, didn't I? What more do you want?'

'I want you to be happy. You *are* happy, aren't you, Michael?' she asked anxiously.

'Of course I am. Come here, I'll show you how much I love you.' He began to tug at her nightdress.

'Michael! It's daylight!' she whispered, deliciously shocked.

'Close your eyes, then, if you want it to be dark.' His hands were busy with her buttons.

'But suppose someone comes in ...' Her voice died as he began to kiss her and as she gave herself up to his lovemaking she understood at last what her sister Grace had meant. Now her happiness was complete.

It was still raining when they arrived at Colchester so he bought her an umbrella, which he held over them both while she hung on to his arm and they laughed together as they tried to keep the drips from running down their necks. They wandered up and down the High Street looking in shop windows.

'I love that coat,' she said wistfully, pointing to a dark blue coat with an astrakhan collar.

'Go in and buy it, then.' He reached into his pocket and pulled out a wad of notes.

'Oh, I didn't mean ... I didn't say that because I wanted you to buy it for me, Michael.' She was horrified that he might think her grasping.

'Don't be silly. If you like it I'll buy it for you. How much is it?' He peered to see the price tag. 'Nineteen and elevenpence. Here you are, here's a pound, that'll cover it. Oh, and here's another half crown. Buy yourself a hat to match.' He laughed at her expression. 'Go on. I mean it.' He gave her a little push.

She still hung back, unsure. 'Aren't you coming in with me to buy it, then?'

'No. I'll wait out here. I don't go in women's shops. So don't be long.' He reached into his pocket for his pipe as he spoke.

The coat was the loveliest thing she had ever had. It was made of the best quality melton cloth and the collar was silky and warm and there was a little astrakhan toque that matched it perfectly. She came out of the shop wearing her new finery, glad that the rain had stopped.

'Well, Michael, how do I look?' She pirouetted in front of him on the pavement.

He grinned at her. 'You'll do, but you'd better take it off or you'll bake. The sun's coming out,' he said, and the way he looked at her she knew he was pleased.

She folded the coat carefully into its bag, then happily tucked her hand into his arm. She knew that as long as she could please him she would be happy.

Rose and Michael returned to Mill House to find that Lissa had prepared the large bedroom for them that Rose had slept in the night she hurt her ankle. It was just across the landing from Eve's room and had the same outlook, overlooking the mill and the creek beyond. It was a lovely sunny room. Rose thought she would never tire of looking at the view from the big bay window. A bowl of roses had been placed on the dressing table, the work of Eve, Rose suspected.

The only thing that she didn't remember was something that looked strangely out of place. It was a dark, leather-covered traveller's chest, rather like a sea chest, standing at the foot of the bed. It was fastened with an iron hasp and padlock.

'That's mine,' Michael said when she remarked on it. 'I asked for it to be brought from my room along the landing so don't you go poking your nose into it, my girl, or you might get more than you bargain for.' He grinned at her as he said it but there was no mistaking that he meant what he said.

Bringing her new-found feminine wiles to bear she looked at him archly. 'I thought there were to be no secrets between us, Michael,' she said.

'That's right. It's no secret that it's my box and it's no secret that you've got to keep out of it,' he said and roared with laughter. 'Now, come on, dear, we'd better go downstairs. The Martriarch's cooked my favourite steak and kidney pudding so we'd best not let it spoil.'

She wasn't happy with his reply but she knew there was no point in arguing so she took off her hat and smoothed her hair and followed him downstairs, regaining her good humour as she looked about her, and thinking with more than a trace of smugness. This is my house now. This is where I live. This is where I belong.

Supper was a pleasant meal. Eve's steak and kidney pudding was delicious and everyone did justice to it, including Lissa, even though she had to keep leaving hers in order to get up and wait on the others.

After supper Rose whispered to her husband, 'Michael, you promised weeks ago to show me the mill and you never have. Now that this is my home I want to see everything.'

He pushed his chair back abruptly. 'All right, then, if you're so anxious I'll take you now.'

'Oh, I didn't mean right this minute,' she protested, sensing that for some reason he had been slightly irritated by her request. 'Just some time. Any time.'

'Well, now is as good a time as any. But I don't know that you'll like it much. You'll find it's a bit dusty,' he warned.

'That's all right. This dress is quite old.' She laughed as she smoothed the faded gingham.

'Yes,' Eve said thoughtfully, 'We shall have to do something about your wardrobe, my dear. We can't have the new Mrs Dowland looking shabby, can we?'

Something in her tone put Rose on the defensive, she couldn't have said why, and she said quickly, 'Michael has already bought me the most lovely coat and hat. We bought it when we went into Colchester last week.'

Eve nodded. 'That's good. I'm sure Michael is very proud of you, my dear.'

'Oh, come on.' Michael said with a trace of impatience, 'or the light'll be gone. I don't want to have to light the lamps just to show you over the place. Are you coming, Dan?'

'No.' Dan got up from the table and stacked the dishes by

the sink, 'I want to put some more netting on the blackcurrants. The birds are having a feast out there.' He turned to Lissa. 'Do you need more potatoes, Lissy? Oh, it doesn't matter, I'll dig some anyway.'

'Dan grows lovely vegetables,' Lissy said to nobody in particular. 'And beautiful fruit. He's a rare good gardener and it's a big garden, too. Ever such a big garden. As big as ...'

'Oh, get on with clearing the table, Lissa-dear and don't prattle on so,' Eve said sharply.

Rose walked over to the mill by Michael's side. It was a warm evening and everywhere was quiet and peaceful. A blackbird was singing its heart out on the branch of a nearby tree and the last rays of the dying sun reflected a fiery glow in the windows of the mill and lent a pink tinge to the white weatherboarding.

'It's almost as if it's on fire,' Rose breathed, 'and with the creek in the background it's ... oh, it's so beautiful. I think I should like to paint it.'

'Can you paint?' he asked.

'I don't know. I told you that once before, don't you remember? I've never had time to find out till now.'

He looked down at her, unsmiling. 'What makes you think you'll have time now?'

She blushed and gave his arm a little shake, thinking she knew what was in his mind. 'We're only just married, Michael, remember. It'll be a while before ... well, you know, before I have other things to worry about.' That was the nearest she could bring herself to speaking of having a child.

'Oh, well, you'll see.' He seemed to have lost interest. 'Well, here we are.' He unlocked the mill and bent his head as they stepped inside the low doorway. The first thing she noticed was the smell; the distinctive granary smell of corn and bran. Then as her eyes became accustomed to the gloom she saw that everything was covered with a film of flour, turning everything, even the great beams that supported the whole structure, a dusty grey.

He led her up open wooden staircases with no handrails to the top floor, never thinking to look back to see how she was managing. Fortunately heights didn't trouble her but she had to hold her dress up carefully lest she should stumble and fall.

She was quite glad when they reached the top. Here there were huge hoppers which he explained stored the grain and fed it down to the millstones on the floor below.

'It's all done by gravity,' he said, 'once we've lifted the grain up here. And the sack hoist does that. You've seen it working, haven't you?'

'Yes, I have. I saw you riding up on it, too. I was terrified you'd fall, Michael.' She caught his arm and squeezed it. She leaned over and peered out of the window. 'It's an awful long way down, isn't it?'

'Oh, that doesn't worry me. I often go up with the sacks. It saves having to run up the stairs every time. And it's quite safe. I've done it for years. I just give the chain a twist round my heel and up we go, as sweet as a nut.'

'Well, you just be careful. Remember you're a married man now,' she chided.

'Don't nag, woman,' he said over his shoulder as he led the way down the first flight of stairs to the floor below where two huge pairs of millstones stood.

Rose touched one. 'You mean to tell me that the water wheel makes these turn?' she asked doubtfully.

'That's right. It's all quite simple really. It's done by a system of gears and cogs. But you don't want me to go into all that, do you?'

'No. I probably wouldn't understand if you did,' she said a trifle ruefully.

'No, you probably wouldn't,' he agreed a little too readily. 'Come on, then, downstairs. I'll just show you the office and then we'll go. It's getting a bit dim in here now, anyway, and it's not worth lighting the oil lamps.'

He led the way down to the ground floor, where a corner had been partitioned off to form a room plenty big enough to hold a desk and chair and a cupboard.

'This is the Matriarch's domain,' he said with a trace of bitterness. 'She doesn't think we're capable of handling the financial side of things so she insists on looking after the books herself.' He made a sound that was something like a snort. 'This is where we have to come cap in hand every Friday for our wages. Five bob a week. That's all she gives us for working all the hours God created. I think she's putting mine up to seven and six now I'm married, but only because I threatened to move out. She says we don't need it since we've got a roof over our heads and food in our bellies.' He turned away and gave another snort. 'But she doesn't know every-thing. Oh, no, she doesn't know it all. Not by any manner of means.'

Rose frowned at him. 'What do you mean, Michael?' she said. 'I don't know what you're talking about.'

'Oh, nothing. Come on, let's leave all this for tonight. I shall have to be over here at six tomorrow to start work. Old Jacob's been helping Dan while I've been away but he's well over sixty, so he's not as spry as he was.'

'And George isn't here to help, either,' Rose said.

'You can't count George. He never did much anyway,' he said as he locked up the mill. 'He was a lazy b...'

'He'll have to work hard now, if he's running a pub,' Rose said quickly.

'What? Oh, yes, he will. Serve him right, too.'

Rose was puzzled. For some reason he didn't appear very good tempered. Several times he had been short with her when she asked a question, she couldn't think why. She looked up at him.

'Shall we have a walk by the river before we go in? It'll give us a little more time to ourselves, just you and me.'

'If you like.'

'I do like. I like very much.' She tucked her hand in his arm. They walked across the bridge over the mill stream towards the river bank. 'It's not as calm as this when the mill's working,' Michael said, pausing for a minute to look down into the dark depths. 'It's very deep, too, I'm warning you, so don't you come here with any fancy ideas of dangling your feet in the water when it's hot.'

'I'll remember, Michael. I promise,' she said. 'If I want to paddle my feet I'll do it in the river.' Suddenly she had a strange feeling, as if someone had poured cold water down her back and she gave a little shiver.

'What's the matter?'

'I don't know. I had a funny feeling. A goose must have walked over my grave, I think. Come on, let's go a bit further.'

They walked along the bank of the creek to where it met the

river and then almost to the spot where they had first met before turning back. By the time they got home again it was nearly ten o'clock and Eve had already gone to bed.

Lissa was still in the kitchen, laying the table for breakfast and a tray to take up to Eve, which she covered with a clean tea towel. She looked up as they entered and Rose saw that she was tired out.

'She said if you were going to be out half the night, Michael, she couldn't wait up for you,' Lissa said.

'I never asked her to,' Michael replied with a sharpness that was just short of being rude.

'Lissa, is there anything I can do to help you? You look quite exhausted.' Rose knew how the girl felt. Many and many a time she herself had finished off her day's tasks hardly knowing how to put one foot in front of the other.

'Oh, no thank you. I've only got to finish this and then I'm going to bed.' The girl flashed her a brief, nervous smile.

'Have you seen to the fire?' Michael nodded towards the big range.

'Dan did it for me.'

'That's all right then. As long as you don't let it out. You'll have the Matriarch after you if you do.'

Lissa nodded and hunched her shoulders as if in fear. 'I know.'

When they were in bed and Michael had blown the candle out, Rose remarked, 'She's a funny little thing, isn't she?'

'Who?'

'Lissa.'

'Is she? I hadn't noticed.' He was busy with her buttons.

'Is she afraid of your mother, do you think?'

'I don't know. I don't see why she should be. Shut up and keep still. I don't want to talk about Lissa just now.'

He still seemed rather irritable so Rose did as she was told, but she didn't really enjoy it although of course she could hardly complain.

When she woke the next morning Lissa was standing by the bed with a cup of tea. She rubbed her eyes. 'Oh, my goodness! Did I oversleep? Where's Michael?'

'Oh, he was up before five. He had his breakfast and went over to the mill an hour or more ago,' Lissa said, drawing back

71

the curtains. 'It's only just seven o'clock now. Do you want your breakfast in bed, Miss, I mean Ma'am, I mean,' she hung her head. 'I'm sorry. I don't know what I should call you.'

'You can call me Rose, if you like,' Rose said, sitting up and hugging her knees. 'It's more friendly, isn't it? I don't mind if your mis ... if Mrs Dowland doesn't.'

Lissa nodded. 'Rose. That's a pretty name. Prettier than Lissa. My father ...' She broke off. 'Would you like your breakfast in bed, Rose?'

'Good gracious, no,' Rose laughed. 'I don't expect to be waited on hand and foot, Lissa. I shall get up as soon as I've drunk this tea. I've always been used to working hard, you know.'

'That's good,' Lissa said enigmatically. 'I must go. It's washing day today. I have to help Mrs Slaughter in the wash house.' She went to the door and paused with her hand on the door knob. 'I hate washing day.' Then she was gone.

Eve was sitting by the fire massaging her hands when Rose arrived downstairs. She looked up as Rose entered the room.

'Ah, good morning, my dear. Did you sleep well? Yes, of course you did. You young people would sleep if you were pegged on the clothes line. I only wish I could say the same.' She resumed massaging her hands. 'I wonder if you'd mind making the bread this morning, Rose,' she said apologetically. 'My arthritis, you know. It's very painful today. I think we must be in for a change in the weather.'

'Why yes, of course I will,' Rose said, eager to be of use, 'But I'm afraid it won't be as good as yours. I've never tasted such delicious bread.'

'Oh, don't worry about that,' Eve said, shaking her head. 'It will be perfectly all right. I'll tell you exactly what to do.' She nodded towards the table. 'There's some toast left for your breakfast, then you can make a start.'

Hurriedly, Rose ate the two pieces of cold toast and would have liked more but didn't like to ask because she was already feeling guilty to think she was up late. When she had finished she cleared the table and went over to the sink to wash up.

'Oh, leave that. Lissa will do it later,' Eve called. 'Now, the flour is in that crock beside the dresser ...'

Rose did everything just as Eve told her and much to her

72

relief the bread, if not quite up to Eve's standard, was very good.

When it was done and turned out to cool Eve looked at the clock hanging beside the fireplace. 'Lissa is taking a very long time over the washing today,' she said. 'I expect it's because Mrs Slaughter is out there in the wash house regaling her with all her family troubles. She's a real misery, that woman, and she's so busy complaining that she takes twice as long over her work as she should.' She looked anxiously at Rose. 'It's nearly half past twelve and time for the boys' dinner. I'm sure you won't mind laying the table and getting it ready as Lissa isn't here, will you, Rose? They'll only want bread and cheese and a pickled onion. They don't stop for much during the day.'

'Yes, of course.' Rose began to lay the table. 'I thought perhaps I might go and see my mother after dinner, if it's all right with you, Eve.'

'Certainly, my dear.' Eve gave a little laugh. 'But you don't have to ask me, you know. You're a married woman now. You must do as you wish. Yes, that's right. You'll find the butter and the cheese in the pantry on the marble slab. And the bread's in the bread crock on the floor. Be sure and put the lid on again in case of mice. And pull the kettle forward, will you? I like a cup of tea after my dinner. No, the boys will have beer. The glasses are in the top of the corner cupboard and the beer is underneath.'

Eventually the table was laid to Eve's satisfaction, by which time Lissa had come scurrying in.

'You've taken a very long time this morning, Lissa-dear,' Eve said sharply when she appeared. 'Has Mrs Slaughter gone?'

'No. She's just finishing scrubbing up. She says it'll be an extra sixpence if you please because of the blankets. That's what took the extra time, you see.'

'There's always some excuse.' Eve reached for her purse, which was kept in a little cupboard by the fireplace and counted out the money carefully. 'Here, take that to her. It's an extra threepence. That's all she's getting. Those blankets weren't full size, after all. An extra sixpence indeed! And you can call and tell the boys dinner's ready on your way back,' she added as Lissa went out of the door.

Lissa hurried across to the wash house opposite the back

door and a few minutes later Rose saw Mrs Slaughter leave. She was a small, underfed-looking woman and Rose recognised her as the woman whose husband had died in an accident the previous year, leaving her with six children under ten years old. No wonder she looked underfed, thought Rose.

The boys, as Eve called them, came across for their meal one at a time so that the mill wasn't left unattended. Michael came first. Rose held her face up for a kiss but he didn't appear to notice and sat down and began to eat his bread and cheese. She was disappointed but realised that he was probably too shy to offer demonstrations of affection in front of his mother. She smiled at him, trying to convey that she understood, but all he said was, 'Pass me another pickled onion, will you, Rose. I've got to be getting back. The grain barge'll be in this afternoon.'

As he said that there was a clatter at the hearth as Lissa dropped the lid of the kettle.

'Sorry,' she murmured, blushing. 'I dropped it. It didn't break.'

'It's hardly likely to, as it's cast iron,' Eve said briefly. 'but do be careful, Lissa-dear. You're always dropping things.'

Rose was sitting opposite the fireplace so she could see what Lissa was doing and she saw the girl lift the corner of her apron and wipe her eye. 'I don't drop things,' she heard her mutter to herself. 'I hardly ever drop things. Anyway, it didn't break.'

'What are you saying, Lissa-dear?' Eve turned to her.

'Not saying anything.'

'Then hurry up and make the tea.'

When Michael had gone back Rose didn't wait for Dan to appear but went upstairs to get ready for her visit home. She would have liked to put the new coat and hat on but it was much too hot for that, so she settled for the only other gingham dress she possessed and her old straw hat.

'You're not going out like that, Rose, are you?' Eve said, appalled, when she returned to the kitchen.

Rose looked down at herself. 'It's clean,' she said defensively. 'Anyway, I haven't got much else. I told you that.'

'It's a pretty dress,' Dan said, cutting himself another hunk of cheese. 'Looks nice and fresh and summery.'

'What do you know about it, Daniel?' his mother said. 'Anyway, it's no concern of yours. I shall speak to Michael. We can't have a member of our family going about looking like a tramp.' Eve wrinkled her nose distastefully.

'I don't look like a tramp. My clothes are all clean,' Rose said hotly. 'And they're mended, too. My mother always says there's no disgrace in a darn.'

'There is absolutely no need for you to wear clothes that are darned when you go out,' Eve replied coldly.

Rose lifted her chin. 'There is if I haven't got anything else.'

'This is exactly what I'm saying. Michael must provide you with something else.'

'But he's already bought me a winter coat and hat,' Rose was quick to defend him. 'Anyway, I can't stand here and argue with you now. I'm going to see my mother.' Irritated, she picked up her bag and went out. As she passed the kitchen window she saw Lissa staring at her wide-eyed in disbelief and something that looked suspiciously like admiration.

Chapter Seven

Her mother was in the piggery when Rose arrived home.

'Oh, dear,' Emma leaned on the muck rake and shook her head, when Rose told her what had happened. 'That's a very bad start, Rose. You shouldn't go arguing with your mother-in-law, especially when you've only just started living there. You'll have to learn to curb your temper, my girl. You always did let it get the better of you.'

'Yes, I know I shall. I know I shouldn't have gone on at her like that. I don't know what came over me. But she made me that mad, criticising my clothes.' She gave a sigh. 'I'll take her a bunch of flowers as a peace offering when I go back.'

'And tell her you're sorry.'

'Yes, all right.' Rose gave her mother a wide, cheeky smile. 'Although I'm not sorry, Mum.'

Her mother gave her an affectionate push. 'Well, you should be.' She brushed a strand of hair back with her forearm. 'Your dad found quite a lot of spotted orchids down by the stream. You could gather a few of them for her, if you like,' she suggested. 'He's down there now, I believe. At least, he's supposed to be. He went down to clear the stream this morning.' She shook her head. 'He should have finished it by now, but he's probably forgotten what he went down there for.'

'I'll go and find him while you put the kettle on.' Rose paused at the door. 'It's a lovely house I'm living in now, Mum, with the most beautiful furniture and things. You must come and see, when you've got time.'

Emma threw down the muck rake. 'When I've got time,' she said, in a tone that conveyed that she never would have.

'It's my home now, Mum. I can invite who I like there,' Rose persisted.

'Of course you can, child. Now, go and find your father. He'll be vexed if you've been home and haven't been to see him. He'll show you where the orchids are.'

Chad was down by the stream whittling a piece of wood. 'Rose!' His face lit up when he saw her and he scrambled to his feet. 'How are you, my dear?' he said as he kissed her. 'And how did you like the seaside? The sound of the sea can be very soothing, I've always thought. I remember ...'

'Dad. Aren't you supposed to be clearing this stream?' Rose shook his arm. 'Look, it's little more than a stagnant ditch further on.'

'Ah, yes. That's right. I was just whittling this stick to ... um ...'

'To poke about in the water?'

'Yes, that's right. I thought if I poked it about in the water it would make a channel. It's a pretty shape, though, isn't it? Rather a shame to get it wet, don't you think?' He held it up. 'I think it would make a rather nice candlestick if I fix a base on it. When I've cleaned it up, of course.' He admired his handiwork at arm's length.

'You're right, Dad. It'll make a very nice candlestick.'

'I thought you'd agree with me, Rose.'

'But didn't you bring this fork to clear the stream?' Rose picked up the large garden fork that was lying nearby.

'Ah, yes, now you come to speak of it I believe I did.' Chad scratched his head. 'I must have thought this piece of wood would do it better. But now I'm not so sure ...'

'No, Dad, neither am I.' She began to hitch her dress up. 'Look, it won't take five minutes. It's that branch that's fallen in the water that's the cause of all the trouble.' She slipped off her shoes and stockings and waded into the water. 'This is what's been damming things up. All the bits of straw and rubbish have got caught up in it.' She gave a tug and the branch gave way, catching her off balance so that she fell backwards into the water.

Chad immediately scrambled down the bank to help her out. 'Oh, Rosie, now look at you. Whatever will your mother say?'

Rose looked down at her filthy dress and tried ineffectually to wring out the worst of the muddy water. 'Never mind what will my mother say. What will my mother-in-law say,' she answered ruefully. 'She'll never forgive me if I walk back to the mill looking like this.'

'Oh, don't worry about that. I'll take you on the cart,' Chad said, not realising that this would be almost as bad in Eve Dowland's eyes.

Emma took one look at her bedraggled daughter. 'Good gracious, girl. What in the world have you been doing?'

'Clearing the stream,' Chad said. 'It was my fault. I hadn't quite got round to doing it.'

'I fell in,' Rose added.

'I'd never have known,' Emma said dryly. Suddenly she burst out laughing. 'Now you really *will* be in trouble when you get back.'

'It's all very well for you to laugh,' Rose said, irritated. 'But what am I going to do, Mum?'

'First of all, you're going to have a cup of tea.' She looked at her husband. 'Didn't you pick some orchids for the girl, Chad?'

He looked blank. 'She never asked me.'

'Well, I'm asking you now. She needs them as a peace offering for her mother-in-law.'

Chad raised his eyebrows. 'What? Already?'

'Oh, it's nothing serious, Dad. Eve's a dear, really.' Rose picked up a corner of her skirt, 'But I can't possibly go back like this. She'd never forgive me. I suppose Millie hasn't got anything I could borrow, Mum, has she? She's much about my size.'

Emma pinched her lip. 'Only her bridesmaid's dress. You'll have to wear that. Even Mrs Dowland can't complain that's not smart.'

'Won't it look slightly ostentatious for a Monday afternoon?' Chad asked mildly.

'It'll be better than going back looking as if she'd been in the midden,' Emma said. 'Now, go on, upstairs and get changed, my girl. And, Chad, go and find her some orchids. And leave that bit of wood here, else you'll forget what you've gone for.' Emma watched her big, broad-shouldered husband shamble off like a big shaggy dog, shaking her head affectionately after him as he went.

As Rose walked home later that afternoon, dressed in Millie's mauve shantung bridesmaid's dress, that didn't quite fit and had rather too many frills and tucks in it for everyday wear, she had the feeling that even the large bunch of orchids her father had gathered was not going to appease Eve.

She was quite right. She realised this as soon as she walked through the door, although Eve was never a woman to raise her voice.

She looked up from her lace-making and removed her *pince nez*. 'Rose! What *do* you think you're wearing?' she said, as she looked the mauve shantung up and down in something akin to disbelief. 'Are you deliberately trying to be awkward? Or are you trying to prove something? Whatever it is, you look quite ridiculous in that dress – heaven knows it was bad enough when your sister wore it at your wedding.' She waved her hand in dismissal. 'I suggest you go upstairs right away and take it off.'

Biting her lip hard against a sharp retort Rose said equally quietly, 'No, I am not trying to be awkward, nor am I trying to *prove* anything, whatever you may mean by that, Eve. In fact, I've brought you this bunch of wild orchids because I was worried that what I said before I went out might have upset you.' She held them out but Eve made no effort to take them. 'As for the dress,' she looked down at it and smoothed the frills. 'I can't see anything wrong with it. I think it's a very pretty dress and it's beautifully made.'

'It's common. And far too fussy. Goodness knows where it came from.'

Rose flushed in annoyance. 'My grandmother made it. She's a very good needlewoman, I'll have you know,' she said hotly, remembering all the hours Granny Robins had spent sewing the two bridesmaid's dresses. She took a deep breath and went on in a carefully controlled voice, 'The reason I'm wearing this dress, Eve, is because I had to take my own off. I fell in the stream as I was trying to help my father to clear it and my dress got all wet and muddy. I'm afraid it was a case of either walk home in a state of filth or put this on. It was all my mother could find that would fit me.' She lifted her head. 'I'm very sorry if I've displeased you. But I think you'd have been even more upset if I had walked home through the village all muddy and bedraggled.'

Eve pursed her lips. 'Frankly, I don't know which would have been worse. You should remember that you're a Dowland now, Rose, and that we Dowlands have standards to uphold. I'll thank you not to forget that.' Her features relaxed and she stretched out her hand for the flowers. 'However, it was kind of you to bring me these. And as for the dress, well, I must confess I thought you were being deliberately perverse. Lissa!' she turned to the girl ironing at the table. 'Put these in a vase, will you?'

'It's all right. Lissa's busy. I'll do it,' Rose said quickly.

'No, you will not.' Eve waved her away. 'Do as I say. Go and take that dreadful dress off.' She handed the flowers to Lissa.

'It *isn't* a dreadful dress. It's a very nice dress,' Rose insisted. 'But I will go and take it off because my sister Millie would be furious if she knew I'd borrowed it. I'll put my old gingham back on. Will that do?' The last words were said with barely concealed sarcasm.

'As you've very little choice it will have to, I suppose. And one more thing, Rose.' Eve's voice stopped her as she reached the door. 'I was under the impression that you were going to visit your mother, not to clean ditches. You belong here now, Rose and I shan't expect you to go labouring at Crick's Farm. Please remember that in future.'

'Very well, Eve. I'll remember. I'll remember everything you've said.' She left the room, not quite slamming the door. That was the last straw. No wonder the boys call their mother the Matriarch, she thought savagely as she ran up the stairs, furious at her mother-in-law's ultimatum. She's a real old tyrant. But she won't stop me from lending a hand at home. If there's work to be done when I visit, then I shall help, and she can say what she likes.

She reached her room and sank down on the bed, still fuming. Then she saw the roses in the bowl on the dressing table that Eve had put there for her homecoming and was filled with remorse. She shouldn't have had such unkind thoughts about Eve. She was the kindest mother-in-law a girl could have, and if she was a little fussy and a bit snobbish, well, that was a small thing to endure for the privilege of being married to Michael and living in this lovely house. She got up from the bed and went over and sniffed the roses appreciatively and then began to struggle with the mauve dress, which was difficult to get out of because it had hooks and eyes all down the back.

She was still struggling several minutes later when there was a tap at the door and Lissa poked her head in.

'I wondered if you might like some help, Rose,' she said timidly.

'Oh, yes, please, Lissa. I'm stuck,' she called. 'I was just wondering what I was going to do. Would you mind unfastening these hooks for me? I can't reach.'

A moment later Rose was free and she wriggled out of the offending dress. Lissa picked it up and laid it carefully on the bed. 'I think it's a pretty dress,' she said. 'I thought your sisters looked beautiful at your wedding.'

Rose nodded. 'So did I.' The two girls looked at each other and then both burst out laughing. 'Oh, dear, I really got into hot water downstairs, didn't I?' Rose said.

Lissa nodded, serious again. 'Yes, she was very cross. I thought you were very brave, standing up to her like that.'

'I had to bite my tongue or I'd have said a lot more,' Rose admitted. She pushed a stray auburn lock back. 'I haven't got this colour hair for nothing,' she said with a smile.

'Oh, it was a good thing you didn't say any more,' Lissa said, looking shocked. 'She can be a real tartar, you know.' She looked over her shoulder to make sure the door was shut and took a step towards Rose. 'When I was little she used to shut me in the coal cellar,' she whispered.

'Coal cellar? When you were little?' Rose repeated, frowning. 'However long have you been here, Lissa?'

It was Lissa's turn to frown. 'I don't know what you mean, how long have I been here. I've always been here. This is where I live. I was born here.'

'Where's your mother, then? And your father? Do they work here, too?'

'My father died.' Lissa's expression softened as she began to speak of him. 'He was nice. I liked him. He was ever so kind. He used to fetch me out of the coal cellar after she'd shut me in and he'd give me sweets and then take me for rides with him in the trap.'

'What about your mother, then? Where is she now? Is she dead, too?'

Lissa screwed up her face, trying to understand what Rose was saying. Then her face cleared and she laughed. 'No, silly, of course she isn't. You know very well where she is. She's downstairs.'

'Downstairs?' Rose frowned. 'Downstairs where?'

'Downstairs in the kitchen, of course.' Lissa said, still puzzled.

Rose's jaw dropped. 'You don't mean ... Not Eve! Not Mrs Dowland! She can't be your *mother*, Lissa!'

Lissa nodded. 'Yes, she is. Didn't you know?' She sniffed. 'She doesn't like me much, though.'

'Doesn't *like* you! Why, the way she treats you ... ' Rose sat down on the bed with a thump and shook her head, still reeling from the shock of Lissa's revelation. 'I thought you were just a servant here. It never ever occurred to me ... ' she caught the girl's hand. 'Oh, Lissa, I'm dreadfully sorry I didn't realise, but I'd no idea ... '

'It's all right. Daughters always have to work hard, she told me that after Daddy died. She never said I was a servant, though.' Lissa put her head on one side. 'Did you have to work hard, when you were at home? You're a daughter, like me, aren't you?'

Rose nodded. 'Yes, I did have to work hard. Very hard. But it wasn't the same. My sisters and I weren't treated like you are.'

'What do you mean? I don't understand.'

'Well, you're treated like a skivvy. You're expected to be at everybody's beck and call. You don't have any life of your own, do you?'

Lissa hunched her shoulders. 'Don't I? I don't know. I've always been told what to do so I'm used to it. Everybody treats me like that. 'Cept Dan, of course. He's always nice to me. He's my favourite.'

'What about Michael? Do you know he's never even mentioned that you were his sister.' Rose was shaking her head in disbelief.

'I 'spect he's forgotten,' Lissa said with a shrug.

'But why? Why does Eve treat you the way she does?'

Lissa shrugged again. ''Cause she doesn't like me. 'Cause she never wanted me in the first place, I reckon. She likes the boys best. Specially George. Isn't George ever coming back, Rose?'

'It doesn't look like it. Not now he's married.'

'I'm glad. He used to get powerful drunk. He used to frighten me when he was drunk.'

'Lissa!' Eve's voice came from the foot of the stairs. 'Where are you? What are you doing? Remember there are vegetables to prepare. You'll get all behind with your work if you don't come and get on with it.'

'I'm coming.' Lissa scuttled to the door. 'Oh, dear, I'd better not let her see me leaving your room, Rose, I was only supposed to be putting some things away. What can I do?'

'I'll go down first. You can follow while I'm talking to her, then she won't see where you've come from.' Rose gave Lissa a conspiratorial wink. 'And don't worry, I'll help you with the vegetables.'

Rose went downstairs and back into the kitchen. Eve looked up as she entered and smiled at her. 'That's better, my dear, even though it is very faded,' she said kindly and Rose knew she regretted their little quarrel as much as Rose did herself. 'What are you going to do now?' she asked as Rose went over to the sink.

'I'm going to help Lissa prepare the vegetables.'

'There's no need for that, you know. Lissa is quite capable and it gives her something to do.'

Rose didn't reply and although Eve pursed her lips in disapproval she made no further objection but sat with her lace bobbins whilst Rose and Lissa prepared the evening meal. It occurred to Rose that hands that had been unable to knead bread only that morning seemed to have no difficulty in doing such fine work but she pushed the thought from her as being uncharitable.

Whilst Rose and Lissa were scraping potatoes Dan came in with a basketful of produce from his garden.

'There, that's the last of the strawberries,' he said, putting them carefully on the table. 'But there are still plenty of raspberries. Do you want to make jam, Mother?'

'Yes. Lissa can make it tomorrow,' Eve said, looking up from her embroidery. 'Have you finished at the mill for today, Daniel?'

'Yes, we've done what we set out to do. The tide's gone now.'

'Where's Michael then?'

'He's still aboard the barge with the skipper, Jim Barnes. But I should think he'll be in soon because the Cap'n wants to get away on the ebb tonight.'

Lissa dropped the potato she was scraping and turned round. 'Cap'n Barnes?' she said. 'Isn't it Cap'n Joel's boat?'

Dan laughed. 'Steve Joel's on the *Perseverance*, Lissy. The barge tied up now is the *Patience*, hadn't you noticed? The *Perseverance* will be along next week or the week after.'

'Oh.' Lissa went back to her potato but Rose noticed that there were two spots of colour on her cheeks.

Nothing was changed in the kitchen of the Mill House, yet to Rose everything was different in the light of her new knowledge about Lissa. Now she could see that Dan, whom she had thought behaved in a rather over-familiar fashion with the girl, was only acting in a perfectly natural brotherly manner. As for Eve, it would seem that Lissa could well be right in thinking her mother resented her birth. As far as Eve was concerned a daughter appeared to be of little more account than a servant – perhaps this was the way she herself had been treated as a girl, Rose mused.

Then there was Michael. He had never spoken of Lissa as his sister and he certainly didn't treat her as such. Or maybe that was how he expected to treat a sister. Rose sighed. Perhaps her own family had strange ideas and the Dowlands reflected most families. No, that wasn't the case she was sure. Even though she and her sisters had always been used to working very hard, they were always treated as equals and never as menials, like Lissa was.

We've always known we were loved, Rose realised with a flash of insight. And that's what Lissa is missing.

'I reckon we've done enough now, don't you, Rose?' Lissa said as Rose picked up another large potato. She shook the pan. 'Look, we've done tons. I reckon there'll be enough there to fry up for the boys' breakfast tomorrow.'

'What? Oh, yes. I wasn't thinking.' Rose smiled at Lissa. 'I'd have done the whole lot if you hadn't spoken, Lissa.'

'You really have no need to prepare vegetables at all, Rose,' Eve repeated from her place on the settle by the stove. 'Lissa is quite capable.'

'I know that, Eve, but I'm quite happy to help where I can,' Rose replied cheerfully. She turned back to Lissa. 'I'll lay the table, shall I?'

Lissa stole a slightly nervous look in her mother's direction before nodding. 'If you like,' she whispered.

Half an hour later the meal was on the table but Michael still hadn't put in an appearance.

'We won't wait,' Eve announced. 'There's never any telling when he'll arrive. You can put his supper over a saucepan, Lissa-dear.'

Lissa-dear, Rose repeated in her head. It was no term of endearment, that was certain.

When supper was over and Rose had helped Lissa to wash the dishes Eve went to bed. '"Early to bed, early to rise,"' she quoted as she gathered up her embroidery bag, '"makes a man healthy, wealthy and wise." I like to think that applies to women, too. You'd do well to observe it, Rose. It could improve your temper.' Eve smiled as she spoke but Rose realised that she hadn't yet quite been forgiven for the afternoon's outburst.

After Eve had gone to bed Dan sat down on the settle to read the newspaper and Rose sat down at the table with a book. Lissa was flitting round the kitchen like a little bird, still busily tidying up although there was nothing out of place. It seemed as if she didn't know how to stop working.

'Rose thought I was a servant, Dan,' she said suddenly, laughing as she spoke. 'Wasn't that funny? She didn't know I was your sister.'

Dan lowered the newspaper and looked at her for a minute before shaking his head. 'I'm not really surprised, Lissy,' he said, 'that's how you get treated most of the time, you poor little mawther.'

Lissa hunched her shoulders. 'I don't mind. At least she

85

doesn't lock me up in the coal cellar any more,' she said thoughtfully. 'I didn't like that.'

Dan shook his head. 'You don't understand, Lissy, do you?' he said, and there was a wealth of affection in his voice. 'You don't know what life's all about.' He looked up at Rose. 'How can she, poor mite? She never goes anywhere to see how other people are treated. All she knows is working her fingers to the bone here morning, noon and night.'

Lissa went over and sat down at Dan's feet, resting her head on his knee. 'Do you think it'll matter if I don't finish the ironing tonight, Dan?' she asked anxiously. 'There's such a lot and I'm ever so tired.'

'I'll help you with it tomorrow, Lissa,' Rose said quickly. 'You run along to bed. You look worn out.'

'I always get tired on wash days.' Lissa yawned. 'I've still got the fire to rake out and the coal to get in for the morning.'

'I'll do that, Lissy. Do as Rose says and run along to bed,' Dan said, stroking her hair as he spoke.

'Where do you sleep, Lissa?' Rose asked as the girl got to her feet. After what she had learned today she wouldn't have been in the least surprised if Lissa had said she slept under the table.

'Upstairs, in the attic,' Lissa said proudly, carefully lighting a candle to take with her 'I've got my own little room.'

Sadly, Dan watched her go. 'I feel so sorry for her, poor little Lissy,' he said as she closed the door behind her. 'She was the apple of my father's eye. He was so delighted to have a little daughter after three sons that he couldn't bear her out of his sight. Used to call her his little Melly, I remember.'

'Melly?' Rose said in surprise.

'Yes, her name's Melissa, really. He chose her name. He said it was the prettiest name he could find for the prettiest little girl in the world.' He folded the newspaper carefully. 'I was about six when she was born. Of course, I didn't know much about it at the time but I guess my mother thought she had finished with childbearing; she'd given my father three sons and as far as she was concerned that was it. She couldn't have been pleased to find herself—' he hesitated, '—well, with a babe-in-arms again. Especially a girl. She never wanted a girl. All she wanted was sons. At the same time, I think she was jealous because my father thought so much of Lissy. He absolutely idolised her.'

'How old was she when he died?'

'Lissy? Nearly eight. It was ten years ago.'

'Then she's about the same age as my sister Babs. She's eighteen, too, but Babs seems older, somehow.'

He nodded. 'Lissy's young for her years.' His faced softened. 'She's not terribly bright, as you can see. But I'm very fond of her.'

'What about Michael?'

He looked up surprised. 'What about him?'

'How does he feel about Lissa?'

He hunched his shoulders. 'I dunno. I've never asked him. Anyway, most times he's not here. And when he is he doesn't have much to say.' He smiled. 'Do you know, Rose, he's been at home more in the few days you've been here than he has for years.'

'Where does he usually spend his time, then?'

'Out on the marsh. Or down at the Miller's Arms. He knows a lot about birds and wild life and he goes punt gunning at certain times of the year,' he grinned, 'as you'll find out when he brings wild duck in for you to pluck and dress!' He shrugged. 'He's quite friendly with a chap called Silas Hands. He's a bit of a rough diamond and I wouldn't trust him far, myself, but Mike seems to get on well with him. They go bird watching together. Or so they say. But I don't ask questions and Mike's not one to say a lot, so I dunno, really. As long as he's there when there's work to be done at the mill it's not my business what he does other times.'

'Well, I must say I'm getting a bit anxious about him tonight, Dan,' Rose said. 'It's nearly ten o'clock and he hasn't even been in for his supper. Do you think I should go and look for him?'

Dan shook his head. 'No. He wouldn't like that. In any case, where would you look? The last I saw of him was on the *Patience* but she'll be long gone. There's no telling where he's gone since then although I'd give a guess at the Miller's Arms. I shouldn't wait up for him, Rose. He'll come home when he's ready and not before. I'm afraid you'll have to get used to that.'

'But he's a married man now. He's got me to consider,' Rose said huffily.

Dan smiled at her and lifted his hand as if to fend off a blow. 'You'll have to take that up with him. Far be it for me to interfere between man and wife. I'm only telling you how he used to be.'

'I see. Well, I'll just put a little more water in the saucepan where his supper is keeping hot or it'll be all dried up and then I might as well go to bed.'

She couldn't sleep. There was so much to think about. Almost every day seemed to bring something new, something that made her realise that things at Dowlands' Mill weren't quite what she had thought. She lay staring up into the darkness. First there was George going off like that and now there was Lissa. Melissa. Yes, it was a pretty name. She frowned. Eve had seemed such a kind, gentle woman that it was almost impossible to believe that she could treat her own daughter as a servant in her own house. Poor Lissa, it was all very sad.

Her thoughts turned to Michael. It was well after half past ten now. Where could he be?

Chapter Eight

She was just dropping off to sleep when she heard Michael's foot on the stairs.

'Where on earth have you been, dear?' she asked, getting up on one elbow as he came through the door. 'Have you eaten your meal? Lissa left it over a saucepan for you.'

He yawned widely. 'Yes, I've eaten it,' he said, throwing his boots down. 'Go to sleep, woman. It's late.'

'Not till you tell me where you've been, Michael. I'm your wife. I've a right to know.'

He didn't reply, but continued taking off his clothes and putting on his night-shirt.

'Have you been with your friend Silas?' she persisted.

He still didn't answer, but climbed into bed beside her. 'Now listen to me, my girl,' he said, leaning over her with one hand either side of her shoulders, 'have I asked you what you've been doing with yourself every minute of the day today?'

'No, but ...'

'Then I don't expect to have to report every move I make to you. Is that clear?'

'I wasn't out till nearly eleven o'clock. I should expect you to question me if I was, dearest,' she said, trying to sound reasonable. 'Your supper must have been dried right up.'

'That's my concern. I ate it. It was all right.' He began pulling at her night-dress.

She clutched it to her. 'Not till you tell me where you've been, Michael.' She laughed, trying to turn it into a joke.

'Oh, no, my girl. I'm not having that.' He wasn't laughing

89

as he dragged her hands away. 'You're my wife, remember.'

He was not gentle and she felt used and somehow defiled because when he had finished with her he rolled away without a word and less than two minutes later began to snore. He still hadn't told her where he had been all evening. Not that he needed to. She had smelled the spirits on his breath.

It was a long time before she slept. She had so much wanted to talk to him, to ask him about his sister, Melissa, but he had seemed different, somehow, almost like a stranger. Was that what drink did to him? She realised that there was still a great deal she didn't know about her new husband.

When she woke the next morning he was already up and gone although it was not much after six o'clock. Hurriedly, Rose scrambled out of bed, determined to be up before Lissa had a chance to bring her tea in bed. That was one task she would spare her new found sister-in-law. After all, she had been used to getting up early all her life. Nobody slept late at Crick's Farm, so it would be no hardship.

When she reached the kitchen she was surprised to see that Eve was already there, looking her usual immaculate self, eating toast and marmalade, whilst Michael and Dan tucked into large plates of bacon and eggs, with fried bread and fried potatoes. Lissa was at the stove making more toast.

'Would you like bacon and egg, Rose?' Lissa asked turning round.

'No, toast will be fine. And I can make it myself. You sit down and have yours, Lissa.'

'Lissa is making toast for everyone,' Eve said. 'I'll have another piece whilst you're about it, Lissa-dear.'

Rose poured herself a cup of tea and then sat down.

After barely more than a nod in her direction, Eve continued with what she was saying to Michael and Dan.

'I think it's time one of you went to Ipswich again to try to find George. After all, there must be someone who knows where he is. Some of his drinking friends, for instance. They'll know, I'm sure.' She paused for long enough to take a bite of toast and swallow it before going on, 'George is my eldest son. My heir. He needs to be found. He can't simply walk away from his inheritance.'

Michael dropped his fork with a clatter, at which she waved her hand in his direction. 'Oh, you and Daniel will both get your share, never fear. Don't imagine I don't appreciate the work you do. But this has gone on long enough. George is my eldest son and I want him back here.' She looked at Dan. 'Will you go to Ipswich today and make enquiries about him, Daniel?'

'I can't possibly go today. I've got one of the stones to dress,' Dan said. 'I might be able to go later in the week.' It was obvious that he was reluctant.

Eve turned to her other son. 'You, Michael. Will you go today?'

'I will not.' Michael spread his hands. 'What's the point? He told me he didn't want to come back. Why should I go trailing round half Suffolk searching for him? He never liked milling, you know that. And if he's happy keeping a pub, well, good luck to him is what I say. I just hope he doesn't drink all the profits and bankrupt himself.'

'But you said he was married,' Eve persisted.

'So? That's all the more reason why he won't want to come back here, I should think.'

'But suppose he has children?' Eve put her cup down with a clatter. 'I have to think about my will,' she said.

'Haven't you got that all sorted out?' Michael asked. 'Heaven sakes, you spent long enough closeted up with old Mr Bradshaw, Father's solicitor, after Father died.'

'Of course I have,' Eve said irritably. 'But if George is determined to stay away, well, that could change things.'

'Oh, I see.' Michael looked up from mopping his plate with a piece of bread. 'You want me to go and find George and tell him to come home or he'll be cut out of his mother's will. Is that it?'

'I didn't say that,' Eve said huffily.

'Well, it sounds as if that's what you meant.' He took a long draught of tea. 'No, I won't do it. When I last saw him he made it quite plain he didn't want me to know where he was living and I respect that. If you want to find him you'll have to put out a search warrant. I'm not doing it and that's flat.'

'Daniel?' She turned to him enquiringly.

He shook his head. 'No, I think Mike's right. We have to respect George's wishes.'

Eve got up from the table. 'Very well, if that's how you both feel, I shall go myself. I need to talk to him, if nothing else,' she said. 'Lissa. Go and tell old Jacob to have the trap ready by ten. There's a train from Bramford to Ipswich at eleven, so that should give me plenty of time.'

'I really don't know what you intend to do when you get there, Mother,' Dan protested. 'I wouldn't put it past George to put the pub, wherever it is, in his wife's name. If he's done that you'll have no chance of finding him.'

'At least I'm making an effort. Which is more than can be said of either of you,' she replied sharply.

At ten o'clock old Jacob brought the trap to the front of the house.

As Eve climbed into it she was calling, 'Remember you've got the ironing to finish, Lissa-dear. And since I've got to go out you'll have to pick the raspberries and make the jam. Rose might like to help you when she's made the bread.' She was still shouting orders as the trap clattered away.

'Of course I'll help you pick the raspberries, Lissa,' Rose said after she had gone. 'I'll enjoy that.'

Lissa didn't return the smile. 'Remember, you've got the bread to make, Rose. You'll find that will be your job every day now. Don't you realise my mother sees you as just another servant to order around?'

Thoughtfully, Rose followed Lissa back into the house. It was not true of course; Lissa was imagining things. Why, only last night Eve had tried to stop Rose from helping to prepare and clear up the supper, saying that Lissa could manage perfectly well on her own. It had been Rose herself who had insisted on lending a hand. As for making the bread, surely that was a small enough task to carry out daily, if that was what Eve wished. It would be no hardship. Heavens, she had been used to working from dawn till dusk almost without respite when she had lived at home. She looked down at her hands. In the short time since her marriage to Michael they were already becoming softer. She must remember to cream them well each night, then perhaps Eve would teach her to do fine embroidery, or even the intricacies of lace-making. They could sit together and sew. Whatever Lissa might say, she was sure Eve would like that.

And as for Lissa ... she looked at the girl's thin back in her faded gingham dress as she went through the door. Could it be that she was jealous? Could it be that she was trying to poison her new sister-in-law's mind against the mother she hated? Rose shook her head. Lissa seemed so guileless, so genuine, that it was impossible to believe her capable of such behaviour.

As the day wore on it became even more difficult to imagine Lissa as a trouble-maker because she seemed so genuinely happy to be working with Rose in the absence of her mother and she sang as she went about her tasks.

When everything was done, the ironing finished and the linen pulled up on to the big airing rack and the bread cooling, she said eagerly, 'If we leave the boys' dinner all ready for them we could take a picnic with us when we go to pick the raspberries, couldn't we, Rose?'

'Is it far, then?' Rose asked, surprised.

'No, not very. Just the other side of the mill pond.' Lissa shrugged her thin shoulders. 'But I thought it might be a nice thing to do. I've seen people picnic along the river bank and thought how lucky they were. But it was only an idea. It doesn't matter.' Her expression showed that it did.

Rose smiled. 'I think it's a lovely idea, Lissa. It'll be a treat to be out in the sunshine. I'll cut some bread and cheese for us and you can find a basket to put it in.'

Lissa's face brightened again. 'And we'll take a bottle of Dan's cider. He always makes cider with the apple drops. It's very good, too.'

'Will he mind?'

'Oh no. But I'll call in at the mill and tell him.' Lissa hummed happily under her breath as she collected together the things they would need.

Rose waited on the little wooden bridge over the mill stream while Lissa went into the mill to see Dan. The water was surprisingly deep and so still that she could see pebbles, white, black, sandy coloured and all shades in between patterning the bottom of the stream and her own image was reflected in the sunlit surface. Yet in spite of the sunshine the bridge had a chill, almost eerie feeling about it and she gave a little shudder as she peered down into the water.

Suddenly, she felt two arms round her and she was swung off

the ground. 'Do you fancy a swim, then?' a voice said, and she found herself suspended over the handrail above the deep water.

She gave a little scream and her arms went round her husband's neck. 'Oh, Michael! What are you doing? Stop it! You'll drop me!' she cried, clinging to him, half laughing, half fearful.

He took a step backwards and put her down beside him, still keeping his arms round her. 'Of course I wouldn't drop you, you silly little goose.' He laughed and kissed the tip of her nose.

'Not on purpose. But you could have slipped, Michael,' she said sternly, annoyed that he should have frightened her yet pleased he was in a happier mood than last night.

He gave her a squeeze. 'No, of course I wouldn't. And if I had I'd have dived in after you. I promise I wouldn't have let you drown.' He roared with laughter.

'Thank you very much. That's a real comfort.' She laughed with him and gave him a playful push.

He leaned over and looked down into the clear depths, his arm still circling her waist. 'At least it's calm today. It isn't always as calm as this, you know.' He looked sideways at her. 'When the mill's running there's a terrific force of water going through here. That's what makes the wheel turn. Makes a hell of a noise. It always amazes me what a noise water makes. And the power of it, too.' He looked round at her and said, his voice serious, 'I warn you, Rosie, if you were to fall in here when the wheel's going you wouldn't get out alive.'

She shuddered and gave a nervous laugh. 'Oh, Michael, don't say such things.'

'Why not? It's true.' He stamped his feet, laughing. 'But you don't have to worry, Rosie. The bridge is quite sturdy, so it's not likely to collapse under your great weight.' Before she could think up a rejoinder to that cheeky remark he changed the subject, pointing to the basket on her arm. 'Where are you off to, then?'

'I'm going to pick some of Dan's raspberries with Lissa. We're going to picnic in the field.'

'Ah. While the cat's away ...' He nodded.

She bridled. 'Not at all. Lissa thought it would be a nice idea, that's all.'

'All right, don't get all hoity toity. I don't blame you. And it'll do Lissa good. She doesn't often get out of the house.' He kissed the tip of her nose again. 'Just don't sit in the sun for too long, it'll make your nose peel.'

'And you won't love me with a peeling nose?' she asked, putting her head on one side.

'It won't make any difference to me, but it'll tell the Matriarch what you've been doing.' He tapped the side of his own nose and grinned. 'And that might not be such a good idea. But I can't stand here talking all day, I've got work to do. The *Perseverance* will be in this afternoon so there'll be grain to unload.' He turned away as Lissa came running along, holding her hat on, her face pink with excitement.

'Oh, Michael,' she called, 'I've just told Dan, we've left your dinner on the table all ready for you. We're going on a picnic, Rose and me.'

Michael raised his hand and started to walk away. 'Enjoy yourselves, then, and don't eat more raspberries than you pick.'

He went off and the two girls carried on over the bridge. Rose noticed that Lissa was almost pretty now that she was excited. She felt a stab of pity. Poor girl, her life must be very drab if a picnic in a field was all it took.

Over the bridge they skirted the mill pool, which was bordered by weeping willows and covered a deceptively large area. At the far end Lissa led the way through a little wicket gate into what she called 'Dan's field'.

It was a big field, laid out in carefully cultivated rectangles with grassy paths between.

Rose paused and gazed at the neat rows of vegetables; peas and beans carefully staked, currant bushes covered with nets against hungry birds, rows of mounded up potatoes, a patch of onions with the tops carefully folded over, tomatoes hanging in ripening bunches with lettuces growing round their feet. 'Does Dan do all this?' she breathed.

'Yes, he spends most of his spare time here. He likes gardening,' Lissa said. 'He grows all our vegetables and fruit. Look, the apples will soon be ripe.' She pointed to the small orchard in one corner. 'We could sit over there under the trees where it's nice and shady and have our dinner, couldn't we?' She looked hopefully at Rose.

'I think we'd better pick some raspberries first, don't you?' Rose laughed.

Lissa made a face. Suddenly, she looked like a mischievous child. 'I s'pose so,' she said with a grin.

The raspberries hung on the canes like huge pink rain drops and it didn't take the girls long to pick what they needed. As they picked, Lissa said, 'Did I hear Michael say that the *Perseverance* will be in later on?'

'Yes, I believe he did.' Rose reached for a raspberry as she spoke. 'Why?'

'That's Cap'n Joel's boat.' Lissa blushed. 'He's ever so nice looking, Rose. You wait till you see him.'

Rose looked round at her. She blushed again and started busily picking. 'I see him sometimes if I take a cup of tea over to the mill,' she said, trying, and failing, to sound nonchalant.

'Is he nice, as well as nice looking, Lissa?' Rose asked.

'Oh, yes,' Lissa breathed. 'He's ever so nice. I like him much better than the other barge skippers.'

'And does he like you?'

Lissa shrugged. 'I dunno. I don't s'pose so. I don't think he notices me much. I'm not very pretty, am I?'

Rose regarded her, with her head on one side. 'You don't make the best of yourself, Lissa.'

Lissa shrugged again. 'I don't know what you mean.'

They picked on in silence. Rose realised that what Lissa had said was true. She didn't know what Rose had meant. She had no idea how to make the best of herself. Yet she was not the simpleton everyone had seemed to suggest, Rose had already discovered that.

When they had picked a basket full of raspberries and the sun was high in the sky they flung their hats off and sat under the trees to eat the bread and cheese Rose had packed and drink Dan's cider.

'Oh, I wish we could do this more often,' Lissa said, licking her fingers after dipping into the raspberry basket. 'Will you ask her if we can, Rose?'

'Who? Your Mother?' Rose had noticed that Lissa rarely called her mother by name which was probably why it had taken so long for her to learn what the relationship was. 'Yes, I will if you like. But can't you ask her yourself, Lissa? She might even like to come too.'

Lissa shook her head. 'She'll say no if I ask her. She always does. And anyway, it wouldn't be the same if she came. She'd want to bring a parasol to keep off the sun and a chair to sit on, for a start. She wouldn't sit on the grass, like this. And she wouldn't let us, either. It wouldn't be fun any more if she came.' She dipped her hand in the raspberry basket again.

Rose gave the back of her hand a playful slap. 'If you eat them all we shall have to spend the afternoon picking more,' she laughed.

But Lissa didn't laugh. Her face crumpled as she drew her hand away and held it with her other one. 'I'm sorry, Rose,' she said, nearly in tears. 'I didn't mean to do the wrong thing, really I didn't. You won't tell her, will you? Please don't tell her.' She scrambled to her feet. 'I'll pick some more. I didn't eat many. Only two or three. Not many. Truly, I didn't eat many.' She was shaking her head violently.

Rose got to her feet and put her arm round Lissa, who was trembling now.

'It's all right, Lissa,' she said, her voice soothing. 'Sit down again. I didn't mean to hurt you.' She drew Lissa down beside her again and stroked her hand gently. 'I was only joking when I slapped you. It didn't really hurt you, did it? I didn't mean to, I promise.'

Lissa looked at her suspiciously. 'You're not cross with me? But you ...' she fingered the back of her hand.

'I'm sorry, Lissa,' she said gently. 'It wasn't meant to hurt you. I'm really not cross with you, honestly I'm not. It was only a playful slap.' She laughed. 'After all, it really doesn't matter how many you eat because we can easily pick some more, can't we? There's no shortage.'

'A playful slap,' Lissa repeated, puzzled. 'I've never heard of that. Slaps are for hurting, not playing.'

Rose shook her head. 'That one wasn't meant to hurt you. But I shouldn't have done it. I'm very sorry, Lissa. I didn't realise it would upset you like that. I won't do it again. I promise.' She leaned forward and kissed Lissa on the cheek.

Lissa put her hand up to the spot Rose's lips had touched

and her eyes filled with tears which she tried to brush away without Rose seeing.

Rose took the cue and busied herself packing up the picnic, pretending not to notice. It was painfully obvious that the poor girl wasn't used to demonstrations of affection. 'Well, come on,' she said briskly, when she had finished, 'I suppose we'd better go back and make a start on this jam or we'll both be in trouble, won't we?' She got to her feet and picked up the basket.

Lissa followed suit and as she stood up she caught her hair in the low branch of the apple tree they had been sitting under.

'Ow.' She tried to pull herself free.

'Wait a minute. Let me ...' Rose pulled the rag that was tying back Lissa's hair and freed her.

Lissa shook her hair. 'Thank you. That's better,' she said, reaching for the rag.

But Rose held on to it. 'You know, you've got pretty hair, Lissa,' she said, fluffing it out, with her head on one side. 'It's a lovely pale colour and quite thick and wavy when it's not scragged back into that rag. You should wear it loose like that sometimes. It suits you. Gives you a kind of elfin quality.'

Lissa fingered it for a moment, then flicked it back. 'I couldn't wear it loose. It would get in the way when I'm working,' she said.

'Yes, I know. But when you're not ...'

'I'm never not,' the girl said simply.

Sadly, Rose gave her back the rag and she dragged her hair back into it then jammed her hat back on. It was true. Lissa was 'never not' working.

By the time they had got the jam bubbling on the stove Lissa had regained her good spirits and was chattering away to Rose as they washed the jam jars in hot water ready to receive the hot jam.

Suddenly, she stopped talking and she seemed somehow to shrink into herself.

Rose frowned. 'Lissa? What's wrong? Are you ill?'

Dumbly, Lissa shook her head. 'No. Listen.'

Rose cocked her ear. In the distance she could hear the clop of hooves.

Lissa nodded and sighed deeply. 'She's back.' She gave a quick look round the kitchen, rushed over and plumped up the cushions on the settle and then pulled the kettle forward on the stove. 'The first thing she'll want is a cup of tea,' she whispered. 'Get the cups down, Rose.'

'I will when I've finished these jars,' Rose said.

'Oh, leave them. You can do them later.' Lissa was still scurrying about.

'No. Eve will have to wait a few minutes for her tea. She can see we're busy. Put the rest of the jars here so I can finish pouring the jam into them. We don't want it to set in the pan, do we?' Rose nodded towards the hot, sparkling jars. 'Come on, now. It's not as if we've been sitting and twiddling our thumbs. We can't leave it now we've got it this far.'

'Oh, dear. Oh, very well.' Obviously torn, Lissa took away the full jars and put empty ones in their place.

'There, it's done now,' Rose said, scraping the last few drops out of the pan. 'Now, we'll have time for a cup of tea.' As she spoke the door opened and Eve walked in, followed by Jacob carrying several parcels.

'I hope there's a cup of tea ready. I'm very dry,' she said as she sank on to the settle.

'I'm just making it,' Lissa said, scurrying over to the stove.

Eve fanned herself with her handkerchief. 'That's right, Jacob, put the things down there. Thank you. You can go now.' She waved her hand in dismissal.

Jacob touched his cap and shuffled out.

'Wouldn't you like a cup of tea too, Jacob?' Rose called after him. 'It's a very hot day and you must be parched.'

He turned in amazement and looked from Rose to his mistress and back again. 'Thankee ... ' he snatched his cap off and started to come back into the kitchen but Eve said smoothly, 'Jacob's wife will have tea ready for him, I'm sure. Thank you, Jacob. That will be all.'

The old man replaced his cap and went off with a slightly crestfallen look.

Lissa looked at her mother, appalled. 'But Jacob's wife *died* six months ago, Mummy. Had you forgotten?' she said, her voice barely above a whisper.

Eve raised her eyebrow. 'Oh, yes, to tell the truth I had.' She shrugged. 'Well, it's no wonder. She'd been housebound for such a long time we never saw her. Well, never mind.' She turned to Rose. 'It was your fault, Rose, because it was a very silly thing to do. One doesn't entertain servants in the house, not even in the kitchen. It would only embarrass them.'

'I don't see why,' Rose said with a shrug, 'Jacob looked as if he could do with a cup of tea. And there's plenty in the pot, so we could easily spare one for him. Especially if his wife ...'

'That's hardly the point, Rose. Jacob is a servant. That's what you must remember.' She waved her hand. 'Of course, it's not something you would know about, living the way you did at Crick's Farm,' she said, thrusting in another barb. 'But you'll learn. In time. Ah, thank you, Lissa. A cup of tea is just what I need. Did the jam turn out all right?' She looked about her. 'Where is it?'

'On the table, there. Look. We've just put it in the jars,' Rose said briefly, determined not to be rattled.

Eve frowned. 'What took you so long? I would have expected it to be all finished and done with long enough ago. After all, it's gone four o'clock.'

'We did have other things to do, you know,' Rose said.

'But there are two of you,' Eve said.

Rose caught Lissa's eye and saw her raise one eyebrow almost imperceptibly as if to say, 'There. What did I tell you? You're a servant here, just like me.'

Rose said nothing. It was quite plain that Eve had returned from Ipswich in a bad mood and having already upset her by offering Jacob a cup of tea she didn't want to antagonise her further. So she busied herself quietly with clearing up after the jam making. Fortunately the jam was a beautiful rich colour and looked as if it would set perfectly. At least Eve wouldn't be able to complain about *that*, she thought smugly.

Supper was taken almost in silence. Dan and Michael were both there and they talked a little about the price of grain and exchanged various bits of news that Stephen Joel had brought from Ipswich and Woodbridge.

Lissa fetched a large apple pie from the dresser. 'Is Cap'n Joel still here?' she asked casually, blushing scarlet as she spoke.

Dan smiled at her. 'Yes, he'll probably be here all day tomorrow, too, and go out on the evening tide.' He leaned over and whispered. 'Shall I tell him you asked?'

Lissa shook her head vigorously and with a quick glance in Eve's direction whispered back, 'Oh, no, Dan. You mustn't ... He wouldn't ...'

Dan grinned. 'It's all right, Lissy, I'm only teasing.'

'What's all that?' Eve asked from the other end of the table, her face like granite.

'Nothing, Mother. I was just teasing Lissy,' Dan answered easily. He smiled. 'Well, Mother, since you don't seem anxious to tell us I'd better ask. Did you have a useful day in Ipswich?'

She pursed her lips. 'If you mean did I find George, the answer is no.'

'I never thought you would,' Michael said. 'In fact I told you as much.'

'At least I made some effort to find him,' she snapped, 'which is more than I can say of either of you.' She held up her hand. 'No, thank you, Lissa. No apple pie for me.'

'That's not fair,' Rose said hotly. 'Dan did try to find him. I remember he'd gone to Ipswich to look for him the first day I came here. And Michael saw him and talked to him and tried to persuade him to come home the day we got engaged. So you can't say they haven't bothered, Eve.'

Eve turned a cold eye on her. 'I don't recall asking for your opinion, Rose,' she said. 'This is a matter between me and my sons, if you don't mind.'

'All the same, Rose is right,' Dan said pouring cream on his pie. 'The fact is, George has taken himself off and from what he told Mike he has no intention of coming back.'

'That's right,' Michael agreed. 'And you might as well face up to the fact that he was no good to us when he was here, Mother.'

'Michael! How can you say that about your brother!' Eve glared at him.

'I can say it because it's true. Only you would never admit it, because he was always your blue-eyed boy. He never did a day's work except when you were watching and I couldn't count the number of times he's slept off his drunken bouts up

101

on the top floor of the mill on a pile of sacks. He was a lazy, drunken sod and he's got what he deserved.'

'What do you mean by that?'

Michael shrugged uncomfortably. 'I mean if he's having to work hard in the pub he's taken because his wife keeps a beady eye on him and won't let him drink the profits, then it's no more than justice.'

'George wasn't that bad, Mike,' Dan protested. 'I'd say he was a bit weak, that's all.'

Rose looked from one brother to the other and then to Eve. The picture she was building of the missing George was a complex one. It was plain that he was the apple of his mother's eye, that Dan regarded him with a tolerant affection and that Michael had no patience with him at all. She wished he would return so that she could see for herself and form her own opinion of what he was really like.

Chapter Nine

The meal was almost over when Eve suddenly said casually, 'I went to see Mr Bradshaw, my solicitor, whilst I was in Ipswich. He suggests putting a piece in the local paper, asking George to come forward. If nothing happens after a reasonable time then, well, I shall have to consider what I shall do.'

Michael put his mug of tea down carefully on the table. 'You mean you'll alter your will.'

She stared at him, 'I didn't say that, Michael. I merely said I shall have to consider what I shall do. Nothing more than that.'

Michael looked at Dan and raised his eyebrows. Dan just shrugged.

Eve turned to Lissa. 'Lissa-dear, I want you to take those parcels up to my room. No, not that square one at the side, it's for Rose. Leave it here. But take the others. Rose, you can open that one. I hope you'll like it. I think you will. I always shop at the best places.'

'Something for me? Oh, that's very kind of you, Eve.' Excitedly, Rose untied the string on the brown paper parcel and opened the box. There, carefully folded in tissue paper was a dress of pale green silk. It was fairly plain, the only trimming a dark green ribbon four inches up from the hem under which was a border of lilies of the valley. A matching green bow at the V-shaped neck and a collar scattered with more lilies of the valley gave the dress an elegant, well-cut look. Rose held it up against her and saw that it was exactly the right length, reaching just to her ankles. 'Oh, Eve, you shouldn't have,' she said, her eyes shining. 'It's the most beautiful dress.'

'It's not for every day, you understand,' Eve said with a satisfied smile. She was obviously pleased to have bought Rose a present, 'but I thought the colour and style would suit you. You can wear it when we go to church on Sunday and if you visit your parents.' An expression of distaste, so fleeting that Rose almost missed it, crossed her face. 'It will not be suitable for clearing out ditches and the like, you understand.'

'No, Eve. Of course not. May I go and try it on?'

'Yes. But I'm so confident it will fit you that I've ordered two more to be sent.'

Rose hurried upstairs. She hadn't expected such kindness from her mother-in-law. She wriggled out of her old gingham and into the new dress. It was quite stylish, it's very plainness giving it a look of quality. Rose put on her best black shoes and went downstairs.

'My, that looks nice,' Dan said admiringly, making her blush.

'Yes, it looks all right,' Michael nodded. 'I suppose you'll be asking me to buy you some beads to go with it next,' he said with an exaggerated sigh and Rose wasn't quite sure whether he was laughing at her or whether he was serious.

She put her hand to her neck. 'Do you think it needs beads?' she asked tentatively. 'It's true, I haven't got any.'

'There you are, what did I say?' Michael slapped his knee and turned to his brother. 'Don't you ever get married, Dan. It's an expensive old business.'

'Well, you're not short of a copper, Mike. I daresay you could manage a string of glass beads from the market without a lot of trouble,' Dan laughed. 'Come on, we'd better get back to work.' With a last swig of tea he left and Michael followed.

Eve had taken no notice of the banter between the two men but was surveying Rose with her head on one side. 'Yes, it suits you. That's good. I knew I could trust my own judgement,' she said with a trace of smugness. 'Now go and take it off and hang it up, then you can help Lissa to finish the washing up.'

Rose didn't move for a minute. She looked round the room, at Eve sitting at the head of the table, and then at Lissa, who was already busy at the sink, her old faded gingham torn at the hem and her hair scragged back with rag that didn't even match the dress. She had seen the look of admiration on Lissa's face when she had come into the room and also the stark envy she hadn't been able to hide and she felt pity well up for the girl. She bit her lip, half afraid to speak, then said in a rush, 'But what about Lissa? Didn't you bring anything for her?'

Eve raised her eyebrows. 'No. Why should I? She had a new dress for your wedding.'

'But you said you'd ordered two more for me. That's hardly fair ...'

'Lissa has what clothes she needs.' Eve waved her hand. 'Go and take the dress off.'

'What does she wear to church on Sunday?'

'Lissa doesn't come to church. She has to cook the Sunday dinner. She doesn't need smart clothes.'

'But it isn't fair ...'

'*I'll* judge what's fair in this house.' Her voice was like a whiplash. 'Now, do as I say and take off the dress.' Her voice softened. 'Arguing with me is hardly a fitting way to say thank you, Rose, is it?' she said, and her tone was almost wheedling now.

Immediately contrite, Rose said, 'You're quite right, Eve. I'm sorry. I shouldn't have said what I did. I'm very grateful for the dress, really I am. I'm afraid I let my tongue run away with me sometimes.'

'Then you must learn to curb it, my dear, or it will get you into trouble.' Eve smiled at her and waved her hand in dismissal.

Rose discovered that she was expected to accompany Eve to church every Sunday without fail. Occasionally Dan came too but Michael and Lissa never did. Lissa was always too busy cooking the roast dinner that was expected to be on the table when they returned and Michael ... sometimes Rose wondered exactly what Michael did when he was not working at the mill. She seemed to see less and less of him as the weeks went by. He was usually up and gone before she was awake in the morning and she was often asleep before he came to bed at night. It was not at all as she had imagined their life together would be; he seemed to have made no concessions to marriage, his life hadn't changed at all as far as she could see, except when he woke her up – often after having had a bit too much to drink – to make love to her. Only there wasn't much love in the rough way he handled her. Sometimes she would lie staring up into the darkness when he had finished and lay snoring beside her and a tear would trickle down past her ear to fall on the pillow. This was not how she had imagined marriage would be. This was not how it was for her sister Grace, blissfully happy even though she lived in a poky little farm labourer's cottage. She tried to think back to the days before she and Michael were married. He had been quite loving and attentive then so why should he have changed? It irked her that there never seemed to be an opportunity when she could talk to him and ask him what was wrong because they were hardly ever alone together. Not that it would have made any difference, she suspected. Michael was not a man to discuss his deeper feelings, even with his wife.

So she tried to content herself at Mill House, helping Lissa to care for the beautiful furniture and china and trying not to do anything to displease Eve, who was so good to her. It quite clearly pleased Eve that she put on the green dress and her best black hat and accompanied her to church every Sunday morning. Although it was not something Rose had ever been used to, she found herself looking forward to the ride in the trap behind old Jacob and she enjoyed singing the hymns and psalms in her clear soprano voice. She also learned to listen carefully to the lessons and sermon because Eve was quite likely to comment and question her afterwards.

As they left the church at the end of the service Eve would look neither to right nor left except to incline her head graciously towards the vicar. She never, ever stopped to speak to anyone and when one day Rose tentatively remarked on this Eve replied, 'I go to church to worship my Maker, Rose, not to socialise with all and sundry. You would do well to follow my example.'

Rose was very tempted to remind Eve of the fact that the lesson that day had included the words, 'Inso much as ye have done it unto the least of my brethren, ye have done it unto me,' but over the months she had lived at Mill House she had learned, not without pain, that some things were best left unsaid. She had learned, too, that Eve's religion was apart from and not a part of her daily life.

For just as she had been careless of the fact that old Jacob might be lonely in his recent bereavement, indeed, had quite forgotten his wife had died, so she was able to dismiss Mrs Slaughter from her service without a moment's hesitation, although knowing full well that the woman depended on the few coppers she earned doing the laundry and rough work at Mill House.

It was the one time Rose heard Lissa standing up to her mother.

She had come in from the garden with a linen basket full of snowy white sheets and pillow cases that she and Mrs Slaughter had washed that morning and hung out to dry.

'Why did you tell Mrs Slaughter not to come any more, Mummy?' she asked, dumping the basket down on the table. 'She works very hard and she has six young children to support, you know.'

Eve picked up a pillow case and examined it. 'The number of children Mrs Slaughter has is no concern of mine,' she said without looking up. 'I feel no responsibility towards her on that account.'

'But she's a widow. Her money has to feed the children. She doesn't have a husband to support her,' Lissa protested.

'That's her look-out. Not mine.' Eve's face was hard. 'I see no reason to waste good money paying somebody to do work that can be done perfectly well by you and Rose. Better, in fact. Look at this. There's a mark on this sheet that should have boiled out.'

'That mark's been there for ages. It's iron mould. It won't come out,' Lissa said.

'Lemon juice might shift it,' Rose put in, anxious to change the subject.

Eve turned to her. 'Very well, you can try it, Rose, since you seem to know what to do. You can take Mrs Slaughter's place and help Lissa with the laundry from now on. It will be no hardship to you since I remember you telling me you were used to hard work when you came to visit me before you and Michael were married.'

Rose looked down at her hands. They were beautifully white

now and the nails were no longer blackened and broken. She had been creaming them carefully in order to soften them in the hope that Eve would offer to teach her fine sewing. Spending hours scrubbing laundry would ruin them again. She lifted her head. 'It's quite true, I've never been afraid of hard work, Eve,' she said quietly. 'But I should hate to think of young children starving because I had taken their mother's livelihood.'

'Nonsense. Of course they won't starve. The woman will find work elsewhere. Her sort always do.' She gave a smug smile. 'That's settled, then.'

'Only if Michael says so. I must ask my husband if he minds, Eve.'

'Mind? Why should he mind? I'm going over to the mill now to look at the accounts. I'll tell him.' Eve went out, banging the door behind her.

Lissa spread her hands. 'What did I tell you, Rose?' she said ruefully. 'You're another servant in this house. Just like me.'

Rose sat down at the table and rested her head on her hand. 'She was so nice to me when I first came here, Lissa. I thought she really liked me. And I was so thrilled to be coming to live in this lovely house. I thought ...'

'My mother can be charming.' Lissa's mouth twisted. 'But only when it suits her.' She picked up the corners of a sheet and Rose noticed that like several of the others in the basket it was well patched. 'Come on, help me fold these, then we can go across to the wash house and put them through the mangle before it's time to get the supper. I shall have to watch my step for a few days now and make sure I don't get behind with my work.'

'Why?'

'Because I argued with her, of course. Lissa is supposed to do as she's told, not have opinions of her own.' She grinned at Rose. 'That's what you've done for me, Rose. A few months ago I wouldn't have dared open my mouth, but ...' her expression turned shy as she went on, 'now I've got you for my friend ... you are my friend, aren't you, Rose?'

Rose nodded and smiled warmly. 'I very much hope so, Lissa.'

Lissa leaned forward. 'Then shall I tell you a secret? I've never told anyone else.'

'Not unless you really want to, Lissa.' Rose looked at her doubtfully.

'Oh, I do.' She put her hands up to cover her mouth. When she took them away again she was smiling. 'You know Cap'n Joel, skipper of the *Perseverance*?'

'I believe I've heard you speak about him.' Rose nodded.

'Oh, he's a wonderful man and so handsome, Rose,' Lissa clutched a pillow case to her chest, creasing it. 'You wouldn't believe. And,' a flush spread across her face, 'I think he likes me, too. He nearly always comes and says hello to me when he's here.'

'That's nice.' Rose looked at the girl, her plain face alight with the thought of her handsome sea captain, her hair, obviously brushed in a hurry when she first got up, tied back anyhow with a piece of rag. She smiled at her. 'Come up to my room, Lissa,' she said on impulse.

'What now? We've got these sheets to do.'

'We'll do them in a minute. Come on, I want to try something.' Rose caught her hand and hurried her, half-protesting, up the stairs.

In the bedroom she shut the door and sat Lissa on the bed. 'Close your eyes and sit still,' she commanded. With long, careful strokes she brushed the girl's fair hair and carefully wound it into a soft bun on the top of her head, leaving it loose enough to wave gently round her face. It made Lissa look older and more mature and emphasised the smooth line of her jaw. It was enough to turn her from the plain little skivvy she had always been to an attractive young woman. Even Rose was amazed at the transformation. She stood back, smiling. 'There. Now you can look at yourself.'

Lissa turned and looked into the mirror. 'Oh, Rose! Is that really me?' she breathed.

'Yes, it is. And you can always look like that. I'll show you how to do it for yourself. Look, all you have to do is brush it up – like so – and pin it – like so. See? You'll easily manage it.'

'Oh, thank you, Rose.' Lissa's eyes sparkled, animating her whole face. She turned her head this way and that, admiring herself with complete unselfconsciousness. 'I wonder if Cap'n Joel will notice any difference,' she said, almost to herself.

'Oh, I'm sure he will, Lissa,' Rose said with a laugh. 'I don't see how he could fail to. Didn't Dan say his boat is in now. Which is it, the *Perseverance*? Or is he on the *Patience*?'

'His boat is the *Perseverance*.' Lissa's mouth twisted. 'To tell you the truth I get a bit mixed up between the *Perseverance* and the *Patience*. When one of them comes in I'm never sure which it is because they both look alike.'

'But their names are quite different,' Rose laughed again.

But Lissa didn't laugh. She looked up at Rose. 'They might be to you. But not to me.' She hung her head. 'You see, Rose. I can't read.'

'Can't read?' Rose said, shocked. 'Oh, Lissa, why not? Is there something wrong with your eyes?'

'No. I've just never learned how.' She shrugged her thin shoulders, still not looking up. 'I had a governess once. When I was little. Miss Mantle, her name was. Well, she was more of a nursemaid than a governess, I think. I don't remember much about it.' She frowned. 'But, you see, everything changed so much after my father died. Miss Mantle was sent away. I remember that because I cried and cried. After she'd gone my mother said I was too stupid to learn. She said it wasn't worth wasting money on me because I wasn't clever like the boys. She said I was simple. She called me the runt of the litter and said I should never have been born. She's never liked me,' she added, stating it as a fact, without any hint of self-pity. She chewed her lip for several minutes, then she looked up. 'I don't think I am simple, do you, Rose? I might not be clever like the boys but I think I could learn if I was taught.'

Rose put her arms round the girl and hugged her. 'No, you're not at all simple, Lissa. I'm quite sure you can learn to read. And write. I shall try to teach you, although I may not be a very good teacher, because I've never done anything like it before.' Rose hugged her again and laughed. 'We'll learn together, Lissa. But I'll promise you this. You'll be able to read and write before very long. And now we'd better go and sort the linen out or we'll both be in trouble.'

Lissa put her hands up to her hair to take it down but Rose stopped her. 'No. Leave it. It's a new beginning.'

Lissa laughed delightedly. 'It'll be a new end, too, if she comes in and finds those sheets still in the basket.'

It worried Rose that she managed to find the time to go to see her parents at Crick Farm less and less. She realised that Eve was obviously and quite deliberately trying to sever her connections with her old home, always finding some excuse to keep her at the mill whenever Rose suggested she might visit them. But Rose was determined that she would not succeed although it was not easy and she had to wait until Eve paid another visit to her solicitor in Ipswich one day in early November before she could slip away.

It was depressing. Crick's Farm seemed to be going from bad to worse although the work load was less because the land was slowly being sold off and the animals were going the same way, if they didn't die first. But the mess and muddle were the same.

'Are you happy in your new home, my girl?' her mother asked as Rose exchanged her own clothes for an old skirt and blouse of her mother's so that she could help Emma by scrubbing the kitchen floor.

Rose was silent for a moment as she filled the bucket with water from the stove and got down on her hands and knees to start on the floor. Her mother would only worry if she knew the truth. 'Oh, yes, I'm happy enough, Mum,' she lied. 'But things aren't quite what I'd expected at Dowlands' Mill. Eve rules it with a rod of iron, even though she's so tiny and the boys are so big. It's no wonder George took himself off like he did.'

'Why do you think he went? The other two have stayed.' Emma was washing up at the sink as she spoke.

Rose sat back on her heels. 'I don't know, Mum, but I shouldn't be surprised if he went away because he couldn't live up to his mother's expectations. From what I can make out he could do no wrong in her eyes although Michael and Dan say he drank like a fish and never did any work. Perhaps he left before she could find out what he was really like.' She resumed scrubbing for several minutes. Then, as she wrung out the cloth she said. 'It's poor Lissa I feel sorry for, Mum. To think it took me weeks before I realised she was Eve's daughter! That shows how she's treated. And she never has anything new. Eve says she doesn't need new clothes because she never goes anywhere.'

111

'Why don't you bring her to tea next Sunday? Would she like that, do you think?'

Rose brushed a strand of hair away from her face with her forearm. 'I'm sure she would, Mum. But I don't reckon Eve will let her come. Nor me, neither,' she added glumly. 'She hates it if I say I want to come home and always finds some reason why I shouldn't. That's why I don't come very often.'

Emma turned to study her daughter. 'Are you sure everything's all right with you, Rose? I always thought you married in a bit of a hurry, seeing as how you didn't *have* to, as the saying goes. They say "marry in haste, repent at leisure". I hope that's not the case with you, my girl.'

Rose bent her head over the scrubbing. 'No, Mum, of course it isn't. Mill House is a beautiful place, although I must say it's a bit shabbier than I realised. Some of the curtains ...' she hesitated, not willing to admit even to her mother how shocked she had been to find how worn and faded the long velvet curtains were and how threadbare much of the linen was. 'But the furniture is really lovely, all old and highly polished. And you should see the beautiful china ...'

'That's not quite what I meant, Rose,' Emma said. 'You've told me about the house before. I meant you and Michael ...'

'Oh we're all right, Mum,' Rose said, a shade too quickly. For how could she explain to her mother that Michael was moody; that sometimes he hardly spoke to her – indeed was hardly at home, yet at other times he could be loving and caring. She fingered the green beads at her neck. Hadn't he only last week bought her these to go with the green dress that she no longer wore now that the weather had turned cold. She'd found them with a message on the dressing table the day after he'd stayed out all night. It was a peace offering, either that or a bribe to prevent her from asking where he'd been, she wasn't sure which.

She finished the floor and threw the dirty water out into the yard, where it ran in rivulets down the ruts in the frozen earth. 'Where's Dad?'

'In his office. He spends most of his time there when it's cold.' Emma sighed. 'He never was one to be out and about the farm in the winter, as you well know.'

'I'll go and see him.' Rose dried her hands and untied the

sack apron she had been wearing and went to the office at the end of the barn.

Chad was bending to put something away behind the desk as he heard her coming.

'Ah, Rose, my dear. Come to see your old Dad, have you?' he said with a bright smile.

Rose looked at him. Something didn't seem quite right but she couldn't put her finger on what it was. Chad was still the same big, untidy man she had always known, with the elbows out of his jacket although his dark hair seemed more liberally streaked with grey than she had noticed before. 'Is everything all right, Dad?' she asked uncertainly.

He leaned back in his chair and steepled his fingers. 'We rub along, Rose, we rub along,' he said. 'I've worried a bit about Millie and Babs having to work so hard, but I think I've resolved that by selling some of the land. At least they won't have so much to do, and we've only half the pigs and sheep now.' He gave a satisfied nod. 'It's given me some capital to work with, too, so it's all worked out for the best.'

'So you've been able to pay all the bills, then?'

'We . . . ll not all of them, perhaps. But several. Yes. Several.'

She sat on the end of the desk, swinging one leg. 'It's like eating your own tail, isn't it, Dad?' she said gently.

He moved some papers on the desk. 'I don't know what you mean.'

'Yes, you do, Dad. And it can't go on, you know. What will you do when you've no more land, no more animals to sell? You need to make it all work for you, not just sell it off.'

'It's only a temporary measure,' Chad said, squaring his shoulders. 'Just till I find myself in funds again.'

'And when will that be?' She spoke on a sigh.

'When my book is published.' He tapped an exercise book on the desk.

She raised her eyebrows. 'You're writing a book, Dad? Does Mum know? What's it about?'

'Yes and no, in answer to your first two questions. And it's about my life, in answer to the third.'

'But you haven't *done* anything, Dad. How can you write about what you haven't done?'

'I'm forty-eight. I've lived forty-eight years. You wait till it's finished. Then you'll see whether I've done anything or not.'

'And this is what you do all day while Mum and the girls slave on the land?' Rose knew she was being cruel but she couldn't help it.

'I'm doing it for them. When it's published we shall be able to leave this place and find ourselves a little house some-where . . . ' His eyes took on a glazed look.

She picked up the exercise book and flicked through it. It was more than half full of her father's small, neat writing. She had always been surprised that such a big, untidy man could produce such meticulous handwriting. She read a sentence here and there. The grammar was perfect and his use of English was clever. But he had nothing to say. It was a diary of a dull life. He didn't even write about the joys of nature. Yet his life hadn't been all that dull; if he'd spoken about some of the hardships he and his family had faced it would have made more interesting reading. Rose put the book carefully down.

'When do you expect to finish it?' she asked.

'Oh, I daresay I shall fill at least two more of these exercise books before it's done,' he said happily.

She shivered. 'Aren't you cold in here? You've no heat and the place is full of draughts.'

He reached down under the desk. 'I have internal fire,' he said, holding up a whisky bottle. 'When I get chilly I have a little nip, you understand. I would never drink to excess.'

'No, Dad, of course not.' She left him, wondering just how much further he could delude himself, and tramped back to the house.

Babs and Millie were there now, trying to warm frozen fingers at the stove. Rose greeted them warmly and tried to ignore the trail of dirt across her newly scrubbed floor.

'I shan't be here when you come next time,' Millie said cheerfully. 'Aunt Madge has got me a job at the Co-op drapery in Ipswich and I'm starting on Monday.' She looked up towards the ceiling. 'Oh, God, I can't wait to get out of this hole.'

Rose saw the look of pain that crossed her mother's face, but all Emma said was, 'I don't blame you, my girl. This is no life for you.' She turned to Rose. 'She's walking out, too, Rose. What do you think of that? She's got herself a young man.'

114

Millie blushed. 'He's a salesman at the Co-op so I shall be able to see him often.'

'Where did you meet him?' Rose asked.

'I met him when I went to stay with Aunt Madge. She introduced us. She thought me and Henry would be jest right for each other.' She giggled. 'We thought so, too.'

'And what do you think about it, Babs?' Rose said, turning to her youngest sister.

Babs shrugged. 'I don't care. I've got my own interests.'

'She's just like her father,' Emma said with a sigh of resignation. 'Always got her head in a book.'

'Only I'm going to do what Dad wanted to do and never got round to. I'm going to be a teacher and nobody's going to stop me,' Babs said defiantly. 'Miss Chamberlain at the village school lends me books and she says I can go there as a pupil teacher.' Her lips set in a determined line. 'I'm going, too. Miss Chamberlain even says I can lodge at her house if I don't want to live at home.'

'When are you going?' Rose asked.

'After Christmas. I can't go till there are a few more children at the school. As soon as there are too many for her to teach on her own she can ask for a pupil teacher and she'll take me on.' She flung her arms wide. 'Oh, Rose. I can't wait!'

'So it'll just be you and Dad,' Rose said to her mother. 'Does Dad know they're both going?'

Emma shook her head. 'Not yet. I'll tell him when the time is right.' She sighed. 'I'll be glad to see them both out of this,' she said. 'It's no life for them. Anyway, things won't be quite so hard when there's just the two of us.'

'Except that you'll be the one who has to do all the work,' Millie said bluntly.

'I don't mind that. I'm used to it. Come on, you girls, lay the table. Let's have some tea. I made some pork brawn from the pig we killed. It's good stuff.'

Rose helped to lay the table. The kitchen was much the same as it had been when she lived there, the kitchen range needed black leading, the mantelpiece held an assortment of bits and pieces, ornaments that had been there ever since Rose could remember, a butter dish with a pat of butter on it, a clock that had stopped, with several letters stuffed behind it, a packet of pills, two pipes belonging to her father and two Staffordshire dogs, one at each end, guarding the rubbish between them. Every chair had to have something moved from it before it could be sat on and the armchair in the corner sagged beneath the weight of a pile of ironing waiting to be done. A large cobweb hung between the corner of the room and the cornice of the dresser. The dresser itself didn't bear close scrutiny.

'Shall I go and call Dad?' Rose asked when the table was set.

'No, I shouldn't bother. He'll come in when he's hungry. He doesn't like to be disturbed. I expect he's busy with his memoirs,' Emma said.

'You know about his book, then?' Rose raised her eyebrows.

'We all do,' Millie said with a laugh. 'It's only Dad who thinks it's a secret.'

Rose shook her head. 'Why do you let him get away with it, Mum?'

Emma cut several slices of bread before she answered. Then she looked up and said, 'Life hasn't been what your father would have wanted. He hates farming. He's no good at it and he knows it. He feels he's a failure. So, if he thinks he can make something of himself by writing a book do you think I'm going to shatter his dream before he's finished dreaming it?'

'Have you seen it?' Rose asked.

Emma shook her head.

'It's rubbish.'

'That's only your opinion.' Emma's jaw had a stubborn set to it. 'He's a clever man. Cleverer than you'll ever be.'

'That's true.' If her mother was sharing the dream it was not for Rose to shatter it, either.

Chapter Ten

At seven o'clock Rose changed back into her own clothes and put on the coat and hat Michael had bought her when they were on honeymoon barely four months ago, although it seemed like a lifetime, and left Crick's Farm. She saw the envy on her sisters' faces as she buttoned up her coat and she knew that they were doing the right thing in getting away from the place.

'Tell Grace I'll go and see her when I can,' she said as she left. 'She must be getting near her time now.'

'Oh, she's still got nearly three months to go. The baby's not due till the end of January,' Emma said. 'But I'll tell her you asked after her.'

'Is she happy?'

'I've never seen anyone as happy and contented.' Emma sighed. 'Thank God at least one of my girls seems to have done the right thing.'

'I'm sure Millie and Babs are, too.' Rose smiled and kissed her mother.

'But what about you, my girl? What about you?'

'Don't you worry about me, Mum. I'm all right.'

Rose got on her bike quickly, without giving her mother the chance to question her further and cycled down the frosty lane from Crick's Farm to the road. It was pitch dark apart from the lamp on the front of the bike, and that wasn't as bright as it might be because the battery was running low. But the darkness had never worried her when she lived at the farm. She had been used to wandering round the outbuildings, shutting up the hens and making sure the pigs were safe without a second thought. She had to admit, though, that the long lane

117

from the main road down to Dowlands' Mill was a different matter. It was narrow and tree-lined and she sometimes felt quite unaccountably nervous on the rare occasions she had ridden along it in the dark.

She reached the entrance to the lane and in her imagination she thought she saw a figure standing there among the trees. She began to pedal faster.

'Hey, wait a minute,' a familiar voice said. 'Don't go so fast. I've come to walk you down the lane. I know you don't like going down there in the dark.'

She nearly fell off her bike. 'Oh, Dan! Thank goodness it's you! I thought ... well, I didn't know what to think!'

He caught the bike as she wobbled and she got off to walk beside him. They walked in silence for several minutes, then she said, 'It's very good of you to meet me, Dan, but where's Michael? Did he ask you to come?'

'No, he didn't. He's gone out on the marsh.'

'What on a cold, dark night like this? What on earth does he do out there?'

'You'd better ask him.'

'He wouldn't tell me if I did.'

'No, Michael is a very private person. He doesn't like people prying into his affairs.'

Rose wanted to cry out, 'But I'm not *people*! I'm his *wife*. He shouldn't have secrets from me.' But she said nothing. How could she admit to Dan of all people that things were not as she would have wanted between her and his brother.

Dan didn't accompany her into the kitchen when they arrived back at Mill House, but muttering something about 'having things to do' he went off in the direction of the mill. Rose suspected, quite rightly, that he was not anxious for the rest of the family to know he had met her at the top of the lane, although she knew he had only done it out of the kindness of his heart.

The kitchen was warm and the scene was almost the same as the first time she saw it. Eve was sitting on the settle with her work – she was crocheting a new altar cloth for the church – and Lissa was at the table with a pile of mending. Only this time Lissa's needle was idle and she was sitting with her head in her hands.

'And where have you been, might I ask?' Eve lifted her eyebrows as she looked up at Rose.

'I've been to see my parents. I hadn't seen them for several weeks so I thought it was time I paid them a visit.' Rose turned her back on her mother-in-law as she took off her coat and hat and laid them on a chair ready to take upstairs with her later. Her heart was thumping but she told herself there was no reason for her to feel guilty. She was a married woman and should be able to come and go as she pleased. She went to the mirror over the mantelpiece and patted her hair. 'Did you have a good time in Ipswich, Eve?' She managed to smile at her mother-in-law's reflection in the mirror as she spoke.

Eve didn't return her smile. 'I didn't go to Ipswich to have a *good time*, whatever you might mean by that. I went on business.' She gave a sniff. 'I must say I find it rather irritating that you should run off to your family the minute my back's turned, Rose. Couldn't you find enough to occupy yourself here?'

Rose mentally counted to ten, then said lightly. 'I only spent the afternoon and early evening at home ...'

'*This* is your home now,' Eve interrupted.

'I know that. But I wasn't aware that it was also a prison, Eve. Surely, I'm allowed out sometimes.' She spoke gently, and smiled again, albeit through gritted teeth and had the satisfaction of seeing that Eve was at a loss for words.

Instead, she stabbed the crochet hook in viciously, annoyed that her words had neither cowed nor apparently irritated the girl. 'Pull the kettle forward and make some tea,' she said after a few minutes. 'Lissa doesn't seem inclined to do it, although I've asked her twice.'

At that Lissa dragged herself to her feet and said wearily, 'Oh, I'm sorry. I didn't hear you. I'll do it.'

At the sound of her voice Rose spun round. 'Goodness, Lissa, you look terrible. Whatever's the matter? Aren't you ...?' She didn't finish the sentence but shot round the table to catch the girl as she collapsed back on to her chair.

'Oh, Rose, I've got the most dreadful headache ...' Lissa leaned against her, glad of the support.

Eve looked up, irritated. 'I don't wonder. It's that silly bun thing you've been wearing recently. It's unnatural. You shouldn't twist your hair up like that. That's what's making your head ache.' There was no hint of sympathy in her voice. 'Anyway,' she added spitefully, 'it looks ridiculous.'

'... and I ache all over,' Lissa went on as if she hadn't heard. 'And I'm so cold, Rose. So dreadfully cold.' She hugged herself and shivered, her teeth chattering.

She looked a sorry sight. Her face was pinched and grey and her hair was wisping out of its pins. Rose put her hand over Lissa's and found it was deathly cold, yet when she touched her head she found it was burning.

'Oh, you poor love,' she said softly. Then over her shoulder, 'Lissa's ill, Eve. She should be in bed.' She turned back to Lissa. 'Come on, Lissy, what you need is bed and a hot water bottle. I'll help you upstairs, then I'll bring you some hot milk and a powder.'

Eve watched over the rim of her gold spectacles, frowning. 'She didn't say she felt ill. How long have you felt like this, Lissa-dear?'

'Since this afternoon. It's gradually been getting worse.'

'Then why didn't you say so, child? You could have gone to bed before.'

Lissa didn't reply but the look she exchanged with Rose spoke volumes. She dragged herself to her feet and went to the door. Rose followed, carrying the hot water bottle and a candle in a holder. 'I'll come back for the milk. Perhaps you'd like to be warming it, Eve,' Rose said as she went.

She followed Lissa up the wide, sweeping stairs, their feet muffled by the thick carpet, then along the landing to a door at the end and up a narrower flight where the carpet was of poorer quality and had seen better days. At the top of these stairs were two doors. Lissa opened the one on the left and went in. There was a single iron bed and a painted chest of drawers with a mirror on it and a chair under the high attic window. Two peg rugs, one by the bed, the other in front of the chest of drawers, covered grey lino dotted with indeterminate blue flowers. The walls were distempered in ice blue and the temperature in the room matched its colour. Like the rest of the house, everything was scrupulously clean and tidy. Rose slipped the hot water bottle between the sheets and helped Lissa to undress, then she went down to fetch the milk, which, surprisingly, Eve had warmed as she had asked.

It seemed an awful long way up to the attic the second time and Rose wondered briefly if she was simply tired or whether she, too, might be sickening for 'flu, like Lissa. But her head didn't ache and she didn't feel feverish, just very tired and faintly queasy in the stomach. She draped Lissa's cardigan round her shoulders to keep her warm as she sat up in bed and gave her the milk.

'Oh, Rose, you're so kind to me. Nobody's ever fussed over me before,' she said, her teeth chattering against the rim of the mug. 'Oh, and you've put some sugar in it, too. It's delicious.' She took several sips, then said, 'I'll have to miss my lesson tonight. My head aches too much ...' Since she had discovered Lissa's secret, Rose had been sitting with her for half an hour every night after Eve had gone to bed, teaching her to read and write.

'Never mind. We can start again when you're better. You won't have forgotten what you've learned. Now, drink up your milk. And don't forget to take the powder.' While she waited Rose gazed round the room. The candlelight made it look a little less cheerless, but the curtains were drab and there were no pictures on the wall, only a sampler over the bed bearing the legend *Home Sweet Home*, which Rose felt was singularly inappropriate. She sat down on the bed and watched while Lissa drank her milk.

'I'll bring you some books to read tomorrow. You'll probably be surprised how much you can read for yourself now,' she said thoughtfully.

'Oh, I shall be better tomorrow.' A look of alarm crossed Lissa's face. 'I can't stay in bed. It's the day for cleaning all the brass and she gets cross if it isn't done on the right day.'

'Oh, Lissa, you don't have to worry about that,' Rose waved her hand. 'I'll give it a rub over with a duster. I'm sure it doesn't need cleaning every week. No, you stay in bed till you feel quite better.'

Lissa frowned, still struggling with her sense of duty even though she felt so ill. 'But that will mean you'll have to do everything. And look after me as well.' She finished her milk and handed the mug to Rose. 'No. I couldn't let you do that. I'll be better tomorrow. You'll see.' She didn't sound very convincing. 'And all those stairs ...' her voice trailed off.

'Well, perhaps you can come down into Michael's old room. That would make things easier, wouldn't it? And better than this cold attic.'

Lissa smiled weakly. 'Oh, yes, that really would be lovely. Michael's old room is nice and big and not nearly as cold as this one because it's right over the kitchen.' She shook her aching head slowly from side to side. 'But she'll never agree to that.'

'Well, we'll see. When you come to think of it, it's ridiculous, you being up here in the servants' quarters when there's an empty room on the floor below.'

'But that's exactly what I am, Rose. A servant. A maid of all work.' Lissa slid down under the bed covers, too tired to argue further.

'You're the daughter of the house and it's high time you were treated like it.' Rose tucked her in and dropped a kiss on her hot forehead. 'Now, go to sleep, dear. There's no telling what tomorrow might bring.'

Lissa gave her a weak but grateful smile. 'I'm glad you're here, Rose. Things don't seem half so bad now you've come to live here.' With a great sigh of contentment she closed her eyes.

Rose watched her for several minutes, then said, 'Are you warm enough or shall I get you another blanket?'

She gave a shudder. 'Another blanket would be nice. I'm so dreadfully cold.' She didn't open her eyes.

'All right. I'll be back in a jiffy.'

By the time Rose had made the journey down to the blanket chest and back up again to the attic and then down the two flights of stairs to the kitchen she was quite out of breath and feeling rather strange herself.

She sank down into a chair by the table, all the colour suddenly draining from her face. 'Oh, dear, the room seems to be going round. I think ... a drink.'

She tried to get up, but she had no strength. Eve looked up and said sharply. 'Sit still and put your head between your knees. It's not a drink you need, it's smelling salts.' She fiddled in her bag and hurried over to wave the pungent bottle under Rose's nose. 'There, is that better?' she asked after a few minutes.

Rose sat up, her face still ashen. 'Yes, thank you, I'm much better now.' She gave a little laugh. 'I don't know what came

122

over me. I've never felt like that before. I expect it was running up and down all those stairs.'

Eve fetched her a drink of water and peered at her as she drank it. 'I hope you're not sickening for something, too. It would be most inconvenient if you were to be ill as well as Lissa.'

'No, I don't think I am. I just felt ... strange for a minute.' She made a face. 'It's a long way up to Lissa's room, you know. It's cold up there, too. If she's going to be ill ...'

'She'll be better tomorrow.' Eve's tone suggested that it couldn't possibly be otherwise. 'Now, would you like a cup of tea? I've just made a pot.'

'Thank you.'

'And then I suggest you go to bed, which is where I'm going. It's already past my usual bedtime.' She poured the tea, muttering all the while, 'I daresay you worked your fingers to the bone at your mother's house while you were there. It won't do, you know. They're not your responsibility any more. Your responsibility is here, to your husband.'

My husband, who I hardly ever see these days, Rose thought bitterly. But she said nothing as she drank the tea Eve had made and then lit a candle and went up to bed.

She undressed slowly although she was desperate to get between the sheets. She hadn't realised how tired she was. As she put on her night-gown and got into bed the thought crossed her mind that Eve would never manage to look after one sick person, let alone two and she prayed, as much for Lissa's sake as for her own, that she would have recovered by the morning. She closed her eyes. The past four months had not been at all what she had expected. She had come to Mill House as a bride, full of hope for the future, excited at the thought of living in such a beautiful house and determined to make Michael a perfect wife because she loved him so much.

She paused in her thoughts as a little worm of doubt crept in. Did she love him? *Had* she really loved him when she married him? Or had she simply been dazzled by his attentions and seduced by the house he lived in, because it was so different from the squalor of her own home?

She turned over and thumped her pillow. What stupid ideas. Of course she loved Michael. Her mind went back to their courtship. He had swept her off her feet just as the heroes did in the penny romances, flattering her with his attentions and not giving her time to consider anything except that he was the most handsome man she had ever seen in her life. Of course she loved him. She had been besotted by him. Not *had* been, she still was, she reminded herself sternly. Only he wasn't often there to besot her these days, he was always out, either working or off with his cronies.

And when he came to bed she was often asleep, although she had lain awake for hours hoping he would come home, aching for his touch. Yet when he was there his lovemaking – if such it could be called – lacked any tenderness and left her unsatisfied. He seemed to have forgotten the joys of their honeymoon. But perhaps this was what marriage was all about. Perhaps she was expecting too much. There was nobody she could ask. Not Lissa. She had no experience of such things. Not Eve. Never Eve. Rose suspected she had no experience of joy in marriage, either, despite having had three sons and a daughter. Certainly not her own mother, although there was, and had always been a tender affection between her parents that was obvious to everyone. Grace. There was always Grace, of course. But it was so difficult to get away from the mill that she hardly ever *saw* her these days, let alone found time to talk about anything important to her.

Tired of trying to make sense of her life, Rose blew out the candle and was nearly asleep when she heard Michael's foot on the stair. He came into the bedroom and paused. Then, without lighting the candle he went quietly over to the chest at the foot of the bed and unlocked it. After a few minutes she heard the chink of metal, then he locked it up again, undressed and got into bed.

'Lissa's ill,' Rose said quietly. 'I think she's got 'flu.'

She felt him stiffen. 'I thought you were asleep,' he said. Then, 'What did you say? Lissa's got 'flu? But what about you? The Matriarch left a note to say it was you that wasn't well. Are you feeling better now?'

Rose hesitated. She was tired and her head ached, but there had been a tenderness in his voice that she hadn't heard lately. Perhaps ... 'Yes, thank you. It was just a passing thing. Probably running up and down all those stairs making Lissa comfortable. I'm all right now.' She reached for his hand. She wasn't going to let a queasy stomach get in the way of what she hoped might follow.

'That's good.' He released her hand and patted it, turned over and was soon snoring.

It was a long time before Rose slept.

Consequently, she woke late in the morning. It was nearly half past seven before she opened her eyes and she got out of bed and dressed herself quickly, conscious that she felt even more queasy this morning than when she went to bed the night before.

She went up to the attic to see Lissa before going downstairs. She was still asleep, the bed rumpled, her face flushed and her hair matted on her forehead. Clearly she had had a restless night. She left her to sleep and hurried down to the kitchen.

Dan and Michael were finishing their breakfast.

'We're late today. Had to cook it ourselves,' Dan said with a grin. 'Are you better, Rose?'

'Yes, I think so, thank you.' She stopped speaking and swallowed deeply. The smell of frying eggs and bacon seemed to catch at her throat.

Michael looked up. 'You're still looking a bit peaky. Come and sit down and I'll get you some toast.'

'I told them you and Lissa were both unwell so they would have to fend for themselves,' Eve said. She was standing at the stove making toast for herself.

'Lissa is still asleep,' Rose said. 'She still looks feverish. I wondered if perhaps we could bring her down ...' she swallowed again, '... down into Michael's old room. It would save me running up and down quite so many stairs.'

'Oh, I don't think that's necessary at all,' Eve said quickly. 'She's perfectly all right where she is.'

'Her room is very cold,' Rose said. She began to nibble the toast Michael had given her, but her delicate stomach couldn't take it and suddenly she made a dive for the sink, retching as she went.

Nobody moved and when she had finished she wiped her mouth and went and sat down again. 'I'm sorry,' she said, 'I should have ...'

'It's all right. Don't worry.' Michael got up and fetched her a glass of water. 'Do you feel better now?'

She gave him a wobbly smile. 'Yes. I think so, thank you.'

'You're not taking Lissa's 'flu, are you?' Dan said anxiously.

She frowned. 'I don't think so. I don't feel feverish. Just a bit sick ...'

'It must have been something you ate at your mother's yesterday,' Eve said, eyeing her. 'Not that I'm surprised,' she added under her breath.

Rose nibbled a little more of the toast, this time managing to keep it down and drank some more water. After a bit she began to feel a little better.

'I must take Lissa some breakfast,' she said, getting to her feet. 'She's probably awake by now.'

'Hang on.' Dan got to his feet, too. 'I think it would be a jolly good idea to bring Lissa down from the attic. I've never liked the poor little mite being up there under the eaves, and now she's ill and there's your old room spare she might as well have it, mightn't she, Mike? Is the bed made up and everything?'

'Of course it is,' Eve said coldly. 'but I really don't think ...'

'Good. Then if she's awake I'll carry her down now, before we go over to the mill. She doesn't weigh more than a penn'orth of tea. I'll do it now. We shan't have time later on because *Perseverance* will be in on the tide.'

'I think you're making too much fuss. She's probably better today,' Eve said sharply.

'I don't think she is. She still looks feverish to me,' Rose said.

'Well, I'll see when I get up there, won't I? If she's better, well and good, if she isn't I'll bring her down to Michael's room.'

'If she isn't better it's you that'll have to see to her, mother,' Michael said firmly. 'My wife isn't well. I'm not having her running up and down to the attic all day.'

Rose looked up in surprise. It wasn't often that Michael stood up for her like that and she was grateful. She smiled at him and rested her head on her hand. She no longer felt queasy but she certainly didn't feel very energetic – fragile was the word that sprang to mind.

Eve stared at her for a minute, then gave a shrug. 'Oh, very well, Daniel. Bring her down. She may as well have Michael's old room since he's not likely to need it any more.'

'I'll put a hot water bottle in her bed,' Rose said, pulling herself to her feet.

'I'll do that, you sit still,' Michael said uncharacteristically, so she sat down again.

When the two men were out of the room Eve looked at Rose long and hard.

'How long is it since you've been *like that*, Rose?' she asked, frowning.

'Like what?' Rose frowned back at her, irritated at such an ambiguous question.

'How long is it since you've seen your – womanlies?' Eve flushed faintly, unhappy at speaking of such delicate matters.

'Oh that!' Rose bit her lip. 'I don't know, exactly. I forgot to make a note of the date, but I know it's a bit late. Quite a bit late, in fact. I thought it was because ... ' Suddenly, her face cleared and she smiled with delight. 'And this morning I was sick! Oh, I must be ... '

Eve nodded, a faint smile was all she allowed to show that she was pleased. 'Yes, it looks very much like it. I shouldn't be at all surprised if you are *enceinte*.'

Rose put her hand on her flat stomach. 'A baby. Oh, how wonderful. Michael *will* be pleased.'

'I should wait until you're absolutely certain before you tell your husband,' Eve warned. 'Go and see Dr Holmes before you say anything to him. After all, you could be mistaken. It could be simply a stomach upset, couldn't it?'

Rose shook her head. 'Oh, no, I'm sure it isn't,' she said with conviction.

As she spoke Michael and Dan came back into the room. Ignoring her mother-in-law's advice she got to her feet and went over to her husband and put her arms round his neck. 'Oh, Michael. I'm not ill. There's nothing wrong with me except that I'm having a baby! That's why I was sick this morning. Isn't that wonderful?'

He looked down at her and a slow smile spread across his

127

face. 'Well, I never did,' he said, as if it wasn't the most likely thing in the world that she should have his child. 'Well, I never did.'

Dan thumped him on the back. 'Well, congratulations, brother. We'll have someone to carry on the family name now, won't we? If it wasn't only eight o'clock in the morning I'd suggest a tot of brandy to celebrate. But we've got a hard day's work ahead of us so we must keep our heads level.' He rubbed his hands together. 'But just wait till tonight! You've still got some brandy in that cask over at the mill, haven't you, Mike?'

Michael's face darkened for a second. 'How did you know about that?'

'Well, if it was supposed to be hidden you didn't do a very good job of it. It was only behind a grain bin, for goodness sake.'

'Is Lissa settled in Michael's room?' Rose asked, sensing trouble between the brothers.

'Yes. But you'd better go up and give her a look. I think she'd like a drink,' Dan said. 'She doesn't look too clever, poor kid.'

'You go, Mother,' Michael said. 'We don't want Rose running any risks.'

Eve looked at him, aghast. '*Me*? What about my arthritis?' She gave an uncomfortable shrug. 'Rose is not *ill*, Michael. Having a child is not in itself an *illness*.'

'All the same ...'

'It's all right. Of course I'll go. Don't worry, Michael, I shan't take any harm.' Rose knew Lissa would rather see her than her own mother.

Rose went upstairs. Lissa looked very small but very comfortable in Michael's big old bed.

'It's much softer than mine,' she said, snuggling even deeper between the covers. 'Dan wrapped me in the eiderdown and carried me down. He's ever so strong. He says Cap'n Joel will be in later today.' She sniffed. 'But I shan't see him.'

'Never mind, I'm sure he'll be back another time,' Rose said encouragingly. 'Now, is there anything you'd like?'

'No, only a drink and you've brought me that. No, don't draw the curtains back, the light hurts my eyes and makes my head worse.' She turned her head slowly from side to side.

'This is a nice room. Thank you, Rose. I like it here. But, I wish I didn't feel so ill. I hurt all over.' An anxious look crossed her face. 'Is she very cross because I'm ill? I've never been ill before.'

'Of course not. You can't help being ill, Lissa.' Rose smiled down at her. 'Anyway, you'll feel better tomorrow, I'm sure.'

'I'm afraid Cap'n Joel will be gone by then.'

'I'll give him your love if I see him,' Rose said wickedly.

Lissa struggled up on to one elbow. 'Oh, no, you mustn't do that. He doesn't ...' she fell back, exhausted with the effort.

Rose laughed. 'Oh, Lissy, I was only teasing.' She stayed for a few more minutes, debating with herself whether to tell Lissa the wonderful news about the baby. But she decided it would only worry the girl to think Rose was having to bear the burden of extra work while she was in bed so she said nothing and left her to rest.

When she got back to the kitchen Dan had gone but Michael was still sitting at the table.

'So what did Mr Bradshaw say, then?' he asked and Rose got the impression that he was repeating a question he had asked before and not received an answer to.

Eve was clattering dishes at the sink. 'He said there had been no reply from the notices he put out.' Her tone was grudging.

He slapped his knee. 'I told you there wouldn't be, but you wouldn't listen. I'll bet it cost you a pretty penny, too, putting notices in all the papers.'

'Not all the papers, Michael,' she contradicted, her voice tart. 'Only the local ones.'

'Well, you know what I mean.' He shifted in his chair. 'I knew damn well you wouldn't find him, wasting your money like that.'

'Oh! I'm glad you realise it was *my* money, to spend as I choose.'

He ignored that. 'So, what are you going to do now, Mother?'

'In what way?'

'About your will. Look here, if ... now I'm going to have a son, it's only natural that I want to make sure his inheritance is secure and not likely to be taken from him by some long-lost uncle who turns up at your death-bed like the prodigal son.'

Eve was silent for several seconds. Then she turned round. 'It's all in hand, if you must know. At Mr Bradshaw's advice I've altered my will, much against my inclination, I must admit. I still cherish the hope ... However, Mr Bradshaw says it's not likely that George will ever come back, so my estate will be divided between you and Daniel, with you, being the eldest now, getting the larger part. I arranged it all yesterday, before I had any inkling that Rose was to have a child.' She lifted her chin. 'I hope you're satisfied now. It's what you've been hankering after, isn't it?'

Michael got to his feet and it seemed to Rose that he relaxed, although she hadn't been aware of any tension before. 'I must go and do some work,' he said and left without another word.

Chapter Eleven

Eve was in a temper, there was no doubt about that. Her face was like a thundercloud and she snapped at all and sundry. At first Rose thought that Lissa was the cause. To Eve, her daughter's illness was nothing but a nuisance. The fact that the poor girl hadn't chosen to be ill and was lying in bed feeling like death would cut no ice with her mother.

It took Rose some time to realise that Eve's ill humour had nothing to do with Lissa. It had a more subtle root, directed towards Michael. For days, ever since her trip to Ipswich, she had hardly spoken a civil word to him and it could only be that she was furious with him because he had forced her to admit that she had changed her will.

Neither had she made any further reference to Rose's pregnancy. In fact, it seemed she was deliberately ignoring it, insisting that the house must still be kept in its pristine state, the washing, ironing and cooking done, even though with Lissa ill in bed there was only Rose to cope with it all. It was also left to Rose to tend Lissa. Eve refused to go near the sick room, saying loftily that it would be unwise at her age to risk catching influenza.

Rose made no word of complaint, but stoically went about her work singing, which she knew annoyed Eve. And when she was sick, as she was every morning, she managed to hide it from everyone, either hurrying out to the privy next to the wash house or heaving over the chamber pot in the privacy of her bedroom.

But it was hard. She had no appetite herself and the food she cooked for the others made her stomach churn. Every night she crawled into bed feeling ill and deathly tired, glad that Michael was seldom there to force his attentions on her. But she was determined Eve should not see her weaken and she continued to scrub and polish the house even though she was beginning to hate the very things she had so coveted when she first visited Mill House.

Nevertheless, she always made sure to put on a smile when she went in to Lissa. Time enough when the girl was better to tell her about the baby.

'This is a man's room,' she remarked one day when she had settled the girl by the fire Dan had lit earlier. Eve had watched Dan carrying the coals upstairs with unconcealed horror. Nobody was allowed a fire in the bedroom at Mill House unless they were dying and she had clucked and tutted and muttered about the price of coal but had luckily fallen short of actually forbidding it. Rose suspected that she was afraid Lissa might come downstairs before she had properly recovered if she was not allowed a fire in her room and she had discovered that Eve was pathologically afraid of illness.

Lissa looked up as Rose spoke. She was painfully thin and still rather weak, but she had recovered enough to sit by the fire in the armchair Dan had brought down from the attic for her. She closed the book Rose had given her, keeping a finger in to mark the page. The one good thing about her illness was that it had given her time to practise her reading and she was enjoying it, eagerly lapping up all the books Rose found for her, even though she still painstakingly pointed to each word and mouthed it as she went along. 'What do you mean, a man's room?' she asked frowning.

'Well, look at it. No pictures. No ornaments.' Rose gazed round at the heavy mahogany wardrobe and dressing table and the wash stand in the corner. Like the rest of the house the furniture was of very good quality but the room was large and had an austere look about it.

Lissa smiled. 'Well, Michael didn't go in for things like that. Men don't, do they? But I don't mind. The bed's bigger than my old one. More comfortable, too. And there's a carpet on the floor.' She wriggled luxuriously further into the armchair. 'And this chair's lovely.'

'All the same, I think I'll go and have a look in the attic.

132

There might be a few ornaments up there that would brighten the place up. And is there anything you want brought down from your old room, Lissy?'

'No. I can fetch my clothes down when I'm better. You do quite enough running around for me, Rose.' She put her head on one side. 'You look dreadfully pale. You're not sickening for this awful 'flu, are you? I hope not. It makes you feel really rotten.'

'Yes, I know, dear. But no, I'm not ill. I'm just a bit tired, that's all.' She smiled conspiratorially. 'I'll go upstairs and see what I can find while Eve is over at the mill.' She tapped the side of her nose. 'What the eye doesn't see ...'

Lissa laughed aloud. 'Well, she's not likely to see anything that comes into *my* room because she never even looks inside it.'

'Oh, it's nice to hear you laugh, Lissy. You're really beginning to feel better, aren't you?'

Lissa nodded. 'But I'm sad that I missed Cap'n Joel. I always take him cups of tea when his boat's in.'

'Oh, I nearly forgot!' Rose beamed at her. 'He left you a note before he left. Dan gave it to me to give you.' She felt in her pocket and pulled out an envelope and gave it to Lissa.

Lissa looked at the letter inside, frowning with concentration.

'Can you read it?' Rose asked.

'Some of it. But I'm not very good at reading joined-up writing yet.' Lissa handed it to her. 'Will you read it to me, Rose?'

Rose grinned. 'Are you sure you want me to read your love letters, Lissy?'

'Silly. It isn't a love letter,' Lissa said, blushing. 'Go on. What does he say?'

'It says, "Dear Miss Dowland. I was very sorry to hear that you are ill. I very much hope that you will be better soon. I look forward to seeing you when I come next time. Yours respectfully, Stephen Joel."' She looked up. 'Did you know his name was Stephen, Lissy?'

Lissa nodded. 'Yes, I've heard Dan call him Steve. It's a nice name, isn't it?' She took the letter and read it through for herself, still frowning in concentration over every word. Then

133

she folded it carefully and smiled happily up at Rose. 'Wasn't it nice of him to write to me?'

Rose left her and went up to the attic to see what she could find. After nearly half an hour she came down again with three pictures and some pretty china. She set out the china, a pair of candlesticks in the shape of a shepherd and shepherdess, a delicately patterned dressing table set and a tall Doulton flower vase. 'There, that's better,' she said, standing back to look at it all. 'I'll get Dan to hang the pictures when next he comes in.' She turned to Lissa. 'Do you like what I've done, Lissy?'

Lissa nodded but she looked anxious. 'Yes, it's lovely. Makes the place look more homely. But I worry about you doing so much for me. You do look most dreadfully tired.' She caught Rose's hand. 'I promise I'll make it up to you when I'm better, Rose. You know you're the best sister a girl could ever have. I don't know what I'd do without you now.'

The sincerity in Lissa's voice brought a lump to Rose's throat. It was little enough she was able to do for the girl and it made her realise what a drudge her life had been before. Unable to speak, she dropped a kiss on Lissa's forehead and left her. She was still holding Stephen Joel's letter in her hand.

Rose never passed her own bedroom door without slipping in for a few seconds just to stand and gaze at the view over the mill and the creek. It was a view she never tired of and now she stood for several minutes just drinking in the scene. The tide was nearly full and the winter sun sparkled on the water and on the frosty marshes beyond. She could hear the gulls wheeling in the distance and at the door of the mill Old Jacob stood waiting by Duke's head while Michael loaded the trap, bringing the sacks of flour out of the mill on his back to be delivered to the baker's in the village. She realised with a rush of pride that her husband was a very strong man.

She turned back into the room and her eyes rested on the shabby old chest at the foot of the bed. It was leather-covered, with a domed lid, the kind travellers used in the days of stage coaches. The dark brown leather was scratched and pitted and although it looked as if it had seen good service in the past it looked quite out of place among the polished bedroom furniture. She had often wondered why Michael insisted on having it in the bedroom at all. What could it possibly hold that was so precious he couldn't let it out of his sight?

And that he didn't want anyone else to see! She remembered that he had not been at all pleased the other night when he discovered she was still awake when he opened the chest. She pursed her lips. Husbands shouldn't have secrets from their wives. She went to the chest and rattled the padlock, trying to undo it. Of course it was locked, she wouldn't have expected otherwise.

She straightened up, rubbing her back, and as she did so something caught her eye just under the foot of the bed. When Michael had taken off his trousers the night before everything had fallen out of the pockets and he had cursed as he crawled round the floor picking things up. She bent down and with a smile of triumph picked up a small key. The key to the chest. In his fuddled state Michael had overlooked his most precious possession. She gave a quick glance out of the window to make sure he was still occupied and with shaking hands put the key in the padlock and turned it. Now at last she would find out what it was he kept hidden there.

She lifted the lid and peered inside. Years ago the chest had been lined with thick striped paper which was now brown and faded and torn at the edges and it had a strange fusty smell, predominantly of moth balls but also of something else that she couldn't identify. She stared into it for several seconds, then sat back on her heels, disappointed. Because the chest appeared quite empty except for a few packets of cigarettes strewn in the bottom. She leaned in and picked up one of the packets. It was not a make she recognised, but that wasn't surprising, her father had never smoked at all and Michael and Dan smoked pipes. She put the packet back, disappointed and turned away, the musty, closed-up smell of the chest making her delicate stomach churn.

Suddenly she heard the clip clop of Duke's hooves across the yard, warning her that the flour was loaded. She got to her knees and glanced out of the window to see Michael coming towards the house. Quickly, she locked the chest, her fingers fumbling in her haste. Then she put the key under the foot of the bed where she had found it. By this time she could hear him coming up the stairs and she scrambled to her feet and went over to the mirror and began tidying her hair.

135

'What are you doing here?' he said, obviously surprised to see her when he came into the bedroom. 'Fine time of day to be primping and admiring yourself. Haven't you got anything else to do?' It was plain he wasn't pleased to see her.

'I wasn't admiring myself, I was tidying myself up,' she said, sounding more calm than she felt. 'I've just been up to the attic to find a few bits of china to make Lissa's room nicer and it's a bit cobwebby up there.'

'Isn't she better yet?'

'Getting better. It wouldn't hurt you to pay her a visit, Michael. She only sees Dan. And me, of course. She's sitting by the fire Dan lit in her room now, reading.'

'Reading! Don't be daft. Lissa can't ...'

'Can't read? Oh, yes she can, Michael. I've been teaching her. You could have done the same, years ago, if you'd had the inclination.'

'I never had the time. Anyway, she's ...' He screwed his finger at his temple.

'That's where you're quite wrong, Michael. Your sister isn't stupid. The only thing that's been wrong with Lissa is that nobody's ever paid any attention to her. She's far more intelligent than you give her credit for. She's learned to read very quickly. And to write.'

But he was no longer listening. He was frowning, his eyes on the floor, obviously trying to search for something without appearing to. She smiled to herself. She knew exactly what he was looking for and was almost tempted to tell him where it was but thought the better of it and simply said, 'Well, I'd better get on with my work. Eve will be running her finger along the mantelpiece in the dining room looking for dust. She likes to keep the servants up to scratch.'

He turned to her and said angrily, 'Don't talk like that, Rose. You're not a servant in this house. You're my wife.'

She gave something approaching a snort. 'You'd better tell your mother that, Michael. I think she's forgotten.'

'It's just her way, Rose. She doesn't mean anything.' His tone now was almost apologetic. 'She's a bit out of sorts these days.' He shrugged uncomfortably. 'I think she misses Lissa about the place.'

'Rubbish. As long as the work's done she doesn't care who

does it.' Rose shook her head and said more slowly. 'No, Michael, your mother's bad temper's got nothing to do with Lissa. I think she's furious because you made her admit she'd changed her will. She didn't want you to know that, did she? You had to almost wring it out of her.'

He scratched his head, perplexed. 'I don't see why she should be so touchy over it. If it's done, it's done and I don't see why we shouldn't be told. Anyway, it was time she did something about it.'

'Ah, but what about if George was to come back? She'd want the old one to stand, wouldn't she? So if nobody knew she'd made this new will she could tear it up and nobody would be any the wiser.'

'Mr Bradshaw must know.'

'Yes, but Mr Bradshaw will do as he's told. But you made her confess, so now you know, too. And that's why she's furious with you.'

'George won't come back,' he said with a shrug. His eyes narrowed slightly as if he was looking into the future. 'No, George won't come back, so when she goes the mill will be mine. Dan won't want it, he's more interested in his garden.' He nodded to himself, forgetting she was there. 'I shall install rollers when she's gone. They're the thing now. They grind finer than stones and that's what people want. Fine flour for fine bread. I shall have an engine, too. I shan't rely on tides for my milling, steam's the thing.'

'I think you're getting ahead of yourself, Michael.'

He almost started at the sound of her voice, so deep had he been in his dream. 'What do you mean?' he said.

'The mill isn't yours yet.'

'No, and if my mother doesn't listen to me and modernise the place it won't be anybody else's, either. She's so mean we still light the place with oil lamps because she won't pay to have electricity installed. Electricity! She won't even have gas! God, we're miles behind the times here in Stavely Creek. No wonder the place doesn't pay!' He turned away impatiently. 'I keep telling her we need to get up to date but she won't listen. And while she holds the purse strings I can't do much. But she won't live forever. And I've got my plans made all ready.'

Rose stared at him. His face was set and she realised with

137

something of a shock that he hated his mother. 'You shouldn't say things like that, Michael,' she said in a hushed voice.

He looked her up and down and then turned away. 'There's no sin in having plans.'

'It depends what they are.'

He pointed to her flat stomach. 'I've got my son to think about, haven't I?'

But she knew it wasn't his son he was thinking about. Sickened, she went down the stairs and into the dining room. She had seen a new side to her husband and she wasn't sure that she liked what she had seen.

The dining room was the same size as the drawing room opposite. Although both were kept in pristine condition neither room had ever been used to Rose's knowledge. The dining room was furnished with a long mahogany dining table with brass claw feet and six upholstered chairs stood round it. To one side was a sideboard with a tantalus holding cut glass decanters and to the other a china cabinet full of cut glass. A pair of rose lustres with a large brass clock between them stood on the mantelpiece. Rose sighed. Every week the room had to be polished, although you could already see your face in the table, yet it was a total waste because the Dowlands never entertained and lived exclusively in the kitchen. She rubbed the table with a duster in a token gesture. That was all it would get today. She was tired and she felt sick. The rest of the furniture got the same arbitrary treatment and she smiled wryly as she recalled how awe-stricken she had been when she first came to Mill House, how she had gone home to Crick Farm dreaming of living in such a beautiful, ordered place, so different to the muddled, squalid existence she was used to, and how she had longed to be allowed to touch and to care for the lovely things she had seen. She little realised then what the reality would be. It was like living in a museum. Now she longed for nothing more than the comfortable squalor of her old home.

She went across the hall to the drawing room. It was cold, like the dining room and smelled of wax polish and soot from the damp chimney. As she began to dust the fussy little ornaments on the chiffonier she recalled the conversation she had had only an hour ago with Michael. It had shown her a side of her husband that she hadn't known existed. A cruel, selfish streak that pointed to a man who would do anything to get his own way.

A thought began to take shape in her mind. A thought that was so terrifying that it hardly bore entertaining and she had to sit down on the nearest chair whilst, in spite of herself it developed.

Michael was waiting for his mother to die so that he could take control of the mill. His recent words made that quite plain. Now that his brother George was not coming back she was the only obstacle. But how long was he prepared to wait? 'She won't live forever and I've got my plans made,' was what he'd said. The thought of what might be in his mind was so horrifying that she shrank into herself, shivering with terror.

She pulled herself together with a great effort. You've been reading too many fairy tales, my girl, she told herself firmly. Else you're letting Dowlands' Mill turn your brain. She got to her feet and resumed her dusting, determined to put the whole matter firmly where it belonged. Right out of her mind.

That evening after supper Michael didn't go out but stayed at home reading the newspaper. When it was time for bed he accompanied her up the stairs and his lovemaking was tender.

Afterwards he smoothed her hair back, saying, 'I know life isn't always easy for you here, Rose. But one day things will be better. I'll make it up to you, I promise.' He laid his hand on her stomach. 'And you're not to work too hard. If the Matriarch complains you can tell her I said so. You're to do nothing that might harm our son. Remember that, Rosie.' He kissed her again and nestled her head in the crook of his arm.

She closed her eyes. This was the Michael she had married. The Michael she loved. The Michael she had feared she had lost. How could she ever have doubted him?

Lissa's recovery from her illness was slow, it had taken its toll and left her even thinner than before. With her hair piled up the way Rose had shown her and with her huge blue eyes in a face that was still pale, she had an attractive, elfin look about her which was appealing.

Not that her mother noticed. She hardly asked if Lissa was feeling stronger before giving her a list of chores to be done.

Rose realised that it had indeed been wise to keep her confined to her room for longer than had been strictly necessary.

And Rose would have kept her out of the kitchen for longer still but for the fact that she fainted one day when Lissa was helping her to change the sheets on the bed and had to confess that she was pregnant.

'And you've let me stay up here in my room, doing nothing but read and be generally lazy, while you were struggling to do my work as well as yours, Rose! And feeling so dreadfully ill, too! Oh, Rose. How could you? How could you let me be so selfish?'

'You've been ill, Lissy. Really ill. There was one night when I nearly called in Dr Holmes, but Dan said wait and see how you were in the morning. And by that time you were a bit better.' Rose smiled at her. '*I'm* not ill, Lissy. I'm having a baby. That's not being ill.'

But Lissa wouldn't be comforted. 'I kept saying to you that you looked tired and didn't look well. Why didn't you *tell* me, Rose? I wouldn't have let you wait on me hand and foot like that ... Well, you're not doing it any more. I'm coming downstairs right now. This instant. And I'll carry the dirty sheets, too.'

'Do you really feel strong enough, Lissy? You won't get any quarter from Madam, you know.'

'I'll manage. Don't you worry about me.'

Rose sighed. 'I confess I'll be quite glad of your help, Lissy. It's washing day today.'

The two girls worked with less than their usual energy, with frequent stops to rest. Lissa wasn't quite as fit as she had thought and Rose was perpetually tired these days. It was quite late in the morning before the sheets were ready to be pegged on the washing line. As they struggled with them against the cold December wind, suddenly Lissa called,

'Oh, look, it's *Perseverance*. It's Cap'n Joel's barge. I know it's *Perseverance*, I can read the name for myself now. And look, he's seen us,' Lissa waved back excitedly to the man at the helm. 'I didn't realise he would be coming back again so soon.' She flushed with pleasure. 'I'll be able to thank him for his letter, won't I?'

They finished pegging out the washing and went back to clear up the wash house, Lissa chattering all the time, thrilled to think her captain had returned. By the time they had folded the linen that was already dry and put it through the mangle the barge was tied up at the jetty and it was time for the midday meal.

Eve had laid the table as she sometimes did when the girls were busy with the laundry and there was bread and cheese and pickled onions, their usual midday fare.

'I'll make some tea. I daresay Cap'n Joel can do with a cup after his long journey.' Lissa said, going to the stove.

'Don't you think the Captain has the facilities to make tea for himself on board his boat, Lissa-dear?' Eve asked, a little too sweetly. 'In any case, no doubt he would prefer beer like Michael and Daniel.'

'Oh, yes. Of course. I didn't think.' Lissa's shoulders slumped with disappointment.

You could go and tell the men that dinner's ready,' Rose suggested.

'Yes, I'll do that.'

Lissa hurried from the room and Rose made a mental note to warn her not to be quite so eager when the captain was about because Eve had eyes like a hawk and missed very little.

'She's pleased to be up and about again after being confined to her room for so long,' Rose said, to explain Lissa's exuberance.

'Yes. She was up there for nearly three weeks. Far too long. I'm sure she wasn't as ill as all that.' Eve sat down at her place to wait for the men.

Rose was sorely tempted to remark, How do you know? You never even bothered to come and see her, but she was learning to hold her tongue and said instead, 'She was really quite poorly, Eve. I nearly called Dr Holmes in one night.'

Eve sat up straight in her chair. 'I'm very glad you did no such thing, Rose. Doctors have to be paid for.'

'So do funerals, Eve.' It was out before she could stop herself.

'Cut some bread.' Eve's tone was icy.

Lissa came back. 'Dan and Michael are going up to the Miller's Arms with Cap'n Joel. They'll have their bread and cheese when they get back, and they'll bring the captain with them,' she said happily.

'Very well. Sit down and eat yours.'

The meal progressed in silence and Rose knew she had offended Eve but didn't know how to put the matter right.

Suddenly, Eve said, 'I've been invited to the Church Ladies' Guild this afternoon to show them my altar cloth.' She couldn't quite keep the pride out of her voice. 'It isn't quite finished yet, but I'm hoping to have it done in time for the Christmas services next week.'

'It's very beautiful. I've never seen such intricate work. All those tiny stitches ...' Rose said, desperately trying to make amends.

'Naturally one puts one's best work into something that is to grace the Lord's Table,' Eve replied with a sanctimonious air that put Rose firmly back in her place. She turned to Lissa.

'I have to be there at half-past two. Lissa, go and tell old Jacob to bring the trap at a quarter-past, will you?'

'I'll go.' Rose got to her feet, anxious to escape and was gone before Eve could argue.

Chapter Twelve

Old Jacob lived in a tiny cottage next to Duke's stable, on the other side of the wash house. Rose could see through the window that he was deep in his afternoon nap, his feet stretched out on the hearth and his old cat curled on his lap. The room was spotlessly clean, and a newspaper spread across the end of the table held the plate on which he had had his bread and cheese and his empty stout tankard. It seemed a pity to disturb the poor old man, but it was already nearly two o'clock. She tapped on the window.

At the second tap he woke in mid-snore and opened his eyes, getting to his feet as fast as his old bones would allow when he saw who it was.

'Yis, yis, orl right,' he nodded, still only half awake as Rose gave him the message. 'But the Missus mighta said a bit earlier. Wait a minute while I find me boots. Where are they now? Dearie me, I'm all of a flummox.'

'Is there anything I can do, Jacob?' Rose asked anxiously.

'No, no, me dear. Well, yis, jest fetch me coat. Thass on the back o' the door there. Thass right.' He shrugged himself into it while she held it for him. Then he wound a muffler several times round his neck and finished off by planting a battered old bowler hat on his head. He shuddered as he reached the door. 'By, thass cowd out today, ain't it? That play up my roomaticks suthin' cruel.' He turned back to the cat, who had made himself comfortable in the old Windsor chair Jacob had been forced to leave. 'You keep house till I git back, Blackie. I shan't be long.' He grinned a one toothed grin at Rose. 'Not if I know it, anyway. The Missus might hev a different idea. But if she thinks I'm a-go'in' to set outside to wait for 'er, wherever she's goo in', she's got another think comin'. I'll goo back an' fetch her but I on't wait, an' thass flat. Not in this cowd wind.'

'I don't blame you, Jacob,' Rose said. 'Shall I say you'll be round in ten minutes?'

He winked. 'Say a quarter of an hour. Then I'll be early and I shan't git in the wrong with her.'

Rose laughed aloud. 'Oh, Jacob, you're a crafty one, aren't you?'

'Ain't no good growin' old if you don't grow artful,' he chuckled as he shuffled off to the stable.

When Rose got back to the house Eve was already putting on her hat and coat.

'I've been thinking. It would be better if Captain Joel had his meal on his boat, since I shan't be here,' she was saying to Lissa. 'It's hardly right for you girls to entertain a strange man alone.'

'But he's already been invited,' Lissa protested, her face showing her disappointment.

'And we shan't be alone,' Rose said, surprised. 'Michael and Dan will be here.'

'Nevertheless, I hardly think it would be seemly.' Eve adjusted her hat to her satisfaction.

'Are you saying that as a married woman, with my husband present, giving a meal to a barge captain who is delivering grain to the mill would not be "seemly"?' Rose's voice was rising with every word. 'And with his brother here, too? Oh, Eve, what are you thinking about? This is the twentieth century, not the Dark Ages.'

'Please don't raise your voice to me, Rose. You really must learn to control your temper. And I'll have you remember that this is my house and what I say goes.' Eve gave vent to her feelings by jabbing a hatpin in so hard that it snapped. 'Drat. Now I shall have to find another one.' She hurried off upstairs.

'Jacob is here,' Rose said, when she re-appeared. 'He's been waiting several minutes. You don't want to be late to the Church Ladies' Guild, do you?'

Flustered now, Eve took a last swift look in the mirror over the mantelpiece, picked up the bag which held the precious altar cloth and her handbag and hurried out.

'I hope you have a pleasant afternoon, Eve,' Rose called after her, but Eve didn't reply.

Lissa sat down at the table, looking despondent. 'It's a shame we shan't be able to give the captain his lunch with the boys,' she said.

'Don't be silly, of course we shall. We'll do as we planned. I never heard such nonsense. Lay the table. We'll have it all ready for them when they get back.' Rose went to the dresser and reached down plates.

'But what will she say if she finds out?' Lissa said, hovering uncertainly by the knife rack.

'She'll never know if we don't tell her.' Rose tossed her head. 'Anyway, if the boys invite the captain in we can hardly refuse to feed him, can we?' She winked broadly and Lissa, quite willing to be convinced, burst out laughing.

'No, of course we can't,' she agreed.

In the event the three men and Alfie, the cabin boy, didn't stop to eat at all when they returned from the Miller's Arms. Anxious to make good use of the short winter daylight, they got straight on with unloading the grain. Now and again Rose glanced out of the window and saw the sacks being carried down the gangplank off the barge and stacked by the side of the mill under the lucam and she realised that they couldn't be taken up into the mill by the sack hoist until the tide was right for turning the wheel. Everything depended on the great water wheel, she mused, even the hoist to take the grain up to the top floor. It was no wonder that Michael wanted to modernise and improve things. It would make life so much easier for both him and Dan.

But it wouldn't happen while their mother lived. She stifled the thought even as it formed in her mind.

Lissa came and stood beside her.

'I don't suppose I shall see Cap'n Joel at all, this trip,' she said disconsolately. 'He'll probably be gone on the tide tomorrow.'

'Never mind. I'm sure he'll be back again before long.' Rose turned and looked at her. 'You're still looking very pale, Lissa. Why don't you take a little walk along the river wall before the light fades? It would do you good to get some fresh air.'

'Oh, I can't do that, Rose! I never go out for *walks*,' Lissa gave an incredulous laugh, amazed that Rose should even suggest such a thing.

'Then it's high time you started. Now don't argue. Just put your hat and coat on. And a scarf, because the wind's chill. But it'll be dark in half an hour or so, so you'd better hurry.' Rose took down Lissa's coat from the peg behind the door and held it for her. 'Come on, and if you're worried your mother might come home before you do, you can bring in the washing on your way. It'll save me going out for it.'

She bundled Lissa out of the door and watched as she crossed the bridge over the mill stream. Then she made a pot of tea, poured four mugs and took them over to the mill.

As she reached it Captain Joel was just coming out of the door. He was a man of about Michael's age, she judged, and of equal height, with dark hair that curled round the cheese-cutter cap perched on the back of his head. He was wearing dark moleskin trousers and a navy roll-necked jumper with the word PERSEVERANCE curved in large white letters across the chest.

'You must be Mrs Dowland,' he said with a smile, his teeth showing very white in his weatherbeaten face. 'I've heard about you.' He had a rakish, devil-may-care appearance and it was not difficult to see why Lissa had fallen for him. Rose had a moment's misgiving. Lissa was so young, so innocent, she wouldn't want her to get hurt.

'And you'll be Cap'n Joel.' She smiled back. 'I've heard about you, too.'

'That's the introductions over then. Ah, I see you've brought us some tea. I must say that's very welcome.' He smiled, then his look turned to one of concern. 'But what about the other young lady? Miss Dowland? She usually brings the tea over. Is she still under the weather?'

'No, she's much better now, thank you. But I've sent her for a walk along the river wall. It'll do her good to get a little fresh air as long as she doesn't stay out too long.' She stepped past him into the mill. 'Are the others inside?'

'What? Oh, yes. Tell them I'll have mine later, will you?' Stephen Joel loped off, making no attempt to hide the fact that he was going in the direction Lissa had taken.

Dan was just inside the mill. When he saw Rose with the tea

he shouted up the stairs, 'Mike! Alfie! Tea's up,' then turned back to Rose.

'You don't usually bring the tea, Rose. Where's Lissy? It's not like her to miss an opportunity to see Steve.' He looked round. 'Where is he, anyway? He was here a minute ago.'

Rose gave a sheepish smile. 'I sent Lissy for a walk.'

'A *walk*! Lissy doesn't go for walks.'

'Well, she has today. I suggested it. I thought it would do her good. And when Captain Joel asked where she was, I told him. He seems to have disappeared ...'

Dan roared with laughter. 'Oh, Rose. You're matchmaking, aren't you?'

She didn't join in his laughter. 'I'm afraid I acted without thinking,' she said, her face sober now. 'Now I've seen him ... He looks a bit of a ... Oh, it was a silly thing to do. I didn't even stop to find out if he might be married.'

'But you haven't done anything, Rose. All you did was to tell him where Lissy had gone. The rest was up to him,' Dan said. 'And for your peace of mind, Steve isn't married. Not any more. His wife died in childbirth two years ago. He's a decent bloke, Rose. A bit of a rough diamond but a decent bloke for all that. And lonely.' He nodded, smiling at her. 'Don't worry, it'll be all right. You'll see.'

'I hope you're right,' she said, still looking anxious.

'Well, if it's any consolation to you, I'd be happy to have Steve Joel as a brother-in-law. He's fond of Lissy, you know. He always looks out for her when he's here.'

She bit her lip. 'All the same ...'

She needn't have worried. Half an hour later, when she was at the sink preparing vegetables for the evening meal, Lissa came into the kitchen with a bunch of hot house roses in her hand. Her face was rosy with cold and excitement.

'Stephen brought me these,' she said, showing them to Rose. 'Aren't they lovely?' She buried her face in them, then she looked up. 'He happened to see me on the sea wall, wasn't that lucky. Oh, he's such a nice man, Rose. We'd never really had the chance to talk properly before and we found such a lot to say. He was ever so concerned because I'd been ill. He said I still looked pale and he was worried in case I stayed out too long but I know he didn't really want me to come in so he took me back to his boat because he wanted to give me these. Aren't they beautiful?' She held them out for Rose to admire, then went on, hardly pausing for breath, 'He said he bought them for me in Ipswich this morning and he was going to give them to Dan for me if he didn't see me himself. Oh, and he said he liked the way I'd done my hair.' She began to dance round the room. 'He really likes me, Rose. He must, mustn't he? Or he wouldn't have brought me these lovely roses!'

'I'm sure he does, dear. But you'd better hurry and take them up to your room,' Rose said peering out of the window. 'You don't want your mother to see them, do you, and she'll be home any time now. In fact I think I can hear the trap coming now.'

'Oh, I must be quick, then. I've got that Doulton vase you brought down from attic. They'll look lovely in that, won't they? Oh, dear, I don't know whether I'm on foot or horseback I'm so happy.' She clapped a hand to her mouth. 'The washing! I forgot to fetch the washing in.'

'Don't worry, I'll go and get it,' Rose said with a smile. 'Go and see to your roses before your mother sees them and thinks they're for her.'

By the time Rose came in with the washing Lissa was downstairs and Eve was there, taking off her coat and hat. She was in a benign mood because she had been complimented by the Church Ladies' Guild on her fine work on the altar cloth.

'The vicar's wife begged me to join the Guild, but of course I declined,' she told them with obvious satisfaction. 'It's not the kind of place one would want to visit on a regular basis.' She patted her hair into place before settling herself in her rocking chair.

'I'm sure the ladies there would be pleased if you did,' Rose remarked.

'No doubt. But apart from the vicar's wife and Dr Holmes's wife there was nobody there I would wish to be associated with. I don't consort with village women, as you well know.' She turned to her daughter. 'You're looking very much better, Lissa,' she said, not unkindly, firmly changing the subject.

'Rose suggested that I should go for a little walk along the sea wall,' Lissa said truthfully. 'It was lovely.'

'It obviously did you good. Perhaps you should do it more

often,' Eve said, causing Rose to raise her eyebrows in astonishment. 'You, too, Rose. A walk now and again wouldn't do you any harm. A short one, of course. It wouldn't do to walk too far, in your condition.'

It was the first time for days that Eve had mentioned the baby and Rose could only conclude that she must have had a very good afternoon indeed.

'I thought I might walk as far as my mother's tomorrow afternoon, as it's nearly Christmas,' she said, striking while the iron was hot. 'I've been wanting to go to tell her about the baby.'

An expression of distaste crossed Eve's face. 'That's rather further than I would advise.'

'I don't see why. I'm on my feet all day as it is, working about the house. At least I'll be out in the fresh air.'

Eve sighed heavily. 'Very well. I daresay Lissa can manage here for a few hours.'

'She hates me coming home,' Rose told her mother as she took off her smart blue coat and hat. 'It isn't that I don't want to come more often, Mum, it's that I can't get away. You know that, don't you?'

'Yes, my girl, of course I do. But your loyalty lies with your husband now. I know that, too.' Emma was looking more scrawny than ever, her sparse hair screwed into a knot and her always spare frame thinner and becoming less upright. She had been in the dairy when Rose arrived, although there were no cows left on the farm now but she came indoors, kicking off her boots and wiping her hands on her sacking apron.

She pulled the kettle forward. 'It's always good to see you, my girl. We'll have a cup of tea and you can tell me all your news.'

'I won't have tea, thanks, Mum. Hot water'll be fine.' Rose blushed as she said it.

Emma turned to look at her and a smile spread across her face. 'Like that, is it? I'm glad to hear it, child. When's it due?'

'Oh, I'm not sure, really. I hadn't ...'

Emma raised her eyebrows. 'You mean to say your mother-in-law hasn't helped you to work it out?' She tutted as Rose shook her head. 'Well, when was your last monthly?'

Rose frowned. 'I can't really remember. October, I think. About the middle of October.'

Emma made the tea in silence and poured Rose a mug of hot water. Then she poured herself a cup of tea and sat down. 'That'll put it sometime next July, I should think,' she said finally. 'That'll be nice. A summer baby. Easier for drying the washing and it'll give the baby a good start in life if it's born in the warm weather.'

Rose sipped her hot water gratefully. It was the only thing that seemed to keep the dreadful feeling of nausea at bay. 'How's Grace? I must go and see her and tell her about the baby when I can get away.'

'Yes, you must. She'll be pleased to see you, Rose. She doesn't get out much now because she finds it a bit of a job getting about. She's quite a size. Getting near her time, you see. But she's as happy as a lark. Why don't you pop and see her today? You've got time, haven't you?'

Rose looked doubtful. 'Well, yes. But I came to see you, Mum.'

'I know. But I can spare you for half an hour to go and see your sister. I know she'd like to see you. You go along there now and I'll finish what I was doing in the dairy. I'll have the tea laid for you when you get back. It'll only be bread and dripping, mind.'

'That'll do me fine, Mum. I don't have much appetite these days and it's a long time since I had bread and dripping.'

Rose set off across the field to see her sister, walking carefully in the frost-hardened ruts. Grace was sitting by the fire in her little kitchen, sewing. She lumbered to her feet when she saw Rose.

'Oh, look what the cat's dragged in,' she said with something approaching a sneer. 'Thass took you long enough to get here, ain't it.' She looked Rose up and down, taking in the smart blue coat with its astrakhan collar and matching toque. 'Quite the smart miller's wife, ain't we? Lady Muck from Turd Hall.' Her lip curled as she spoke.

'Oh, Grace, don't be like that,' Rose said, going over to her and planting a kiss on her cheek. 'I've come as soon as I could.'

150

'You've bin married near on six months,' Grace reminded her. 'You coulda come afore.'

'That's all you know about it!' Rose snapped. 'But if this is all the welcome I'm going to get I'm glad I didn't. And don't worry, I can go as quickly as I've come.' She turned back to the door.

'There's no need for that.' Grace laid a hand on her arm. 'I'm sorry, Rosie. I didn't mean to upset you. Come an' sit down and I'll make some tea. If you don't mind slummin' it, that is.'

'Slumming it?' Rose stared at her and said sharply, 'Grace! Whatever's the matter with you?'

Grace shrugged. 'Well, you don't come hie nor by me for months and then suddenly turn up in your posh clo'es, talking all cut glass. You ain't like my sister Rose any more.'

'I don't talk all cut glass, do I?' Rose said amazed.

'Not much you don't.' Grace gave an exaggerated imitation of the way Rose's speech had altered since living with the Dowlands.

Slowly, Rose took off her hat and coat and laid them over the back of a chair. 'I suppose I've learned to copy the way they speak at the Mill. I hadn't noticed,' she said thoughtfully. 'But I haven't changed inside, Grace. I'm still the same Rose, really I am. And it's not my fault I haven't been to see you before. I've wanted to come, but you wouldn't believe the hard job I have to get away even to go and see Mum.' She sighed. 'I can't do just as I like, you know.'

Grace, busy now with the kettle nodded. 'I'm not really surprised. That man of yours looks a bit ...'

'Oh, it isn't Michael. It's his mother. She hates me coming home ...' Before she could help herself Rose was telling Grace all about Eve and how she was treated as no better than a servant in the house. She told her about Lissa and her illness and even about Captain Joel.

'Mind you, when you see the way she treats her own daughter you can't wonder that she treats me as a servant, too.' She sighed. 'Just imagine, when I first went there I had no idea Lissa was her daughter.' She gave a little mirthless laugh. 'When I went there I didn't know a lot of things, did I? I thought Dowlands' Mill House was the most wonderful house

151

in the world. All that lovely furniture and china, beautiful carpets in every room; long velvet curtains everywhere ... And when I married I thought I was the luckiest girl alive to be living there. But it doesn't mean anything. It's all show. It's not a home at all. Just a showplace. And a showplace that's shabby and moth-eaten into the bargain, when you look closely. Only that doesn't matter, because nobody ever goes there to see it.' She looked round Grace's homely little room. 'Do you know, Grace, I'd give my eye teeth to live somewhere as cosy as this, with a husband who loved me like Albert loves you.'

Grace had listened to Rose's outburst in silence. Now she shook her head. 'But surely Michael ...? I mean, look at all the things he bought you before you were married ...'

Rose shrugged. 'Oh, I suppose he loves me, in his way. But he's hardly ever there. He's either working or out on the marsh ...'

'What on earth does he do out there?'

'I dunno. Watches birds, I think. And if he's not doing that he's down at the Miller's Arms.' She looked up. 'Don't tell Mum what I've told you, Gracie. You won't, will you?'

''Course I won't if you don't want me to.'

'I never intended to spill it all out like that. I dunno what came over me.' She looked round the room again. 'I suppose it was seeing you here like this, so happy and contented, although you haven't got much money, have you?'

'We manage all right,' Grace said. 'We don't want for much but what we don't know it.' She roared with laughter at her own joke. 'Now, I've got some nice little fruit scones I made this morning. You'll hev one, won't you, with your cuppa?'

'No tea for me, Grace,' Rose said. 'Just hot water.' She blushed. 'That's partly why I came. To tell you I'm like you.' She pointed to Grace's swollen stomach.

'Oh, Rosie!' Grace squealed. 'When?'

'Mum reckons about July.'

Grace did rapid calculations. 'So there'll only be about six months between yours and mine. Oh, ain't that nice now! They'll be able to play together, won't they?'

'I hope so.' Rose's voice was flat. 'They will if I have my way.' She bit into a scone. 'My, these are nice,' she said, more cheerfully. 'I can see now why you're getting as fat as butter. And I don't mean the baby, either. Look at you, you've got a double chin!'

'Thass what happiness does for you,' Grace said, reaching for the teapot.

'I guess I shall never get fat,' Rose said.

'No, I guess you won't.' Grace finished her scone and reached for another one. 'If I was you, Rosie, I wouldn't stand for Michael goin' off like that an' not tellin' you where he's goin'.'

'I don't see what I can do about it. He just tells me to mind my own business. It's like the chest in our bedroom ...' She was off again, telling her sister about the chest at the foot of the bed.

'Do you know what I think?' Grace said, when she'd finished.

Rose shook her head.

'I think there's suthin' fishy goin' on.'

'Like what?'

'I dunno, do I? But if it was me I'd make damn sure I found out. Why should he wanta keep cigarettes in a big ole chest? If you ask me that ain't all he keeps in there. He wouldn't keep it under his nose all the time if he didn't. And he can't be bird-watching all the time out on that marsh, can he?'

'He knows ever such a lot about birds,' Rose said doubtfully.

'So he might. But he can't do a lot of watching when thass dark, can he? No, there's more to it than that, I'll be bound.' Grace nodded sagely.

Suddenly Rose burst out laughing. 'Oh, Gracie, you've been reading too many penny dreadfuls. I'm sure there's nothing sinister in what Michael does. I reckon he goes for long walks with his friend Silas when he's not birdwatching. Or out in his boat. He's got a big rowing boat he tows the punt with when he goes out for wild duck.' She waved her hand. 'The punt has a gun on the front and he has to paddle it with his hands so it doesn't make a noise and disturb the ducks till he gets near enough to fire. Or so Dan told me.' She took another scone and bit into it. 'All I know about it is he doesn't catch all that many ducks and his boots get that muddy you wouldn't believe.'

'And I suppose it's your job to clean them.'

'Well, it saves Lissy a job, doesn't it?'

Grace put her head on one side. 'Oh, Rosie, whatever's become of you? And to think I was jealous of you.'

Rose didn't tell her mother of her conversation with Grace, and Emma assumed they had talked babies and asked no questions. But as she walked back to Mill House Rose went over in her mind what Grace had said and seeds of suspicion began to grow.

Grace was right, of course. Michael couldn't be out bird-watching all the time he was out, especially in the dark, although he nearly always had a pair of binoculars slung round his neck. But if he wasn't doing that, what was he doing?

The answer came to her in a flash. Of course. The binoculars were just a blind. He didn't go out to watch birds he went to meet another woman! That was why he was always so evasive when she questioned him. That was why he was often so late home. It all made sense now. It all fitted together.

A strange feeling came over her, and she thought for a minute she would choke. She stopped and undid the top button of her coat so that she could take some deep breaths to calm herself. She put her hand on her still flat stomach. How could he? How could he spend all his spare time with another woman, leaving his pregnant wife to the mercies of his harridan of a mother. The strange feeling didn't leave her, it seemed to be getting worse, then she recognised it for what it was; not jealousy, but blind rage.

She strode on, looking neither to right nor left, the fury seething inside her looking for an outlet. When she came to the lane leading down to the mill she picked up a thick stick and beat at the frost-rimed hedgerow as she marched along in an effort to give vent to her feelings.

Then, just as suddenly, the fury left her. She stopped in her tracks, quite calm, her head clear. She knew exactly what she would do. She nodded to herself, threw away the stick, straightened her hat, and went on at a more leisurely and dignified pace.

Chapter Thirteen

After supper that evening Michael got up from the table and shrugged on his coat.

'Where are you going, dear?' Rose asked, as she always did.

'Out.' It was what he always replied.

'Will you be late?'

'I might be. Might not.'

'Very well, dear.' She began to clear the table as he banged out of the back door.

A few minutes later she whispered to Lissa, 'I've got to run to the privy. Will you finish here?'

'Yes, of course. Are you all right, Rose?'

'I will be. I think I must have eaten something that didn't agree with me.'

'I'm not surprised. You've been to your mother's today, haven't you?' Eve said, her sharp ears missing nothing. 'I wonder you haven't been poisoned before now.'

'There's nothing wrong with my mother's food,' Rose retorted, as she took a shawl from behind the door. She would like to have said more, because Eve never missed a chance to make snide remarks about her family, but she had other things on her mind. Wrapping the shawl round her shoulders she hurried out of the house.

But she didn't go to the privy. She slipped across the yard and over the mill stream bridge behind Michael. She shuddered as she crossed the bridge. There was always a feeling of icy cold there, even on a summer's day, let alone in the middle of winter. It was an unnatural, eerie cold, it seemed to her, and she quickened her pace, the darkness increasing the sense of what she could only describe as evil that surrounded the bridge and mill race below it.

She hurried on, glad to leave it behind, out on to the river bank, keeping a safe distance behind him. As she walked, the frosty path was sharp and uneven through her thin house shoes, and she pulled the shawl more tightly round her against the cold night air. It was a moonless night, and the habitual thin mist rose from the marsh, but as her eyes became accustomed to the darkness she could see the ghostly outlines of stunted trees and bushes along the way. She could see Michael striding on ahead of her, looking neither to right nor left as he went.

A large boat went past the end of the creek, on its way to the docks at Ipswich. She could hear the throb of the engines across the water and in the dim light of the lanterns on board she saw him silhouetted clearly. He had just reached the end of the creek, where it widened out into the river and now he stopped, looking about him. Rose stopped, too, and crouched down behind a bush, watching. It was a brave woman he was meeting, if she was prepared to face this bleak, lonely marsh by herself, she thought with a shiver. She gazed around. Everywhere was deathly quiet and the trees and bushes had begun to assume queer, grotesque shapes in the misty darkness. The gullies were glistening with water snaking in from the rising tide. She tried not to think of her own adventure on the marsh, how petrified she had been that night, and how easy it was to let the imagination run riot. Even now she found herself shivering with fear at the memory. It was only the fact that Michael was not far away that gave her the courage to remain where she was, even though she knew she couldn't call on him.

Suddenly, in the stillness, she heard approaching footsteps and someone hurried past her, so close that she could have put out her hand and touched him. Because it was a man, she was in no doubt of that, she could smell the stale tobacco as he passed. He reached Michael and the two figures were silhouetted clearly against the dark sky as one of them lit a lantern, swung it to and fro several times and then extinguished it. She frowned. Clearly, Michael was not meeting another woman, which was a relief, but what on earth was all that about?

She heard the murmur of voices, and crept a bit closer to try and hear what was being said, but the two men moved away and disappeared into the darkness. A few seconds later she heard the splash of oars and saw the dark shadow of a boat moving out into the river. The sound of the oars grew fainter and fainter until she could no longer hear it and she realised that now she was quite alone on the marsh.

For a long time she remained crouched where she was, trying to make sense of what she had seen, filled with a mixture of relief that Michael was with a man and not a woman and curiosity as to what they might be doing out on the river at this time of night. She was becoming chilled and knew she must soon summon up the courage to go back to the house. It wasn't far to run, less than a quarter of a mile, and she could see the light from it shining dimly through the mist, but in her total isolation all her fears and fantasies crowded in and she felt rooted to the spot. An owl hooted, adding to the eerie desolation, and then all was quiet, deathly quiet, except for the sound of the water lapping the bank.

She knew she must move. The cold was eating into her bones and her teeth were beginning to chatter, although more with terror than cold. She knew Lissa would soon begin to wonder why she was spending such a long time in the privy and would go and look for her. Added to that, Michael might come back and if he found her spying on him there was no telling what he would do. He had never yet struck her, but lurking at the back of her mind was the feeling that he was quite capable of it if he had a mind to. She chafed her frozen limbs. She would freeze to death out on this bleak marsh if she didn't move soon. She told herself all these things in an effort to pluck up the courage to go back the way she had come, through the thicket of brambles where anyone – anything – might be lurking and over the bridge which she had now convinced herself was haunted, but she wasn't sure her legs would carry her.

Suddenly, she heard a twig snap. It was probably a heron nesting in a nearby tree but she didn't wait to find out. As if all the devils in hell were behind her she made a dash for the mill. As she ran along the river bank ghostly fingers clawed at her hair, but heedless of the pain she managed to jerk it free, realising afterwards that it was only a bramble, then the shawl came off, caught up in a bush, and with shaking hands she had to stop again to untangle it. At last, sobbing, she reached the mill yard, where she waited for a minute to compose herself and steady her breathing before stepping into the welcome warmth of the kitchen.

'Oh, I was just coming to see if you were all right, Rose. Are you better now?' Lissa asked anxiously. 'You look awfully white.' She was just finishing the washing up and Rose realised with a shock that she had only been gone ten minutes. It had seemed like a lifetime.

Eve frowned at her. 'Yes, you are looking a bit peaky. Is it raining? Your clothes look damp.'

'It's a bit misty. I stood outside for several minutes to get a breath of fresh air.' That much was indeed true.

'Well, I think you should go straight to bed. And be careful what you eat in future. Remember you have your child to think of. My grandson.'

For once Rose was glad of Eve's aversion to illness. 'Yes, I think I will go to bed,' she said, passing a hand across her brow in an effort to calm herself.

'I've already put a hot water bottle in your bed,' Lissa said, fussing round her. 'So it'll be nice and warm for you.'

'Thank you, Lissa.'

After she got into bed Rose lay for a long time staring up into the darkness. Now she was safe and warm in bed she felt calmer and could turn her mind to what she had seen out there on the marsh and try to make sense of it all. Who had Michael's companion been? Probably his friend Silas Hands. It was nobody she had ever seen before, she was sure. And where could they possibly have been going in a rowing boat, in the dark, on such a bitterly cold night? There were no houses on either side of the river bank for miles and it was hardly the night for fishing.

She cuddled the hot water bottle Lissa had put in her bed, gratefully feeling the warmth seep back into her frozen body. At least Michael wasn't seeing another woman, she thought drowsily, although what he was doing was still a complete mystery. And she knew better than to ask him for an explanation. Perhaps Dan would know. Come to think of it, it would have been much more sensible to ask Dan than to follow Michael out on to that dark and treacherous marsh. She should have thought of it before. She would speak to Dan. Tomorrow. She fell asleep.

She didn't hear Michael come to bed and when she woke in the morning he had gone. Only the dent in his pillow showed that he had been to bed at all.

The morning followed its usual ritual of washing, getting dressed, being sick and forcing down a piece of dry toast. After that, she began to feel better and could face the day. Grace had told her that she would soon stop feeling so dreadful, that it only lasted about three months, but it had become so much a way of life now she couldn't imagine ever feeling any different.

'I suppose the boys have both gone over to the mill,' she said to Lissa, leaning her head on her hand.

'Michael has. Dan's gone to the garden to pick some Brussels sprouts for supper tonight.'

Rose got to her feet and looked out of the window. 'It's a lovely morning, isn't it? I think I'll take a walk. I might be able to give Dan a hand, too.'

'Good idea.' Lissa nodded approvingly. 'A walk will do you good. Are you feeling any better, Rose?'

Rose made a face. 'Difficult to say. I always feel awful in the morning. But it'll pass.' She took down the shawl from the back of the door and went outside.

The sun was shining in a clear sky although it was cold and the frost still rimed the trees and bushes. She hurried across the bridge, shuddering as she always did as she went, and through the wicket gate that led to the garden. Dan was at the far end, picking sprouts into a bucket. He straightened up when he saw her.

'Hullo, Rose, are you better today?'

She didn't speak until she reached his side. Then she said, 'I wasn't ill last night, Dan. It was only an excuse. I followed Michael out on to the marsh.'

He looked at her and shook his head. 'Now, what in the world did you want to do that for, Rose?' he asked chidingly.

'I wanted to see where he went. I thought he might be

159

seeing another woman.' She felt foolish as she said the words.

'And would you really mind if he was?'

The words shocked her. She stared up at him. 'I— of course I would.' She hesitated as his words sank in. 'I don't know— I hadn't thought—'

'Poor little Rose. My brother isn't very nice to you, is he?' His voice was gentle and his blue eyes were full of compassion. 'I've noticed, you know. Life at Mill House isn't quite what you had expected, is it?'

She shrugged, embarrassed at his perception. 'I'm getting used to it. I had to work hard when I lived at home, you know.' She smiled at him. 'At least you're kind to me, Dan.'

'There's a reason for that.' He turned away from her and continued picking the sprouts.

The way he spoke sent an odd fluttering feeling in her heart which she thought it best not to analyse. Instead she said, 'Like I told you, I followed Michael out on to the marsh. I saw him meet another man and I saw them both go off in a rowing boat. I don't understand it, Dan. I thought you might know where he was going.'

Dan straightened up. 'I'll have a word with him.' He shook his head and gave a sigh. 'I've already told him ...'

'Told him what?'

'Never mind it, Rose. It's no concern of yours. You've satisfied yourself that there's no other woman involved, now take my advice and leave it there.'

'But he's my husband, Dan. I ought to know. Is he in some kind of trouble?'

'No, he's not. But he will be, if he's not careful.'

'What do you mean?'

He took both her hands in his and she noticed with some surprise that although he was picking ice-cold sprouts they were warmer than her own. It felt safe, and comforting. 'It's best you don't know what I mean, Rose. I've told you I'll have a word with him, now leave it at that, there's a good girl. There's no point in ... well, I wouldn't want you getting yourself involved, that's all.'

She frowned. 'I don't understand.'

He smiled at her, his blue eyes warm. 'Good. Now, take these sprouts back to the house or we'll have the Matriarch shouting for them.' He gave her hands a little squeeze before letting go of them. 'Trust me, Rose.'

They walked back to the mill together.

'I hate this bridge,' she said as they crossed it. 'It gives me the creeps.'

'That's probably because of the rate the water rushes through. Do you know, when I have to get down there to look at the wheel – because sometimes things get tangled up in it, bits of weeds, broken branches of trees, and things like that stop it from turning properly – well, when I get down there into the water I have to tie five pound weights to my boots to keep me on an even keel so I don't get swept away.'

'Goodness me. No wonder it looks dangerous.'

'It *is* dangerous when it's in full spate.' He looked at her and smiled. 'I don't wonder at you getting the creeps, Rose. It's easy enough to imagine all sorts of horrible things when the mill wheel's churning the water up, but I can assure you nothing nasty's ever happened yet. All the same, the first thing we'll have to do when we've got a baby toddling round the place is to put a stout fence round it.'

Rose looked down into the black water and shuddered. 'Indeed we shall.'

She went back into the house. She was glad she had spoken to Dan about Michael but it seemed he already knew. And didn't approve. For some reason the fact that Dan knew made her feel better but she still wondered what on earth it was that Michael was up to.

In spite of the fact that there were only three days to go to Christmas nothing different was happening indoors, except that Eve was spending all her time putting the finishing touches to the altar cloth. Lissa was cleaning the brass, as she did every Thursday, so Rose picked up a cloth to help her.

'We always put paper trimmings up for Christmas at home,' she said in a low voice to Lissa. 'And we deck everywhere with holly.'

'Pagan customs,' Eve said. 'Christmas is a religious festival and should be treated as such.'

Rose sighed. There was nothing wrong with Eve's hearing. 'Don't you even have a turkey?' she asked in her normal voice since there was no point in whispering.

Lissa shook her head, amazed at the idea.

'We shall have our normal Sunday roast, since Christmas Day is on a Sunday this year. And we shall all attend church in the morning.'

'All of us? Even Lissa?' Rose asked.

'Yes, as it's a special occasion. I've bought her a new coat from my catalogue.'

'Oh, how lovely. As a Christmas present? You shouldn't have told her, Eve,' Rose clapped her hands delightedly. 'You should have kept it as a surprise.'

'We don't exchange Christmas presents in this house, Rose,' Eve's voice dripped ice. 'It's another pagan custom.'

'Well, in that case, I shall go and visit my parents on Christmas afternoon,' Rose said. She turned to Lissa. 'And perhaps you would like to come with me, Lissa. And see what other pagan customs we follow.'

Lissa's face lit up, but fell again when she saw her mother's disapproving expression.

'Well, if nothing else is going on we shall neither of us be missed, shall we?' Rose remarked. 'We can leave the tea laid ready so all you have to do is make the tea, Eve. You'll be able to manage that, won't you? After all, I don't suppose Michael will be here. He rarely is, these days.'

Eve pursed her lips but said nothing and Rose knew she had won the day.

For the rest of the day she sang about her work. She looked forward to taking Lissa home with her and at lunch time she managed to have a quiet word with Dan to ask him if she could take some of his best D'Arcy Spice apples as a present to her family. She had no money so she couldn't buy presents and she had had no time to knit or sew anything. Her hands were too rough for such work, anyway, but she knew her presence would be gift enough.

During the afternoon she went upstairs to her room to hang Michael's clean shirts in the wardrobe. While she was there she went across to look out of the window, as she always did and was surprised to see her father sitting on his cart in the yard. He rarely came to the mill these days since there was no longer corn to be ground at Crick's Farm. She hurried from the room and down the stairs. She was glad she had seen him because it would be a good opportunity to send a message to her mother to tell her the good news that she and Lissa would be home for tea on Christmas Day. She knew Emma would be delighted.

'Where are you off to now?' Eve asked grumpily as she threw her shawl round her shoulders. 'You're always flitting off somewhere, these days. Is your stomach still upset?'

'No, it's better today. But my father is in the yard. I want to speak to him. I haven't seen him lately.'

She was out of the door before Eve had a chance to object and she ran across the yard towards him. Chad was already back up on the cart and Michael was standing beside him. As she approached Rose saw what looked like a small keg pass between then, which Chad bent down and tucked swiftly under the seat.

'Ah, Rose, my dear,' he said, straightening up as he saw her. 'How nice to see you. I came for some chicken feed and I wondered if I might be lucky enough to catch sight of you. How are you, my dear?' He spoke quickly, and had what almost amounted to a furtive look about him. But she was too full of her own exciting news to pay much attention to it.

'I'm well, Dad, thank you.' She smiled up at him. 'And I've got some good news. Will you tell Mum I shall be home for tea on Christmas Day? And that I'm bringing Lissa with me? I know she'll be pleased.'

'Indeed she will. And so shall I, my dear. It will be nice to have all my daughters round the table once again. Because Grace and Albert are coming, too, if she can walk that far.' He turned to Michael. 'And you, my boy? Will you be accompanying them?'

Michael shook his head. 'I shall be too busy.'

'On Christmas Day?' Chad raised his eyebrows. 'Surely that's the one day in the year when industry can legitimately take second place to idleness.'

'Maybe. Anyway, I'm not one for social gatherings,' Michael said. 'But Rose is welcome to come if she likes.'

'Thank you very much,' Rose said dryly. 'I hadn't realised I was expected to ask your permission.' She looked up at her father and said eagerly, 'Now, you won't forget to tell Mum,

163

will you? I know what your memory's like.'

'As if I would.' He looked at her reproachfully. He picked up the reins. 'Come on, Socrates, we've got a message to deliver. We mustn't tarry.' He touched his hat to Rose and waved to Michael. 'Thank you, my boy. Thank you, indeed,' he called as he left the yard.

'Did he pay for it?' Rose asked when Chad was out of sight.

'Pay for what?' An expression something akin to alarm crossed Michael's face.

'The chicken feed, of course. I know he isn't very prompt in settling his accounts, especially now I'm not there to keep him up to scratch.'

Michael's expression relaxed. 'Oh, that. He'll settle up at the end of the month, I expect. I'm not worried.' He saw her give a little shiver. 'You're getting cold. Go on in. It's freezing out here.'

It wasn't until she was in bed that night that Rose had time to sort out the events of the day in her mind. Her conversation with Dan that morning hadn't been at all helpful. She had been so sure he would reassure her about what Michael was up to out on the marsh, but he hadn't. Instead he had hinted that it was best she knew nothing about it.

She turned over and thumped her pillow. Sometimes Michael went duck shooting early in the morning. Dan didn't approve of that and they had had several arguments over the breakfast table about the folly of lying in wait in lonely creeks for flocks of ducks and then shooting at them, scattering them in all directions and killing as many as possible.

But it couldn't be that because this time Michael hadn't gone early in the morning, he'd gone late in the evening. And he'd slept in his bed for at least a part of the night. There were no ducks waiting to be plucked out in the wash house, either. So he hadn't gone duck shooting.

Tired, her mind going round in circles as she tried to work out what Michael had been doing, she turned her thoughts to more pleasant things. She would be going home for Christmas tea and Lissa was coming, too. And Dan had said she could take some of his apples. Dan was nice. It was a relief to know he was always there if she needed a friend. Another thought began to nag at her. Why should she need a friend when she had a husband?

She hoped her father would remember to tell her mother they were coming. Not that it mattered too much, there was always a good table at Christmas even if they sometimes went a little short at other times through the year. But Chad had seemed a little preoccupied today. And what was it he had hidden so swiftly under the seat of the cart? Something he hadn't wanted her to see? It had looked like a small keg. Of brandy? Smuggled brandy? Her heart began to beat so fast that she thought she would choke. Dear God, not that. Surely not that.

Christmas Day dawned bright and clear. In contrast to other Christmas mornings Rose had known, when the bedroom rang with squeals of excitement as she and her three sisters scrabbled in stockings half filled with tiny gifts, lovingly made for each other out of scraps and a bright farthing at the toe, this Christmas morning was exactly like any other Sunday morning of the year, except that both Michael and Lissa as well as Dan accompanied them to church.

Rose smiled to herself at the way Eve graciously acknowledged the compliments she received on her altar cloth, which nobody could fail to notice as they approached the Communion rail. For once she was happy to dawdle in the church yard after the service, having sent Lissa ahead with the boys so that she could be preparing the dinner, chatting briefly with those whom she regarded as worthy of her attention.

'But I don't know who was responsible for all that greenery in the church,' she remarked distastefully, when finally they reached the lych gate where Jacob was patiently waiting with the trap. 'Fancy decking the Lord's house with holly and ivy. It's pagan.'

'There's a carol about the holly and the ivy,' Rose said. 'We often sing it at home.'

'You would! I don't suppose you realise the significance of it all,' Eve said with a sneer.

'It's a very religious carol,' Rose protested. 'It says that Mary bore Sweet Jesus Christ to redeem us all. I've never quite known what that meant,' she added thoughtfully. 'The only kind of redeeming I know is getting things back from the pawn shop.'

'It's not that kind of redemption. We're all sinners. That's why we need redeeming.' Eve said.

Rose raised her eyebrows, 'What, you as well, Eve? You're not a sinner, are you?'

'We're all sinners,' Eve repeated.

'Oh. I suppose that's why you made the altar cloth. So you get redeemed.'

'Don't be impertinent, Rose.' Eve didn't speak again.

At three o'clock, when all the washing up was done and the tea was laid ready with a white cloth spread over it Rose and Lissa got themselves ready to go to Crick's Farm.

'Are you walking?' Dan asked.

'Yes, it's a nice afternoon,' Lissa said, so excited she could hardly do up the buttons on her new coat.

'What time will you be coming back tonight?'

'I don't know. About eight, I should think,' Rose said.

'I'll come and meet you. I know you don't like the lane when it gets dark.' He turned to his brother, half asleep by the fire. 'Or will you be going, Mike?'

Michael shook his head. 'No. They won't take any harm. There's two of them.'

Dan winked. 'I'll be there, don't worry,' he said softly.

For some inexplicable reason, Rose felt an extra lift to her spirits and she couldn't help wishing, although she knew it was disloyal to have such thoughts, that Michael was a little more like his brother.

Chapter Fourteen

Crick's Farm was in its usual Christmas pandemonium of muddle and excitement. Paper trimmings were strung round the rooms and bunches of holly had been stuck untidily behind pictures, all adding to the happy confusion. Millie and Babs were flitting about, with sprigs of mistletoe in their hair, trying to look busy but too excited to actually do much, whilst in the midst of the confusion Emma was stoically putting the finishing touches to the Christmas cake on the kitchen table.

'There. That's done.' She stood back to admire it, her head on one side, all the time wiping her hands on her apron before going over to kiss Rose and Lissa.

'Oh, it's lovely to see you, my dear,' she said, giving Lissa a hug. 'We've heard that much about you I feel I know you already. Now, take your things off and give them to Babs.' She turned to Rose. 'Take her into the front room. Millie got the fire going early this morning – it takes an age to get the chill off that room, I s'pose it's because we don't use it but once a year. Grace is in there with Albert's mother.'

'Albert's mother?' Rose's eyebrows shot up in surprise.

She shrugged. 'Well, what could I do? I had to invite the old girl here else Albert would have had to go and spend the day with her and that wouldn't hev suited Grace. And not to blame her, either.'

Rose nodded. 'No, that's right.' She put her arm round Emma's shoulders and gave her a squeeze. 'You're a good sort, Mum. Can I give you a hand with anything?'

'No, it's all done now. The ham is all sliced and the celery washed – I hate that job – and the beetroot's peeled. Millie made the jellies and blancmanges yesterday for me. No, you go on into the other room, go and meet Millie's young man. She's got a surprise for you.' She dropped her voice. 'They're engaged!'

'What already? But, Mum, they haven't been walking out five minutes!'

'They seem to know what they're about,' Emma said with a shrug. 'Anyway, you're a good one to talk, aren't you? You and Michael hardly knew each other afore you was wed.'

'That's true.' More true than her mother could ever know.

It was a motley crowd that sat round the tea table that Christmas night. Millie flashed her rather vulgar engagement ring and gazed adoringly at her Henry, a slightly self-opinionated young man in Rose's view, with mannerisms and a small moustache, whose hair was sleeked back like a tailor's dummy. Grace, plump, contented and very pregnant sat between her husband, Albert, a small wiry man with a weather-beaten face and very blue eyes, who looked uncomfortable in his Sunday suit and stiff collar, and his mother, who was as miserable and ailing as ever. Mrs Giles even lined up her bottles of pills ostentatiously beside her plate so she shouldn't forget to take them. Babs, growing into a passably pretty girl in spectacles, tried to be sociable, whilst at the same time poring over a book on disciplining children that Miss Chamberlain had given her for Christmas. Chad smiled benignly to think his entire family was present and thought how well the scene would go when written up in his memoirs.

Lissa sat shyly in Rose's shadow, drinking everything in and saying very little but obviously delighted to be there. She had never seen so many people gathered in a room before and she was amazed at how happily they all chattered and laughed together. And nobody seemed in the least worried when a cup of tea got spilled, or even when a spot of beetroot stained the tablecloth.

After tea they all sat round the fire and cracked nuts and played silly Christmas games and Lissa forgot to be shy and joined in with the others, shrieking with laughter just like the rest when the blindfolds came off and they saw what stupid things they had done.

Then Chad decided everybody should have a Christmas drink.

'I've got something a bit special,' he said mysteriously. 'I'll go and get it.'

'I'll come and give you a hand, Dad,' Rose said.

'No, no, child, you remain here. I can manage very well on my own,' he waved her aside.

'Yes, let him get on with it. It'll be the first time he's lifted a finger today,' Emma said with a laugh.

Nevertheless, Rose followed Chad out into the kitchen and reached down glasses from the corner cupboard, turning just in time to see him putting a small keg back under the dresser. She picked up the jug standing on the table. It was full of amber liquid.

'What's this?' she asked.

'It's nectar,' he answered proudly.

She sniffed it. 'It's brandy.' She nodded towards where he had hidden the keg. 'Where did it come from?'

'Never you mind. I got it from a very good friend of mine for whom I did a favour. I thought it would be a little treat to give everyone a taste, as it's Christmas.'

'But brandy's expensive, Dad. You can't afford...'

He tapped the side of his nose. 'It's a case of wheels within wheels, Rose dear. And you don't know what I can and can't afford now, do you?'

'I reckon I've got a pretty good idea.' She looked at him suspiciously. 'You got this brandy from Michael, didn't you? No, don't trouble to deny it because I saw him give it to you.' She stared at the jug on the table. 'Now, why should he do that? And, more to the point, where did he get it from?'

'Ask no questions and you'll be told no lies, Rose. Now, pour this out and take it through to the others.' He had already poured himself a generous measure and now he threw it down his throat in a chillingly practised way.

'Not until you tell me what's going on, Dad.' She sat down at the table and stared at the jug of brandy for several minutes. Then she shook her head and said slowly, 'Or better still, I'll tell you. This is smuggled liquor, isn't it?' She rested her head on her hand. 'Oh, God, I hate to say it but I can see now. My husband is a smuggler. That's what he was doing the other night. He—' She looked up. 'And was it you he was with, Dad?' She shook her head. 'No, it couldn't have been, the man I saw with Michael wasn't tall enough for it to have been you. Well, whoever it was, he and Michael must have rowed out to that big boat I saw going past the end of the creek to take whatever it was they were smuggling in before the boat docked and the customs men could get at it.' She frowned. 'I couldn't think where Michael might be going in a rowing boat at that time of night, but of course, this explains it all. It even explains those cigarettes in the chest at the foot of our bed!' She leaned her head on her hand again. 'Oh, God. He'll end up in prison. My husband'll end up in prison. No wonder his brother said it was better I shouldn't know what he was up to.' She closed her eyes. When she opened them again she noticed that her father's hand was trembling as he poured himself more brandy and that the colour had drained from his face.

'Are you sure? Do you really think this is contraband brandy, Rose?' he said anxiously, staring at it before drinking it in one gulp.

'Oh, yes. Of course it is. Where else would Michael get it from?' she said impatiently. 'Didn't you know that, Dad? Didn't you realise?' She frowned. 'But what puzzles me is why should Michael have given it to you? Because I know you couldn't afford to pay for it, could you, Dad?'

He lifted his chin. 'He gave it to me because I did him a small favour, that's all, Rose.' He shrugged. 'It was nothing much. He just asked me if I had an outhouse he could use to store things in.'

'When?'

'Oh, I don't know, a couple of months ago. Maybe more. Well, there are plenty of empty buildings about the place, so I couldn't see why he shouldn't use one.' He scratched his head with the stem of his pipe. 'To be quite honest, I never thought to ask him what he wanted it for. It certainly never occurred to me that he might want it to store contraband goods.'

'Not even when he kept you supplied with brandy?'

He shrugged. 'No. I thought the brandy was just his way of paying me for the use of the barn.' He gave a sheepish grin.

'He knows I'm partial to a drop of brandy.'

'Don't we all!' Rose said on a sigh.

He sat down and leaned towards her, twisting his hands together as the enormity of what he had done hit him. 'What shall I do, Rose? I promise you I had absolutely no idea ... I would never have got involved if I'd thought for a minute ... You know I could never be a party to matters outside the law.' He leaned back and wiped his brow on his sleeve. 'Oh, my goodness, whatever will your mother say? We've always been good, law-abiding citizens, as you well know.'

'Is there anything stored there now?' Rose asked.

'Where? Oh, I don't know. I've never looked. To tell the truth, I don't even know which barn he uses.'

'Well, we'd better take a look round, hadn't we? I'll get my coat.'

'Take them a drink first,' Chad insisted. 'We might as well drink it now we've got it.'

'All right.' Rose suppressed a smiled as she handed the drinks round. She could see the humour in watching Albert's mother and Millie's priggish young man extolling the virtues of contraband liquor.

By the time she got back to the kitchen Chad had lit a lantern and together they toured the outhouses. There was nothing suspicious to be found anywhere, although outside the barn farthest from the house the ground was churned up and there were frozen footprints in the mud.

'Ah, this must be the one they used,' Chad said, stating the obvious. 'But whatever it was they stored here, it's all gone now.'

'And I'll make sure Michael and his cronies don't come here again,' Rose said grimly. 'If they want to end up in gaol themselves, there's no reason to take you with them, Dad.'

'No. No. Indeed no.' Chad was having to trot to keep up with her as she strode back to the house. 'But, Rose,' his voice was pleading. 'What shall I do? If I don't let him use the barn he won't keep up my supply ...' His voice died as she turned and glared at him in the light of the lantern.

'Good. You'll be better off without it, Dad.'

'But you don't understand, Rose. It helps me with my writing. It clears the brain ...'

She shook her head. 'No, it doesn't.' Her voice softened. 'You're deluding yourself, Dad. And you know it. You're an intelligent man.'

'Yes, you're right, I am deluding myself.' He looked at her and his shoulders sagged, so that for a moment he reminded her of a penitent sheepdog. 'I'm a bit of a failure, really, Rose, aren't I? I sometimes wonder why your mother puts up with me.'

Rose was silent for several minutes, then she said, her voice gentle, 'She puts up with you because she loves you, Dad. But that doesn't mean she doesn't know your shortcomings. And it doesn't mean she wouldn't be happier if you were to pull your socks up and do a bit of real work. She's killing herself, trying to keep things going for you, Dad, do you realise that? And all you do is dream and drink your days away. It isn't fair to her, is it?'

'No, Rose, it isn't fair to her.' He straightened his shoulders. 'I've been a damn fool, but I swear to you, Rose, that I'll turn over a new leaf.' He nodded firmly. 'As soon as that keg of brandy's empty.' He set off back to the house.

'You've got to do better than that, Dad,' she called after him.

He stopped and looked back, surprised. 'Well, we can't waste good Napoleon, can we? That really would be a crime.'

'We'll see about that,' she muttered, and when he had gone to join the rest of the gathering in the front room she fished behind the dresser for the brandy keg and poured its contents down the drain.

The evening came to an end much too quickly for Lissa and as she and Rose left to go back to the mill all she could say was, 'Oh, Rose, I wish we didn't have to go home. I've never enjoyed myself so much in my whole life. I really haven't.'

'Not even when you've been with Cap'n Joel?' Rose said wickedly.

'That's different.' She was quiet for a minute, then she said, 'Dan says he'll be coming back in a few days, so I shall see him again. He really likes me, Rose. He said so.'

'I'm not surprised, Lissa. You're a lovely girl,' Rose said, squeezing her arm.

'Do you really think so?' She still sounded doubtful.

Dan met them at the end of the lane and escorted them

home, Lissa chattering all the while about the wonderful time she'd had at Crick's Farm.

'We only had tea and played a few silly games,' Rose said apologetically.

'I'm sure it did Lissy good. I only wish I could have come, too,' Dan said and Rose thought she detected a wistful note in his voice.

'You could have done. I'm sure my mother . . .' she stopped. Of course Dan couldn't have gone home with her. What was she thinking of? It wouldn't have done at all.

The girls received a frosty reception from Eve when they got in, a total contrast to the warm and generous atmosphere at Crick's Farm. She wouldn't even listen when Lissa tried to tell her what had gone on. Michael wasn't there.

'Have you been alone all evening, Eve?' Rose asked trying to sound sympathetic.

'Dan has been here most of the time.' Eve nodded coolly towards her youngest son. 'But unlike many people I'm quite content with my own company, Rose.' She gathered together her work. She had started on another piece of embroidery now that the altar cloth was finished. 'However, as I never keep late hours I think I shall retire for the night. Good night to you all.'

'Good night, Eve,' Rose replied. 'And a merry Christmas,' she added under her breath.

She waited until Lissa, too, had gone to bed before she spoke to Dan of her father's unwitting involvement in Michael's smuggling.

Dan sat rocking himself back and forth in the rocking chair as she told him her story and how after talking to her father she had pieced together for herself what Michael had been doing out on the marsh a few nights ago.

'I didn't want you to know, Rose,' he said, shaking his head. 'I've been trying to stop him, ever since he started.'

'When was that?'

'I'm not sure. Some time last year, I think. He and that pal of his, Silas Hands, were in it up to their necks at one time.' He paused and then went on, 'I thought I'd put a stop to it when I stopped him from storing the stuff, mostly tobacco, cigarettes, spirits and stuff like that, in the mill. Being right out of the way as we are I suppose they thought the mill would be the ideal place. But once I found out, which I admit took me several months, because they were very clever the way they went about it, I wasn't having any. I told him I wasn't going to be incriminated with him and if he brought any more stuff to the mill I'd inform the police.'

'So he took it to Crick's Farm. And nearly turned my father into a drunkard for the privilege,' Rose said bitterly.

Dan got up, so suddenly that the chair continued rocking. 'Well, he won't be carrying on his rotten trade from Stavely Creek any more,' he said savagely.

She looked up in alarm as he began to shrug on his reefer jacket. 'Dan. What are you going to do?'

He stared at her. 'I'm going to knock a hole in the bottom of his bloody boat and sink it,' he said. 'That'll put a stop to his games. I ought to have done it months ago.'

'But Dan, it's dark out there.'

'So much the better.'

She got up from her chair. 'I'll come and hold the lantern for you.'

He took her wrist as she put out her hand for the lantern. 'No, Rose. If Mike should come back while I'm doing it and you're there with me there's no telling ... ' He looked down at her, his eyes warm. 'He hasn't ever laid a finger on you, has he, Rose?'

She shook her head. 'No. He never has. But I've always had the feeling ... ' her voice died away in uncertainty.

He nodded. 'I know. Mike's got a vicious temper.' He put a finger under her chin and tilted up her face. 'If he does ever raise a hand to you, Rose, you must tell me,' he said quietly. His mouth assumed a grim line. 'And I'll thrash the living daylights out of him, so help me, God.' He looked down into her eyes and then very slowly bent his head and his lips brushed hers. 'Merry Christmas, Rose,' he said inconsequentially.

'Merry Christmas, Dan,' she whispered back.

After he had gone out she stood for several minutes with her hand pressed to her lips as if to seal the place where his lips had been. Then she turned and went up the stairs to bed, tears glistening in her eyes. She had been married five months almost to the day. To the wrong man.

*

174

For the next few days Rose went about in a daze. Nothing was different, yet everything had changed. Not that Dan made any reference, either by word or gesture, to what had happened on Christmas Night. After all, why should he? It had only been a perfectly innocent Christmas kiss, she argued to herself. But in her heart she knew better. Dan was in love with her and, God help her, she returned that love.

She lived in fear that Michael would suspect something. He didn't care about her, she realised that – in fact sometimes she wondered why he had married her at all – but that didn't mean he wouldn't care if another man paid attention to her. Especially his own brother.

Oh, it was all such a muddle. At night she tossed and turned in bed, worrying and wondering what would happen if Michael was to suspect anything, and it was always her first thought in the morning.

But as the days went on she began to cheer up. It was the beginning of a New Year and there was the baby to look forward to. She laid a hand on her stomach, just beginning to swell. Things would be better when the child was born, she was sure. But somehow, however hard she tried, she couldn't imagine a baby at Dowlands' Mill.

She got up and went downstairs. Now that the sickness had passed she was always ready for a good breakfast before beginning the day's work.

Lissa was at the stove cooking bacon and eggs and Eve sat at the table delicately nibbling toast and marmalade. She finished it just as Rose walked in.

'I'm going over to the mill to see to the accounts,' she announced, dabbing her mouth with her napkin. 'I'm afraid they rather got neglected over Christmas, whilst I was busy finishing the altar cloth.'

After she had gone Lissa put a plate of bacon and eggs in front of Rose and sat down opposite, leaning her elbows on the table. 'There was a fearful row here this morning, did you hear it?' she asked.

'No.' Rose didn't look up from her breakfast. Eve was always having rows with somebody or other. 'What was she complaining about this time?'

'Oh, it wasn't *her*. It was the boys.'

At this Rose did look up. 'What were they quarrelling about?' she asked, her tone guarded.

'Well, it seems that Michael hadn't been able to find his boat. You know he's got a big old skiff thing that he messes about the creek in. Well, it apparently disappeared over Christmas and when he did eventually find it, it was almost buried in the mud. Somebody had chopped holes in the bottom and sunk it!' Lissa's eyes were round with horror. 'Can you believe that! And do you know who did it?'

Rose shook her head.

'It was *Dan!* He owned up! Oh, Rose, I thought Michael was going to kill him. He was *furious*. Well, you can imagine, can't you? He says it'll take him ages to repair it.'

'Oh, it can be repaired, then?' Rose helped herself to more bread. Her heart was thudding but she tried not to show it.

'Yes. Michael says he'll get his friend Silas Hands to help him.' She rested her chin on her hand, her brow creased into a deep frown. 'It's not at all like Dan to do a thing like that, is it? I wonder what came over him. It was a dreadful thing to do, wasn't it, Rose?'

'I suppose he must have had a good reason.' Rose said, trying to sound nonchalant as she took a bite of bread.

'You haven't put any butter on your bread,' Lissa pointed out, laughing.

'Oh, no. I thought it tasted funny. How stupid of me.' Rose reached for the butter dish.

'I heard Dan say something about "that'll stop your little game",' Lissa said thoughtfully. 'But Michael only uses his boat for shooting duck. I can't see any harm in that, can you?'

'No, there's no harm in that,' Rose said levelly.

Lissa sat biting her lip for several minutes. Then suddenly, she shook her head and smiled. 'Dan expects *Perseverance* today or tomorrow. You know what that means, don't you, Rose?'

'Indeed I do.' Relieved at the change of subject, Rose got up and began to clear the table. 'It means we'd better wash your hair, because you'll want to look your best for Cap'n Joel.'

'Don't tease me, Rose.' Lissa fingered a stray strand of hari. 'Nobody's ever paid me any attention before,' she said dreamily.

176

Rose bent and kissed her. 'I'm not teasing, Lissy. I'm very happy for you. But are you sure ...? After all, you're only eighteen and Captain Joel ...'

'I'm quite sure,' Lissa interrupted. 'Stephen and I have talked about it. He's got a house in Manningtree so I'll have somewhere to live when he's away. And he says I shall be able to go with him on *Perseverance* sometimes – it's ever so comfortable inside, Rose. Have you seen it?'

'No, I haven't.' Rose stopped on her way to the sink, the teapot in her hand. 'When did you go on board, Lissa?' she asked suspiciously.

Lissa blushed. 'Oh, he showed me his quarters last time he was here. I told you, don't you remember? He took me on board to give me those roses.' She gave a little smile that was almost apologetic. 'I've still got them in my room.'

'But surely they must be dead by now.'

'Yes, they are. But I'm still keeping them. Nobody's ever given me roses before.'

Rose began the washing up. It hadn't been a good start to the day and she didn't know which was the most worrying, Lissa's infatuation – it couldn't be more than that, could it? – with Captain Joel, or the quarrel between Dan and Michael.

Not that the quarrel between the two men had anything to do with her. Or so she thought.

As usual, Michael still hadn't returned home when she went to bed. When he finally came into the bedroom she feigned sleep, like she always did, mentally holding her breath to see whether he would roll into bed and begin to snore straight away or whether he would begin to fumble with her nightgown and wake her up with his rough attentions.

But tonight he did neither. He came round to her side of the bed and stood there for so long that in the end she opened her eyes. He was holding a candle and staring down at her. In the dim light his expression was malevolent.

'It was all your doing,' he said, his eyes narrow. 'Wasn't it? It was all your doing.'

She sat up, pulling the covers up to her chin against the cold night air. 'I don't know what you're talking about, Michael. Come to bed. You've had too much to drink.

Whatever it is, we'll talk about it in the morning.' She made to lie down again but he got hold of her hair, coiled into the thick plait she wore it in at night, and yanked her back into a sitting position.

'Not a drop has passed my lips tonight. I'm stone cold sober,' he said. 'And don't come the innocent with me, mawther. You know very well what I'm talking about. Chad Bentley's barn. That's what I'm talking about. He's said we can't use it any more. That's your doing, isn't it? Not that it'll make any difference, we'll use it if we see fit and he won't stop us. He just won't get paid, that's all.'

'You're not to involve my father in your sm ... whatever it is you do,' she said savagely, trying to wriggle free. 'He's a respectable, law abiding man. Find someone else to do your dirty work for you.'

'Like you did!' He gave her hair another yank.

'I don't know what you're talking about. And let go my hair, you're hurting me.'

His grip tightened. 'I'll hurt you even more if I find you playing around with my brother,' he said, his face only inches from hers.

'Oh, Michael, don't be so ridiculous.' She laughed in his face. 'For goodness sake come to bed.'

'He sank my boat.' He sounded like a petulant small child.

'Well, that had nothing to do with me,' she said, trying to sound reasonable and keep the tremor out of her voice. 'That's between you and him.'

'If you hadn't told him ...'

She raised her eyebrows. 'Told him what, Michael? That you're a smuggler? But he already knew that, didn't he? He didn't need me to tell him.'

'He sank my boat,' he repeated.

'Good. Now let me get some sleep.' She tried to lie down but he was still holding her hair. 'Please let go.' She put her hand up to loosen his fingers but he caught it in his other hand and dragged her out of the bed.

When she was standing in front of him he caught both her arms, bruising her with his grip. 'If you play around with my brother I'll kill you,' he whispered. 'You're *my* wife and don't you forget it!' With that he gave her a shake and a push that

178

sent her off balance and she fell, catching the side of her face on the chest at the foot of the bed.

She sat there, rubbing her cheekbone. 'You're jealous, aren't you, Michael?' she said wearily. 'But you've no need to be. Nothing's ever happened between Dan and me. He's kind to me, that's all, which is more than you are these days. But there's nothing suspicious in that, is there? After all, unlike you, Dan's kind to everybody.' She got to her feet. 'Now, may I get back into bed?'

He stood to one side, his temper gone. He hadn't intended to hurt her but his pride wouldn't allow him to admit that he was sorry for what he'd done. 'Yes,' he growled. 'Get some sleep.'

She crawled in and lay on the edge of the bed as far away from him as she could, staring up into the darkness. What had happened to the charming man who had courted and married her those few months ago? What had changed him? And how could she recapture the man he had been? She let her hand creep across to find his. 'Michael?' she whispered.

But her only reply was a snore.

Chapter Fifteen

'Whatever's the matter with your face, Rose?' Predictably it was Lissa who drew attention to the angry blue bruise on Rose's cheekbone the next morning at breakfast.

'Oh, it's nothing much.' Rose fingered it without looking up. 'I tripped as I went into the bedroom and struck my face on the chest at the foot of the bed. It was very careless of me.' It wasn't a complete lie, she consoled herself.

'Lift your head up. Let me see,' Eve said from her position at the head of the table. She regarded Rose for some time, her face expressionless, before saying, 'You must have struck it very hard. It's badly bruised. You should paint it with oil of arnica.'

'I'll get it for you. It really does look very painful.' Lissa got up from the table.

'No, please sit down, Lissa. I'll do it after breakfast.' She gave an embarrassed laugh. 'I'm sure it looks much worse than it is. Would you pass me another piece of toast, please?' She spoke quickly, anxious to change the subject. From the corner of her eye she could see Michael watching her, an expression of guilt turning to relief on his face. Dan was staring at his brother and it was plain that he realised exactly what had happened. She prayed that it wouldn't bring added conflict between the two men.

Michael gulped the rest of his breakfast, got up and left. 'Don't forget to paint that bruise with arnica,' he muttered as he reached the door.

When he had gone Dan carried his plate over to Rose, who had begun swishing suds in the sink preparatory to beginning the washing up.

'Please don't say anything to Michael,' she managed to whisper to him. 'It will only make things worse. It was an accident, truly it was.'

'I don't believe you, Rose. It was no accident. I saw his face. I could kill the bastard.' He spoke through gritted teeth.

She shook her head. 'No. Please, leave things be, Dan.'

He sighed. 'Very well. But if it happens again . . .'

'It won't, Dan. It won't. Unless . . .'

'Unless what?'

'Nothing. It doesn't matter.' How could she tell him what Michael had said? But Dan's concern gave her a warm feeling inside.

The next day the weather turned wet, with a howling gale that sent the rain lashing at the windows. It was depressing. The kitchen, where Lissa kept the big range stoked with the coals that Dan got in first thing every morning was warm, but everywhere else in the house had a cold, damp feel about it and the dining room table developed a bloom that no amount of polishing could erase.

'It's a waste of our time, trying to make things shine when the weather's like this,' Lissa said, straightening up and pushing a strand of hair back behind her ear. 'And if she complains I'll tell her so.' Eve was always 'her' or 'she', never 'my mother'.

'You'd better not,' Rose said with a laugh, 'I've noticed the way she looks at you when you answer her back sometimes. One of these days you'll overstep the mark and you'll be out on your ear.'

'I don't care,' Lissa said with a toss of her head. 'When Stephen comes back . . .'

'When's he due?'

'Soon. He said he'd be here early in the New Year. But it depends on the weather, of course. Could be weeks, I suppose.'

'Might even be months.' Rose turned from dusting the ruby lustres on the mantelpiece. 'And even then . . .'

'Oh, I know. He might not want me.' Lissa chanted. 'You've said it all before, Rose.' She grinned at her. Nothing, it seemed, could shake her confidence in her captain.

Rose lifted her shoulders. 'All right, Lissa. But it doesn't alter the fact that you're still under age. You can't get married unless Eve agrees.'

'Ha! Do you imagine she's going to object? She'll be glad to get rid of me.' Lissa gave the table a finishing swipe. 'There. That'll do for that. Come on, let's get back to the kitchen where it's warmer and I'll make us some cocoa. She won't be back yet. Old Jacob's taken her into the village in the trap.'

'Yes, I saw them go. She must be barmy. Who'd want to be out in weather like this?'

Lissa shrugged. 'You know what she's like. She got some bee in her bonnet that the vicar's wife wanted to see her so it wasn't likely that a bit of rain would stop her.'

'I don't call this "a bit of rain", it's absolutely throwing it down. It's not fit for man nor beast to be out. Especially old Jacob. His rheumatism is dreadful, you know. And he's got the most dreadful cough. I could hear it as he waited for her.'

'Yes, I heard him coughing, too. But if she wants to go anywhere he has to take her. It's part of his job, along with fetching and carrying for the boys. The trouble is, if he doesn't work he'll have to give up his cottage and then what will he do? I know he'd rather die than end up in the workhouse.'

'Surely, the boys would let him stay on in the cottage, even if he couldn't work, after all these years of service. After all, it isn't as if anyone else needs it.'

'Oh, the boys would let him stay, but they don't have any say in it. You ought to know by now, Rose, it's my mother who rules this place and I can't see her letting Jacob stay if he's not working. She'd rather leave the place empty. Ah, speak of the devil ... here they come.' She made a face. 'Oh, blow! They're back early. That means we shan't get our mug of cocoa, Rose.'

Eve came in, shaking her umbrella and expecting to be fussed over.

'It really is the most awful afternoon,' she said, taking off her hat and coat and giving them to Rose to drape by the fire. 'Yes, please, Lissa, I'll have a cup of tea. I had one with the vicar's wife but she doesn't have Earl Grey and I'm very partial to that, as you know. Rose, fetch my house shoes for me, will you, dear? No, I don't think my feet are wet, I only had to walk as far as the trap. I must say the Vicarage is rather *shabby*. Not at all what I had expected ...' She ran on, giving out orders in between a commentary on her visit to the

Vicarage so it was nearly half an hour before Rose could pick up an old umbrella and slip away to knock at the door of Old Jacob's cottage. He had just got in after stabling the horse and trap and was hanging up his wet coat, coughing and wheezing as he did so.

'I came to see if there's anything I can get you, Jacob,' she said as he opened the door. 'With that dreadful cough you should have been in bed this afternoon, not hanging about in that old trap waiting for Mrs Dowland. Look at you, you're wet through. Did you have to wait outside all the time she was there?'

'No. I had a cuppa tea with the vicar's groom in the tackle room. He'd got a nice fire goin' in there.' He broke off, coughing.

'But you still got pretty wet.' Rose pointed to his shirt, where the rain had seeped right through his overcoat. 'And look at you, you're shivering with cold.'

He nodded. 'Tell ye the truth I don't feel all that special, Mrs Michael,' he confided, hugging himself. 'In fact, I was jest goona warm meself a drop o' milk and put a little snifta o' whisky in it and then I was goona turn in. See if I could warm meself up a bit.' The poor old man looked nearly dead on his feet.

'I think that's a very good idea, Jacob. Now, is there anything you need? Anything I can do for you?'

'No, thankee kindly. I've got all I want.' As he spoke he staggered and clung to the door post for support. 'Mercy me, I've turned a bit giddy all on a sudden.'

She put down her umbrella and went inside to help him to his chair by the fire. 'You sit there quietly and I'll warm the milk for you. Then I'll go over and get one of the boys to help you up to bed. Now, where do you keep your milk? And the whisky?'

'Thass all in the cupboard alongside the fireplace there.' He watched as she put a little saucepan on the hob and found the milk and the whisky, glad that he didn't have to make the effort to do it for himself.

Rose noticed that everywhere in the little cottage was immaculately neat and clean, with everything in its appointed place. When it was warmed through she put the milk in an enamel mug and poured in a generous amount of whisky. Jacob wrapped his hands round it gratefully and she left him to drink it while she hurried across to the mill.

She had expected to see Dan, but to her dismay it was Michael who was there, moving sacks of flour ready for delivery. They had hardly exchanged a word since the night he had struck her and she wasn't anxious to ask a favour of him.

'Is Dan here?' she asked.

'Why? What do you want him for?' he picked up another sack.

'I want to ask him to come across and put Old Jacob to bed,' she said coolly. 'The poor old chap's quite ill.'

Now he stopped what he was doing and looked up. 'What's wrong with him?'

'He took your mother out in the trap in all this rain and it's chilled him right through. He's got the most awful cough, too. I've warmed him some milk and then he's going to bed, but I don't think he'll manage to get there on his own. He's not very steady on his pins.'

He dusted the flour off his hands. 'No need to call Dan. I'll come and give the old boy a hand.' He stood looking at her for a minute, then took a step towards her. 'Are you all right, Rosie?' he asked uncertainly.

'Of course I'm all right. Why shouldn't I be?' she answered, her face wooden and her tone to match.

'It's just that ... I've never said I was sorry about what I did to you the other night. I'm afraid my temper got the upper hand. It was a dreadful thing to do.'

She looked at him in surprise. She had never expected an apology; Michael was not a man to admit he was ever in the wrong. 'It's all right, Michael. It's over and done with now.' She spoke quickly, for some reason strangely embarrassed. But he refused to be put off.

'I didn't mean to hurt you, Rose. Really I didn't. I wouldn't willingly do you any harm.'

'I know. I know you didn't mean it, Michael. We won't speak of it again. We must go ...'

He didn't move, but caught her arm and pulled her to him and stood looking down at her, smoothing her hair away from her face. 'I don't know what came over me that night, treating you like that. I must have been out of my mind. But it won't happen again, Rose. I promise.' Gently, he kissed the ugly discoloration on her cheek.

She closed her eyes, feeling herself weaken as he bent his head and kissed her again. She didn't know what had prompted this uncharacteristic show of tenderness, but this was more like the old Michael, the man she had fallen in love with. The relief brought a lump into her throat.

'You know I wouldn't rightly do anything to harm you, Rose,' he murmured, sliding his hand down until it rested gently on her stomach. 'Nor our son.'

'I know that, Michael.' She rested her head on his shoulder, thanking God for whatever had brought on this sudden change in him and praying that things would be better from now on. He cradled her in his arms, his cheek resting on her hair and they remained like that for several minutes, both reluctant to move apart. But at last, remembering Old Jacob, she pulled away from him a little so that she could look up into his face. 'We really ought to go and see to Old Jacob, Michael,' she reminded him.

He smiled down at her and gently pushed a strand of hair away from her face before bending his head to kiss her once, then several times more. 'Yes, I suppose you're right,' he said with a sigh.

He held the umbrella over them and kept his other arm tightly round her as they hurried across the yard to Jacob's cottage. She didn't look back. If she had, she might have seen Dan standing at the mill door, shaking his head, an enigmatic expression on his face.

Michael put Jacob to bed and there the old man remained for nearly two weeks. Rose and Lissa made him tempting soups and junkets, which for the most part he could only pick at, while Dan and Michael took it in turns doing the things he would be too embarrassed to let the girls do for him.

'I hope he realises how much trouble he's causing,' Eve said, as Lissa ironed his night-shirt while Rose sieved soup for him. 'You're both neglecting your own work and goodness knows how much time the boys are spending on him.'

'Well, it's our Christian duty to look after him, isn't it?'

Rose said. 'We heard that in church on Sunday, didn't we? The story of the Good Samaritan? Don't you remember?'

Eve sniffed. 'There are limits,' she said, then swiftly changing the subject, 'Look, that bread on the hearth will be over-risen if you don't see to it right away.'

'It won't hurt for another two minutes.' Rose finished sieving the soup and then turned her attention to the bread, pummelling it fiercely to relieve her frustration with her unfeeling mother-in-law. She couldn't understand Eve. She seemed to have no consideration at all for Jacob, who had been with the family for years and years. In fact, even Dan said he couldn't remember a time when he hadn't lived in the little cottage behind the wash house.

It was while Jacob was ill that Captain Joel returned. The weather had turned cold and dry and a white hoar frost coated the leafless trees and bushes with filigree icing and transformed the landscape into a kind of frozen fairyland under a brilliant blue sky. On such a morning *Perseverance* glided in on the tide with every sail set, like a great red butterfly.

Lissa, returning from Jacob's cottage nearly dropped the tray she was carrying in her eagerness to tell Rose the good news.

'See, I told you he'd be back,' she said gleefully. 'I wonder how long he'll be here for. I must go and see him and find out.'

'Just be careful,' Rose warned. 'You don't want to upset your mother.'

Lissa made a disgusting face that conveyed more than words ever could.

But fate was kind to her. That night a thick fog rolled in, sliding silently up the river and into the creek, shrouding the trees by the mill pond into ghostly shapes and completely hiding the barge tied up at the jetty from the house. The air was freezing and still, and with not a breath of wind to blow the fog away, let alone fill a sail, *Perseverance* was weatherbound for a whole week.

Lissa was unashamedly delighted at the dreadful weather and in spite of Rose's warnings, hidden by the fog she stole away at every available opportunity to board *Perseverance*, and see her captain. Stephen Joel was equally happy at being able to spend time with his Lissa but his happiness was tempered with annoyance at having to kick his heels waiting for the fog to lift and a fair wind.

'You see, my darlin', although I'm happy to be here with you and I don't want to leave you, the trouble is, while I'm stuck here in Stavely creek I'm not earnin' any money. An' I need money if I'm goin' to support a wife, don't I now?' He smoothed her brow as she lay in the crook of his arm on the bunk in his living quarters. 'Don't frown, darlin'.'

'I was just thinking, Stephen. I've never had money and it's never really worried me before because I've never had anywhere to spend it. But now I wish I had, because then I could give it to you.' She twisted round so that she could look up at him. 'Not that it really matters. I don't think I cost much to keep.'

He bent his head and kissed her. 'But I want to spend money on you, Lissy,' he said softly. 'I want to buy you pretty clothes, darlin'. I want you to have all the things you've missed over the years.' He waved his hand. 'There's a big wide world out there you don't know anythin' about. I want to take you an' show you.' He kissed her again. 'I love you, Lissy, and I want to marry you and take care of you.'

She clung to him. 'Oh, I wish you could.'

'I will. I promise.' He tried to break away. 'You must go back to the house, Lissy. You mustn't stay here any longer or I shan't be responsible ...'

She silenced him with a kiss. 'I'll go back soon. But I love you so much, Stephen. All I want to is be with you. To be your wife.'

'That's what I want, too, darlin'.' He tried to put her from him but she still clung. 'We mustn't rush things, Lissy. We have to wait ...'

'I don't want to wait, Stephen ...'

Unlike Lissa, Rose heaved an unashamed sigh of relief when the fog cleared at last and Stephen Joel was able to leave. It had been a difficult week. In spite of Rose's warnings, Lissa had been going around singing to herself and with such an ecstatic expression on her face that Rose was sure her mother must suspect something. She was certainly becoming suspicious of Lissa's frequent and prolonged attentions to Jacob.

'Jacob can't be *that* ill, that she needs to spend so much time there,' she complained when Lissa had once again slipped across to *Perseverance*. 'I notice my brass hasn't been cleaned this week.'

'Yes, it has, I did it myself. Lissa's giving the cottage a clean,' Rose lied on both counts. 'She wants it to be spick and span ready for when Jacob comes downstairs.'

'And when will that be, I should like to know.'

'Soon. He's getting stronger every day.' She offered up a silent prayer that the fog would lift before Jacob's recovery meant finding another excuse for Lissa's absences.

Her prayer was answered. One morning they woke to find everywhere fresh and sparkling in bright sunshine. It was as if a curtain had been rolled away, revealing the tide just leaving the creek and, to Lissa's consternation, carrying *Perseverance* with it.

'He never even said goodbye to me,' she said to Rose, her lip trembling, as they carried the laundry over to the wash house and began the weekly wash.

'Probably just as well. You'd have cried buckets and then Eve would have begun asking even more questions,' Rose replied, trying to keep her voice brisk and matter-of-fact. She grinned. 'As it was she was beginning to get suspicious about the amount of time you were spending with Old Jacob.'

'Is that where you told her I was? Thanks, Rosie.' She made a brave attempt at a smile but the tears threatened to spill over. She bit her lip. 'I mustn't cry. Stephen will be back again as soon as he can,' she said, with a lift of her chin. 'And then we'll be married.'

Rose paused and rested her hands on the wash board where she had been scrubbing a shirt. 'Oh, Lissy, don't set your hopes too high. You know what Eve's like. What if she says no?'

Lissa gave a mirthless laugh. 'What, and have to wait another three years to be rid of me? Don't be silly, Rose. Anyway, Stephen's going to speak to her next time he comes.' He'll win her round. You'll see.' Her tears had gone and her eyes were sparkling with happiness now.

Rose leaned over and kissed her, unwilling to blunt Lissa's optimism, but less certain about what Eve's reaction might be. 'I do want you to be happy, Lissy.'

Lissa gave her a hug. 'Oh, I am, Rose. I am. I think I must be the happiest girl in the world.' She gave a little skip as she picked up the copper stick and pushed a sheet under the water in the copper in the corner. 'Or at least, I will be when Stephen comes back for me.'

Rose said nothing but continued scrubbing the shirt collar. Since Lissa was clearly so happy and filled with confidence why did she, Rose, have such a feeling of misgiving nagging at the pit of her stomach? And why did the old proverb, 'There's many a slip ...' keep revolving round and round in her brain to the rhythm of the mill wheel turning just across the yard?

'Isn't it time you stopped cosseting Jacob? I thought you said he was better now,' Eve said later that day, frowning as she watched Rose pouring onion soup into a jug ready to take to him. 'Do you realise you've both been waiting on him hand and foot for nearly a fortnight? In fact at one point Lissa hardly ever seemed to be away from his place. I wonder she didn't take her bed over there. It's not good. He'll expect it, you know and then where shall we be?'

'Oh, he's much better than he was. Dan's lit his fire and Michael's going to help him downstairs again so he can sit by it,' Rose said. 'Would you like to go and see him, Eve? You can take him this soup, if you like, while I fetch the washing in.' She held out the jug.

Eve wrinkled her nose distastefully. 'You know I can't bear illness, Rose. But you can give him my regards and tell him I hope he'll soon be fit to work again.'

Rose leaned against the table, the jug in her hand. 'Jacob is an old man, Eve, and he's really been quite ill. I doubt whether he'll ever do much work again,' she said carefully.

Eve raised her eyebrows. 'Not work again? What are you saying, Rose? Of course he'll work again. Good heavens, he's nowhere near seventy yet, although I must say he looks it. Anyway, looking after the horse and driving the trap aren't exactly onerous tasks, are they?' She made clucking noises with her tongue. 'Some days he doesn't have to go out at all so it's little enough he has to do in exchange for living in the cottage. *And* we pay him a wage, too.' She obviously regarded herself as some kind of Lady Bountiful as far as Jacob was concerned.

'His chest is still very bad. And lying in bed hasn't helped his rheumatism,' Rose pointed out. 'His joints have stiffened up alarmingly. He's in a great deal of pain from them.'

'You don't have to tell me about painful joints.' Martyred, Eve held out her hands, which nevertheless still managed intricate needlework. 'Tell him from me that the best thing for painful joints is to use them. So the sooner he's back at work the easier they will be. I want him to take me to Bramfield next week, so I shall expect him to be recovered by then, tell him.'

Rose took the soup along to Jacob. Michael was still there. He had just settled the old man in his chair by the fire.

'I'll just put a few more coals on, Jacob, then I must be off,' he said. 'My wife'll look after you.' He sniffed the jug Rose had put down on the table. 'Mm, onion soup. That smells good, Rosie. I hope you've left some for us.'

Rose fetched a bowl and poured Jacob a little soup. 'There. I haven't given you too much, so you'll be able to eat it all,' she said, giving it to him.

'Aye, thass a drop o' good, Ma'am, thankee kindly,' he said, sipping it noisily.

She sat down on the chair on the other side of the hearth and waited till he had finished and come up for a second helping. 'You're really on the mend now, Jacob, aren't you?' she said, handing it to him.

'Aye, I'm feelin' half tidy now, thankee. But I can't seem to git th'owd knees an' feet workin'. They're mortal painful,' he said, shaking his head. 'I can't seem to git about much at all.'

'You'll improve with the weather, I daresay,' Rose said cheerfully.

He didn't answer but slurped in silence. Then he shook his head. 'I'm afeard my workin' days are about done. I'm gettin' on for sixty-six, y'know, Mrs Michael.'

'You mustn't say that, Jacob. Sixty-six isn't old. Why, only today Mrs Dowland was speaking about you getting back to work again,' Rose said. 'In fact, she sends her regards to you and says she hopes you'll be well enough to drive her into Bramfield next week.'

'Hmph.'

Rose laughed. 'What's that supposed to mean, Jacob?'

Jacob finished the soup and wiped the bowl round with the remains of his bread. Then he leaned over and put the bowl on the table. 'Jest what I say, Ma'am. Hmph. 'Cause I know what the Missus is gettin' at although she ain't put it in so many words. Drive me into Bramfield next week or you'll be out on your ear, Jacob. Thass what she's a-sayin', plain as a pikestaff. I can read 'er like a book.' He gave a great sniff and reached for his pipe. When he had lit it he spent several minutes coughing before he could speak again. 'I know 'er of owd. I don't fergit even if she do,' he panted finally.

'I don't think you should smoke that pipe, Jacob,' Rose said doubtfully. 'It's making your cough worse, I'm sure.'

'Don't matter if it is. Ain't got much else in life now my canary's gone.'

'Oh, did you have a canary, Jacob? I've never seen a bird here.'

He shook his head. 'I don't mean a bird. Thass what I ollus called my owd lady. My missus. She was my canary. Bin dead near on a year now, she hev.' A tear glinted in his rheumy old eye. 'Near on forty years we was tergether, jest the two of us, 'cause we never had chick nor child. I still miss 'er.' He drew on his pipe and coughed again. 'Never mind. I shall soon foller, I dessay.'

'No you won't. You're much better now,' Rose insisted.

He stared at her. 'Thass as maybe.' Then shook his head. 'But y'see, thass like this. If I can't work I on't be able to stay here. She'll turn me out. An' I'd rather drop dead termorrer than be sent to the Spike. The work'us,' he explained, seeing her bewilderment.

'Oh, I'm sure it wouldn't come to that. Not after all these years, Jacob. Mrs Dowland wouldn't be so unkind ...'

'Thass what you think. But you don't know 'er. Not like I do.' He stared into the fire and puffed on his pipe for several minutes, wheezing horribly in between. 'I knew Mrs High an' Mighty Dowland when she was no more'n Evie Pryke, showin' her knickers to the boys for a lick o' their lollipop.' He shook his head. 'Nah, you can't tell me nothin' about Mrs Dowland. She think nobody know what she was like afore she come up in the world. But she's wrong. I remember her even if she don't remember me. And I ain't forgot. Nor never likely to.' He looked Rose straight in the eye. 'I'm like a elephant. I don't fergit nothin'.'

Jacob sat puffing his pipe and staring into the fire. Rose waited for him to go on but he seemed to have forgotten she was there.

'Were you and Mrs Dowland at school together, then?' she asked at last, hoping to prompt him.

He dragged his eyes away from the fire and looked up at her, at the same time giving a little barking laugh. 'School? Me? No, I never had no schoolin', bless yer. I ollus had to help on the farm. Me dad was stockman and there was nine of us kids so me mother could do with all the extra coppers us boys earned.' He shook his head. 'But I knew Evie Pryke, all right. Her mother was the dairy maid, a toffee-nosed gal called Ethel.' He gave his barking laugh again. 'She made out she was a widder, but we all knew diff'rent. We all knew Evie was born the wrong side o' the blanket. Ethel 'ad bin in service out Claydon way, y'see an' got turned out 'cause she was in pod. That was either the father or one o' the sons at the house where she worked, we reckoned, put 'er that way, but o' course she never said. Made out 'er 'usband was a sailor, drownded at sea.' He gave a wheezy chuckle. 'But we knew that worn't the case. Boys ollus find these things out and anyway my mate Jemmy Harker 'ad a cousin what worked as scullery maid at the same place as Ethel so we knew all about it. Caused a rare owd how-de-do at the time, that did.'

This didn't tie up at all with the Eve Dowland Rose knew. She frowned. 'Are you sure you've got the right person, Jacob? After all, it is *Eve* Dowland and she's quite well educated. She does all the mill accounts. Surely, if she was a dairy maid's daughter ...'

'Oh, aye, she's clever, right enough. She had schoolin'. 'Er mother saw to that. Right from the start she was determined to make suthin' of Evie. Used to beat 'er from here to next week if she didn't do her learnin'. Cor, you shoulda heerd the poor mite shrick sometimes when 'er mum got in a paddy an' lambasted 'er. Thass a wonder she didn't beat the brains out of 'er. Lucky for Evie she was a bright little thing or she'd never hev lived to tell the tale, if ye ask me. Us lads felt right sorry for 'er sometimes.'

The air was becoming thick with acrid tobacco smoke from Jacob's pipe, but although it made her feel slightly nauseous Rose was loath to complain, or to leave, before Jacob had finished his intriguing tale. 'So what happened next?' she prompted.

'I dunno, really. I lost track of 'er when we grew up a bit. I went in the army and served in India for ten years or more. When I come out I worked on the farm again, but that didn't suit me, hoein' turnips an' sechlike, so I left. I'd heerd they wanted a groom at Dowlands' Mill an' that suited me right down to the ground 'cause I was used to workin' with hosses. Specially as this cottage went with the job too. That was jest right for me an' my canary since we was lookin' for somewhere to live. But I was suthin' flabbergasted when I see Evie was workin' 'ere, I can tell ye. She was housemaid, if ye please.'

Rose leaned forward. 'What did she say when she saw you, Jacob?'

'Oh, she never reckernised me. I worn't surprised.' He fingered his grizzled beard. 'I'd bin clean shaven in them days an' she'd never knowd me all that well anyway, 'cause she was a good bit younger'n me. But I knew her all right. She hadn't changed. Still as hoity toity as ever, mincin' about with her cap tails flyin' and never so much as a How-de-do to the likes o' me or my missus.' He shrugged. 'Well, that didn't take me long to git 'er measure. Anyone with half a eye could see what was in the wind. She'd set her sights on Mr George, the master's son. Well, the Dowlands was quite well-to-do, nice house an' all that, an' you could see she fancied 'erself as the miller's wife. She played up to the poor boy suthin' shockin' and that worn't long afore she was in pod. She'd done it deliberate, schemin' bitch. Everyone knew that. 'Cept 'im, o' course. Poor beggar couldn't see it. He never stood a chance against 'er. Nice feller, 'e was, too. A real gent. Too good fer the likes o' she.' He stopped and puffed on his pipe again. Suddenly, he began to chuckle.

'Gawd, there worn't half a row when th' owd Missus found out Evie was up the spout. She wanted to turn 'er out, but young George said he was goona stand by 'er and if she went,

193

then so would he. You never heard sech gooins on. Anyway, the upshot of it was, he got 'is way – well, he was th'on'y child an' his mum an' dad doted on 'im – an' they was wed. Posh weddin' it was, too. Well, within a twelvemonth th'owd chap, his father, was dead an' 'e was hardly cold in 'is grave afore madam, – Evie, that is, although now she was all fer bein' called "Eve" if ye please – 'ad sent the missus packin'. Don' ask me how she managed it, for I dunno, although I reckon if the truth be told the missus was glad to get outa 'er way. Anyway, she went to live out Ipswich way. I drove 'er to the new place, I remember.' He assumed a high, falsetto voice. '"Jacob," she say, "I shall never set foot in my old home again while that woman is there." ' He went on in his own voice. 'And she never hev. Not to blame 'er, neither.' He leaned over and knocked the dottle out of his pipe. 'So there y'are. Evie got the run o' the place, jest as she wanted, 'cause she could twist George round her little finger.'

He was silent for several minutes, then added thoughtfully, ''Cept when it come to the little gal, o' course.' He chuckled. 'Cor, Evie weren't half suthin' savage when she found she was up the spout again. You could hear her shoutin' at George right out in the yard. She said she reckoned she'd done 'er bit givin' 'im three strappin' sons 'ithout hevin' to go through all that palaver again. And when the babby turned out to be a little maid she turned right agin' 'er. An' what made it worse was that George thought so much of 'er, 'cause Evie was as jealous as fire is hot. Reg'lar doted on the child, 'e did. Couldn't do no wrong in his eyes. That was a shame 'e died like 'e did.' He looked up. 'That was a heart attack. Dropped dead in the yard carryin' a sack o' meal on his back. Wunnerful way to go, mind yew.'

He sucked on his empty pipe for several minutes, shaking his head before he went on, 'Oh, that was cruel the way Evie treated the little gal arter 'er dad died. I reckon she thought she'd git her own back on account of him thinkin' so much of his Melly. Thass what 'e used to call 'er. His little Melly. Nobody called 'er that after 'e died. She was ollus Lissa after that.' He looked up and smiled, his one remaining tooth sticking up like an ancient tombstone. 'All the same, she's growed up a bonny gal, ain't she? Pretty as a picture. And she's bin lookin' arter me pretty well these past days, same as yew hev, Mrs Michael. I wouldn't want yew to think I ain't grateful for all what yew've done for me, 'cause I am. I reckon I shoulda bin dead be now if that hadn't bin for yew all.' He closed his eyes, rolling his head wearily from side to side. 'Oh, dear, I dunno wass come over me, runnin' on like that. Yew shouldn't hev let me run on the way I hev, wastin' your time, Mrs Michael, I reckon I let me tongue run away with me. That musta bin the soup, loosened me jaw.'

'I'm glad you did, Jacob, because now I shall be able to make sure you never get turned out of your little cottage,' Rose said with a smile.

His eyes snapped open in alarm. 'You ain't gotta tell th'owd woman what I've towd you. She don't know to this day that I reckernised her when I first come 'ere. If she found out she'd hev me down the Spike afore I could whistle.' He twisted his pipe in his hand. 'I s'pose you've gotta hand it to 'er, in a way ain't ye?' he said thoughtfully. 'Arter all, she set out to better 'erself an' she managed it, didn't she? She's a owd bitch, but I can't help feelin' sorry for 'er, all the same. 'Cause I don't reckon all 'er schemin's brought her much joy.' He closed his eyes. 'Dearie me. I'm mortal tired arter all that talkin'.'

Rose got up to go. She patted him on the shoulder. 'I'll leave you to have a sleep then. And don't worry, Jacob, your secret's safe with me. I promise I'll see to it that you'll never be turned out. You'll end your days here, never fear.' She gathered up the things she had brought and put another coal on the fire, then crept out, to mull over quietly the things he had told her about Eve.

She didn't doubt the truth of what he had said, she knew from experience that Eve was – what had he called her? – a scheming bitch. Because it had become increasingly plain over the past months that the reason she had been so charming and so eager for Michael to marry was the thought of an extra, unpaid skivvy. On the other hand, Rose couldn't help feeling a certain admiration for her. Because nobody would ever have dreamt that Eve Dowland, the autocratic, highly-respected widow of the well-to-do miller, was the illegitimate daughter of a dairy maid.

Chapter Sixteen

Later that night, when Dan went in to help him up to bed, Jacob was still sitting there, just as Rose had left him, a contented expression on his face and his pipe in his hand. As she had promised, but sooner than anyone had expected, he had ended his days in his own home.

Secretly, Rose wondered if unburdening his secret to her had somehow released him so that he could die in peace. She longed to be able to share it with someone – Lissa, Michael, even her own mother, but she couldn't because she had promised Jacob that she would keep silent and anyway what good would it do? As Jacob had said, you had to hand it to Eve that she had risen above her past, even if her manner of doing so wasn't entirely admirable. But it was a weapon lying ready to be used should the need ever arise. And that was a comfort.

Jacob's funeral was a quiet affair. He had no relatives so there was only Michael and Dan to follow him to his final resting place beside his 'canary'. Rose and Lissa prepared a tea of ham sandwiches and fruit cake and followed the service in the prayer book while they had gone.

'I really don't see the need for all this fuss,' Eve looked disapprovingly over her spectacles at the food spread on the white tablecloth.

Rose regarded her thoughtfully. She saw her mother-in-law in an entirely new light now. Not that she found her any less hard and unyielding, but at least she could understand a little of what had made her that way.

'No, I don't suppose you do,' she said, 'but surely even Jacob deserves some mark of respect at his passing.'

'I saw to it that he didn't have a pauper's funeral,' Eve reminded her. 'I don't know what more you expect.'

'*I* expect the boys will be glad of a bite to eat when they get back,' Lissa said, warming the teapot. 'It's a bitterly cold day today to be standing at a graveside.'

As if on cue Dan and Michael walked in, flapping their arms to get some warmth back into their bodies.

'Old Duke seems to know Jacob's gone,' Dan remarked. 'He hardly lifted his head all the way to the grave yard and back.'

'We shall have to advertise for another groom, I suppose,' Dan said, helping himself to a sandwich.'

'I think not,' Eve's voice was decisive. 'Yes, please, Lissa, I will have a cup of tea and a *small* piece of cake. Yes. Thank you.'

'What do you mean, Mother? You think not. Who's going to drive the trap now Jacob's gone?' Michael asked.

'You and Dan, of course.' She bit daintily into her cake.

'Don't you think we've got enough to do?' Dan said with a sigh.

'We could get Silas Hands. He's helping me to repair my boat. He might be glad of the work,' Michael offered.

Dan turned and looked at him suspiciously. 'What does Silas Hands know about horses?'

Michael shrugged. 'Not a lot. But ... '

'I'm not employing anybody else.' Eve's voice cut across their conversation like a whiplash. 'I've carried Jacob for years, paying him, letting him live rent free, when all he did was tend the horse and do a bit of fetching and carrying.'

'Who'll take you to church on Sundays, then, Mother?' Dan asked mildly.

'You can.'

Dan got to his feet. 'We'll see. But we haven't got time to discuss it now. There's work to be done. Come on, Mike, let's get changed. The tide's just about right to start work.' The two brothers left and went upstairs to put on their white overalls and caps.

'The very idea, expecting me to employ another hand,' Eve grumbled after they had gone. 'Milling isn't that prosperous these days ... ' She broke off frowning as there was an urgent tap on the back door. 'We're not expecting anybody, are we?'

'What a question! Are we *ever* expecting anybody?' Lissa murmured under her breath to Rose as she got up to answer it.

'Please, is my sister there? I've got a message for her.'

Recognising Babs' voice and guessing why she had come, Rose hurried to the door.

Babs immediately enveloped her in a bear hug. 'It's a boy, Rose! Grace has got a little boy!' She couldn't contain her excitement. She began to dance her round the room. 'We're aunties! You and me, we're aunties, Rose! Isn't that just wonderful?' She held Rose away from her to see her reaction.

'Oh, Babs, yes! When was he born? Is Grace all right? What are they going to call him? Oh, just fancy, our Gracie a mother!' They hugged each other again. 'Oh, I can hardly believe it.' She didn't know whether to laugh or cry.

'Well, it's true. He was born at two o'clock this afternoon. I went to see him as soon as school was over and then I hopped on my bike and came over to tell you. Oh, he's the most gorgeous baby, Rose. With the biggest blue eyes you ever saw.'

'Perhaps your sister Barbara would like a cup of tea, Rose. I daresay there's still a cup in the pot.' Eve's voice trickled cold water into the conversation. 'We've just buried our old groom, you understand. His funeral was this afternoon. He'd been with us over thirty years.' She wiped an imaginary tear from the corner of her eye, the first sign of any emotion at all.

'Oh. Oh, I'm sorry. I should have realised.' Babs looked round, taking in for the first time that all three women were dressed in black and biting her lip guiltily. 'Perhaps I shouldn't have come. But I thought you'd want to know, Rose, and ...' her voice trailed off.

Rose gave her a little shake. 'Of course I wanted to know, Babs. I want to know all about it.'

Babs glanced at Eve again. 'Perhaps I shouldn't stay for a cup of tea,' she said doubtfully. 'I can see it's not convenient ...'

'Of course it's convenient. We want to hear some more about the baby, don't we, Rose?' Lissa was already pouring her tea. She seemed to radiate a new-found confidence – Rose would almost have called it truculence – since falling in love. 'And I'll cut you a piece of fruit cake. Come on, sit down, now.' She turned to Eve. 'Would you like another piece?'

'No. You know I never eat between meals although I made an exception today.'

'Might make you a little less sour if you did,' Lissa muttered into the teacups.

'What did you say?'

'I said I wondered if the milk had gone sour.'

'Don't be ridiculous. Milk doesn't sour at this time of the year.'

'It does if it's ten days old. I'll get some fresh.' She winked at Rose. 'Go on. Sit down with Babs, Rose. Then we can hear all about it.' She put her head on one side and looked at Babs. 'You know, it's quite appropriate that you should have come today, isn't it? No sooner is Jacob dead and in his grave that you've come to tell us of the new baby. That's how it goes, isn't it? For every person that dies another one is born. That's how life goes on.' She gave a huge sigh and a wide smile spread across her face. 'Oh, I think it's ever so exciting. A new baby!' Her face took on a dreamy look.

'Don't forget there'll be a new baby here in a few months,' Eve said, her face wooden as she nodded towards Rose's thickening waistline. 'You may find it isn't quite so exciting when there are endless nappies to wash and the child won't stop crying.'

'Oh, I shan't mind.' Lissa refused to have her spirits dampened. She handed Rose and Babs their tea. 'I hope it's a little girl. I'd like to have a little niece to dress in pretty clothes.'

'If it's a girl I shall call her Melissa, after you, Lissy,' Rose smiled up at her.

'You will not!' Eve's voice came from the other side of the room like a whiplash.

Rose raised her eyebrows in surprise. 'Why not, Eve? Little girls are often called after their aunts. Especially if they're Godmothers, too.'

'Oh, am I to be Godmother?' Lissa squealed in delight.

'Of course. Who else?' Rose said with a grin.

Eve shrugged uncomfortably. 'It's ridiculous to have two people of the same name in a household.'

'Brother George was called after Daddy,' Lissa pointed out.

'That's different.'

'I don't see why.'

Rose shot a warning look in Lissa's direction. It wouldn't do for her to become too argumentative. Stephen Joel hadn't yet made her his wife.

'I understand you're a school teacher,' Eve said to Babs, swiftly changing the subject.

'I hope to be. One day. At the moment I'm a pupil teacher. Miss Chamberlain at the village school is training me.'

'Very commendable, I'm sure.' That was the end of the conversation as far as Eve was concerned, but Babs didn't realise this as she warmed to her subject.

'Oh, I really enjoy it. And most of the children are really keen to learn. Of course, Miss Chamberlain's warned me that it's difficult at harvest time, when the children are all needed to help in the fields – the school's practically empty then. And she says the older girls sometimes have to stay at home to look after the little ones when there's a new baby. Then again, the boys are expected to earn a few coppers stone picking to help the family finances so you can't really blame them if their attendance isn't very good.' She spread her hands. 'But what can you do? We just have to teach them as best we can. That's what Miss Chamberlain says.'

'Very commendable, I'm sure,' Eve repeated.

'Oh, it's not commendable. I love it. And I love the children, even if they aren't always very clean. After all, it's not their fault, is it? And we try to teach them ...'

Rose cleared her throat and shot a warning glance at her sister. 'Hadn't you better be getting back, Babs?'

'What?' Understanding dawned and she put her hand up to her mouth. 'Oh, I'm sorry. I'm afraid I tend to get carried away.' She turned to Eve. 'You see I haven't been at the school many weeks, Mrs Dowland. Only since Christmas, in fact, so I'm still finding it all very new and exciting.' She turned back to her sister. 'But you're right, Rose. I'd better be getting back. Mum's with Grace and the baby so I've got to get Dad's tea.' Hastily, she swallowed the last of her tea. 'Not that he'd notice if I missed it. He's that busy ...!'

'With his memoirs?' Rose asked with a twist of her lip.

'What? Oh, no. He's cleaning up the yard! Goodness knows what's given him this change of heart but you wait till you see it, Rose. And old Bessy has just had eleven piglets. Oh, I can tell you, things are looking up on Crick's Farm!'

'Thank God for that,' Rose breathed. 'Long may it continue.'

In a sense Eve had been right. Jacob's death made very little difference to the running of the mill, largely because in recent years, since Jacob's rheumatism had got much worse, the boys – and especially Dan – had done most of the deliveries themselves in order to save him the trouble, although this was not something they had admitted to Eve. But Jacob had always taken Eve to church, dropping her at the lych gate and then going on to while away a pleasant hour or so at the Miller's Arms till she was ready to return.

Dan cheerfully took on this task. On Sunday he harnessed up Duke and brought the trap round to the front door, the only time it was ever opened was on Sunday mornings. Eve and Rose got in and Eve adjusted her black bombazine. The pattern had never altered in the months Rose had lived at Mill House, in spite of offering to take her turn cooking the dinner, so that Lissa could accompany her mother, Eve insisted that Rose should accompany her whilst Lissa stayed at home.

Unlike Jacob, Dan came into church with them. Rose sat between him and Eve and he sang the hymns and psalms in a pleasant baritone that went well with Rose's clear soprano. Eve never sang anything. The only time she opened her mouth during the service was to say the Creed and a definite Amen to the prayers.

Afterwards, as they drove home, Dan said, 'I enjoyed that. I always like a good sing.'

'You don't go to church for "a good sing",' his mother reprimanded him sharply. 'You go to worship your Maker.'

'But we sang the Venite this morning,' Rose said. ' "O come let us sing unto the Lord", it says. So there's nothing wrong in enjoying a good sing. There can't be, if the prayer book tells us to.'

'Don't be impertinent, Rose.' Realising she was losing the argument, Eve fell back on chastising her daughter-in-law.

As always, the dinner was ready when they got home, roast pork with apple sauce followed by plum pie and custard.

Afterwards Rose washed up whilst Lissa put her feet up. Then she got on her bike to go and visit her sister.

It was a bright January day but the frost still rimed the trees and the puddles were still solid with ice where the warmth of the sun hadn't penetrated. When she came to the cart track leading to Grace's cottage Rose got off her bike and walked, fearful that a wheel might get caught in a frozen rut and pitch her over the handlebars.

She propped the bike against the wall and found her mother, in the tiny wash house at the back of the house, boiling nappies and looking hot and flustered in spite of the bitter weather.

Rose kissed her. 'Oh, Mum! And on a Sunday, too!' she said, half joking.

'Better the day, better the deed. Or so they say,' Emma pushed her hair back out of her eyes with her forearm. 'My goodness, you soon forget how much work a tiny baby makes,' she said with a rueful smile.

'But you're thrilled to bits with your little grandson, aren't you Mum?' Rose said, giving her a hug.

'Yes, of course I am. And your Dad's like a dog with two tails. Did you call in and see him?'

'No, I came straight here, because I mustn't be away too long. But Babs told me what he's doing.'

'Yes, bless him, he's really got the bit between his teeth. Not before time, mind you. He reckons on ploughing up the bottom field next week, so the frost'll get nicely into the ground.' She looked her daughter up and down. 'And how are you, my girl?'

'Me?' Rose raised her eyebrows. 'Oh, I'm all right, Mum. I'd like to have come before to see Grace, but on top of everything else we had Old Jacob ill and then he died ...'

Her mother nodded. 'It ain't all honey at Dowland's Mill, is it, my girl?' she remarked perceptively. 'You can't do jest as you like there, can you?'

Rose shrugged but didn't meet her mother's eyes. 'It's all right. I'm not complaining.'

'No. But then o'course you wouldn't. You ain't the sort to complain. But I've got eyes in me head and I can see as far through a brick wall as the next.' Emma sniffed and gave her a little push. 'Go on, then, if you mustn't be away too long. Go up and see your new nephew. He's a bonny boy and no mistake. But don't wake Albert. He's heving a nap by the fire. Poor man, he don't take too kindly to sleeping on the kitchen floor, but he'll hev to make do there for the next six weeks.'

Rose frowned. 'Why, Mum?'

'Well, husbands never sleep with their wives till six weeks after a confinement. It wouldn't be right now, would it?'

'No, I s'pose not.'

Rose crept past Albert, snoring by the kitchen fire, although if a coach and four had driven through the house it didn't look as if he would wake, and climbed the narrow stairs to find Grace lying in bed in the tiny bedroom under the eaves, with her little son in the crook of her arm, and looking the picture of contentment.

She squeezed past the chest of drawers and sat down on the bed, which took up most of the available space in the room.

Grace didn't seem to notice the cramped quarters. 'We're going to call him William Albert,' she said, her face alight with love as she looked down at her little son. 'He looks like a Billy, doesn't he?'

Rose looked down at the little screwed-up face with its pink button nose and smiled. 'He's a lovely boy, Gracie.'

'You can hold him if you like.'

Rose took the warm bundle from beside Grace and cradled the baby in her arms. As she looked down at him he stretched out his tiny fingers with their perfect finger nails and his mouth opened into a tiny, round yawn. Then he moved his head as if to settle himself and fell asleep.

The thought went through Rose's mind, soon I shall have a baby of my own. Just like this. And I shall hold him in my arms, just as I'm holding little Billy, only it will be my baby. And Michael's. She bent and dropped a kiss on the baby's downy head and then handed him back to Grace, who nestled him once again in the crook of her arm.

'I hope you'll have a boy, Rose. It'll be nice. They'll be able to play together.'

Rose got up to go. 'I'll see what I can do,' she said with a laugh. 'But it's a long way ahead yet. It'll be summer before mine's born. Look, you'd never know.' She patted her stomach.

'I'll bet your skirts are getting tight, though,' Grace laughed.

'Yes, that's true.'

'You wait till you can't get down to do your shoelaces up. You'll know it's getting close, then. But you'll be surprised how quick the time goes.' Grace moved her head on the pillow. 'It's not going very quick now, though. I want to get up but Mum says I've got to stay here another week. She won't even let me put my feet to the ground, and Nurse Bennet agrees with her. You should hear the tales they tell of women who drop dead if they get up before they should!'

Rose's eyes widened. 'Oh, you don't want to risk that, Gracie!'

'No, I certainly don't. Mind you, I feel as fit as a fiddle so I feel a bit bad about Mum waiting on me and doing all the work.'

'Who's that talking about me?' Emma came into the room with a tray and two cups of tea. 'It's time you had a drink, my girl,' she said to Grace. 'And I've brought you one, too, Rose.'

'No, I must be getting back. You sit here and drink it, Mum. It'll do you good to take the weight off your legs for five minutes,' Rose got up and made room for Emma. 'Anyway, you know I can't drink tea at the minute.'

'Ah, yes, I'd forgot.' Emma sat down with a sigh of relief. 'Well, *I* can and I can jest do with a cup, I don't mind telling you.'

Rose left the tiny cottage and wheeled her bike back up the track to the road, thinking about the future. She found it much easier to imagine Grace's life than her own. She could see that before many years there would be a bevy of children running around the little cottage. She could picture Grace and Albert growing older, still living there with their family round them, all crowded together, with not enough money and not enough room, yet with all the love in the world to keep them contented.

How could spacious, immaculate Mill House compare with that? What would the future hold for a baby there? She tried to visualise a child at Dowland's Mill but no image would come. All she could see was the neat, well-ordered household she had become used to, with Eve at its head. There seemed to be no place in it for a child. She took one hand off the handlebars and laid it over her stomach. Yet it was to be. The baby was there, inside her, and in a few months it would be born. Nothing could prevent that. So why did she feel a chill inside her that defied explanation?

Chapter Seventeen

By the time Rose had pushed her bike to the end of the frozen track it was getting late and the light was beginning to fade. Once she reached the road there were no ruts so she was able to ride. It was a good thing Michael had bought her the bike before they were married, because things had changed and he would never spend out the money to buy her one now, she thought ruefully as she switched on the head lamp. But she was glad she had it because it was quite a long way from the mill to Crick's Farm, and even further to Grace's cottage. Of course, once the baby was born she would have to walk, but maybe it wouldn't seem so far pushing a pram and talking to the baby.

Filled with these thoughts she cycled the mile along the empty road, past ploughed fields and cottages huddled in isolated groups, with the Miller's Arms standing opposite the church halfway along. At the far end of the village she turned down the long lane that led to the mill. Here the trees overhung the road, nearly meeting, so it was almost like the nave in a great cathedral. There were no leaves on the trees now so what sun there had been earlier in the day had penetrated the black skeletal branches, thawing the ground slightly. But the sun had gone now and the ground had begun to freeze again, covering the ground with a thin, invisible layer of ice. Realising this, she tried to make herself ride slowly instead of instinctively pedalling faster as she usually did, because she was always nervous in the lane. Tonight it was even worse. The light from her bicycle lamp was making the shadows dance eerily in the hedgerow, frightening her into imagining someone was moving along beside her. Trying hard to keep her imagination in check she pedalled on, carefully keeping to the middle of the lane, where the ground was still dry.

But suddenly, when she was almost in sight of the mill, she was startled by the very real sound of a bicycle bell ringing urgently behind her and a voice shouting, 'Look out! Look out!'

Startled, she wobbled to the side to let the impatient cyclist by, at the same time trying to look round to see who was making such a commotion, because cyclists rarely used the lane to the mill and certainly not at this time on a Sunday evening. But in the gathering darkness she hadn't seen the long, solidly frozen puddle at the edge of the lane. The first she knew of it was when her front wheel skidded. She braked and tried to right it but lost control as her long skirt caught in the back wheel. The next thing she knew she was lying awkwardly in the ditch with the bike on top of her.

The other cyclist jumped off and came over to her. 'Oh, bloody hell, whatever's happened, Missus. Are ye hurt? Can ye get up?' He held out his hand, peering down at her. 'Oh, God, A'mighty, thass Mike's wife.'

She looked up and saw the ugly face of Michael's friend Silas Hands staring down at her. She didn't like Silas Hands, she considered him to be a bad influence on Michael. Furthermore, she didn't trust him. He had a shifty look about him and a way of holding his head on one side, hunched into his shoulder, as if he was perpetually on the look out in case he was being followed. But lying here tangled in her bicycle she was at his mercy because she had landed with a bump on the frozen ground and jarred her back so painfully that she didn't think she could get up without assistance. She took refuge in irritation. 'Don't be ridiculous, of course I can't get up until you shift the bike. I can't move a finger with this thing on top of me. Ouch!' She winced as she tried to move and a searing pain tore through her.

'Your leg is it?' he said as he clumsily tried to extricate the bicycle. He was as frightened as she was, because one of her legs was under one wheel and the other was sticking out through the frame.

'No. My legs are all right. I think I must have landed on my back.' She cried out again as, the weight of the bicycle gone, she tried to get up.

'Front wheel's buckled,' he said as he laid the bike on the bank, relieved that she hadn't been too tangled up in it. He'd been afraid she might have broken a leg, then Mike would blame him, although he had only been trying to warn her he was coming along behind her. Daft woman. She hadn't needed to go wobbling all over the lane like that.

He leaned over her and she could smell the spirits on his breath. 'Can ye get up now?' he asked, 'or do ye want me to carry ye to the house?' He sounded reluctant to say the least. 'I was jest on my way there to see Mike about 'is boat.'

'No, I don't want you to carry me. But I'd be glad if you'd help me to my feet, this bank's a bit slippery.' She gritted her teeth against the pain in her back as, none too gently, he took her hands in his and hauled her to her feet.

'Are ye all right now?' he asked, peering at her. 'Thass not far to walk. Not above a hundred yards or so. Can ye manage?' He grinned encouragingly at her, showing brown and rotting teeth.

'Yes, thank you, I'll be perfectly all right now.' She was as anxious to be rid of him as he was to leave her.

'You won't push the bike, not with the wheel buckled like that.'

'It doesn't matter. I'll leave it in the hedge. Michael can fetch it in the morning.'

'I'll walk with ye, if ye like.'

'No, thank you. I can manage.'

'Well, I'll be on me way, then. I'll tell Mike you took a tumble, but that was your own fault, ye know. You shouldn't hev looked back.'

She was incensed. 'I wouldn't have done if you hadn't made such a noise with your bell.'

'That was to let you know I was comin'. I didn't want you swervin' out and knockin' me orf.'

'There was plenty of room in the lane for you to pass. You needn't have come anywhere near me.' She was beginning to feel distinctly faint, so she waved him off. 'Oh, go on, go and do whatever it is you're going to do with Michael.'

He hesitated a minute, took off his cap and scratched his head, then settled it back on his dark, greasy curls, got on his bike and pedalled off. She was glad to see him go in spite of the fact that the pain in her back was getting worse and she was beginning to feel dizzy.

Carefully, she began to walk towards the house. One step at a time, slowly, like a sleep walker she made her way forward. There was nothing to hold on to, nothing she could steady herself with and she could feel herself swaying, and then staggering to regain her balance. What was wrong? She had only fallen off her bike, for goodness sake and landed on her backside, giving herself a nasty jolt. She rubbed her back as she walked, the pain seemed to be getting worse instead of better now that she was on the move, it was as if there was a lead weight in her back, and each step she took was like a knife jabbing into her.

She reached a big elm tree that stood at the entrance to the lane and stood for a minute, leaning against it, summoning up the energy to take the last few steps to the house. She felt terrible, sick and dizzy and now the pain in her back gripped her like a vice, making her whole body ache. She folded her arms across her stomach, praying that the fall hadn't harmed the baby. If only she could get indoors.

She tottered a few steps as Michael ran towards her. He caught her just before she fell.

'Fell off your bike, Silas says,' he said as he swung her up into his arms. He sounded annoyed rather than sympathetic. 'Slid on a bit of ice, he said. Well, you should have come home before it got dark. You knew what the roads were like.'

'It was his fault. He rang his bell. It startled me,' she said furiously.

'He only did it because he didn't want to frighten you. He told me so himself.' He gave an irritated snort. 'You've only got yourself to blame.'

'You would say that, wouldn't you! And you would take notice of your so-called friend's side of the story. You don't care a bit about me, do you?'

'Well, you're a stupid bitch, staying out after dusk when it's icy like this. In your condition, too. You ought to know better.' He put her down as they reached the door. 'I'm not coming in now. I'm busy with Silas. We're going out on to the marsh. But you'll be all right, won't you?'

She leaned against the door jamb, feeling too ill to argue further. 'I suppose so.'

He went off so she pushed open the door and staggered in, reeling across the room to collapse on to the settle by the fire.

Eve looked at her over the top of her *pince nez*. 'Good gracious! What on earth's the matter, Rose? You look as if you've been in the hedge. Have you been drinking or something?'

'No, I haven't been drinking. I fell off my bike into the bank and I've hurt my back a bit.' She pushed her hair back from her forehead. 'I don't know why, but I feel really dreadful. As if I might be going to faint.' She smiled wanly at Eve.

'Here.' Seeing Rose's chalk-white face, Lissa produced a smelling bottle from the dresser and waved it under her nose. 'This should help. There, is that better?'

Rose gave a little splutter as the pungent smell stung her nose. 'Thanks, Lissa. Yes, that's a bit better.' She tried to sit up.

'No, you lie still. I'll make you a drink.'

'Oh, thank you, that would be lovely.' She watched as Lissa busied herself with the kettle. 'I don't know what's wrong with me, that I should feel so awful. I only fell off my bike into the hedge, for goodness sake.'

'How did it happen? Was the road icy?' Eve asked, frowning.

'Yes, but I knew that and I was being extra careful. It was Silas Hands coming up behind me that startled me.'

Lissa gave a wicked grin. 'Seeing Silas Hands in the lane on a dark night would be enough to startle anyone,' she said. 'I think he's a horrible man.'

'So do I.' For once Eve agreed with her daughter. 'I don't know how on earth Michael came to make his acquaintance.'

'In the Miller's Arms, I suppose,' Rose said with a sigh. She shifted her position slightly and winced as the pain seared through her again.

Lissa saw it and came over. 'Here's another cushion for your head, Rose. Do you want one under your back, too?'

'Yes, please. Oh, no, not like that. Yes, that's better.' She closed her eyes. 'Do you know, I feel as if the whole of my insides have been jolted around and wrung out,' she said anxiously, putting her hand on her stomach.

'The fall has obviously shaken you up,' Eve said, still frowning. 'You shouldn't have been out on a bicycle in your condition. It was a silly thing to do.'

'No it wasn't. I should have been perfectly all right if that dreadful man hadn't come along behind me ringing his bell like some demented fire engine and shouting "Look out" at the top of his voice. I turned to see what was going on and skidded on a patch of ice. I hate that man,' she added vehemently.

'I agree, he isn't a very savoury character,' Eve said. 'But what was he doing, coming down the lane at this time on a Sunday afternoon?'

'Coming to see Michael. They've gone out on to the marsh. At least, Michael said they were going out on to the marsh. Silas Hands said he was coming to see Michael about his boat. I don't know which was true.' And I don't care much, she said to herself. Michael didn't show much concern for me so I don't care about him.

Lissa brought her drink and put it on a stool beside the settle. She tried to sit up a little and found that the pain in her insides was getting much worse and she could feel a wet, stickiness when she moved. She realised that something was very wrong.

'I think I should go to bed,' she said anxiously. 'I'm afraid ... falling off my bike like that ... the baby ...' She bit her lip as tears began to roll down her cheeks.

'Nonsense, Rose, you're imagining things,' Eve said briskly. 'You've had a shock, that's all. Now have a drink and lie there quietly. You'll be all right in a little while.'

Rose leaned over and took two sips of her tea. It was sweet and scalding hot and delicious. She quite forgot she didn't like tea. She picked the cup up to take another drink, then put it down with a clatter. 'Lissa,' she said urgently. 'I think I should go to bed. Will you help me, please?'

Lissa put her arm round her and helped her to her feet and in spite of the fact that she was such a little thing she half carried Rose upstairs and helped her into bed.

'I think we should call your mother,' she whispered, seeing the state Rose was in as she helped her out of her clothes and into her night-gown.

'No, we can't do that. She's busy with Grace. I'll be all

right now I'm in bed. I think the pain is better already.' She tried to smile at Lissa.

Lissa shook her head. 'It isn't, Rose, is it? It's getting worse.'

Rose nodded.

'Then I shall call Dr Holmes.'

'Oh, you can't do that,' Rose looked up, alarmed. 'It's Sunday. He won't come.'

'Well, we must do something, Rosie.' Lissa bit her lip. 'I'm afraid if we don't you might lose the baby.' She took a deep breath. 'I'm going to fetch Dr Holmes. You lie still. I shan't be long.'

Lissa was gone a full hour. She came back rosy cheeked from hurrying but on her own.

'He said there's nothing he can do if he comes. You've just got to stay in bed and let nature take its course,' she said. She looked at Rose doubtfully. 'I told him what had happened and he said it was probably just the shock of falling off your bike that did it and you'll be all right in a few days. I only hope he's right, Rosie.'

Rose laid her hand on her aching stomach. 'Oh, so do I, Lissy,' she said.

But Rose wasn't all right in a few days. She was in bed for a fortnight, tended lovingly by Lissa, who held her while she cried for the loss of her child.

'There'll be others, dear. There's plenty of time. And you weren't that far on, only three months,' Lissa tried to comfort her.

'I know. But to think, when it happened I was on my way back from Grace's. I'd been holding her baby and thinking it wouldn't be long before I'd be holding my own. And now it's all finished. There isn't going to be one for me.' Rose began to cry again.

'Yes, of course there will be, Rosie. It just won't be as soon as you thought. That's all. Now eat this nice creamy custard I've made. It'll help you get better.'

'You're a sweet girl, Lissy.'

After she had gone Rose lay looking out of the window. So much had happened in such a short time. There was Jacob, although now the story he had told her about Eve seemed remote, almost dreamlike, yet nevertheless she knew it was true. Then his funeral and on the same day Grace's baby was born. She thought of little Billy, perfect in every detail, born into that tiny cottage with nothing but a life of hardship to look forward to and she recalled the look of love and pride on Grace's face. Lucky Grace. Her eyes filled with tears again but she dashed them away. This was not the end of the world, she was only twenty-three, as Lissa said, there was plenty of time for more babies.

Eve, of course, never came near Rose whilst she was in bed but Michael could hardly do otherwise. He made it quite plain that he was not happy at being turned out of his bed to sleep in his brother's room, although he quickly admitted he had no wish to sleep beside a sick wife.

He came into the room looking distinctly bad tempered and gave her a brief peck on the cheek. 'You should never have gone out on that bike on those icy roads,' he said sternly. 'It was a stupid thing to do.'

She stared at him, wondering if his abrupt manner perhaps masked an inability to show his true feelings. She had expected him to show at least a little compassion, after all, it had been his baby too. But his face was stony.

'But you knew I wanted to go and see my sister and there was no other way I could get there. You wouldn't have taken me in the trap even if I'd asked you, would you?' She spoke sharply, disappointed that he had shown no sorrow for what had happened, only irritation at the inconvenience.

'You could have waited.' She noticed that he didn't answer her question.

'How long for?'

He didn't reply, but stood gazing at the ugly chest that still stood at the foot of the bed, his thoughts clearly miles away.

She waited for several minutes to see if he would speak again. When he didn't she put out her hand to him in an effort to bridge the chasm that seemed to yawn between them. 'I'm sorry about the baby, Michael,' she said softly. 'But we'll have others, won't we?'

He took a step back, out of her reach, and put his hands in his pockets. 'We shall if you take a bit more care,' he said cruelly.

Tears, she wasn't sure whether they were of weakness or anger, coursed down her cheeks. 'It was not my fault your friend Silas Hands frightened me,' she said hotly.

'That's right, blame Silas. If it hadn't been for him telling me you'd fallen you'd have had to walk all the way back, instead of me fetching you, remember.'

'If it hadn't been for him I would never have fallen in the first place!' She waved her hand. 'Oh, what does it matter whose fault it was? It's all over and done with now. And much you care about it.' She turned her head away, too dispirited to say more.

He hovered from one foot to the other, realising he had gone too far now. 'Is there anything you want, Rose?' he asked tentatively. 'Anything I can get you?'

She shook her head from side to side without looking at him. 'No,' she said flatly. 'Nothing you can give me.'

It was his turn to hold out a hand now. 'Rose?'

'Oh, go away. I don't want to talk to you.'

'All right. If that's how you feel ... ' He left the room but after a minute he came back.

'Oh, I forgot. I brought you this.' He threw something on the bed and went out again.

She didn't even look to see what it was but lay staring out of the window. Her relationship with Michael was going from bad to worse. He rarely touched her these days and when he did she had difficulty in not recoiling from him. She thought back to the last time he had kissed her, really kissed her, not just a perfunctory peck on the cheek, and remembered that he had been unusually attentive the day Old Jacob was taken ill. So much so that she was sure that things would be better from then on. But they hadn't been. Looking back, she realised that it was almost as if he had been playing a part that day, his every word and action calculated to impress, although why it should have been so she couldn't think because there was no audience. Not even Dan. Unless Dan had been there ... somewhere out of sight ... where she couldn't see him ... but all the time Michael knew he was there and was staking his claim, proving his ownership, so to speak. Yet why should Michael feel the need to do that? After all, she was his wife so he had no need to feel threatened by his brother. Unless he was jealous. Unless he thought that Dan ... She felt herself flush even as the thought formed in her mind.

Realising her thoughts were taking a dangerous turn, she reached out for the little package Michael had thrown down on the bed. When she unwrapped it she found a little jewel box and inside it a single pearl shaped like a teardrop hanging from a gold chain.

It was very delicate, but the old saying 'pearls for tears' immediately came into her mind and she put it quickly back into its box. She wished he hadn't given it to her because she knew she could never wear it. It would always remind her of her lost baby – it was even shaped like a tear drop – and she had the unreasonable feeling that it was an omen, that her life was to be full of tears. She knew she was being irrational but try as she might it was a feeling she couldn't shake off.

By the time her mother found an opportunity to come and see her Rose was up and about again.

'I'm sorry I couldn't come before, my girl, but I had to see Grace on her feet and I knew you'd be well looked after here,' Emma said, kissing her. She held her at arm's length. 'You're masterful pale, my girl,' she said critically. 'You ain't doing too much, are you?'

'No, we see to it that Rose takes care, Mrs Bentley,' Eve said from her rocking chair, smiling benignly at Rose. 'Pull the kettle forward, dear. I'm sure your mother would like a cup of tea.'

'I can't stop for long,' Emma said, sitting down with an involuntary sigh of relief, 'I've got to get back to give your dad a hand. He's mending the hole in the hedge where the cows got through. Made a rare mess of the winter wheat, they did. But he thinks it'll grow on all right because thass only jest through the ground.'

'Is dad all right?' Rose asked, busying herself with the teapot.

'Oh, yes. Taken on a new lease o' life, he has. I dunno what brought the change in him, but since Christmas he's worked like a good 'un. I've never known him work so hard.' Emma gave a satisfied nod. 'If he goes on like this we shall pull the farm round in no time, me and him together.'

'I'm glad to hear that, Mum. At one time I wondered what was going to happen to you both.'

'So did I, my girl. So did I.' Emma picked up the tea Rose had poured and took a sip. She leaned towards Rose and whispered, 'You hevn't poured any for Mrs Dowland.'

Eve heard. 'I only drink Earl Grey tea, Mrs Bentley,' she said sweetly. 'I shall have mine later on, thank you.'

'Oh, I see.' Emma raised her eyebrows in Rose's direction and was rewarded with a wink. 'Well, everyone to their taste, but I must say this is a very good cuppa, whatever it is.' She took another sip.

Lissa came in with a basketful of clean, dry washing. The wind had whipped colour into her cheeks and blown a strand of hair across her face. She greeted Emma, then said, 'It all dried quickly in this wind,' pushing the strand back behind her ear. She laughed. 'I was watching a barge come up the creek. I thought at first it was *Perseverance* but it isn't, it's *Patience*. She nearly went aground because the tide isn't really far enough up for her to tack yet. I stood watching for several minutes. Is there another cup of tea in the pot, Rose?'

'Yes, I'll pour it for you. Do you want yours yet, Eve? I can make it if you'd like.'

'No, it's rather early for me.' Eve smiled apologetically towards Emma. 'I'm afraid I'm a creature of habit, Mrs Bentley. I don't drink tea till four in the afternoon.'

'Really?' Emma said without much interest. She put her empty cup down. 'Well, I'd better be going, Rose, if I'm going to lend your dad a hand afore it gets dark. I'm glad to see you're on the mend.'

'I'll walk up the lane a little way with you, Mum,' Rose said, reaching for a shawl.

'I'm glad you said that, Rosie,' Emma said as they walked across the yard towards the lane.

'Well, we couldn't talk properly with madam sitting there taking in every word, could we?' Rose tucked her hand companionably into her mother's arm. 'Now, are things really as good as you say between you and dad?'

'Yes. I never hear a word about his memoirs these days, in fact, I don't even know if he's still got them. And, better still, he ain't touched a drop of brandy for weeks. I'm right proud of

216

him, Rosie, because he was never cut out to be a farmer, but he's working real hard. Something must hev shaken him up. I dunno what, but whatever it was it did the trick.' She twisted round. 'Do you know of anything that might hev given him a jolt, Rosie?'

'I don't see it matters what it was as long as it did the trick,' Rose said, carefully not answering her mother's question.

Emma patted Rose's hand as it lay in the crook of her arm. 'I'm sorry about the baby, Rose, but thass not the end of the world, you know. I miscarried twice, no, three times, it was – see? You forget when the others come along. And there'll be others for you, my girl. In time.'

'Maybe.' Rose was non-committal.

Emma was not one to pry so she changed the subject. 'Young Lissa's changed, hevn't she?'

'What do you mean?'

'Well, she was a meek little namby-pamby thing at your wedding and look at her now! Pretty as a picture and got plenty to say for herself.'

'I helped her to make the best of herself. It didn't take much.'

'You get on well together, don't you?'

'Yes, I'm very fond of her.'

'Thass good.' Emma was silent for a while. 'She courting?'

'What do you mean?'

'You know very well what I mean. Is she walking out with a young man?' Emma sounded a trifle impatient.

'No. Well, not exactly. Why do you ask?'

'I jest wondered. She's got that look about her.'

'What look? I don't know what you're talking about, Mum.'

'Don't you? You will. In time.' Emma stopped. 'Don't come any further with me now, thass time you went back.' She sniffed. 'Not that you've got much of a place to go back to. It ain't much like a home, is it?' She burst out laughing. 'Not a place you could throw your muddy boots down in, is it?'

Rose kissed her. 'It's not as bad as all that, Mum. It's all right, once you get used to it.' She thought for a minute, then she said, 'I don't think I'd want to leave.' But as she said the words it was Dan she was thinking of, not Dowlands' Mill.

Chapter Eighteen

Gradually life got back to something like normal. Eve hated the routine of the house disturbed and so it wasn't long before Rose was cooking and scrubbing and polishing as hard as ever. It was as if the baby had never been. But Rose knew that it had. She knew there had been a tiny being growing under her heart and when she lost it she lost part of her reason for living. She took to going out for long walks along the sea wall in order to escape from the house and be by herself. She went in all weathers, huddled in a thick shawl against the cold wind or driving rain, glad to be alone and away from Mill House, where the atmosphere of suppressed hatred seemed almost tangible to her heightened senses.

Since the loss of the child Eve hardly troubled to conceal the fact that she hated Rose, just as she hated Lissa. That it was a hatred born of jealousy Rose was in no doubt, but she couldn't understand why Eve, who had been so sweet and welcoming to her at first, should have turned so spiteful towards her. Even knowing Eve's background did little to answer the questions that nagged as she trudged the lonely marshes. Then slowly she began to understand. Eve was ashamed of her past and the only way she could come to terms with it was to become powerful and dominant, especially towards her own sex and even more especially towards Rose, who had also married the miller's son, but without needing to stoop to the devious measures Eve herself had been forced to employ. No wonder she was jealous. No wonder she was full of hatred. Realising all this, Rose was surprised she had ever been pleasant in the first place.

Not that it mattered, she decided with a sigh. Nothing mattered any more, not even the fact that Michael had shown no desire to return to her bed, although it was nearly two months now since she had miscarried. She was glad, really. Glad to be rid of his drunken fumblings and rough lovemaking. Lovemaking! She gave a little mirthless laugh that was carried away on the wind. There was little enough love in the way Michael had used her.

She stood with her face turned towards the river. The tide was low and the gulls wheeled and screamed and jostled for the tastiest tit-bits in the mud, whilst a heron stood, aloof and motionless at the water's edge. The March wind gusted, sending ripples across the water in the gathering dusk. She pulled her shawl closer and turned away. She had walked far enough, it would be dark by the time she reached home, although that didn't worry her. The marsh no longer held any terrors for her. This was nothing short of amazing when she remembered how terrified she had been on the night Michael had found her out on the marsh, hysterically babbling about having seen a dead body. Now she found the empty, wind-swept saltings a place of comfort, a place to escape to and she had grown to understand that all sorts of flotsam got washed up into the gullies with the tide, only to be left there when it receded. But there was one place that still made her flesh creep and that was the bridge over the mill stream. Even after all these months she couldn't bring herself to cross it except at a run and she never, ever looked back, even in broad daylight. She had never been able to explain this because it was a pretty enough spot, with the water tumbling through from the mill pond, where weeping willows trailed green fingers and a path led to Dan's garden beyond. Nobody else, not even Lissa, felt there was anything in the least sinister there. No one else shared her conviction that it was haunted, that something evil lurked there, waiting ...

Thinking of Dan's garden reminded her that if she didn't hurry Eve would be complaining about vegetables not prepared for supper. She quickened her pace for a few steps, then slowed again. There was no hurry. Lissa was there. She would do them, quite cheerfully, too. These days, nothing seemed to worry Lissa. She went about her work singing to herself, wrapped in a little world of her own, waiting for her captain to come back and take her away, quite impervious to her mother's rantings. And nothing Rose could say, no warnings, could shake her faith in this. Not even the fact that *Perseverance* hadn't been seen in Stavely Creek since the beginning of the year and it was now the end of March.

'Look how awful the weather's been,' she had said when Rose pointed this out. 'Poor Stephen's probably holed up in some horrid little creek in the Blackwater, waiting for the winds to drop.'

'*Patience* has been here. Twice.' Rose had hated saying it.

'*Patience* doesn't go as far afield as *Perseverance*.' Lissa had laughed and given Rose a quick hug. 'Don't *worry*, dear. I've told you. He'll be back.'

'But he hasn't even written to you.'

'No, I told him not to, in case *she* got hold of it. You can just imagine what she'd say. Anyway, he's like me, not very good when it comes to writing things down.'

Rose still worried, though. She couldn't bear to think of Lissa's heart being broken.

She walked on in the gathering gloom. She could see a square of yellow light which was the kitchen window shining through the trees. Soon she would be home. She quickened her pace, ready to run across the dreaded bridge, but then slowed almost to a halt. Because somebody was there, standing in the middle of the bridge and looking down into the water. She blinked and looked again, wondering if her imagination was playing tricks in the fading light. But no, the figure was still there, standing perfectly still, dark-clad, with a kind of cowl over its head.

She clamped her hand over her mouth to stifle a scream, mesmerised by the thing standing there. No wonder she had always felt there was something evil about the bridge. It was haunted.

But there was no other way to get back to the house. The mill stream was fed from the mill pond on one side and it fed into the creek on the other. She stood stock still, her heart thumping in her chest. She couldn't cross the bridge, not while that *thing* was there. Not even if it meant that she had to stay out on the marsh all night. Her thoughts raced as she began to

220

panic. She would find a bush to shelter under, away from the cold rain that was just beginning to fall and she would wait there until someone came to look for her. Sooner or later someone would come because they all knew she liked to walk this way. Slowly, she started to back away, afraid to take her eyes off the thing on the bridge in case it moved, or worse, began to follow her, praying all the time that it wouldn't be long before somebody came, because already her heightened senses were imagining all sort of noises, a creak, a snap of twigs, footsteps, somebody breathing . . .

Then something touched her arm. Cold with terror, she screamed.

'Rose! Rose! Whatever's the matter? It's only me. I've been to the garden. I forgot to bring the sprouts back this morning,' Dan's voice came from behind her, comfortingly normal.

'Oh, Dan.' Weak with relief she leaned against his rough shoulder. 'Thank God it's you.' She began to sob. 'I've seen . . . I've just seen . . .'

'Seen what, for goodness sake? Look at you, you're shaking like a leaf.' He put his arm round her. 'Now, calm down and tell me. What is it you've just seen?'

She buried her head in his coat, at the same time pointing behind her. 'There, on the bridge. Look, there's something there. A figure. A cowled figure.'

He stroked her hair. 'There's nobody there, Rose. I promise you there's nobody there.'

'Yes, yes, there is. It looked like a monk. It was a ghost. I know it was.' She was breathless in her agitation.

'It must have been your imagination. There's nobody there. Nobody at all. Look.'

'No. No, I can't.' Her head was still buried in his coat.

Slowly, he turned her round and made her look.

The bridge was empty.

She gave a little hiccuping sob as she turned back to him, puzzled. 'But there was somebody there, Dan. I saw him – it. Standing in the middle of the bridge and looking into the water.' She looked up at him. 'You must have seen it, too.'

He shook his head. 'I didn't see anything. I've just come from the garden, where I've been freezing my fingers picking sprouts for the past ten minutes.' He smiled down at her, his voice reassuring. 'It's nearly dark now, Rose. I expect it was a trick of the light.'

She swallowed. 'I always have a strange feeling when I cross the bridge, Dan. Even in broad daylight it feels cold and menacing there. I hate it. I've always felt there was something evil about it. I'm not surprised it's haunted.'

He gave her a little shake and said firmly, 'Don't be silly, of course it isn't haunted, Rose. Nobody that I know has ever seen anything strange there. There aren't even any old wives' tales about it. It's just an ordinary wooden bridge over the mill stream. Come on, now, stop being silly. You've got to walk over it because there's no other way back to the house.'

She held back. 'I don't think I can, Dan.'

'Of course you can. I'm right beside you so there's nothing to be frightened of. Now come on.' He took her arm and marched her briskly across to the other side. 'There. Nothing to it, was there?'

She looked back. 'There's something evil there,' she whispered. 'I know there is.'

'Well, all I can say is, nobody else has ever seen it. Come on, Lissa's waiting for these sprouts.'

He kept hold of her arm as they crossed the yard. It was comforting. When they got to the door he gave her the basket of sprouts. 'You can take these in. I've got to finish off over at the mill.' He smiled down at her. 'Are you sure you're all right now?'

She nodded. 'Yes, I'm all right now.'

'Good.' He gave her hand a little squeeze and went back across the yard.

Back in the warm kitchen everything was familiar and ordinary. Blackie, Jacob's old cat was washing himself in front of the fire, the clock ticked steadily, the flame from the oil lamp reflected in its brass weights and pendulum. Eve was putting the finishing touches to an enormous meat pie – she still maintained that Lissa's pastry was like concrete – whilst Lissa peeled potatoes at the sink. As Rose took off her shawl and hung it up her fears evaporated. Now it was easy to believe that Dan had been right, of course she hadn't seen anything on the bridge, it had been her over-active imagination at work. Feeling slightly hysterical, she didn't know whether she wanted to weep with relief or laugh at her own stupidity.

'You've taken your time,' Eve said, bending down to put the pie in the oven. 'You could have made this pie if you'd been back earlier. You always seem to go for walks at the most inconvenient times. You know how my back plays me up if I stand too long.'

'It looks delicious. You make much better pastry than me, Eve,' Rose said, refusing to rise. Privately she thought that it did no harm for Eve to move herself a bit. She was getting fat. 'Dan's given me the sprouts. I met him coming back from the garden. I'll do them, Lissa.'

'Thanks. Yes, he forgot to pick them. Are they icy?'

'No. They're better when they've had the frost on them, anyway.' Rose busied herself with the sprouts, relieved to find that she was no longer trembling.

Half an hour later Dan came in from the mill as Rose was straining the cooked vegetables. He came over to the sink to wash his hands.

'All right now?' he asked softly without looking at her as he rinsed them under the tap.

She nodded. 'You must think I'm very silly.'

'I don't think anything of the kind, Rose, you know that.' He flicked the water from his hands and went to dry them on the roller towel beside the sink. 'I think you've had a rough time, one way and another, and I'm sorry. I just wish there was something I could do to help.'

She bent her head as she emptied the vegetables into their dishes. Dan's kind words had brought her unaccountably near to tears.

'Here, let me take them. I'll put them on the table.' His hand touched hers as he took the hot dish and a tingle ran right up her arm.

Oh, God, she thought, what is happening to me? She glanced at Dan but he had put the dish on the table and was pulling out his chair to sit down, talking to Lissa and quite oblivious of the effect he had had on his sister-in-law.

She took her seat opposite him, carefully keeping her eyes on the table.

Eve was serving the pie when Michael came in.

'You're late. Where have you been, Michael?' she asked without looking up.

He didn't bother to wash his hands but came to the table and pulled his chair out with a harsh, scraping noise. 'I don't have to tell you every move I make, do I?' he said sullenly.

'There's no need to be unpleasant. I only asked a civil question that required a civil answer.'

'All right. I've been talking to Silas Hands, if you must know. He brought me some fitments that I needed.'

Dan looked up sharply. 'Not for that boat of yours, I hope. I thought I'd done for that, well and truly.'

Michael pointed his fork at Dan. 'You mind your own business, brother. And you start knocking my boat about again and I'll start knocking you about, so I'm warning you.' He turned to his mother. 'Silas is helping me to repair it.'

'If you start that ...' Dan stopped. Eve knew nothing of her son's shady activities and it wouldn't do to tell her. 'Just mind and keep it for punt gunning, then. And *nothing else!* Do you hear me?'

'And you can mind your own business. Do *you* hear *me?*' Michael said, his voice beginning to rise.

'That's quite enough from you both, thank you.' Eve's voice was sharp. Then her expression relaxed. 'We've certainly enjoyed the duck you've shot in the past,' she remarked as if the previous interchange had never taken place.

'Silas thought he saw fish in the mill pond, but I told him it must have been his imagination. There aren't any fish there.' Michael was piling his plate with vegetables as he spoke.

'There used to be. Years ago,' Eve said thoughtfully.

'Well, there aren't any there now, I can tell you that.'

Rose was hardly listening. She was thinking about Silas Hands. Silas Hands, with his head buried in one shoulder and his greasy curls. If he'd been standing on the bridge could his silhouette have been mistaken for a cowled form in the fading light?

She looked up and found Dan's eyes on her. He was smiling and his expression said, 'There, what did I tell you?' as plainly as if he had spoken the words aloud.

She returned his smile, feeling rather foolish, then glanced at Michael. He was looking at them both and there was no doubt what was in his mind.

That night Michael returned to his own bed and his treatment of Rose was not gentle. When he had finished with her he rolled away. 'That'll teach you to play around with my brother,' he said grimly.

'You're wrong. There's nothing between Dan and me,' Rose said wearily.

He turned back and slapped her face hard. 'Don't lie to me, woman. I saw the way you were looking at each other over supper tonight. Don't tell me you haven't been fornicating behind my back, woman.'

She put her hand up to her face and rubbed it. 'Why must you be so violent, Michael? You know very well I haven't been unfaithful to you. Apart from anything else, when would I have had the opportunity? Tell me that.'

'Silas saw you together only today, coming out of the bushes.'

'I'd been for a walk on the marsh. I often go walking on the marsh, you know that. It's since I lost the baby. Or had you forgotten about the baby already?'

He didn't answer but countered with, 'And I suppose he'd been for a walk on the marsh, too.'

'No. Dan had been to collect vegetables from his garden. We met by accident. Anyway, it's hardly the weather ...'

'The way he was looking at you over supper would melt ice.'

'Oh, don't be so silly, Michael. You're imagining things. You're jealous.'

He gripped both her arms, looming menacingly over her. 'Too bloody right I'm jealous. I'm not having another man making free with my wife. Specially not my brother, he gives me enough trouble without that. So I'm warning you. Don't ever let me see you giving him the come-on again.'

'I wasn't giving him the come-on, Michael.' She stared up at his shadowy shape in the darkness, knowing full well that she was inviting trouble as she added, 'But at least he's always kind and considerate towards me. Which is more than can be said of you.' She twisted her head away to try to avoid the blows she could sense were coming.

The next morning at breakfast she tried to keep her face down to conceal the ugly bruise that reached from her temple to her chin and blacked her eye. Eve was the first to comment.

'You haven't been falling over again, have you, Rose?'

Rose nodded. 'I tripped over the rug in the bedroom.'

'There must be something wrong with your eyesight. You probably need spectacles.'

'It would be more sense to get rid of the rug, I should think,' Dan said grimly, helping himself to marmalade.

Rose shot him a warning glance but he had his eyes on his plate and didn't look up.

'What are you going to do, Rose?' Lissa asked, sitting herself down in the armchair by the empty grate in the drawing room. The two girls had gone in to give the room its weekly polish but she was not ready to begin yet. They both enjoyed polishing days because it gave them an opportunity to chat away from Eve's eagle eye. The vigour with which they polished depended on the weather; on hot days they gave everything a quick dust, on cold days they put more energy into it in order to keep warm.

Rose sat down in the chair opposite. 'What do you mean, what am I going to do? I'm going to start off with the chiffonier, while you do the table. And don't forget to take all the photographs off before you start.'

'You know that's not what I'm talking about, so don't pretend.' Lissa pointed to her face. 'Michael did that, didn't he?'

Rose fingered it, nodding. 'He's jealous. He's got the idea into his head that Dan and me ... Of course, it's rubbish. It's all in his imagination. There's nothing between Dan and me. Nothing at all.'

Lissa grinned. 'Who are you trying to convince? Me or yourself?' She leaned over and put her hand on Rose's knee. 'I wouldn't blame you, Rosie, honestly I wouldn't. Dan's a lovely man.' She leaned back in her chair. 'It's just a pity you didn't meet him first,' she said ruefully.

Rose shook her head, looking towards the door. 'You mustn't say things like that, Lissy,' she hissed. 'I'm married to Michael and there's an end of it.'

'It doesn't give him the right to knock you about.'

'He doesn't. Well, not much.'

'Last night wasn't the first time, though, was it?'

'No. But he was jealous, that's all.'

Lissa's brow creased with worry. 'Oh, Rosie, I wish there was something I could do.'

'There is. Help me get on with this polishing. I'm getting cold.'

'Oh, all right.' Lissa took the lid off the polish and sniffed it. 'Oh, I do love the smell of furniture polish, don't you, Rose?'

'Yes, it's got a nice lavender smell. Come on, let's spread it around a bit so Madam will think we've been working hard.'

'She won't come in.' Lissa was still sniffing the polish tin. 'She's gone over to the mill to do her office work. Oh, that reminds me, it's your turn to clean the office this week.'

'It never looks any better. Five minutes after it's done there's a film of flour over it again. Still, I don't mind doing it. I love the mealy smell of the mill.'

Lissa made a face. 'I don't. It makes me feel sick.'

They gave the room a perfunctory polish and moved on to the dining room on the other side of the hall. Then they shut both doors whilst they swept and dusted the stairs, polishing the carved mahogany balustrades and newel post.

When they had finished Rose stood back and looked round, at the grandfather clock standing at the foot of the sweeping staircase, at the Chippendale elbow chair that stood in the corner and the gilt framed pictures on the wall. 'This is a beautiful house,' she murmured. 'How can it remain so beautiful when it holds so much hate in it?'

Lissa stared at her. 'What a funny thing to say.'

She sighed. 'Yes, I suppose it was. But a house like this should be warm and light and full of love.'

Lissa pulled the shapeless old cardigan she was wearing more closely round her. 'Well, it's none of those things, is it?'

'It must have been, once. Somebody must have loved it very much. You can tell, can't you?' She rubbed the smooth wood of the newel post. 'I think it's waiting for the love to come back.'

'Well, it won't while *she's* here, that's certain. Come on, you'd better stop daydreaming and go over to the mill. I expect Madam has finished in the office by now.'

They went back to the kitchen. Eve was there, waiting for someone to make her morning coffee. Rose left Lissa to do that and went over to the mill.

The office was on the ground floor in the far corner. As she went across to it she could hear footsteps on the floor above, probably Michael moving about. She hoped he wouldn't come down, she didn't want to see him. In truth, she didn't want to see him ever again, but she knew this was not possible. Everywhere else was quiet because the tide was not yet right to turn the water wheel. She went over to the window in the office. It was only a small window and overlooked the mill race, which was little more than a fast running stream at the moment.

Suddenly, she saw a movement beside the wheel. Dan was there, up to his thighs in water, raking something away from under the wheel. As if he sensed her looking at him he looked up and waved. Then he dived his hand into the water and brought out a handful of weed.

'It chokes up the paddles,' he said, making her understand with a mixture of mime and mouthing.

She nodded and mouthed back, 'I see.' Then she turned to get on with her cleaning.

Not surprisingly, Eve kept the office very neat and tidy. There was nothing on the desk except a blotter, a pen tray with its own inkwell and an oil lamp that was necessary to work by on dull and overcast days. Behind the desk was a large swivel chair and behind that a bank of cupboards and drawers which were kept locked. Grey flour dust permeated everywhere even though the door was always kept closed.

Rose swept the floor and the walls and when the dust had settled she cleaned the window and polished the furniture, such as there was. She even cleaned the brass knobs on the drawer fronts and the handle on the door.

While she was working Michael came to the door. 'Oh, it's you,' he said. He came into the office. 'Are you all right?' he asked.

She straightened up from polishing the rail of the chair and looked at him, lifting her chin so that he could see the extent of the angry bruise on her face. 'What do you think?' she asked. 'And would you like me to show you my arms?'

He shuffled his feet. 'No. I'm sorry, Rose. I lost my rag last night.'

She didn't answer.

'I've said I'm sorry.'

'I heard you.'

'Is that all you're going to say?'

'What do you expect me to say? It's all right, Michael? It doesn't matter, Michael? It didn't hurt, Michael?' Her voice rose. 'Well, it isn't all right. It does matter and it did hurt. I feel bruised all over. And if that's all you came back to my bed for I don't want you there any more.'

He took a step towards her, his face reddening. 'I'll come to your bed when I damn well like,' he shouted, his expression ugly. He caught her arm. 'Just remember, you're my *wife*.' He raised his hand as if to strike her.

She raised her hand to shield her face. 'No, Michael. Please ...' she begged.

'Get down on your knees.'

'I can't, you're holding my arm.'

'Get down on your knees, I said.' He forced her to her knees, wrenching her arm in the process. 'That's better.' He let her go, a gloating expression on his face. 'Now perhaps you'll remember who's master.'

He went out, slamming the door, leaving her still on her knees.

She sat back on her heels and covered her face with her hands. What was to become of her? Was she to put up with his blows and ill-treatment of her for the rest of her life? She began to cry, tears of utter despair.

Suddenly, she felt a hand on her shoulder. She looked up and saw Dan standing there. He was wet almost up to his waist from standing in the mill stream.

'I heard what went on, Rose,' he said. 'I couldn't help it. I was working right outside the window.'

Rose tried to push him away. 'Then you know you mustn't let him find you here, Dan.'

'He won't. He's gone off on his bike to the Miller's Arms. I saw him go.' He helped her to her feet, then put out a finger and gently traced the bruise on her face. 'I could kill the bastard with my bare hands,' he said savagely. 'How could he do this to you!'

She turned her head away. 'Because he's jealous. He's jealous of you, Dan, although I keep telling him he has no reason to be.'

He took her face in both his hands and turned it towards him. Then he bent and gently kissed the angry bruise. 'That's where you're wrong, Rose,' he whispered, his voice not quite steady. 'He's got every reason.' Slowly he drew her into his arms. 'Don't you realise how much I love you, Rose? How much I've loved you almost from the first time I saw you?'

He looked down at her, and she put her hand up and touched his face, wonderingly, as he spoke the words she had so longed to hear.

'Do you love me, Rose? A little?'

Her eyes swam with tears. 'Oh, Dan. I love you so much. So very much.'

He bent his head to gently kiss the tears away, then his mouth found hers and she could taste the salt of her own tears. Tears of complete happiness. A happiness born of the moment, with no thought of what the future might hold.

After a long, blissful moment Dan lifted his head.

'What are we going to do, Dan?' Rose whispered, looking up at him from the comforting circle of his arms. 'How can we carry on as if nothing had happened between us? Look at Lissa. Anyone with half an eye can see she's in love. How can we hide it? I don't want to hide it. I want everyone to know. If it weren't for Michael ...'

'Yes, if it weren't for Michael ...' He was silent for a long time, stroking her hair and dropping kisses on it.

'We must go away,' he said at last. 'It's a sure thing we can't stay here. We'll go ...'

'We could go home. I could take you to Crick's Farm,' she interrupted eagerly. 'I'm sure my parents will welcome us when they know ...' Her voice trailed off as he shook his head.

'We'll have to go further afield than that, my love,' he said. 'Do you think Michael is going to take this thing lying down? If he finds out where we've gone he'll be after us like a shot out of a gun. I wouldn't care for myself, I can look after him, but I wouldn't like to think what he might do to you. No, we'll go into Norfolk, perhaps. That should be far enough away. I daresay I could get work on the land, maybe in time set myself up as a market gardener. And I can dress mill stones. A good many men get their living dressing stones, going from place to place ...'

'We could have a caravan. With a horse.' Her imagination was racing ahead.

He took her face in his hands and kissed her. Then he smoothed her hair back from her forehead. 'This is serious, Rose. This is real life, not a fairy tale where everybody lives happy ever after. I've got to make plans and it'll take a little time. We're not like ordinary people. If you come away with me it'll be as my wife, but you won't *be* my wife, not legally. Are you prepared for that?'

She nodded. 'Yes, Dan. I am. I know what you're saying.'

He shook his head, his face agonised. 'God, I wish it didn't have to be like this, Rose. I hate this hole in the corner business. I want to make you my wife and I want everybody to know.'

She put her finger over his lips. 'I don't mind, Dan. I don't mind anything as long as I can be with you.'

He kissed her again and for a while they forgot everything in their love for each other. Then with a sound that was something between a sigh and a groan Dan drew away.

'You'd better get back to the house, my darling. Even Lissa couldn't have taken this long to clean this place.' He smiled down at her. 'For the time being we shall have to pretend none of this has happened. Do you think you can do that? Pretend the most marvellous thing in the world has never happened?'

She smiled back at him. 'It'll be difficult. I want to shout it from the house tops. But I'll try.'

'It'll only be till I've sorted out the best thing to do. But it's important nobody should suspect a thing.' His jaw set. 'You know Mike. The bastard's already knocked you about for no reason. If he knew there were grounds for his jealousy ... Well, I wouldn't like to be in your shoes. Nor his when I got at him,' he added grimly. He dropped a kiss on the end of her nose. 'I love you, whatever happens always remember that, Rose.'

She hugged him. 'And I love you, Dan.'

He looked down at himself. 'I'd better go and get out of these wet things.'

'Yes, you'll catch cold. You must be frozen.'

He grinned at her. 'I'm far from that, I can tell you!' Another lingering kiss and he was gone.

Rose hurried back to the house. She knew now exactly why Lissa went about singing and with a look of absolute bliss on her face and it was with difficulty that she composed her own features into their usual bland expression.

'You've been gone rather a long time,' Eve said when she walked in.

'I cleaned the window and polished the brass while I was over there,' she said. 'I must say you keep the office very tidy, Eve.'

'Of course. I like to know exactly where everything is.'

She went over to the sink, where Lissa was peeling onions to go with the bread and cheese at lunch.

'Where have you been?' she hissed. 'You've been simply *ages*. And why is the bottom of your dress wet?'

'I had a look at the stream. Dan was clearing away the weed from the mill wheel. It's boggy there.' Some of that was true.

'Did you know the stream runs so fast that he has to tie weights to his feet when he does that, so he doesn't get swept away?' Lissa said in her normal voice.

'Yes. I remember him telling me.'

'What are you talking about?' Eve called from the other side of the room.

'Dan. Tying weights to his boots when he clears the weed out of the wheel,' Lissa said over her shoulder.

'Yes, the stream runs very fast.' Eve resumed her embroidery.

Rose began to lay the table. She was apprehensive. How could she and Dan behave normally after what had happened this morning? When all she wanted to do was to look at him, to touch him, to feel his arms round her? She almost dreaded him walking in the door.

But he came in discussing flour quality with Michael and sat down at the table, still deep in conversation. Rose took her cue from his matter-of-fact manner and found it wasn't as difficult as she had feared. And in the days that followed it was amazing how often he managed to squeeze her hand surreptitiously or wink at her from the other side of the room, so that she knew it was real, that he loved her and was working out a way that they could be together.

As for Michael, he didn't touch her. He shared her bed, but usually didn't come to it until she was either asleep or feigning sleep and he never attempted to wake her. She was glad. The thought of him venting his animal lusts on her made her want to vomit. She hated Michael Dowland with an intensity that almost frightened her and she couldn't wait to get away from Dowlands' Mill to a new life with Dan.

Chapter Nineteen

'You're very quiet these days,' Lissa said one day, nearly a month later. It was a warm April day and they were busy at the wash house with the week's laundry. 'Are you all right, Rose? Is Michael – I mean, does Michael . . . ?' She didn't know how to go on, but stood there, nibbling at the soap.

Rose smiled and said cheerfully, 'I'm quite all right, Lissy, thank you. And Michael hasn't hit me any more, if that's what you're trying to say.'

'Oh, good. I'm glad.' She gave an audible sigh of relief. 'I do worry about you, Rose, you know.'

'Well, there's no need.' Rose stared at her quizzically. 'Lissa, why are you eating the soap?'

Lissa looked at it. 'Because it tastes so nice. Here, have a little bite.' She held it out. 'Sometimes I can't leave it alone. Mmm,' she waved it under her nose. 'Smells delicious. I think it's the carbolic I like.'

Rose studied her anxiously. Lissa was blooming. Her skin was soft and clear and she had put on a little weight. She looked the picture of health so it seemed ridiculous to ask, 'Are you feeling all right, Lissy? Not sick or anything?'

'No,' Lissa said with a laugh. 'I've never felt better in my life. Why do you ask?'

'I just wondered.' Rose continued at the scrubbing board. Suddenly, a thought struck her.

'Lissy, we don't seem to have washed any clouts for you for quite a long time. When did you last have your monthlies?'

Lissa looked up, surprised. 'Can't remember, now you come to speak of it.' She frowned. 'Round about Christmas, I think.'

234

'*Christmas! Lissa!* That's three – nearly four months.'

Lissa scratched her head. 'Well, I've never been very regular, have I?'

'But you've never gone three months!' Rose sat down on an old kitchen chair that was kept in the wash house. 'Lissa, tell me truthfully. Did you and Captain Joel ...?' She began again. 'When Captain Joel was here in January – when he was stuck here in that fog for a week – you went on his barge, didn't you?'

Lissa grinned. 'Yes, I did. That fog was a godsend.'

Rose took a deep breath. She wasn't smiling. She had a nasty hollow feeling in the pit of her stomach. 'Did he ...? Did you ...?' She nodded, not quite knowing how to phrase what she was trying to say.

Lissa nodded too. 'Yes, we did,' she said, understanding perfectly. 'Stephen didn't want to at first. He wanted to wait, but I wanted him to know that I was his. Completely his.' She smiled, a little secret smile. 'He didn't take much persuading.'

'Oh, Lissy. You know what's happened, don't you?'

Lissa put her hand on her stomach and smiled again. 'I think so.'

'But what are you going to *do?*'

'I'm going to marry Stephen when he comes back.'

'Has it occurred to you that he might not come back? It's three months now, you know.'

'He'll come. I know he'll come.'

'Turn sideways.'

Lissa did as she was told.

'I can't think why I haven't noticed before. Your skirt's quite tight, already.' Rose brushed a strand of hair away from her face and stood up. 'Have you written and told him you're having his baby?'

'No. I don't know where to write.'

'Well, you must find out. Ask Dan.' She got up from the chair and took Lissa by the arm and gave her a little shake. 'Don't you understand what you've done, Lissy?' she said urgently. 'Do you realise what your mother will say when she finds out?'

'I shan't tell her.'

'Oh, Lissy, you won't need to. She's got eyes in her head.

Heaven knows why I didn't notice before.' Rose was exasperated with Lissa's lack of concern about her condition. 'Oh, come on, let's get this washing done and out on the line while the sun's shining.' Her voice was sharp with anxiety.

'I'll peg it out, then I can watch for Stephen's boat. He'll be here any day now. I know it.'

But Lissa was wrong. Two weeks later Stephen Joel still hadn't put in an appearance. Rose was worried sick and didn't know who to turn to. She was hardly on speaking terms with Michael and she doubted he would react sympathetically anyway. And she and Dan had tacitly agreed that they would have no private conversation so it was impossible to tell him.

She tried to discover why *Perseverance* hadn't been seen.

'We haven't seen Captain Joel's barge for several months,' she said casually over supper one night.

'He'd got to make a trip to Newcastle when he left us. But when was that? A month or two ago now, wasn't it?' Dan said.

'January. There were bad storms up that way earlier in the year, though.' Michael speared another potato.

'You don't think he got shipwrecked?' For the first time Rose saw fear in Lissa's face.

'Shouldn't think so. He wouldn't go out if the weather promised rough,' Dan said. He held out his plate. 'I'll have another piece of that bacon, Rose, please.' He managed to touch her hand as she handed it back to him.

'When's he due back here?' Rose persisted.

'What's that to you?' Michael glared at her. 'Is he another of your fancy men?'

'Don't be stupid,' she said scathingly. 'It's just that we haven't seen his barge for several months and I wondered when he was due.'

Dan grinned at Lissa. 'I wonder it wasn't you that asked, Lissy. You like Captain Joel, don't you?'

Lissa blushed and got up to clear the plates away and bring out the treacle pudding that had been boiling on the hob. 'Oh, you. You're always teasing,' she said, giving his shoulder a nudge with her elbow as she passed him.

Eve said nothing but Rose noticed her eyes narrow as they swept from Lissa's face to her waistline and back.

Suddenly, she stood up so abruptly that her chair fell over backwards with a clatter.

She pointed to Lissa. 'You little *slut!*' she hissed, her face screwed up in hatred. 'You abominable little *whore!*'

Dan raised his eyebrows in astonishment. 'What's the matter, Mother? What on earth's got into you? You can't speak to the girl like that.'

Michael's lip curled. 'I reckon she can. I reckon you're up the spout, aren't you, girl?'

'Don't be daft, of course she isn't. What a stupid thing to say,' Dan said.

'Yes, I am.' Lissa's chin lifted defiantly. 'And when Stephen comes back we're going to be married.'

Eve was still standing up. Now she rested her hands on the table and leaned forward. 'You stupid little bitch. Has it occurred to you that he isn't coming back?' Her voice was scathing. She gave a mirthless laugh. 'It's no wonder nobody's seen him. He won't come back here any more. Not after what he's done.' She regarded Lissa as she would regard something nasty brought in on someone's shoe. 'You dirty little slut.'

'I'm not a slut. Stephen loves me. He told me so.' Lissa spoke with quiet dignity. 'I don't know why he hasn't been back but I know he will come and then he'll marry me.' She turned and looked straight at her mother, 'And he'll take me away from this dreadful place to somewhere where I'll be treated like a human being and not just a skivvy.'

'He can't marry you, even if he wants to, which I very much doubt,' Eve said spitefully, 'because you're not old enough. And I shan't give my consent.'

'Then I shall live with him till I'm twenty-one. After that I shan't need it.' It seemed nothing could shake Lissa's faith in Stephen Joel.

'You're an imbecile. You're not right in the head. I always told your father you were a simpleton, but he wouldn't have it,' Eve spat. 'But my words have been proved true. You should have been put away years ago. Before you had the chance to bring disgrace on the family.'

Dan went round and put his hand on his mother's arm. 'I think you've gone too far, Mother,' he said firmly. 'There's nothing wrong with Lissa. She's been a bit silly, but she's not stupid. I think you should apologise to her.'

Eve shook his hand off her arm. 'Apologise? Me? To *her*? That I never shall. In fact I shall never speak to her again as long as I live.' She turned her back on Lissa. 'Tell her she can pack her bag and get out of my house. I won't have her under my roof another minute.'

Even Michael had the grace to look shocked. 'You can't do that, Mother. You can't turn the girl out just like that, with nowhere to go.'

'Can't I? Just watch me!' She glared at Rose. In her temper she couldn't look at anybody without glaring at them. 'Tell her to pack her bag and get out,' she commanded.

Rose shook her head. 'No, I could never be the one to tell her to go,' she said quietly. She hesitated, biting her lip. Then she said, choosing her words carefully and watching Eve all the time, 'And I'm surprised you can be so uncharitable, Eve. Doesn't the bible say, "Let he that is without sin among you cast the first stone"?'

Eve froze and Rose knew the shaft had gone home. But she recovered herself immediately. 'I don't know what that has to do with it,' she said with a shrug.

'I think you do, Eve,' Rose persisted. 'And out of Christian love and charity I think you should take back all the harsh things you've said. Lissa needs help, not rejection.'

'Mind your own business. You're not one of the family,' Eve bluffed rudely. 'Michael! Tell her to go.'

Michael shook his head. 'I think we should give the matter more thought. Perhaps we can get in touch with Stephen Joel ...'

'Let her get in touch with him. I want her out of my house. I won't have her under my roof another night. Daniel?'

Dan shook his head. 'You're too hard, Mother. Lissy's only nineteen ...'

'She's old enough to behave like a whore. Let her take the consequences.' Eve looked round at the four faces at the table. 'Very well, if none of you will do it I'll do it myself.' She marched off upstairs.

'What am I going to do?' Now Lissa was frightened. She seemed to have shrunk in size as she huddled in her chair and looked from one to another of them. 'Where shall I go?'

'Buggered if I know. You were a silly little bitch, weren't you?' Michael said, washing his hands of the whole thing.

'This is no time for blame, Mike. We've got to decide . . . '

'*You* can decide, brother. I want no part of it. I don't think she should be turned out, but if that's what the Matriarch's set on, well, so be it.' Michael scraped back his chair, shrugged on his coat and left the house.

Dan scratched his head. 'What about the mill? Could we hide her there, Rose, do you think?' He assumed, quite rightly, that the responsibility was going to fall on the two of them together.

'Is there anywhere she could hide there that Michael wouldn't find her?' Rose asked.

He shook his head and sighed. 'No. I suppose not. He goes all over. He'd find her.'

'Isn't there a shed somewhere?'

He shook his head again.

Lissa was looking from one to the other, depending on them.

Suddenly, Rose's face cleared. 'Of course! I know exactly where she can go!'

Before she could say anything else Eve came slamming back with a carpet bag bulging with hastily thrown in clothes. She got hold of Lissa by the shoulders and marched her to the door and pushed her out, flinging the bag out after her. Then she slammed the door shut, brushed her hands together and resumed her place at the table.

'I think I'll have another sliver of that treacle pudding, Rose,' she said calmly, as if the last fifteen minutes had never happened. 'It's really quite delicious. Your puddings are getting better, aren't they?'

Rose stared at her in disgust. Then she pushed the pudding up the table towards her and got up from the table.

'I have to go to the privy,' she said. 'I think I'm going to be sick.'

'And I have to go back to work.' Dan followed her out.

Lissa was walking across the yard towards the lane, dragging her feet, her shoulders bowed. Rose ran after her.

She caught her hand. 'Come back, Lissy. We're going to

hide you.' Although there was nobody to see or hear she spoke in a whisper.

Lissa looked up at her. Her former assurance was gone and her face was streaked with tears. 'Where? You can't. There isn't anywhere.'

'Yes, there is.' Rose dragged her back to where Dan was still standing in the middle of the yard waiting, wondering what she had in mind.

'She can have Jacob's cottage!' Rose whispered triumphantly. 'It's empty now he's gone. We can keep her there, can't we, Dan?'

'Yes. Of course! Why didn't I think of that! Come on, quickly now, Lissy. Before anyone sees us.'

'Where's Michael? We don't want him to see.'

'I expect he's gone out on to the marsh. He always does that when there's any trouble. He hasn't gone back to the mill, look, the door's still shut.'

'That's all right then.'

They hurried Lissa round the corner to the little cottage that backed on to the wash house.

The door wasn't locked. Inside it was just as it had been when Old Jacob lived there, pots and pans hanging on hooks in the back kitchen, the kettle on the hob, his old armchair still in its place. Upstairs it was the same; the bed neatly made, the chest of drawers beside it with a mirror on top and his hair brushes in front of it. A chair under the window was the only other furniture there.

'Good. Nobody's been here since the old boy died,' Dan said.

'No. We ought to have come in and cleared the place but we never did.' Rose looked round. 'As it happens it's a good thing. You'll be all right here, won't you, Lissy?'

Lissa nodded dumbly. Things were moving too fast and in the wrong direction. She couldn't keep up.

'Now, you must stay here, out of sight,' Dan warned. 'If anyone comes snooping around, go upstairs where you can't be seen. Don't leave anything around downstairs that might let anyone know you're here. In fact, it'll be better if you stay upstairs all the time, don't you think so, Rose?'

'Yes, we'll lock you in if we can find the key.'

'What am I going to eat?' Lissa wailed.

'I'll feed you, don't worry,' Rose promised.

'What about when I want the privy?'

Dan scratched his head and looked at Rose.

Rose said, 'Oh, that's nothing to worry about. I'll find you a bucket.'

'How long have I got to stay here?'

'Till we can decide what else to do with you,' Dan said. 'It's obvious you won't be able to stay here indefinitely. But we'll cross that bridge when we come to it. Now, have you got everything you need?' He looked round. 'Yes, I think you'll manage.'

'Till Stephen comes.' Her optimism was beginning to return and she gave them both a watery smile.

'And that might be sooner than she knows,' Dan said under his breath as he and Rose left the cottage and locked the door behind them.

'Why do you say that?'

'I shall contact the harbour master at Ipswich and see if he can give me any information about the man and his boat. At the very least he ought to be told the predicament he's got her into.'

'Do you think he'll marry her, Dan?'

He shook his head. 'I dunno. I really don't know. He seems a nice enough chap, fond of Lissa, too. I've always thought they might make a go of it, that I wouldn't mind if they did. But after what he's done ... and the fact that he hasn't been near for all these weeks. Well, I must say I do wonder if he's got cold feet and sheered off somewhere.'

'And then what shall we do? She won't be able to stay there with a baby, will she?'

He gave her a ghost of a smile. 'Let's take one day at a time, shall we, Rose? We've got a few months grace before we have to worry about that.' His face changed. 'I love you, Rose,' he said softly.

'I love you, too, Dan.'

'I'd got feelers out for a job in Stowmarket, but ...'

She caught his hand. 'I know, Dan. We can't leave Lissa.'

'It may not be for long.' He laid an arm across her shoulders. 'And then we'll start a new life, away from all this.' He gave her shoulders a squeeze. 'I must get back to work. If Mike comes back and sees us like this ... ' He squeezed her again. 'I'll go now, you can follow in a few minutes.'

He smiled. Then the smile faded. 'I love you, Rose,' he said again and was gone.

She stood in the April sunshine, looking over at the mill pool. It looked calm and smooth with its border of willow trees moving gently in the breeze. She went purposefully over and stood on the bridge, testing herself whilst her mind was still full of the events of the past hour. But it was no use. Even with the trauma of Lissa at the top of her mind she still had the feeling of menace, of something evil at this spot and she shivered, making herself look down into the fast running waters of the mill stream. Something had happened here in the past, now she was more sure of it than ever. She shivered again and went back to the house.

Eve looked up as she entered. 'Do you feel better?' she asked. 'Good gracious, girl, you look as if you've seen a ghost.'

Rose sat down and rested her head on her hand. 'Perhaps I have,' she said. She looked up. 'You're a wicked woman, Eve Dowland. May God forgive you for what you've done to Lissa today, for I never shall.'

'I don't need to seek forgiveness from anybody for what I know is right,' Eve replied smoothly.

'Your mother-in-law showed more compassion towards you, didn't she?'

'What on earth are you talking about?'

Rose's courage failed her. She couldn't face another confrontation, she was too emotionally drained by what had happened to Lissa. 'Nothing,' she said and began the washing up.

Rose missed Lissa. Her presence, the secrets they shared, the little jokes that helped to combat their life of drudgery, all that was gone now that Eve had banished her from the house. The few minutes she was able to spend with her when she smuggled food out to the cottage were all too short and had to be spent reassuring the girl that somehow everything would come right. Because Lissa, spending time alone and for almost the first time in her life with nothing to do, had at last begun to realise that her optimism might have been misplaced and that Stephen Joel might indeed never be seen again.

'What shall I do if he doesn't come back, Rose?' she wept, her eyes swollen. 'I shan't be able to stay here for ever. Where shall I go? And what about the baby?'

Rose picked up the plate of untouched food she had left the last time. It was on the chest of drawers, just where she had put it down. Lissa was lying full length on Old Jacob's bed, her hands behind her head, gazing at the ceiling. She hadn't even combed her hair.

'There won't be a baby if you don't eat,' she said, her voice stern, trying not to let Lissa see how sorry she felt for her.

'That might be a good thing,' Lissa said miserably.

'You don't mean that, Lissa. And if you do you should be ashamed of yourself. Saying it to me, of all people.' Rose's own eyes filled with tears now and she brushed them away impatiently, surprised how much the loss of her own baby still hurt.

Lissa got up from the bed and went and flung her arms round her, immediately contrite. 'Oh, I'm sorry, Rosie, I shouldn't have said it. Of course I don't mean it. But I'm so frightened ... I've already been here nearly a fortnight and all I do is think and think and wonder what will happen to me. And it's so lonely here with nothing to do and nobody to talk to.' She looked at Rose miserably. 'Has Dan managed to find Stephen yet?'

Rose shook her head. 'Not yet. And there's no guarantee that he will come back, even when he does contact him, Lissa. You realise that, don't you?'

'A wife in every port, you mean?' Her mouth twisted and she sat back on the bed with her hands in her lap. 'I really didn't think he was like that,' she whispered, shaking her head. 'He was so ...' she groped for the right word and couldn't find it. 'I really thought I could trust him,' she said instead. 'You must all think I'm very silly.'

'Perhaps we're wrong. There may be some other reason why he hasn't been back. It's possible.' But not very likely, Rose added to herself.

Lissa shook her head again. 'Not after all this time.' She took a deep breath. 'No, you were right, Rosie, and I was wrong. I can see now how stupid I was. But, you see, nobody had ever paid any attention to me before and when he was so nice to me I reckon it just went to my head. I loved him so much and I believed him when he said he loved me.' She laid her hand on her stomach. 'And now I've got to pay for my stupidity. Oh, Rose, what's going to happen to me?' She looked up, and her face crumpled again.

Rose put her arms round her and held her tight. 'You'll be all right here for a few weeks, Lissa, while Dan and I decide what's to be done. We'll think of something between us, don't worry.'

'I wish you'd married Dan instead of Michael,' Lissa muttered, her face half buried in Rose's shoulder.

Rose closed her eyes, half inclined to confide in Lissa, but for the moment the secret was too precious to be shared. She waited a moment, reluctant to leave Lissa so depressed, then patted her arm. 'Now be a good girl and eat this stew before it gets cold. I have terrible trouble getting meals to you, you know what Eve's like, she's got eyes like a hawk, so the least you can do is to eat it now it's here.' She put the plate on her lap.

Lissa gave her a watery smile. 'I'll try. It smells good.'

'You must. And when you've eaten, why don't you turn out Jacob's chest of drawers. It'll give you something to do and sooner or later someone's got to do it.'

Lissa nodded. 'Yes, all right.' She took a mouthful of stew.

'Good, isn't it?' Rose asked, watching.

'Mm. Yes, it is.'

'Then eat every scrap.' She stood over her for several minutes more, then turned to go. 'I'll try and bring you some more books. And some wool. You could knit something for the baby.'

'I can't knit.'

'Well, you'll have plenty of time to learn.' She turned to go.

'Rose.'

'What's the matter?' She stopped and looked back.

'Thank you for looking after me. If it wasn't for you and Dan I don't know what I'd do.' Lissa's eyes were brimming with grateful tears.

Rose went back and kissed her. Now was not the time to remind her that things couldn't go on this way for much longer. Soon she would have to be moved. But where to?

Chapter Twenty

Rose left Lissa. When she got out of the cottage she walked out on to the marsh, automatically holding her breath and hugging herself against her unknown fears as she hurried across the bridge. It was half tide and the gulls were investigating the newly uncovered mud for food, their feet making intricate interwoven patterns as they strutted about. She watched for several moments and then went back the way she had come. The tide was just down far enough for milling to begin and as she crossed the bridge again she started with surprise as the big wheel was unbraked from inside and suddenly creaked into motion, forced round by the weight of water rushing through the mill race. She stopped a moment to look down into the black, foam-flecked cauldron of water boiling round the wheel, shuddering as the familiar prickle of fear ran down her spine, her imagination busy with what awful thing might have taken place here in the past.

Then quickly, she hurried back across the yard, gathering a basketful of washing off the line as she went.

As she opened the door and entered the kitchen, Eve looked up and remarked, 'It took you long enough to get a few sheets in.' She was icing a cake for the Ladies' Guild's May Fair, although she still resisted their invitation to become a member. Eve preferred to remain aloof from the herd and to bestow her bounty as and when she chose.

'I walked out on to the marsh,' Rose replied, dumping the linen basket down on the settle. 'I need to get a breath of fresh air now and again, you know.'

'You can do that easily enough by cleaning the outside of the windows. Goodness knows when they were last done.'

'The sun's on them. They'll smear.' Rose was sorting out the corners of a sheet. 'Will you help me to fold these, Eve, please? I can't do it on my own and Lissa isn't here to help.' She waited with the corners in her hand. 'I can't put them through the mangle until they're folded properly.'

'One of the boys . . .'

'The mill is working. The boys won't be in for ages. I can't leave them like this, they'll get all rumpled.' She held out two corners. 'I've washed them, boiled them, hung them up to dry and fetched them in all by myself. I can't do this on my own and there's nobody else to help me, now that Lissa's not here. You've sent her away, Eve, remember?'

'Don't even mention that name!' Eve came over and snatched two corners of the sheet and helped Rose to fold it in half and shake it, giving vent to her irritation by shaking it so violently that it cracked. Then they folded it again and pulled it into shape, anger again giving Eve such strength that she nearly pulled Rose over. When it was done Rose smoothed it and laid it beside the basket on the settle.

'Don't go away. There are five more,' she said cheerfully as Eve turned to go back to the table.

By the time they had finished, Eve's mouth was in a thin, straight line. 'You give no thought to my arthritis,' she said. 'You've no idea how painful it is for me to do that.'

'Well, someone's got to do it, Eve,' Rose said. 'You'd be the first to complain if I put crumpled sheets on to your bed. There now,' she smoothed the top one and then picked the whole pile up. 'I'll go and put them through the mangle and then they can go up on the rack to air.' She gave an elaborate sigh. 'Although how I'll manage it without Lissa to turn the handle I can't think.' She put her head on one side. 'Do you ever wonder where she went, Eve? Do you ever worry about what might have happened to her?'

'No. Why should I? She's no better than she should be, bringing disgrace on the family like that. If she starves in the gutter it's no more than she deserves.' Eve's face was like granite as she picked up the icing bag again and resumed decorating her cake.

Carefully, Rose laid the sheets down on the end of the table. 'I wonder what your life would have been like if you'd been treated the way you've treated your daughter, Eve,' she said, with her head on one side, her eyebrows slightly raised.

Eve didn't look up. 'Go and get on with your work. I'm busy.'

Rose took no notice but went on, 'But you weren't shown the door when you fell pregnant, were you? After you and the Miller's son had romped in the hay – or more probably on the marshes. You weren't treated the cruel way you treated Lissa, were you, Eve?' she asked quietly.

'I don't know what you're talking about. Stop rambling on and get those sheets mangled before it's time to prepare the vegetables for supper.' Eve still didn't look up but her hand faltered and the line of icing she was tracing had several squiggles in it that had to be lifted off and the whole line begun again.

Rose watched her dispassionately. 'Of course you know what I'm talking about, Eve,' she said. 'I'm talking about you and George Dowland. He married you after you became pregnant even though his parents were against him marrying a servant, didn't he? And after his father died you sent his mother away, so you would have full control of the mill. Which was just what you wanted, wasn't it, Evie?'

Eve looked up sharply. The cake decorating was degenerating into chaos. 'Wherever did you get such a cock and bull story from? I never heard such nonsense.'

'Jacob. Just before he died. He knew you when you were a girl and your mother was dairymaid. He worked on the same farm. Didn't you recognise him when he first came here? No, he said not, because he'd grown from a boy to a man. He recognised you, though. He told me so.'

Eve's eyes widened in horror, just for long enough for Rose to realise that her words had struck home, then she recovered herself and her face resumed its habitual disdainful expression. 'Jacob was an ignorant old fool. He wasn't quite right in the head, that's why we kept him on, because nobody else would have given him work. I never heard such nonsense in all my life.'

'Then you deny it?'

'It's not worth a denial.' She threw down the icing bag. 'And if this is your way of trying to persuade me that I was wrong to turn ... ' she hesitated, '... that girl out of my house, then you're wasting your time. I have no regrets. I never want to see her again.'

'Very well, Eve.' Rose accepted defeat. The woman was pure granite, she had no feeling, no heart, so she would never break. But she would sleep a little less easily in her bed knowing that Rose knew the truth about her past, even though she refused to admit it and had tried to make out that Jacob was simple-minded, which was far from the truth. There was some small satisfaction in this. Rose picked up the pile of sheets for the second time. This time she went out of the door and over to the wash house, where she took out her fury on the mangle, imagining as she fed the sheets through the rollers that she was squeezing an admission out of Eve.

Two more weeks went by. Lissa was becoming pale and listless through lack of fresh air and exercise and it was difficutl to get regular meals to her. Sometimes it was late at night, after Eve had gone to bed, when Rose performed the nightly ritual of emptying her slop bucket, before she could take her food. She worried about her.

'Have you heard from the harbour master at Ipswich yet?' She managed to ask Dan one afternoon. He was on his way back to the mill and she had been collecting the eggs from the chickens when they met in the yard. It was difficult to have any kind of proper conversation with him because Michael watched them both like a hawk.

'No, not yet,' he said, his voice low. Then louder, 'Yes, I shouldn't be surprised if we're in for a storm. Look at the clouds over to the west, there.'

'Lissa hates thunder,' she whispered.

'I'll go to her if it gets too bad,' he promised. He raised his hand briefly and went off to the mill.

Rose went indoors, Michael was just finishing his lunch. He stared at her suspiciously as she closed the door behind her. 'I told you to leave my brother alone,' he warned, pointing the bread knife at her.

She sighed and went over to the draining board to begin wiping the eggs. 'I haven't touched your brother.'

'You were talking out in the yard there.'

'So? He warned me there was going to be a storm. There's no harm in that, is there?'

'Is that all?'

'Oh, for goodness sake, Michael. Don't be so petty.' She finished the eggs and began to clear the table. Somehow she had got to take Lissa some bread and cheese. The girl hadn't had anything since last night and must be starving. Suddenly she had an idea. 'Oh, Dan did say would you take him over a hunk of bread and cheese. He doesn't know what time he'll finish at the mill and he wants a bit to "put him on" as he calls it. I'll put it on a plate and you can take it over with you.'

'But he's only just left. Didn't he have enough to eat when he was over here?' Eve asked.

'Apparently not.' She cut a generous lump of cheese and thick doorstep of bread.

Michael got up. 'Give it here, then.' He eyed it. 'Is he going to be over there for the rest of the week?' he asked sarcastically.

'He said he was still hungry.' Rose was confident Dan would know what the bread and cheese was really for.

Dan was right about the storm. Rose was upstairs on her hands and knees, sweeping the carpet in Eve's bedroom – Eve had complained that it was nearly a fortnight since it had been swept, at which Rose had reminded her tartly that there was only one pair of hands to do the work now that Lissa was gone – when the first clap of thunder rolled. Rose took no notice and carried on, crawling round the floor with the brush and dustpan. Storms didn't worry her, her only concern was for Lissa, whom she knew would be terrified. She could only hope Dan would be able to keep his promise and go to her.

There was a brilliant streak of lightning and a few seconds later another crack of thunder. She sat back on her heels and looked out of the window. The rain hadn't started yet but the sky was black. Soon the heavens would open. As she watched there was another streak of lightning. It forked across the sky and straight down into the river, it seemed. Rose stood up to get a better view.

'Come away from the window.' Eve had come into the room. 'Quickly, help me to cover the mirrors.' She was pulling out

249

towels, tea towels, pillowcases, anything which could be used.

'There's no need for that,' Rose protested. 'It's only a storm.'

'Only a storm!' Eve's voice was rising hysterically. 'Didn't you know lightning is attracted to mirrors? Quick, help me. And the ones in your bedroom.' She flitted from room to room, throwing anything she could find over every mirrored surface.

Rose got down to continue her carpet brushing, although it was so dark that she could hardly see what she was doing. Covering mirrors was only a superstition and she wasn't superstitious. Eve would be covering up all the knives next!

'No. No. Come downstairs with me. Don't stay up here.' Eve had come back into the room and now she got hold of Rose's arm and dragged her to her feet. 'There's the big overmantel in the dining room and the one on the chiffonier in the drawing room.'

Slowly, Rose got to her feet again and followed Eve down the stairs. 'Do you want to cover the face on the grandfather clock? That's glass,' she asked with more than a trace of sarcasm.

'No, it's not a mirror. Yes, wait a minute, it shines, doesn't it? Put this tea towel over it.' She threw a tea towel at Rose and when Rose didn't move screamed, 'Well, go on, do it!'

Eve ducked her head as another streak of lightning was followed almost immediately by the crash of thunder.

'Oh, dear. It must be right overhead. Come along. We'll go into the kitchen now and have a cup of tea. Quickly now.' She kept looking behind her to make sure Rose was close behind.

Storms excited rather than frightened Rose and she was amused to see how Eve cringed every time the lightning lit up the room. Outside the rain had begun now. First with drops that made patches of wet the size of saucers on the cobbles and then, seconds later, the heavens opened and it lashed down with a roar nearly as loud as the thunder that accompanied it.

'What are you doing?' Eve asked. She was sitting huddled in her chair with her back to the window, peeping out from her apron, thrown over her head. 'Where are you going? You can't go out in this.'

'I'm not going out. I'm letting the cat in. He's mewing.' Rose opened the door wide enough to let Blackie in. He rushed in, bringing with him a great spray, just as if someone had tipped a whole bucket of water over him. She slammed the door shut.

The cat went over to the warmth of the stove and began to lick himself dry, purring as the warmth seeped into him. Eve was pale and tight with anxiety, watching as Rose pulled the kettle forward, the rain hissing down the chimney on to the fire.

Rose reached the cups down from the dresser and put them on a tray. Then she made the tea and put the milk in the cups. 'While it's brewing I'll just go upstairs and ...'

'No. No, don't leave me.' Eve put out her hand. 'Light the lamp. It's so dark, just like night ...' she cringed as another flash of lightning lit the room.

Rose lit the lamp and trimmed it. 'You don't like storms?' she said, stating the obvious.

'They terrify me. Always have.'

Rose regarded her without sympathy. 'It's horrible, being frightened, isn't it?' she said conversationally. 'Children are often frightened of the dark. Of being put in cupboards without any light. That's a cruel thing to do, Eve, don't you think?'

Eve didn't reply, but sat twisting her handkerchief in her hands, waiting for the next thunderclap. Rose poured her tea and handed it to her just as the thunderclap came. The tea cup went crashing to the floor.

'It's all right, I'll pour you another, then I'll clear it up,' Rose said.

Eve didn't answer. She didn't even blame Rose for dropping the cup.

Rose sat down at the table, watching the woman by the fire. Gone was the haughty, disdainful, self-contained harridan and in her place was a creature, frightened nearly out of her wits by thunder and lightning. She couldn't help smiling a little as she drank her tea, but she felt no vestige of sympathy or compassion.

Then, above the roar of the rain she heard a knocking sound.

'What's that?' Eve turned frightened eyes to her.

'I think it's somebody at the door.' Rose got up to investigate.

'No, it can't be. Not in this rain.' Eve put her cup to her chattering teeth.

Rose opened the door and a blast of cold wind and rain nearly took it out of her hand. A man stood there. 'Can I come in?' he said. Even in such dreadful weather he waited for her nod before he stepped over the threshold.

He took off his hat and she saw that it was Stephen Joel.

'Captain Joel!' She could do nothing but stare at him.

He looked at the pool of water forming on the floor from his dripping clothes. 'I'm sorry. I'm makin' your floor all wet. May I . . . ?' he began to unbutton his sodden reefer jacket.

'Yes, yes, of course. Take off your wet things. I'll pour you a cup of tea.' Rose handed him a towel and then busied herself with the tea pot as she spoke. 'Please sit down, I didn't realise your boat was in. Did you get wet like that just coming from the jetty?'

'No. I haven't come by boat. I've walked from Bramfield. Caught the train from Ipswich. I thought I'd get here before the storm broke but it was further than I thought. At least, it took longer than I realised it would on foot.' He gave a rueful smile. 'I don't hev much cause to walk a lot as a rule so I was a bad judge.'

'Who is this man?' Eve asked. It was almost comical to see her trying to be imperious when she was eaten up with terror and cowered every time the thunder rolled, which it did, almost continuously.

'This is Captain Joel, Lissa's . . . ' Rose hesitated, not quite sure how to describe him.

'I've come to see Lissa. I got a message from the harbour master at Ipswich to say she was in trouble. He didn't say what sort of trouble but I guessed it must be pretty bad. So I've come as quick as I could.' He looked round. 'Where is she?'

'Gone.' The word was a shout of triumph from the rocking chair.

He frowned and looked at Rose, raising one eyebrow.

Rose pushed his tea over towards him and sat down opposite to him. 'She . . . ' she began.

'She's gone, the slut.' Eve lifted her chin and looked at him as coolly as the storm would allow.

He frowned again. 'I don't understand. Gone where?'

'I wasn't having scandal in my house so I turned her out. I

252

don't know where she's gone and I don't care. Let her die in the gutter and her bastard with her.' Eve was vitriolic.

Stephen Joel stared at her. Then he put his head in his hands. 'Oh, my poor girl,' he moaned to himself, 'what hev I brought on you?' He looked up at Rose. 'She's hevin' a child?'

Rose nodded.

He nodded too. 'I feared it might be somethin' like that. Oh, my poor girl.' He pushed back his chair and stood up. 'Where will I find her?'

'In the gutter, I should think,' Eve spat.

'How long has she been gone? I must go and look for her.'

'Nearly a month,' Rose said. She looked hard at him. 'I'm sure she's somewhere safe,' she said slowly, willing him to understand what she dare not put into words. 'Please sit down and drink your tea. Michael and Dan will be over later. You can't go without seeing them. They've been wondering where you were. It's such a long time since you were last here.'

He sank back on the chair and took a drink of tea. In spite of wiping himself with the towel rivulets of water were still streaming down his face and droplets clung to his curly hair. 'The boat's been in dock,' he said, speaking automatically, his thoughts obviously far away. 'I got caught out in bad weather and got dismasted. Did a lot of damage, I can tell ye. I was lucky to get away with me skin. Thass why I hevn't been by lately.' He drank some more tea and took a bite of the cake Rose had put at his elbow. The storm was still raging, and the rain was pouring like a torrent over the gutters and splashing on the cobbles. Neither of the women spoke, waiting for him to continue.

He swallowed and went on, 'I thought it was a good opportunity to do a bit on the house while the boat was in dock.' He looked up, giving Rose his full attention now. 'I've got a little house in Manningtree, y'see. My wife ... she died near on three years ago in childbirth ... ' He put his head in his hands. 'Oh, God, if anything's happened to my Lissy ... '

Rose got up and went round and put her hand on his shoulder. The rain had soaked through his thick reefer jacket and his shirt was wet. 'I'm sure Lissa's all right, Captain Joel,' she said, squeezing his shoulder, the only way she could think of to let him know she was safe.

'I've painted the house from top to bottom ready for her,' he went on and she had no way of knowing whether or not he had understood her unspoken message. 'Thass why the harbour master had a job to get howd of me. He never thought to look for me there on account of he knew I hadn't been back much since Lucy died.' He sniffed. 'I reckoned the next time I came here, when the boat was back in commission so I was earning again, I'd ask Lissy to marry me and take her there.'

'She's under age, I might remind you,' Eve said coldly.

'Seein' as how you've turned her out I don't reckon that signifies much, do you, Ma'am?' he said, his voice polite. 'If I can find her I shall take her home with me and look after her. I reckon we'll be all right together and when the time comes I shall make a honest woman of her. It's never been in my mind to do anything different.'

'You won't find her,' Eve said confidently.

'Please God I shall, beggin' to contradict you, Ma'am. I shan't rest till I do. I love Lissy. I never meant her no harm, bless her. And if on'y I can find her I shall make up to her for all the misery I've caused.' He covered his face with his hand. 'I knew we shoulda waited. I told her so,' he muttered to himself, but Rose heard.

'You do intend to marry her, Captain Joel?' Rose asked. 'If you can find her, of course,' she added quickly.

'Thass what I said, Ma'am. An' thass why I've come here today.'

'You'll never find her,' Eve repeated, rocking back and forth in her chair.

Rose turned to her. 'If you're so sure of that there can't be any harm in writing a note to say you consent to their marriage, can there, Eve?' she said. 'After all, it would ensure that she didn't turn up on your doorstep at some future time, wouldn't it?'

'There's no point.' Eve ducked her head automatically as another clap of thunder reverberated through the heavens.

Rose fetched a pad and envelope. Then she took down a pen and inkwell. 'I think you should do this, Eve,' she said, standing over her. 'It will make amends, won't it? Like I said once before, Jesus said, "Let him that is without sin among you case the first stone." How can you go to church every Sunday knowing what you've done. Other people know too, you know.'

Rose spoke softly, so that only Eve could hear. At her last words, Eve looked up guiltily. It was impossible to tell from Rose's expression whether she was talking about Lissa or Eve herself. The thunder and lightning were making her feel confused. Did other people know about how she had trapped George all those years ago? Had Rose told them? Or was she talking about Lissa? She didn't know. All she knew was that she was being blackmailed over something and must hold on to her dignity at all costs. Another clap of thunder and she clutched the arms of her chair till her knuckles showed white. She took a deep breath and tried to control her trembling.

'Give me the pen,' she said haughtily. 'You can marry her as far as I'm concerned. I've washed my hands of her. That is, *if* you can find her, which I very much doubt, since she's been gone nearly a month.' With a hand that shook she scribbled her consent and signed it.

He bent and took it from her. 'Thank you, Ma'am,' he said, inclining his head courteously. 'I'm much obliged to you.' He turned to Rose. 'Mrs Michael, hev you any idea where I should start to look for my Lissy?' he asked. 'Do you know where she might hev made for?'

Rose smiled at him. 'I suggest you go out of the back door and across the yard. Behind the stables you'll find a little cottage. It used to belong to the groom, but he died earlier in the year. Just call, Captain Joel, and Lissa will come down and let you in. She's been waiting for you. She always said she knew you'd come for her.'

There was a silence. The storm seemed to have died as quickly as it had begun. Only the sound of rain trickling from the gutters broke the stillness. Rose looked at her mother-in-law. Eve's face was a picture of astonishment mingled with fury to think that she had been so tricked.

Rose smiled at her. Later she knew she would have to pay for this but for the moment victory was sweet.

Chapter Twenty-One

Tight-lipped, Eve watched Rose adjusting her hat at the kitchen overmantel. Since Stephen Joel's unexpected appearance and the realisation that she had been tricked, relations had been to say the least strained between them.

'Where are you going?' she asked, her curiosity getting the better of her.

'To see my mother.'

'There's ironing to be done.'

'It can wait.' Satisfied with her appearance Rose turned away from the mirror and gazed coolly at her mother-in-law. 'Or you can do it yourself.' She went to the door and looked back over her shoulder. 'If you haven't forgotten how.'

She left and fetched her bicycle from the stable. Since Lissa had gone there had been a gradual shift of authority at Mill House. It stemmed from Rose's knowledge that Eve couldn't do without her. Without Rose, she would either have to do all the work herself or pay someone else to do it and it was debatable which course appealed to her least. The thought of spoiling her soft hands by dipping them in carbolic soap and scrubbing floors made her shudder, and she wouldn't know where to begin when it came to washing clothes. The very idea was a nightmare. At the same time, she had no wish to spend money on some inefficient woman from the village.

Rose understood this very well. She knew that this was why there had been no retaliation, no wrathful explosion, after Stephen Joel left, the consent to Lissa's marriage in his pocket. But she knew, too, that underlying Eve's impotence was a seething, brooding hatred, not just of Rose herself, but of her own inability to deal with the situation.

Rose didn't care. That was the difference between them. That and the knowledge, of which Eve had no inkling, that soon she and Dan would be gone, away from the house she had once thought so beautiful but had come to realise that, like a rosy apple, it hid a rottenness at the core.

Now that Lissa was gone there was nothing to stop them once Dan had found work. Because although she insisted that she would be happy living on berries and sleeping in the hedge as long as they were together, this was not what he wanted for her.

'Haven't you heard the old proverb, Rose? When poverty comes in at the door, love flies out at the window?' he'd said. 'I won't have that happening to us, you're too precious to me.'

All her protestations had failed to sway him, so all she could do was to exercise patience until he was ready. Sometimes she found it very hard, especially as they had so little time alone together. And Michael watched them, all the time, waiting for proof of his jealous suspicions.

She sighed as she rode the final few yards up the bumpy track to Crick's Farm and propped her bike against the side of the house. At times she wondered where it would all end.

'Rosie! We was beginning to think you'd forgot all about us!' Her mother was just crossing the yard from the dairy, but her welcoming smile belied her words. She hurried across to Rose and kissed her. 'You ain't been to see us for weeks, my girl.' She eyed her daughter up and down. 'You look right peaky. Is anything wrong?'

'Not any more, Mum.' Rose linked arms with Emma. 'Come indoors and I'll tell you all about it.'

Inside the house the kitchen looked somehow bigger. While her mother made the inevitable pot of tea Rose looked around and realised that it was simply that there was less clutter about.

'Well, there's only the two of us now Babs has got rooms with Miss Chamberlain,' Emma explained when she remarked on it. 'And your dad works that hard!' Her shoulders lifted proudly. 'He's taken on a boy to help with the rough work and he says if things go on the way they are I'll soon be able to hev help in the dairy. What do you think of that?'

'I'm very glad, Mum. It's no more than you deserve.'

'And thass all since Christmas. I dunno what come over him then, but he's worked like a trooper ever since. And,' her voice dropped, 'he ain't touched a drop of liquor. Not a drop. Ain't that a wunnerful thing?'

'It must have been his New Year's resolution.' Rose smiled, remembering the scene with her father on Christmas night.

'Well, whatever it was he's stuck to it, thank the Good Lord.' Emma poured the tea and sat down. 'Come on now, what's your news? You said you'd got suthin' to tell me. I'm all ears.'

Rose told her Lissa's story.

Emma listened in silence. She had no need to speak, the expressions that flitted across her face, from shock at Lissa's pregnancy, horror at Eve's treatment of her, to triumph when Rose tricked her into giving her consent to Stephen Joel, said it all. 'Well, she's not the first and won't be the last to put the cart before the horse. As long as he's ready to stand by her there's no harm done,' she said sagely when Rose finished.

'That was the trouble. He was away such a long time we were afraid he'd gone off and wasn't coming back,' Rose said. 'We were beginning to wonder what to do with her. We couldn't have kept her in that cottage much longer.'

'We?' Emma cocked an eyebrow. 'You mean you and Michael?'

Rose shook her head. 'No, Dan helped me. Michael didn't know anything about it.' Rose hoped her mother hadn't noticed her flush at the mention of Dan's name.

'Why was that? I should hev thought your husband ...' Obviously Emma had noticed.

'Oh, Michael's always busy with other things. Anyway, Dan always had a soft spot for Lissa.'

'And not only Lissa, if you ask me,' Emma remarked under her breath. 'You should hev brought her here,' she said in her normal voice. 'I'd hev looked after the little mawther. I always liked her.'

Rose gazed at her mother. 'Do you know, we never thought of that,' she said. 'Still it doesn't matter now. She's gone.' She sighed. 'I just wish I could have said goodbye to her, but Dan took them both into Bramfield in the trap to catch the train so I never had the chance. He said they were so happy it brought tears to your eyes.'

'I can imagine. Where will they live? On his boat?'

'No. He's got a house in Manningtree. He was married before, you see, but his wife died. He's a nice man. He'll look after Lissy. She deserves it.'

Emma poured herself another cup of tea and one for Rose. 'And what about Madam? What does she make of it all?' she asked.

'She's never mentioned it since Stephen Joel walked out of the door. You'd think the whole business had never happened.' Rose laughed. 'Except, of course, that she's hardly civil with me. She's eaten up inside with fury. She's so mad she doesn't know what to do with herself. Oh, I know her well enough to read the signs.'

'You want to watch out then, my girl. She'll be taking it out on you, if you're not careful.'

'Ah, that's just it, you see. She can't take it out on me too much, I'm too useful. And that makes her even madder.' She laughed again. 'One of these days she'll get so mad the cork'll blow and she'll go off pop. I just hope I'm there to see it.' She drained her tea.

'Just you watch your step, Rose, and don't get too cocky,' Emma warned.

'I won't. Don't you worry about me, Mum, I'll be all right.' She didn't add, Dan will look after me, that was a secret too precious to share even with her mother. She got to her feet and went and kissed Emma. 'Where's Dad? I can't go back without having a word with him.'

'He's down on the bottom field, mending the hedge.'

'I'll go and find him.'

'Take him a bottle of tea. I expect he'll be ready for it.'

Rose waited while her mother poured the tea and milk into a bottle and corked it, then wandered down to the bottom field. It was a beautiful summer day, a skylark was singing his heart out high in the sky and there was a hum of bees flitting among the poppies that were growing up with the corn. The hedgerow as she walked down the side of the field was a riot of yellow buttercups and dandelions, white campion and tiny scarlet pimpernel. It was good to see that the field looked well cared for, with a clear path round it, and the half grown corn looking so healthy. At the bottom of the field, near the ditch into which

Rose had fallen with such disastrous results Chad was mending the hedge, carefully bending and interlacing the branches to make a neat job. He straightened up as Rose approached.

'Ah, Rose, my dear daughter, it's a delight to see you.' He gave her a kiss and then held her at arm's length. 'You're thinner, child. Are you not well?'

'I'm perfectly well, thank you, Dad.' She held out the bottle.

'Tea!' His face lit up. 'Just what the doctor ordered. Come and sit down with me while I drink it. I assume you've already partaken.'

'Yes. With Mum.'

They sat on a fallen log and Chad drank the tea expertly from the bottle. When he had finished he wiped his mouth and said, 'Ah, that's very much better. As they say, the cup that cheers.' He laughed. 'Even if it did come out of a bottle.' His laughter faded and his expression became serious. 'I'm glad you've come, Rose. I'm reluctant to concern you with my problems but I am a little anxious.'

'About what, Dad?' Rose turned to look at him.

'That business we discussed at Christmas.' He didn't return her gaze but picked a blade of grass and put it in his mouth and began chewing on it. 'You know. Michael and my barn.'

'Ah, yes.' Understanding dawned. Then she frowned. 'Oh, Dad, you haven't ...'

He held up his hand. 'No, Rose, I haven't gone back on my decision. I told him and his friend that they could no longer use the barn and as far as I was concerned that was an end of it.'

'Then what ...?'

'As you know, the barn is situated right on the edge of my property. I don't very often have occasion to go there. But when I looked the other week I thought, but I wasn't sure, that the lock had been tampered with – you understand, I took the precaution of putting a padlock on the door when I told them it was no longer available to them. Anyway, since then I've kept an eye on the place and I suspect that they are using it again, in spite of what I said. Oh, no, there's no agreement between us,' he added hastily, seeing the suspicion in Rose's eyes. 'If they are using it they're trespassing on my property. But the grass round the barn certainly looks as if it's been trampled on.' He spread his hands. 'And of course, putting the padlock on was only a gesture. If they're determined to get in it would be easy enough to take a board out, since the place is pretty nearly derelict. I don't really know what to do, Rose. If they are using it, and I'm not absolutely certain that they are at the moment, I could hardly prosecute my own son-in-law, now, could I? At the same time, if I do nothing and contraband goods are found on my property I'll be charged with being a receiver of smuggled goods. I feel I'm in rather a predicament. Of course, I haven't told your mother any of this,' he added quickly.

Rose sat chewing her lip. She had been so preoccupied with Lissa that she hadn't noticed Michael's comings and goings. She knew he and Silas Hands had mended the boat but had assumed – she should have known better! – that they were only using it to tow the punt since the odd duck peppered with lead shot had found its way to the kitchen to be plucked and drawn.

'I'll speak to Michael,' she said, although in truth she didn't know what good it would do.

But it was enough for Chad. His face cleared. 'Thank you, Rose, my dear. I'd be obliged.'

She got up from the log and brushed the back of her skirt. It was one of her favourites, a blue and cream striped cotton that reached just to her ankles and was full enough to give her plenty of room to pedal the bicycle. 'Of course, you could always pull the barn down,' she mused, still intent on getting the dust off her skirt. 'If it's derelict anyway, and you don't use it, that might be the best thing to do. Michael can't use it if it isn't there, can he?' She smiled at her father.

'Mm. I might even do that,' he said. He laughed aloud. 'I wouldn't have to do much more than lean my weight against it and it would go down like a pack of cards.'

'There you are, then. There's your answer.' She kissed him and left, turning to wave to him when she got to the top of the field.

Cycling home she thought about what her father had said. He could easily solve his part of the problem by demolishing the barn, but what about Michael? Was he up to his old tricks? Had he indeed only suspended them until he could get his boat mended? She had been so preoccupied with Lissa over the last weeks that she hadn't taken much thought as to what Michael might be doing. She'd been only too glad when he was out of the way. Come to think of it she had never seen any sign of him during her walks on the marsh. But broad daylight wasn't the time for smuggling.

Perhaps her father was being over-cautious. It could simply have been the local lads looking for somewhere to play. An old barn would make a marvellous den.

Her thoughts went round and round in her head as the pedals went round and round on the bicycle but by the time she reached the mill her mind was no clearer.

After supper that night things followed their usual pattern. Dan went off to work on his garden and Michael picked up the bag that held his binoculars.

'Are you going out?' she asked him quickly.

'Looks like it,' he said, going to the door.

'On to the marsh?'

He frowned at being cross-questioned. 'What do you want to know for?'

'I thought I might come with you. What are you going to do?'

He gave an elaborate sigh. 'I don't see what business it is of yours, but if you must know I think I saw an avocet down by the water's edge the other night. They're quite rare in these parts and I want to see if I can see it again.'

She got up. 'I'd like to come.'

'You'll be bored stiff.'

'What about the washing up?' Eve demanded at the same time.

'No, I won't be bored. And the washing up'll keep,' Rose answered them both as she followed him out of the door.

He didn't wait for her but strode off across the bridge and out on to the marsh. She had to run to keep up with him. Over to her right she had a brief glimpse of Dan weeding the carrot bed in his garden.

'Do you often see rare birds out here?' she asked breathlessly when she caught him up.

'Sometimes.'

'Do you keep a notebook about what you see?'

'No. Why should I?'

'I just thought you might like to have a record.'

'I have. In my head. Now be quiet.' He got out his binoculars and crouched down in the long, coarse grass beside the path.

She crouched down beside him. 'This is near where you found me that night when I'd hurt my ankle. Do you remember?' she whispered.

'Yes. Be quiet, I tell you.'

They crouched there for what seemed to Rose a very long time. Then she sneezed and he turned on her. 'I couldn't help it,' she protested. 'The grass tickled my nose.'

The day had been warm so she hadn't bothered to bring a shawl but a chilly wind had piped up and she began to get cold. And bored.

'Doesn't look as if it's coming today,' she said with a yawn.

'I told you to be quiet. If you can't keep your mouth shut you'd better go home.'

She got to her feet. It was beginning to get dusk. 'I think I will.'

She went back the way they had come. Michael's boat was at its mooring, it had been carefully repaired and given a coat of black paint. The oars were lying in the bottom of the boat. It looked innocent enough. Perhaps her father had been wrong after all.

She walked on. Dan was still at work on his garden, a shadowy figure in the fading light. She hesitated a minute and then pushed open the gate and went in.

'Dan,' she called softly.

He turned and came to her. 'Rose! What are you doing here? Mike'll kill you if he sees you.'

'It's all right. He's out there watching for avocets. I stayed with him till I got bored. Then I saw you and couldn't resist ... I just wanted to ...'

'I know.' He gathered her into his arms and his mouth came down on hers. 'Oh, it seems so long since I've held you like this,' he said, after a long time.

'Can't we go away, Dan?' She looked up at him from the circle of his arms. 'Just leave here and go where we can be together?'

263

'I'm sorely tempted, my darling, but I know it wouldn't be the right thing to do.' He kissed her again. 'Just be patient a little while longer. Things will come right, Rose. I promise.' He turned and led her towards the gate. 'You'd better go back. We don't want Mike coming back and finding us. I'll hang on here for a bit so the Matriarch doesn't get suspicious.'

They reached the gate. 'I hate all this, Dan.' She held up her face for a last kiss.

'So do I, my darling.' For a moment he held her close, then she left him to hurry back to the house, warm in the knowledge of his love.

She had almost reached the bridge when a figure loomed in her path.

'Michael!' She put her hand guiltily to her throat. 'I thought you were still out on the marsh.'

'Well, you thought wrong, didn't you!' He caught her by the hair and dragged her to him. 'I followed you back. I knew what I'd find, and by Christ I was right, wasn't I?' With each word he jerked her head. 'I'll teach you to play fast and loose with my brother, mawther.' He hit her in the face, knocking her to the ground. Then he began to kick her. She screamed and tried to roll away into the hedge but there was no escape, the blows rained relentlessly on, each one accompanied by a curse. She knew there was no escape. He was going to kill her.

Dimly, she heard pounding feet. Or was it blood pounding in her head? Then the blows stopped and she heard Dan's voice.

'You bastard! You bloody bastard!' As he spoke he lifted Michael bodily by his collar from where he was bending over Rose and caught him a blow to the chin that sent him reeling.

Rose didn't wait to see what happened next although as she crawled her way back to the house she could hear the grunts and blows as the two men fought. Oh, dear God, she murmured as she dragged herself to her feet by the bridge railings, what's to become of me? What's to become of all of us?

The next morning she put on a high-necked, long-sleeved blouse, and left her hair loose so that it fell across her face, but she couldn't help wincing as she sat down.

Dan, sporting an ugly bruise under his chin, tried to attract her attention but her eyes never left the table and she avoided any contact with him at all. That bastard had given her a real pasting last night. Well, he wouldn't give her another. He'd laid his plans during a sleepless night. He knew now that he couldn't wait for Mr Humphrey at Stowmarket, who had promised him work in the autumn. They would have to go today. But not until tonight when Michael was off on his nightly jaunt. Then they would steal away and be past Ipswich before anyone knew they had gone. That was the best way. Then there would be no prospect of him following and trying to take her back.

She got up and began to clear the table. He followed her to the sink. 'Get a bag packed. I'm taking you away.'

She didn't look up but shook her head almost imperceptibly. 'It'll only make matters worse. He'll follow us.'

'Not if we don't go till tonight. After he's gone out. Do as I say, Rose,' he whispered urgently.

'Oh, if only we could,' she said on a sigh.

'Trust me.'

'What are you talking about?' Eve asked from her place at the head of the table.

'I was just saying that it always seems to rain when there's a grain barge to be unloaded. And Jim Barnes will want to be off on the ebb tonight so we'll have to get it done.' He went to the door. 'It's only a thin drizzle. May not amount to much.' He managed to wink at Rose as he left.

He loped across the yard. *Patience* was low in the water so she'd got a good load on board. It looked like being a busy day. Michael was already there, running the sacks out of the hold, down the gang plank and on to the shore.

'You can carry on here. I'll get the hoist going,' he said shortly when he saw Dan approach. Clearly he had no wish to work anywhere near his brother, a sentiment Dan heartily endorsed. Dan went on board the barge.

'Young Mike's got the wind up his tail this marnin',' Jim Barnes said. 'Musta had a rough night last night.'

'I shouldn't wonder,' Dan said briefly. Jim Barnes was a real old woman for gossip and he didn't feel inclined to feed his appetite for scandal. He hoisted a sack on to his back and hurried down the gang plank – a bit slippery from the rain, he would have to watch it – to deposit it beside the wall where

Michael only had to hook it on to the chain and hoist it up to the top floor of the mill. As he worked he laid his plans. It wouldn't take him long to throw his own clothes into a bag tonight and he'd got enough money to last them for a bit. They'd need to pay for lodging and food while he looked for work. Transport, too. Catch a train to Ipswich and then where to? Norwich. That's where they'd go. Plenty of mills up there on the broads. He could get a bit of a living dressing stones. He hated dressing stones. He wanted to work on the land.

Back and forth he went with the sacks on his back, his mind working in time with his feet, his fury with his brother lending him extra strength.

In the house, Rose dragged herself up from the table and began to clear the breakfast things away. Every bone in her body ached.

'Have you fallen again?' Eve asked sarcastically, seeing the bruises on her face.

'Yes, that's right.'

'It seems to me you need to be a bit more submissive to your husband.'

'You're probably right.' Rose had neither the strength nor inclination to enter into a discussion with Eve.

'Michael has rather a quick temper. It doesn't do to antagonise him.' Eve pursed her lips. Of course, Michael should never have beaten her but she couldn't help a feeling of vicarious triumph that the girl had been taken down a peg. Several pegs in fact, by the look of her. 'Did he hurt you much?'

Rose turned and looked her full in the face, pulling aside the curtain of hair that she had arranged to hide the worst of the injuries.

Eve drew in a quick breath as she saw Rose's black eye and the blood congealing on her badly grazed cheek. 'Have you bathed it?'

'No.'

'Well, you should.'

Rose turned away. She couldn't be bothered to argue. Thank God by tonight she would be away from Dowlands' Mill and all it stood for.

She left the kitchen and went upstairs to her bedroom to begin packing, pulling out drawers and throwing her things in a heap on the bed while she searched for a bag of some sort to put them in. Mustn't take too much because there was no telling how far they would have to walk, but must take enough because there would be no money to buy clothes until Dan found work. She allowed herself a little smile. She'd always told Dan she would be happy sleeping in the hedge as long as they were together. It might very well come to that.

As she passed the window she paused for a moment and looked out. Through the thin drizzle of rain the water in the creek looked calm and tranquil, a far cry from the turmoil in Mill House, she thought wryly. Jim Barnes was standing on the deck of *Patience*, he considered himself too old to hump sacks of corn so he watched while Dan did it. Dan was very strong, he hefted the sacks as if they hardly weighed anything and ran sure-footed up and down the gang plank. Her heart swelled with love for him.

She turned her attention to Michael. He was up to his old trick, hooking his heel into the chain of the hoist and riding up with the sack. It looked dangerous and she remembered how she used to worry in case he should fall. Her lips twisted bitterly. She wasn't worried now. She wished he would fall. She wished he would fall and break his neck so that she could dance on his grave. She caught her breath and put her fingers to her lips, shocked at the viciousness of her own thoughts.

Anyway, things like that didn't happen, she consoled herself. Problems were never solved that easily. She turned away from the window, but as she moved she heard a shout that turned into a terrified scream. Then there was a thud. Then silence. Hardly daring to look she stole a glance out of the window. Everywhere was deathly quiet and still. Michael was lying on the concrete, a sack of corn had partly broken his fall and was spilling its contents over him and over the ground. The great iron hook from the hoist was swinging back and forth just below the lucam.

She put both hands to her mouth. 'Oh, God,' she whispered, horrified. 'I wished him dead. It was my fault. I wished him dead. And now he is.'

267

Chapter Twenty-Two

For several minutes Rose stood, rooted to the spot, too shocked to move. She could hardly take in the sight before her eyes. Michael was lying there on the ground, twisted and still, where he had fallen as he travelled up on the hoist with the corn sack, something he had done thousands of times before. It wouldn't have happened if she hadn't wished him dead, she thought dully. It was all her fault. She had killed him as surely as if she had driven a knife into his heart. She couldn't believe it, just as she couldn't move from where she was standing. It was as if time was suspended and she was watching a sequence of events that had nothing to do with real life. She saw Dan and Jim Barnes go to where Michael lay and bend over him. It seemed to her that they moved very slowly, although in reality they lost no time. She watched Dan feeling for a pulse and then nodding up at Jim.

So Michael wasn't dead. She hadn't killed him with her wicked wish. Her shoulders sagged as relief flooded through her, relief that was tinged with something she hardly recognised – and would never dare to name – disappointment.

She turned away from the window and made her way stiffly down the stairs as fast as her bruised limbs would carry her.

Eve was sitting where she had left her, in the rocking chair. It seemed she hadn't heard Michael's dreadful scream.

'There's been an awful accident. Michael's hurt,' Rose said, and to her own ears her voice sounded flat and lifeless. She carried on, zombie-like, through the kitchen.

Eve looked up and hurriedly got to her feet and followed her out of the door and across the yard.

Dan was kneeling beside Michael and Jim Barnes was crouched beside him. 'He's still breathing, thank God,' Dan said without looking up.

Jim made way for Rose. Michael was lying at a strange, unnatural angle and was unconscious, his face ashen against his dark hair. Corn was still trickling slowly out of the sack which had partly broken his fall. Automatically, she smoothed his hair back from his cold, clammy forehead. This was the man she had fallen in love with, thinking he was the most handsome man she had ever seen. Yet as she gazed at him now there was no love, in fact no feeling at all for him, not even pity, in her heart. He had beaten it all out of her.

'What happened?' she asked.

Dan shook his head. 'We can't tell. He'd gone up on the hoist like that hundreds of times, so whether he hadn't fixed the sack properly, whether it burst, whether ... oh, I don't know what could have happened. All I'm sure of is that the chain didn't break. It wasn't the hoist that failed.'

'Has someone gone for the doctor?' Eve asked. Even now her voice was imperious.

Rose scrambled stiffly to her feet. 'I'll go,' she said. 'I can go on my bike.' The bike Michael had bought her.

Dan nodded, still staring at his brother. 'Yes, that's probably the quickest. Jim'll help me to get him into the house while you've gone.' He looked up now and his face was white with shock. 'But stay with him while I go and get the door off the office to use as a stretcher.'

'I'm his mother. I'll stay with him.' Eve had somehow managed to get down and was kneeling beside him. She took his hand and kissed it, the first gesture of affection Rose had ever seen from her. 'Quickly, Rose,' she said over her shoulder. 'And tell Dr Holmes to hurry.'

Rose fetched her bicycle and pedalled off up the lane as fast as her bruised body would allow, her thoughts a jumble of horror, pity and apprehension. It was unbelievable how suddenly life could change. One minute Michael had been a normal, active man, going about his daily work and the next he was an unconscious heap on the ground, hanging on to life by a thread. She sped along the village street, and suddenly noticed Dr Holmes's pony and trap standing outside the school. That was lucky! Then she remembered, he was one of the school managers.

She propped the bike against the school railings and hurried inside, where she could see her sister Babs in the classroom, gold-rimmed spectacles perched on the end of her nose, writing something on the blackboard and the children putting up their hands, clamouring to answer her questions. She hurried to the door when she saw Rose, calling instructions to the children over her shoulder as she came. A small piece of Rose's mind registered that Babs was well on the way to being a very good teacher.

'Oh, Babs, I'm looking for Dr Holmes,' she said breathlessly. 'I saw his trap outside so I thought he might still be here.'

'Yes. He's with Miss Chamberlain.' Babs took in Rose's distraught face. 'I won't stop to ask what's wrong, you can tell me as we go along. This way.' She led the way, saying over her shoulder, 'What is it? Your mother-in-law?'

'No, it's Michael. He's fallen off the hoist. He's unconscious.'

'Oh, Rosie, how dreadful!' She slowed her step. 'Will it ...? Is he ...?'

'We don't know. That's why I've come for Dr Holmes.'

'Yes, of course.' Babs walked on swiftly to Miss Chamberlain's office where she knocked briefly and opened the door. Miss Chamberlain and the doctor were sitting either side of her desk, drinking tea and discussing the school's finances.

The doctor immediately got to his feet, draining the last of his tea as he listened to what Rose had to say, then asked a few brief questions as she followed him out to the trap.

'Were you involved?' he asked when they reached it.

'No. I wasn't anywhere near,' she said, surprised.

'Then how come that black eye?' He put his hand under her chin and turned her face to the light.

'Oh, I walked into a door. Can you hurry, please. He's very bad.'

'Walked into a door, did you? Walked into a fist, more like. I've seen that kind of injury before.' He studied her for a long minute but she didn't waver before his gaze. Then he nodded. 'Did you say they're moving him?' He asked briskly.

270

'Yes, Dan's taking the door off the office to carry him in on.'

He heaved himself up into the trap. 'Best they'd left him where he was till I got there,' he said. 'But it can't be helped. You get on your bike and go on ahead. Tell them I'll be there in a jiffy.' He clicked at the pony. 'Walk on, Hamlet.'

She flew back to the mill, bumping and rattling over the pot holes in the lane. When she arrived Dan and Jim Barnes had already carried Michael into the house and had lain him, still on his makeshift stretcher, on the kitchen table. He hadn't regained consciousness. Eve was with him, still holding his hand. She looked suddenly old and haggard.

Dr Holmes was not long in following. His face was grim when he eventually straightened up after making his examination.

'I'd recommend sending him to Ipswich hospital, but I fear he wouldn't stand the journey,' he said, shaking his head. 'I'll have to set that arm and leg as best I can, they can't be left like that. Then we shall just have to wait and see.'

'He'll live, Dr Holmes,' Eve said. It was a statement rather than a question and carried with it the implication that the old doctor would be to blame if he didn't.

Dr Holmes turned and faced her. 'That, Madam, is in the hands of the Good Lord. I can only do my best for him.' He turned back to Michael and felt his pulse for the umpteenth time. 'You have another son, I believe, as well as Daniel, here.'

'Yes. George.'

'Well, I think he should be sent for. Meantime, we must make Michael as comfortable as we can. Someone go and fetch Nurse Bennet. You may find her at Mrs Crow's, she's just had her eighth. Tell her I'm going to need her for what I've got to do here. The rest of you had better arrange for a bed to be brought downstairs for him. It'll save a lot of running up and down. He's going to be laid up for some time, I fear.'

Dan and Rose exchanged agonised glances. The doctor's words seemed to toll a death knell.

For three days Michael's life hung in the balance. He lay in the bed Dan and Rose had put up in the dining room, pushing the big dining table up against the wall and rearranging the rest of the furniture to accommodate it, looking like a ghost. Rose

271

tended him, washing him and seeing to his needs, with a kind of deadness inside her. There was still a sense of unreality about the whole business, and at times she wondered if the shock of Michael's accident had affected her mind and she was quietly going insane.

On the fourth day, he regained consciousness and Dr Holmes breathed a sigh of relief. 'He's not out of the wood yet, by any means,' he warned the family, 'but at least he's in the land of the living again now. He's a tough 'un, there's no doubt about that.' He turned to Eve. 'Is your other son coming home?'

'We haven't managed to get in touch with George yet,' she said, not willing to air family disagreements in front of Dr Holmes. 'But Daniel is going to try and see him tomorrow, aren't you, Daniel?'

'That's right. If you think it's safe for me to leave, Doctor.'

'Yes, I think you should go. Probably the best tonic for the boy would be to see his elder brother,' the doctor said.

'I wish you didn't have to go, Dan. I don't know how I'm going to manage without you,' Rose said that night as Dan was helping her wash up the supper things after Eve had gone to bed. Suddenly, she couldn't bear the thought of him not being there and she realised that it was only because of him that she had been able to cope with this nightmare.

He put down the tea towel and came and stood behind her, his hands on her shoulders. 'I have to go, Rose. You heard what the doctor said. George ought to be told about Mike and it might make all the difference to Mike if he saw George.'

'But you said yourself that they didn't get on,' Rose protested, 'so it might even make matters worse if he came back.' She was desperately trying to find an excuse to keep him there.

'They're still brothers, Rose. At times like these disagreements are forgotten,' he said. 'Anyway, I might have better luck at finding him now. It's getting on for a year since he went off so one of his friends might know where he's settled. You never know, he might even be wishing he could find some excuse to come back without losing face.'

'Yes, I suppose you're right. You might find someone who can tell you where he's living.' Her head was bowed over the sink.

Dan gave her shoulders a squeeze and then dropped his hands to his sides. 'I won't be gone long, only a day, but I must go, Rose. And even if I don't manage to find him tomorrow I can put a piece in the local paper, telling him of Michael's accident and asking him to get in touch. If he reads it he'll be sure to come back. So there's always a chance there.'

'Yes, I suppose so.' She turned round to look at him and gave a little smile. 'I've heard so much about him, it would be nice to meet him at last. Is he like you, Dan?'

'No, he favours Mike, if anything. He's dark, like Mike is.' He gave a little grin. 'I've always got on all right with both my brothers, but George and Mike never saw eye to eye. I think Mike was always a bit jealous of him being the eldest. Not that they wished each other any harm, mind you, and if George knew Mike was ill I'm sure he'd come back. That's why I have to make one last effort to find him. You do understand, don't you, Rose?' He watched her for a moment, then his arms went round her and he bent his head and kissed her, long and hard. 'I swore I wouldn't do that, not while Mike's lying there so ill,' he said unsteadily. 'It seems somehow, I don't know, underhand. Disloyal.'

'Yes, I know. I feel the same. But it's so hard.' She clung to him a moment more. 'I just don't know how I'll manage without you, Dan,' she whispered.

'I'll only be gone for a day, darling.' He smiled and smoothed her hair away from her face. 'And who knows, I might even bring the prodigal son back with me.'

She smiled back at him. 'Yes, I'm being silly, aren't I? I do hope you'll find him, Dan.' She bit her lip. 'I'll miss you while you're gone.'

He kissed her again. It was meant to be brief but it got a bit out of hand. At last he lifted his head. 'I'll miss you, too,' he whispered. 'But it won't be for long. I promise.' He laid his cheek on her hair. 'And soon, when this is all over and Mike's back on his feet we'll go away as we'd planned. Like you said, my darling, even if we have to sleep under a hedge and live on roots and berries it'll be worth it if we're together.' He leaned away from her and his mouth twisted. 'Ironic, isn't it, that this should have happened the very day I was going to take you away. When I saw what he did to you last night I knew we couldn't stay here a day longer.'

She nodded. 'I was upstairs packing my bag when he fell.' She shuddered and said, her voice barely above a whisper, 'I'd been watching him and wishing he'd fall and break his neck, Dan. And then he did fall. I almost saw it happen.' She swallowed painfully. 'I thought it was my fault. I thought I'd killed him by wishing him dead.' She looked up at him. 'It does happen sometimes, doesn't it, if you wish hard enough it comes true.' She put her head wearily back on his shoulder and went on, her voice muffled, 'But he isn't dead, so it wasn't my fault after all.' She gave a great sigh.

'We can't leave him, Rose. We can't go away. Not now. Not till he's better. You realise that, don't you?' he said bleakly, stroking her hair.

'Oh, yes,' she said, her voice flat. 'I realise that. Just as I realise that something always seems to happen to keep us here, Dan. First it was Lissa. We couldn't leave while we'd got her hidden away. And now she's gone we'll have to stay till Michael's better. Perhaps we shouldn't even be thinking of going away. Perhaps we're not meant to be together. Perhaps it's our punishment for falling in love.'

He gave her a little shake. 'Don't talk like that, Rose. It's not like that at all. It's just that we've got to be patient for a bit longer. But God knows how we'll manage it.' He pulled her to him again, kissing her hungrily.

Michael was not a good patient. With one arm and one leg in splints he was practically helpless and he took his frustration out on anyone who was nearby. Surprisingly, considering her terror of the sickroom, this was more often than not his mother. She sat by his bedside for long hours, putting damp cloths on his aching head and giving him sips of water to moisten his dry lips. He accepted her ministrations grudgingly, swearing impatiently and complaining if she didn't anticipate his every need.

But it was Rose, with Dan's help, who washed him and changed his bed. The day Dan was in Ipswich she had to manage alone, because Eve hadn't the strength to help her.

'You'll have to help yourself a bit,' Rose said, using the

brisk tone she adopted with him now. 'Without Dan's help I can't lift you on my own.'

She took no notice of the curses which accompanied every word he spoke. It was his only means of venting his fury on a fate that had dared to make him even temporarily helpless.

'Come on, then,' she said, her impatience matching his own. 'Move your good leg, for goodness sake, so I can get the sheet from under you.'

'I am moving it, you stupid bitch.'

'No, you're not.' She gave his good leg a slap.

Surprisingly, he didn't swear at her. 'Do that again,' he said.

'Willingly.' She slapped his leg again.

'Harder.'

She slapped again. 'Why, what's the matter?'

'I can't feel it. Christ, I can't feel it! I can't feel a thing.' There was absolute terror on his face.

'Don't be silly. Wiggle your toes.' Her alarm matched his.

'I'm trying. I can't! I can't move it! I can't even feel it!' He gave a great cry. 'Oh, God, I'm a cripple. I shall never walk again. Oh, God, why didn't I die in the first place instead of being condemned to this living hell!'

She drew the covers over him. 'It's probably only a temporary thing,' she said, her voice gentle, although inside she was quivering with fear that he might be right. 'Dr Holmes would have said if he'd suspected anything, I'm sure.' She looked down at him. 'Does your back hurt?'

'I don't hurt any bloody where, except my arm. I wish to God I did. I wish I was in bloody agony. Oh, God.' He turned his face away and began to cry like a child.

Rose looked helplessly at Eve, who had witnessed the whole scene. Tears were running down her cheeks and she wiped them away with a lace handkerchief.

'I think we could all do with a cup of tea,' she said in a thin, wavery voice that was not at all like her usual tone. 'It's a good thing Daniel's gone to fetch George. He'll be needed here more than ever, now.'

But George wasn't with Dan when he arrived home later that evening. All his efforts to find him had proved fruitless.

'In fact, his old cronies were asking me if I'd seen him,' he said, shaking his head.

'He'd taken a public house. You told them that,' Eve said. 'Didn't they know where it was?'

'No. I reckon he must have left the district altogether. Some of his so-called friends know every pub for miles.'

'But you put a notice in the newspaper?'

'Yes, Mother, I did that.' He looked up at Rose as she put a plate of meat and vegetables in front of him. 'Ah, that looks good, Rose.' He dropped his voice. 'It's the best thing I've seen all day.'

She smiled at him. She knew he wasn't referring to the meal on his plate.

It wasn't until after he had eaten that the two women broke the news that Michael was paralysed. Rose told him that when Dr Holmes had visited earlier he had shaken his head and told them that this was what he had feared might be the case. Michael's back was broken and there was no hope that he would ever regain the use of his legs.

'He'll spend the rest of his life in a wheelchair,' Eve moaned. 'My poor boy. And he does so love the outdoor life.'

Dan sat staring into the fire, which never went out, summer or winter. 'There are some things he won't be able to do,' he said at last. 'But there'll be plenty that he can. If I lengthen a few strings he'll be able to watch the mill when it's running. It's just that he'll sit at it instead of standing.'

'You can't expect him ever to *work* again!' Eve said, shocked.

'Yes, I shall, Mother. It'll be the best thing for him. Even though he'll be in a wheelchair he won't want to feel he's useless. And he won't be. We'll still be able to run things between us, Michael and me. And George, of course, when he comes back.'

In those words Rose heard the last of her hopes dashed.

The weeks that followed were bleak. Michael improved. His broken arm and leg mended, the headaches lessened and his bruised body recovered, but there was neither use nor feeling in his legs and he lay in his bed alternately weeping bitterly and refusing to speak or roaring his frustration out on anyone who came near, throwing whatever was to hand at them, from a book to a plate of food. It was debatable which was the most difficult

276

to deal with. If Rose went near him he cursed her, if she didn't he accused her of neglect. Nothing she did was right.

Life would have been difficult enough for her if she had loved him, she would have been prepared to put up with his rages and insults. But she didn't love him. She hated him. She hated him all the more because his crippled state bound her to him more tightly than the strongest marriage vow.

'Get out of my room!' he snarled at her when she took the bowl in to wash him – always a dangerous operation because he was likely to hurl it across the room if he could get his hands on it.

'If I don't wash you you'll stink,' she said, putting it out of his reach.

'Then I'll stink. I'm not having you messing about with my private parts.'

'Don't be stupid. I've done it all the time. Who else do you think has kept you clean?'

'I don't care. You're not doing it any bloody more. Get Dan.'

'He's over at the mill.'

'Then I'll wait till he's finished.' He turned his face away.

She stood looking down at him, wondering why she couldn't summon up even an ounce of pity for him.

Suddenly, he jerked his head round. 'Get Silas. Silas can look after me.' There was a look of triumph on his face. 'I'll have him. He can live here and look after me.'

She ground her teeth together. 'Of course he can't,' she snapped. 'Your mother will never allow him in the house.' Thank God, she added under her breath. Weasel-faced Silas Hands would be the absolute last straw.

'She'll bloody well do as I say!' he barked. 'Now get out.'

Rose went back to the kitchen. Eve was sitting in her rocking chair rubbing cream into her hands. She had aged since Michael's accident. Sitting by his bed and listening while he cursed everything from her to the fate that had brought him to such a state had taken its toll on her. Knowing her abhorrence of sickness Rose couldn't help admiring her for maintaining her vigil.

'He won't let me wash him,' she said with a sigh. 'He wants Silas Hands.'

Eve wrinkled her face in disgust. 'That dreadful creature!'

'He says he wants Silas Hands to come and live here and look after him.'

'I'm not having that man in my house. Nothing would be safe. I'm sure he's a thief. You can tell, just by looking at him.'

Rose sat down and rested her head on her hand. 'You'd better tell him that. He won't listen to me.'

'I will.' Eve got up and went through to Michael. Five minutes later she came back.

Rose was still sitting in the same position. 'He wouldn't listen, would he?' she said wearily.

Eve sat down. 'I suppose we could put a bed up in Michael's room for him,' she said thoughtfully. 'He could stay there. He could eat his meals with Michael so he wouldn't need to come through here to eat. And if we gave him a key to the front door we wouldn't need to see much of him at all.' She looked up. 'It would help Daniel, too, wouldn't it? He wouldn't have to lift him about if Silas was there to do it.'

Rose's mouth dropped open in surprise. 'But ...' she began.

'You must have noticed how tired Daniel is looking,' she went on. 'It's difficult enough having to run the mill single-handed without what he has to do for Michael.' She made an impatient gesture. 'Oh, I wish George would come home, it would make things so much easier all round.'

'But until he does, you think it might be an idea to ask Silas Hands?' Rose gave a little mirthless laugh. 'One thing to be said in his favour is that he knows just as many obscene words as Michael does so they can swear at each other.'

'Daniel won't like the idea,' Eve said, 'but with Michael in his present mood, I really think it might be the best solution. Till George comes back, anyway.'

Surprisingly, Dan wasn't against the idea.

'If it'll help him to have his old crony there then I think we should indulge him,' he said. 'I must say, I'm fed up with being sworn at every time I go near him. Perhaps Silas Hands'll sweeten his temper a bit.'

'I just wonder if he's honest,' Eve said anxiously.

'Oh, I wouldn't think so for a minute,' Dan answered, cheerfully. 'But that's just a chance we shall have to take. I'll go and see him tonight.'

Rose went and told Michael. He was lying propped up on his pillows gazing out of the window and for a second, before he composed his features into their habitual snarl Rose caught a glimpse of the vulnerable, frightened man underneath.

'Dan has gone to fetch him now. Do you think he'll come?' she asked.

'Not if he's got any bloody sense. He won't come anywhere near.' He turned his face to the wall and refused to speak again. Rose left him to sulk.

An hour later she went back to him. 'Well, your friend Silas obviously hasn't got any sense, Michael. He's coming across the yard with Dan now.'

A moment later they came in at the door and Silas greeted Michael with a stream of obscenities. Michael replied in like manner.

Rose looked at the man who had come in with Dan. He stood there, his head hunched into one shoulder as it always was, yet he looked different, somehow. Rose realised why. He was clean. He had washed himself, his hair had been cut and he was wearing a relatively clean shirt and new moleskin trousers. But underneath he was still the same shifty, weasel-faced Silas Hands who made her flesh creep.

'We can put a bed up in that corner for Silas if we move the table out,' Dan said, looking round the room.

'And I want my bloody box. I keep asking for it but nobody takes any notice. I want it standing at the foot of my bed, where I can see it.'

'There hasn't been room for it,' Rose said.

'Then make room.'

'Yes, all right. We'll make a space for it.' Dan raised his eyebrows at Rose.

'Bring it first. Now. I've been asking for it for weeks.'

'All right. When we've taken the table out, there'll be room for it. Silas, you can give me a hand,' Dan said.

When the table was deposited in the drawing room opposite Dan followed Rose up the stairs and into the bedroom.

'Will you be able to manage the box?' he asked when he saw it. 'Only I wasn't anxious to let Silas Hands upstairs to help me with it.'

'I'm glad. I wouldn't want that dreadful man in my bedroom, even for a minute. And the box shouldn't be too heavy because it's practically empty.' She grinned at him. 'I looked in it one day when he'd left the key. It hadn't got anything in it except a few packets of cigarettes and I expect he's smoked them by now.'

They carried it down the stairs and along the hall into Michael's bedroom.

When Michael saw it he became more animated than he'd been at any time since the accident. 'Put it there, at the foot of the bed where I can see it. That's right.' He lay back on his pillows, exhausted by the effort of holding his head up. But he was smiling.

Chapter Twenty-Three

Much though the rest of the family disliked Silas Hands, it had to be admitted that he and Michael got on well together. Silas could manage him as nobody else could. When Michael swore at him he swore back, cursing him for being bloody useless, lying in bed all day expecting to be waited on hand and foot. At the same time he was always attentive to Michael's needs, combining a surprisingly sensitive gentleness with a rough and ready approach which seemed exactly to suit Michael. Things were working out better than anyone could have expected, apart from the fact that there was not, nor ever would be, any improvement in Michael's condition. His back was broken. He would never stand or walk again. Even Silas Hands hadn't the courage to tell him that stark truth but allowed him to foster the idea that he was improving week by week.

Silas went out most evenings, either to the Miller's Arms or on other, more questionable expeditions. When he came back, letting himself in through the front door and going straight to Michael's room, there would be sounds of raised voices and inebriated laughter. There was no doubt Silas's presence was good for Michael, even if he did encourage him to drink too much.

With the rest of the family he was morose and monosyllabic.

Nevertheless Eve always paid him a daily visit, choosing to go in the evening when she knew Silas would be out. She would sit and talk to him about the day's events but she never knew whether he listened to what she was saying because he usually lay with his eyes closed, taking not the slightest notice of her. Rose felt sorry for her. She knew how Eve hated the sick room, yet she forced herself to go there because Michael was her son and she loved him. The weary anguish on her face as she left him bore witness to the fact that she realised her devotion was neither appreciated nor returned.

But at least Michael didn't scream at her to get out and leave him be as he did Rose. It seemed he couldn't bear her near him and he habitually shouted abuse at her when she brought meals for him and Silas and removed the dirty dishes afterwards. He wouldn't even allow her to tidy up, saying that Silas did it well enough for his needs. As she picked up the supper tray one evening Rose paused long enough to glance round the room. The dust lay thick everywhere, the ruby lustres on the mantelpiece were dull through lack of cleaning, there were fingerprints in the dust where Silas had steadied the brass clock while he wound it, and piles of newspapers were heaped on Eve's best dining chairs. There was a heap of dirty clothes and bed linen in the corner and empty whisky bottles littered the fireplace. The whole room reeked of stale tobacco. She marvelled at her mother-in-law's forbearance at allowing the room to degenerate into such a state, remembering how much elbow grease she and Lissa had been forced to expend on it in days gone by.

'Don't stand there gawping, mawther. You've got the tray, now get out,' Michael shouted, seeing her standing there.

'All right. I'm going.' She turned towards the door, screwing up her face in pain. Why was he so horrible? But it was understandable, imprisoned as he was in bed with half his body lifeless. She took a deep breath and turned back. 'Will you let me come and clean this room up a bit, Michael? It really is in an awful state and I'm sure you'd feel much better ...'

'No, I bloody won't. Silas does what's needed.'

'Well, is there anything else you want? Anything I can get you? You don't look very comfortable. Your pillows have slipped. Let me ...' She put the tray down on the chest at the foot of the bed and took a step towards him.

'No! Leave me be. Get out! I don't want you touching me!' He put up his arms to fend her off.

'Oh, very well.' With a sigh she picked up the tray again and left the room. She would come back for the heap of washing later.

Dan was just coming along the hall to pay his evening visit to his brother. His face lit up when he saw her although he didn't touch her. 'Are you all right, Rose?' he asked softly.

She nodded soberly. 'Yes, I'm all right.' Her face creased into a frown. 'I've been thinking, Dan,' she said, 'Michael's room is awfully cramped. That truckle bed in the corner can't be all that comfortable for Silas Hands, and that great ugly old chest stuck at the foot of Michael's bed takes up a lot of room.'

Dan took the heavy tray from Rose and rested it on a nearby table. 'I wouldn't worry too much about Silas Hands, Rose. The room might look a bit cramped but it's a darn sight better than the hovel he was living in, I can tell you.' He pointed to the empty plates on the tray. 'He must think he's died and gone to heaven, living somewhere like this, being paid for his trouble and with three good meals a day thrown in.'

'We can't grudge him that. He earns it. He doesn't appear to mind what he does for Michael and he seems to have found exactly the right way to treat him, swearing at him and complaining all the time about how useless he is. He doesn't treat him at all like an invalid. Only the other day I heard him yelling at him and telling him to "put a bit of effort into it".' She grinned. 'Only with the usual embellishments, of course.'

Dan grinned back. 'Of course. That goes without saying.' His grin faded and his look turned to one of concern. 'But what about you, Rose? How are you managing?'

She shrugged and glanced back at the closed door of Michael's room. 'I don't like Silas Hands. I don't like having him in the house.' She shuddered. 'He's shifty. Weasely. But Michael wants him here so I must just put up with him. No, not just put up with him, I should be grateful to him. And I am. Anyway, I don't have to see all that much of him, thank goodness.' She bit her lip and stared at the wall. 'I'm trying to face the fact that this is how life is always going to be, Dan. Dr Holmes says there's no reason why Michael shouldn't live for years, even though he'll never walk again.' She gave a resigned sigh and went on in a flat, unemotional voice. 'So Silas will continue to stay and look after him, you'll continue to run the mill and I'll always be here because he's my husband and I can't leave him. It's never going to be any different, is it? You and I are never going to be able to go away together, are we?'

'Don't talk like that, darling.' Dan shook her arm. 'We'll find a way ...'

She shook her head and looked up at him, her eyes bleak. 'You know that's not true, Dan. I realise now that we were never meant to be together because something has always happened to stop us. First it was Lissa. We couldn't leave because of her. Now she's sorted out we can't leave because of Michael.' She turned away. 'I'll never be able to leave him, not the way he is, and you'll never be able to leave the mill.'

He put his hands on her shoulders, gently rubbing the sides of her neck with his thumbs. 'Don't talk like that, Rose. You mustn't give up hope. When George comes back ...'

She twisted away. 'When George comes back! But George isn't coming back, is he? Why should he, for heaven's sake? Why should he give up the life he's chosen for himself in order to come back here?' She gave a mirthless laugh. 'After all, it's worse now than when he left. A mill he hates and a mother who still insists on holding all the reins, only now he's got a crippled brother thrown in for good measure. My God, if I was George I wouldn't come within a mile of the place.'

'You can always leave, Rose, if that's how you feel,' Dan said quietly. 'You could walk out of the door now, this very day. Nobody would blame you.'

She hung her head. 'You know that's not true,' she said and her voice was full of weariness. 'God knows I'd be glad enough to get out, but how could I leave without you, Dan? While you're here I have to stay.'

He pulled her back into his arms and cradled her head against his shoulder. 'You're right, Rose. We're wasting our lives here. It's not right that you should be made to suffer like this, while I slave my insides out running a mill that's twenty years behind the times because my mother's too mean to spend money on it. I'll take you away. We'll start a new life together, just you and me.'

'Oh, if only we could. But it's no use, Dan. We could never do it. How could we be happy, knowing we'd walked out and left our responsibilities behind? And it would kill your mother.' She sighed. 'No, we'll just have to put up with things as they are.' She gave a wintry smile. 'At least we see each other. We can talk and sometimes I can even rest my head on your shoulder like this.'

He took her face in both his hands and turned it up to his. 'I don't know why you should consider my mother and brother for a moment after the way they've both treated you, Rose, but I love you for it.' He bent his head and kissed her, then said in her ear, 'But it's not enough. God knows we deserve a little happiness together and there's a limit to how long we can wait for it. Rose, may I come to your room tonight?'

'Oh, please, Dan. I'll be waiting for you,' she whispered. Then she broke away from him and picked up the tray and hurried back to the kitchen.

The next morning when she woke the whole world looked brighter. Dan had left her while she still slept but the memory of his presence was still with her and she lay for a while re-living the gentleness of his touch, the warm strength of him, and their joy in one another as they melted into one. Afterwards, drowsy with love she had slept like a baby in the loving comfort of his arms. She felt no sense of disappointment that he was no longer by her side. There would be other nights.

She climbed out of bed and drew back the curtains. The July sun seemed to shine more brightly, sparkling on the water of the creek like thousands of diamonds, the trees seemed greener and even the mill itself looked quaint and picturesque bathed in the day's brightness. She saw Dan cross the yard in his white miller's overalls, his cap set back on his curly hair and love for him welled up inside her like a gushing fountain. As if he sensed her eyes on him he turned and looked up, waving and smiling, then touching his finger to his lips and waving again.

She stretched luxuriously and then turned back into the room and began to pull on her clothes. Even the thought of the pile of dirty sheets waiting for her in the wash house couldn't dampen her spirits.

'You're very cheerful this morning,' Eve said acidly, listening to Rose singing as she fried rashers and eggs for Silas and Michael. 'I don't know what you've got to sing about, with your husband lying crippled for life in the next room.'

Rose paused with the slice in her hand. 'My being miserable isn't going to make him any better, is it?' she said, 'So I might

285

as well try and keep my spirits up. Anyway, it's a lovely day and hadn't you remembered? Michael's wheelchair is coming today. That should make a world of difference to him. You know how he frets about not being able to get out on to his beloved marsh.'

'That's true. That man will be able to wheel him out.' Eve never referred to Silas by name, always as 'that man'.

'He'll be able to take his meals with us, too.'

Eve frowned. 'I'm not having that man at my table. I'm sure his table manners are atrocious.'

Rose didn't answer that. 'Dan is hoping Michael will be able to go back to working at the mill once he gets his wheelchair,' she said instead.

'That's out of the question. Daniel should realise that. Michael is ill. He's an invalid. He can't be expected to work again.'

'Michael isn't ill. Not any more,' Rose said patiently. 'His legs are useless. That's all.'

'Isn't that enough, for goodness sake?' Eve's voice was sharp.

Rose took a deep breath. 'I didn't mean it like that. What I meant was, the fact that he can't walk needn't necessarily mean he can't work. There's nothing wrong with his arms. Nor his brain. It would do him good to have something to occupy his mind.'

'You're heartless, Rose. Quite heartless. I would never have thought to hear you speak in such a way of your crippled husband.' Eve pursed her lips, the conversation at an end as far as she was concerned.

Breakfast over, Rose washed up and went over to the wash house. Dan had lit the big copper earlier and the water was already bubbling. Rose immersed the sheets in the dolly tub and got to work with the dolly legs. It was hard work and seemed harder now that Lissa was no longer there to share the tasks with, to chat and to giggle with. She missed Lissa more and more, not just to share the work load but because they had become such good friends. She wondered whether she was happy in her new life. Lissa had never written since the day she left with her Stephen. Rose had never expected her to, because Lissa knew that Eve always received the post into her own hands and the chances were that a letter addressed to Rose would never reach its destination without first being steamed open and read. But every day Rose watched for the big red sails of *Perseverance* to appear in the creek, knowing that Stephen Joel would bring news of Lissa when he came. So far he hadn't come but sooner or later he would. She prayed earnestly that Lissa was happy now. She'd had little enough happiness in her life.

When the sheets were blowing on the washing line Rose went back into the house. The wheelchair had arrived and Silas had lifted Michael into it. He was smiling, but when he saw her his face composed itself into its usual scowl.

'Are you going for a walk now, Michael?' she asked. 'Out on to the marsh?'

'No,' he said with exaggerated patience. 'I'm not going for a walk. I can't walk, remember? Silas is going to take me for a walk. He's going to wheel me like a babe in a push-cart. That's what's going to happen, if you must know.'

'Well, I just hope the fresh air will sweeten your temper a bit,' she flashed back at him.

'If it don't I'll shove the bugger straight in the river, Ma'am,' Silas said with a wolfish grin. 'Come on, ye old bastard. Let's git the wheels rollin'. I've got suthin' I wanta show you . . .'

They went off across the bridge and she could hear Michael talking eagerly. So he was pleased with his wheelchair even if he was at pains not to let her know it. She got out her bike and went off to visit her mother.

Emma was down on the field with several of the village women, helping with the harvest. Chad and three men from neighbouring farms were cutting the corn, rhythmically swinging their long scythes so that the great swathes fell neatly, all the same way, ready for more men following behind to gather into sheaves. Then the women came along to prop the sheaves into stooks, where they would be left until they were taken into the barn for threshing.

Emma was busy traving, as it was known locally, with the rest of the women. Her face broke into a smile when she saw Rose. 'Hullo, my girl. Thass nice to see you. Hev you come to lend a hand?'

'Oh, I'd like to. I'd really like to,' Rose said warmly. 'But . . .'

'Oh, come on. You can spare an hour, I know right well.' She straightened up and rubbed her back. 'You can hev a bite o' bread and cheese with us first. We shall be stopping directly. Look, Grace is over there under the hedge feeding young Billy. Go and hev a word with her while we finish this bit.'

Grace was sitting in the shade with her baby at her breast. 'He couldn't wait any longer for his dinner,' she said, stroking the little downy head fondly. 'He's a right little piggy, aren't you, lovey?' She looked up at Rose. 'How's Michael?'

Rose sat down beside her sister and pushed her hat to the back of her head. 'He's all right. Well, as all right as he ever will be. His wheelchair came today. Silas Hands has taken him for a walk on the marsh.'

'I wonder you didn't go, too,' Grace said. 'I would if it had been my Albert.' Adding under her breath, 'God forbid that he should ever come to such a state.'

'Oh, Michael doesn't want me with him. All he wants is Silas Hands.'

Grace didn't answer for several minutes until she had shifted the baby to the other breast. When he was settled there she said, 'Funny, ain't it? I thought you was the luckiest one of us four girls, Rose, marrying Michael Dowland and going to live in that lovely house. But now I ain't so sure. Babs seem right settled where she is at the school. She loves teaching the children and she gets on well with Miss Chamberlain. I don't reckon she'll ever get married, meself. I don't think she wants to. She's as happy as a lark where she is. Not like Millie. She can't wait to get wed. She's head of her department at the Co-op and saving hard for her bottom drawer.' She made a face. 'I can't say I care much for her young man. He seem a bit smarmy to me. Not the sort to get his boots dirty, let alone his hands, but they seem suited to each other so thass all that matters.'

'Do you see much of her?'

'Who? Millie? No, she don't visit us much. She said she can't think why we choose to live across a ploughed field. I told her choice didn't come into it. We live where the cottage is and glad and thankful to hev it seein' as it's rent free.' She laughed. 'I 'spect she and her intended'll go in for a posh new semi in Ipswich. An' good luck to 'em, I say.'

'Is that what you'd like, Gracie?'

Grace turned and looked at her in amazement. 'Me? Live in a town? No thanks. I'd die.' Her expression softened. 'People might not think I've done all that well marryin' my Albert but we're all right, Rose. An' we've got our little Billy.' She lifted him up and buttoned her dress. 'What I say is, if you don't ask for much you ain't disappointed if you don't get it. Not but what me an' Albert ain't got all we want.' She looked at Rose. 'Thass what I mean, Rosie, when I say I reckon you've come off worst outa the four of us. Because you can't be very happy. Not with your man the way he is, apart from everything else.'

Rose shot her a look. 'What do you mean, apart from everything else?'

'Well, if you want me to put it into words, losing the baby like you did. It'd hev been born about now, wouldn't it?'

'Yes. But perhaps it's as well ...' Rose took Billy from Grace and cuddled him and unexpectedly a sudden tear fell on his head as she thought of her own lost baby. Quickly, she brushed it away and said briskly. 'But you're right, of course. Things haven't turned out the way I'd expected. It probably serves me right. I thought I was marrying into money, marrying into the Dowland family. I thought I loved Michael Dowland. And what's more to the point, I thought he loved me.'

'But the Dowlands' hev got money, hevn't they?' Grace looked at her in surprise.

She gave a laugh that was more of a snort. 'If they have I've never seen it. Eve Dowland keeps her hands firmly on the purse strings, I can tell you. Every penny has to be accounted for.'

'I'll bet you've got gas.'

'You'd lose your bet.'

Grace hadn't heard. She was too busy with her own thoughts. She went on, 'Nearly everybody's got gas except us. Even the street lamps are gas now.' She brightened. 'But Mr Bowcher's hevin' gas put on at the farm and he said he might get them to bring it as far as us if it didn't turn out to be too expensive. Oh, it'd be suthin' wunnerful not to hev to fiddle around with oil lamps.' Her expression was blissful.

'Oh, yes, wouldn't it!' Rose agreed.

Grace turned to stare at her. 'You mean ... You *hevn't* got gas?'

'No. I told you you'd lose your bet. The house and the mill, everywhere's lit by oil lamps. Eve says gas is dangerous and she won't have anything to do with it.'

'Well, I never.' She took the baby and laid him in the little nest she had made for him in the straw. 'Fancy you, of all people, hevn't got gas.'

'See? Like I found out, things aren't always what they seem. Ah, here comes Mum. She said I could stay and have a bite of bread and cheese and help with the harvest. I'll enjoy that.'

Emma came across to them, wiping her face on her pinafore. 'My word, it's hot work today, girls,' she said as she sat down and opened the basket that held the food.

To Rose, bread and cheese had never tasted so good. Nor had the beer, which had been cooling all the morning in the running water of the stream. And although she was tired at the end of the afternoon spent in the field she couldn't remember when she had enjoyed herself so much. It occurred to her as she cycled home, hot and dusty but very happy, that for the first time in a year she had relaxed. There had been nobody watching her to see she did things the right way. Nobody scolded her if she dropped an aitch – although she didn't think she had, Eve's vigilance had paid off – and she had laughed more in one afternoon than she had for months. She couldn't wait to tell Dan in bed tonight. A rosy flush spread over her cheeks at the thought. She never doubted that he would come to her.

As she cycled down the lane humming to herself she saw above the trees the red sails of a barge tied up at the jetty. She began to pedal faster, hoping it might be *Perseverance* with news of Lissa. She put her bike away and hurried over. To her delight it was and Stephen Joel was standing at the door of the mill talking to Dan.

'I'm real sorry about your husband, Mrs Dowland,' he said, when he saw her. 'Dan here's jest been tellin' me about the 'accident.' He shook his head. 'Mike had been warned enough times about going up with the chain like that, but thass cold comfort to say that now thass happened, I reckon.'

'Yes, it's a bad business. But his wheelchair came today, so at least he can get out in the fresh air. He's hated being cooped up inside the house.' She turned to Dan. 'Are they back yet?'

He shook his head. 'Lucky if we see them before dark.' Then to Stephen, 'Silas Hands looks after him, Steve. Did you ever meet Silas Hands?'

Stephen raised his eyebrows in surprise. 'I met him a time or two in the Miller's Arms. He didn't strike me ...' he stopped and cleared his throat before he said more than was prudent.

But Dan understood. He gave a wry smile. 'No, Steve, I know what you mean. He isn't the sort of man we'd have chosen, either. But Mike insisted on having him and I must say they get on well together.'

'He won't let anybody else do anything for him. Only Silas Hands,' Rose said bitterly. Then she smiled and caught Stephen's sleeve. 'But what about Lissy. How is she? I've been dying for you to come so that I could ask.'

He grinned at her. 'Go and see for yourself.' He nodded towards *Perseverance*.

'You mean she's with you on the barge?' Rose's face lit up.

'Yes, but we're only here for a few hours. We came in on the tide and we must go back on the ebb. Tell you the truth I wasn't sure we'd be welcome.'

'You'll always be welcome as far as we're concerned, won't they, Dan?' She turned eagerly to Dan.

'Of course,' he agreed. He smiled at Rose. 'You go and talk to Lissy while Steve and me unload. You've got a little while.' He winked at her. 'I'll tell the Matriarch you haven't got back from your mother's yet if she asks where you are.'

Rose hurried up the gangplank and into the big comfortable cabin. Lissa was sitting at the table, knitting. As soon as she saw Rose she got up and flung herself into her arms.

'Oh, Rosie, it's so good to see you,' she said when the first greetings were over. 'I've missed you so much and I've got so much to tell you.'

Rose held her at arm's length. She looked radiant with

health and very pregnant. 'Tell me, then. Are you and Stephen married yet?'

Lissa held out her hand with its wide gold wedding band. 'Of course. We were married as soon as he could arrange it. Oh, Rose, he's so good to me. So gentle. So loving. Oh, I'm so happy there are not words to describe it. And his little house at Manningtree is perfect. It's up a little alley and has geraniums on all the window sills. He said he'd change anything I didn't like but it's all so perfect I don't want to alter a thing!'

She hugged Rose again. 'I don't usually come with him on the boat but when he said he was coming here I asked if I could and he was ever so pleased. He says he doesn't know which is nicest, having me with him on the boat or looking forward to seeing me when he gets back. I'm very happy, Rose,' she added unnecessarily.

'I can see that,' Rose said with a laugh. 'Oh, Lissy, I'm so glad for you.'

'I thought of writing to you but then I thought *she* might get hold of the letter so I didn't.'

'You could always write to me at my mother's house,' Rose said, suddenly thinking of it.

'Oh, yes. I'll do that.' She laid her hand on her stomach. 'Stephen is a bit worried. You see he lost his first wife in childbirth but I've told him there's no need. I'm sure everything will be fine.'

'Have you seen a doctor?'

'Oh, yes. Stephen insists that I see the doctor at least once a month, although I'm sure it's a waste of time.' Her expression turned dreamy. 'Just think, in less than two months we'll have our own baby. Stephen wants a little girl so that's what I want, but I don't really mind.' She clapped her hand over her mouth. 'Oh, what am I thinking of. I haven't offered you a cup of tea. Look, Stephen's got everything he needs here.' She went to a cupboard by the side of the stove. It was stocked with blue and white striped china and underneath were fresh supplies of food. She busied herself boiling the kettle, chattering all the time. As she handed Rose a mug of tea she glanced out of the port hole behind her. 'Whoever's that in a wheelchair, being pushed over your property? Don't they know it's not a public right of way?'

Rose twisted round and saw Silas Hands pushing Michael across the yard.

'Hasn't Dan told you about Michael yet, Lissy?' She could see from Lissa's blank expression that he hadn't, so in carefully measured tones she told her about her brother's accident and about Silas Hands being paid to nurse him.

When she had finished Lissa took both her hands in hers. 'It's not fair, is it, Rose?' she said, her face full of pain. 'You've had nothing but misery ever since you arrived at Dowlands' Mill.'

'It's funny you should say that,' Rose said, a little half smile playing round her lips. 'My sister said exactly the same thing, only this afternoon. I suppose it's true, in a way.'

'Why don't you leave, Rose? You could come and live with Stephen and me.'

Rose burst out laughing. 'Indeed I never could. How do you think I'd feel, playing gooseberry to you two love birds?'

Lissa flushed. 'I suppose you're right.' She shook her head. 'But I'm sure you could find somewhere to go, couldn't you?'

'I expect I could. But I could never leave, Lissy.'

'Why on earth not. Remembering the way Michael treated you when I was here I can't imagine why you want to stay.'

'Can't you, Lissy?' Rose looked her straight in the eye. 'Can't you guess what keeps me here?'

For a moment Lissa looked blank. Then she breathed, 'My brother, Dan?'

Rose nodded. She said softly. 'We'd planned to go away together. To Norfolk, perhaps. Then the accident happened and trapped us both in our different ways. But at least we know we have each other. It helps.'

'I always said it was a pity you didn't marry Dan,' Lissa said. 'But now it's too late.'

'Yes. Now it's too late because I could never leave Michael. Not the way he is. And Dan can't leave the mill.'

'No, I suppose not. I'm sorry, Rosie.'

'You needn't be. As long as I have Dan I can cope.' She grinned. 'At least Michael can't knock me about now if he sees me talking to his brother.'

'And is that all you do, Rose? Talk?'

Rose blushed scarlet. 'No,' she admitted.

'I'm sorry. I shouldn't have asked. It's none of my business. But I'm glad for you, Rosie.' She took Rose's hand. 'You must be careful though, Rose. Michael might not be a threat but I wouldn't trust that Silas Hands any further than I could throw him.'

'And that wouldn't be far, in your present state,' Rose said with a laugh. 'But I know what you mean.' She glanced out of the port hole. 'I must go. If her ladyship knows you're here she'll raise the roof.' She hugged Lissa again.

'I'll keep your secret,' Lissa whispered. 'I'm glad you've trusted me enough to tell me.'

'Well, we've been through a lot together in our time, haven't we?' She went up the stairs to the deck. 'Don't forget. Write to me at Crick's Farm. And I'll write to you.'

'Maybe one day you and Dan will come and see us at our little house, Rose.'

'Maybe. One day.' Rose waved to her and hurried off the barge just as Eve came out of the back door to cross to the mill.

Chapter Twenty-Four

Eve and Rose came face to face halfway across the yard. But even before they met Eve had begun her tirade.

'Where have you been? I've been looking for you all afternoon.' She stopped and stared open-mouthed at Rose. 'What on earth do you think you've been doing? You're filthy and you look as if you've been pulled through a hedge backwards!' Her eyes travelled over Rose's head to the barge behind her and then back to Rose's face. 'I know where you've been! You've been on board that boat, haven't you?' she said triumphantly. 'And I don't need two guesses as to what you've been up to as well, you little slut. My word, you just wait till your husband hears about it. And he will, because I shall make it my business to tell him.'

Rose waited, her head on one side, till Eve was finally forced to stop and draw breath. Then she said, 'Your guess is quite wrong, Eve. If you must know I've spent the whole afternoon in the field, harvesting with my mother and sister.' She gave a sigh of contentment. 'It was hard, dusty work but oh, I really enjoyed myself. It was just wonderful to be able to spend time working in the sunshine with the others, laughing and talking and knowing that nobody was following behind me ready to complain about every move I made.' She lifted her chin. 'But you're right about one thing. I have been on board that boat, although not for the purpose your evil mind imagines. If you look at the name on the bow you'll see it's Stephen Joel's barge, *Perseverance*. I've been on board to see my sister-in-law. Lissa. Your daughter.' She shrugged her shoulders. 'You can tell Michael if you like. I can't imagine he'll be particularly interested.'

Eve's eyes narrowed, her face a picture of impotent fury. 'Lissa! You've been – she's here! How *dare* she set foot on my land, brazen hussy that she is.'

'She hasn't set foot on your land, Eve. She's on her husband's barge,' Rose pointed out, adding softly, 'She's seven months pregnant and so happy it brings tears to your eyes.'

'It won't bring tears to *my* eyes.' Eve pushed past her and strode towards the boat.

She had reached the foot of the gangplank when a voice behind her said politely, 'If it's me you're wanting to see, Mrs Dowland, I'm here, right behind you.'

Eve shot round and found herself looking at Stephen Joel. 'No, I was going to speak to *her*.' She jerked a thumb in the direction of the boat.

He took her arm. 'By all means. I'll willingly take you aboard. I'm sure my wife will be only too pleased to be reconciled with you, Mrs Dowland.' His grip tightened although his voice remained pleasant and polite. 'I'm sure that's what you have in mind, because I know you wouldn't want Lissy to be upset in her condition any more than I would. In fact, I wouldn't allow it, Mrs Dowland. You understand that, don't you?'

Eve shook her arm free. 'I've changed my mind. I've important things to do in the house.' She hurried back across the yard.

Sadly, Rose watched her go, suddenly sorry for her. She was a sad woman, so eaten up with stupid pride and hatred that there was no room left in her life for compassion and love. For Eve, love meant to possess and to dominate. She had never learned that love must be freely given, with no strings attached. She turned to Stephen.

'I'm sorry about that, Captain Joel. I'm afraid my mother-in-law ...' she stopped. There were no excuses for Eve's behaviour.

Stephen Joel's jaw was set as he stared after Eve. 'I won't hev my Lissy upset,' he said grimly. 'She insisted on comin' when she knew I was bound for Stavely Creek because she was desperate to see you, but I'll see it doesn't happen again. We'll be gone within the hour and I shan't bring her back here again.' His expression relaxed as he turned to Rose. 'But you'll be more than welcome at our little house any time you care to come, Mrs Dowland. I know nothing would please Lissy more than to show you our home. And anything that makes her happy makes me happy.'

'Thank you, Captain Joel.' Rose smiled at him. 'If I may say so, Lissy's a lucky girl to have married you.' She turned as she sensed someone looking at her and saw Eve's face framed in the kitchen window. 'I must go before my mother-in-law starts throwing things,' she said with a rueful smile. 'Somebody's got to bear the brunt of her frustration.'

'I'm afraid it's my fault. I upset her,' Stephen said.

'It would have been even worse if she'd got aboard your boat. Then Lissy would have been upset, too.' She smiled at him again. 'But don't worry. We shall keep in touch. Lissy's going to write to me at my mother's address.' She went back across the yard to the house.

As she had expected the atmosphere in the mill kitchen was icy and the rest of the day was spent for the most part in frosty silence. Eve hardly spoke and answered in monosyllables when she was spoken to.

It didn't help that she had been looking forward to Michael eating with the family now that he could be wheeled to the table but this he flatly refused to do unless Silas was included.

'He looks after me better than any of you would. He's one of the family now. If I eat in the kitchen then so will he.' He argued his case quite reasonably. Silas had taken him for a long walk on the marsh and the fresh air, the salt tang from the river and the familiar surroundings had put him in a surprisingly good mood.

'I won't have that man at my table,' Eve hissed. 'He's little better than a tramp.'

'All right. If that's how you feel Rose can bring our supper in like she always does. Makes no difference to me where we eat.' As far as he was concerned the matter was closed.

But Eve wouldn't let it rest. 'Don't you want to join your family again? Don't you want a change from that pig sty of a room?'

'Not if it means Silas has to eat there on his own. He's a good bloke. He's done a lot for me and I won't have him shoved on one side and treated like a servant.'

'But he *is* a servant. I pay him to look after you, and that makes him a servant. Don't you realise that?'

'Well, you get your money's worth and more besides. That's all I've got to say.' He raised his voice. 'Silas!' he bawled. 'Come and take me away. I've had enough socialising for one day.' Silas came, reeking of the filthy weed they both smoked and wheeled him out of the kitchen and back up the hall to his room. 'And you needn't bother to come and sit with me tonight, Mother. I'm tired so I expect I shall go to sleep early.'

Eve's disappointment manifested itself in bitter complaint. All through the meal she kept up a monologue of the things she had done for Michael and his ingratitude towards her.

'I allowed my best dining room to be turned into a bedroom for him and what is it now? Nothing more than a better-class slum because he won't let anyone in to clean it and *that man* isn't capable of doing it. And I allowed *that man* to come and live here because that's what he wanted, although I live in mortal fear for my possessions and I make sure my bedroom door is locked at night.'

At this Dan caught Rose's eye and they both had difficulty in containing their laughter.

'I'm sure you're quite safe, Mother,' Dan said mildly when he could trust himself to speak. 'And you must admit Silas is clean now. He washes himself under the pump every morning and his clothes are respectable, even if they aren't quite what you'd like him to wear.'

Eve screwed up her face in disgust. 'I should think not. Those moleskin trousers! And that cap! It wouldn't be so bad if he hadn't taken to wearing it back to front. It makes him look as if his head is joined on to his shoulders and he hasn't got a neck at all.'

'The poor man can't help it if he's got a slight deformity,' Rose said.

'It makes him look shifty.' Eve pushed her plate away, her shepherd's pie half eaten. 'And another thing. That wheelchair cost me a lot of money. I bought it so that Michael could spend some time with his family.'

'Then you bought it for the wrong reason,' Dan pointed out. 'The wheelchair should be for Mike's benefit, not yours.'

She shrugged. 'Well, of course, I meant that as well.' She

turned her attack to Rose. 'It doesn't seem to bother you that Michael spends all his time with *that man.*'

'No, it doesn't. I'm glad he's got Silas and if you think back to the way he used to treat me you won't be surprised. Silas doesn't mind being sworn at, he gives as good as he gets. And if they choose to live in a pig sty, then it saves me the trouble of cleaning the room.'

'That's no way for a woman to speak of her husband. You married him for better or worse ...'

'Well, I had plenty of "worse" and now it's a bit better, so I'm not complaining.'

'You're *glad* Michael's a cripple. You're *glad* he had that accident!'

'Oh, Mother, don't be ridiculous. Of course Rose isn't glad,' Dan said with a trace of exasperation. He got up and went round to her and put his arm round her. 'You're over-wrought. Why don't you go up to bed? Rose will bring you some warm milk. Things will look better in the morning.'

Stiffly, Eve got to her feet. 'Yes, I am a little tired,' she admitted. 'I'm sure nobody realises how much worry I live with, what with the mill, and Michael's accident, then George refusing to come home ...'

'George might not even know he's needed here,' Dan pointed out.

'He must have seen the notices in the newspapers. No, I can only think he's deliberately staying away.' She took out her handkerchief and blew her nose. 'Oh, it's all too much. I'm too old for all this worry.'

She left the room and they heard her making her way slowly up the stairs.

'I'll give her a few minutes, then I'll take her this milk,' Rose said, going over to the stove and putting the saucepan on the hob.

'You can give me a few minutes first.' Dan pulled her to her feet and put his arms round her. 'I don't know how I've kept my hands off you all day,' he murmured next to her mouth. 'It may have been a mistake, letting me come and make love to you last night. It's made me want more.'

She wound her hands round his neck. 'I want more, too, Dan. But we must be careful. If Eve were to find out she'd turn me out of the house. Oh!' She wrenched herself free just in time to rescue the milk from boiling over.

He gave her a last kiss. 'I've got to go over and close the mill up. I left in a hurry when supper was ready.' He looked down at her. 'But I won't say goodnight until later. All right?'

She nodded and smiled at him. 'Oh, yes, Dan. It's very all right.'

Eve was sitting up in bed. Even her bed jacket matched the blue and cream decor of the room and had tiny blue bows at the neck and wrists. But Eve herself looked haggard and Rose suspected she had been crying.

'Put the milk on the table there,' Eve pointed to the bedside cabinet that held the small oil lamp she kept burning all night and her bible. Rose noticed that she was still wearing her rings and they had twisted round on her thin fingers as if the stones were too heavy. 'Thank you. Now come and sit on the bed.' She patted the bed cover.

Puzzled, Rose did as she was told.

'You think I'm a bad tempered, ungrateful old woman, don't you?' Eve said, giving her a piercing stare that demanded a truthful answer.

'I sometimes think you're a bit hard,' Rose answered.

'And so would you be if you'd led the life I've led. Things have come easily to you. You're very lucky, Rose.' She picked up the mug of milk and took several sips. 'Ah, this is nice. Did you put whisky in it?'

Rose nodded. 'I thought you needed it. It will help you sleep.'

'Thank you. You're very kind.' She cradled the mug between her hands. 'Although I don't know why you should be kind to me. I know I'm not very kind to you at times.'

Rose gave a shrug and made a sound that was neither affirming nor denying Eve's statement.

Eve appeared not to have noticed and went on, 'I couldn't expect you to understand. You've come from a loving family. And Michael married you for love – Oh,' she waved her hand, 'I realise something went wrong between you, but he married you because he wanted to, not because he had to, so he must have loved you once.' She sighed. 'It must be a wonderful thing to be loved. Really loved. It's something I've never known.'

She plucked nervously at the blue and cream bed cover. 'I don't know just how much Old Jacob told you about me ...?' She looked up questioningly.

'He told me all he knew. He'd worked at the farm your mother came to after you were born when he was a lad,' Rose answered. This was not the time for prevarication.

She nodded. 'I thought as much. I thought I recognised him. But what he probably didn't know was that my mother was raped repeatedly by the son of the house where she was formerly employed as parlour maid. Naturally, when it was discovered she was pregnant she was dismissed. Oh, she'd tried everything she could to get rid of me, she told me that herself. She left me in no doubt that I had blighted her life. Yet she made sure I had an education; in fact she taught me to read and write herself.' Her mouth twisted. 'You could say she beat the three R's into me because she didn't spare the rod. I didn't have a happy childhood. I cried myself to sleep every night because nobody loved me.'

She took another drink and a deep breath. 'But gradually I convinced myself that I didn't care. I learned to look after myself and not to worry about what other people thought of me. When I was old enough I went into service. I had several positions before I came to work for the Dowlands but when I came here I knew this was what I wanted. A beautiful house and a prosperous mill. I was determined to stay. And to make sure I would never have to leave I set about it the only way I knew.

'George Dowland was an only son. He'd been spoiled and pampered all his life, but he was a kind man and I was fond enough of him even though he lacked backbone. And when I got pregnant he did the right thing by me – as I knew from the start he would, I wouldn't have risked it otherwise – against the wishes of his parents. But I knew he didn't love me. He married me because he had, as he put it, "shamed" me. But he was a good man and he treated me well. Better than I deserved. As you know I bore him three sons. They all respected me, but I would hardly claim they loved me. Then Melissa was born. My husband idolised her, the child that nearly cost me my life, and I hated her because she enjoyed the affection my husband had never felt for me.'

'Maybe if you'd loved her ...' Rose ventured.

Eve shook her head. 'By the time she was born I think I was incapable of loving anyone. The most I've been able to command in my life is a certain amount of respect. And not much of that, I suspect.' She finished her milk and handed the mug to Rose, staring at her with an almost puzzled expression on her face. 'I don't know why I've said all that to you, Rose. I'm not in the habit of confiding in anyone, let alone ...' she didn't finish the sentence.

'I expect it's because you're tired and a bit disappointed,' Rose said. She leaned over and gently kissed Eve's cheek. 'Sleep well.'

Eve's eyes were half closed. She put her hand up to the spot Rose's lips had touched. Then her eyes fluttered open. 'You won't tell anyone what I've said, Rose?'

Rose shook her head. 'No, I won't tell anyone.' She went out of the room and quietly closed the door.

It was past midnight when at last Dan crept to Rose's bed. As she had lain waiting for him, knowing that he would eventually come, she went over her conversation with Eve. It explained so much and she could only hope that confessing would be Eve's first step to opening her own heart and letting love swallow her pride.

She heard the door open and held out her arms as Dan slid into bed. He was tired. Running the mill single-handed was beginning to take its toll. She held him close, savouring the familiar mill aroma that always clung to him. She was content. As long as she could go to sleep each night holding him like this, whether it be sleepy from love-making or weary from the days' work, she knew she could cope with anything that happened during daylight hours.

Eve soon began to notice the difference in her, how she sang about her work, how she refused to be ruffled, and how patient she was with Michael's harsh words to her. She even mentioned it to Dan.

'I'm afraid Michael must have been more cruel to Rose than we realised before his accident,' Eve remarked. 'Have you noticed how much happier she seems these days? I'm sure it's because she's no longer afraid of him.'

Dan was washing his hands and he kept his back to his

mother as he dried them. 'No,' he lied, 'I can't say I've noticed any difference in her.'

'Oh, yes. She sings about her work and she seems to have boundless energy. She's even been helping you in your garden, hasn't she?'

'Yes. She says she likes being in the open air and I can do with a hand. I haven't had much time for gardening since Michael's accident. Mind you, I'm planning on getting him back to work before long. If I make a few adjustments he'll be able to keep an eye on things when we're milling and apart from helping me it'll do him good to feel useful again.' He sat down at the table, yawning. 'Anyway, we'll see what happens.' He looked round. 'Where is Rose, by the way?' he asked innocently, as if he didn't already know.

'Gone to her mother's. She seems to spend more time there than she does here, if you ask me.'

'She only goes once a week. You can't grudge her that. Ah, here she is now.' He smiled at her as she came in the door. 'Did you have a good afternoon, Rose?'

'Yes, thank you. My sister was there with little Billy. He's becoming quite a handful now he can crawl about.' She took off her hat and coat and tied on her pinafore. 'The dinner's all in the oven. I'll have it dished up in no time.'

'There's no hurry. You're only ten minutes late,' Eve said. A new, more relaxed relationship had grown between the two women lately.

'Speak for yourself, Mother. My stomach's flapping against my back bone,' Dan said with a grin.

Rose laughed. 'If you're that hungry you could have been dishing it up yourself.'

'I'll give you a hand, anyway.' Dan came over to the stove.

'Lissa's got a little girl. They're calling her Rose, after me,' she whispered, unable to contain herself. 'Born last Thursday. The letter was waiting when I arrived at Mum's.'

'What are you two whispering about?' Eve demanded.

'We're not whispering. I was telling Dan to hold the pan steady. He's all fingers and thumbs,' Rose said over her shoulder. Then to Dan, 'Do you think I should tell her?'

He nodded. 'But wait till I'm not here. She might take it better.'

303

After the meal Dan winked at Rose. 'I'll just go and collect Mike and Silas's tray and then I've got to go and shut the chickens up,' he said. 'I shan't be long.'

When he had gone Rose began to clear the table. 'I went to my mother's this afternoon,' she began.

Eve got up and began to help her. 'I know that, dear. Is she well?'

'Yes, thank you.' She turned and leaned against the table. 'Lissa has been writing to me at my mother's house.' She watched her mother-in-law's face. Her expression changed from jealous fury to pain. Then, with an effort, she composed her features and smiled. 'I didn't know that. And how is she?'

Rose didn't take her eyes off Eve's face. 'She has a little daughter. Born last Thursday.'

Eve caught her breath. 'October the nineteenth. That's my wedding anniversary.' She didn't speak for a long minute, obviously struggling against tears. Finally she looked up at Rose. 'Are they both well?'

'Yes. Lissa and Stephen are calling her Rose, after me.'

Eve nodded. 'That doesn't surprise me.' She resumed gathering the plates up.

'Eve?'

'Yes?'

'Do you think you could bring yourself to write to her?'

Eve pursed her lips as she carried the plates over to the draining board.

'Somebody's got to make the first move,' Rose said gently. 'And Lissa would be so happy if it was you. I know she'd love you to see your little granddaughter.'

'My granddaughter.' Eve's expression softened. She turned and looked at Rose. 'You'll never know how much I was looking forward to your baby, Rose. I was so disappointed when you lost it. I thought a grandchild might love me, even if nobody else did ...'

'Well, now you have a grandchild to love you. And for you to love.'

Eve nodded. 'I'll write to Lissa.' She hesitated. 'I still have my children's christening robe upstairs. I made it myself. It's all broderie anglaise. Do you think she might like it for her little Rose, Rose?'

Rose's eyes filled with tears at Eve's pathetic eagerness.

'I'm sure she would, Eve.'

Eve had gone to bed when Dan came back. He kissed Rose and drew her down by his side on the settle by the fire.

'I love this time of day when there's only you and me,' he said softly into her hair.

'We should be careful. One of these days Silas will come past that window on his way from the marsh.' She giggled. 'Then we'll have blackmail on our hands.'

'He doesn't go to the marsh. He goes to the pub.' He began to kiss her thoroughly.

'Sometimes he goes to the marsh. Perhaps we should go to bed,' she murmured.

'Yes. In a minute. What did the Matriarch say about Lissa?' He nuzzled her neck, not really interested in the answer to his question.

'She's going to look out the family christening gown for her.'

He shot up. 'What?'

Rose nodded, her eyes shining. 'Yes. But first she's going to write to her. Your mother's mellowing, Dan.'

'It's all your doing, you minx.' He began to fumble with her buttons.

She caught his hand. 'Not down here, Dan. We agreed we wouldn't. In fact, we agreed we'd save all this for my bedroom.'

He gave a groan. 'I know. But I can't keep my hands off you.'

She nibbled his ear. 'I'm pregnant,' she whispered.

His head shot up. 'What did you say?'

She smiled at him. 'I'm pregnant, Dan. I'm having your child.'

He stared at her open-mouthed without speaking.

'But what else did you expect?' She gave a little giggle at his expression. 'You've hardly missed a night coming to my bed for the past two months and more.'

He shook his head, quite out of his depth. 'I don't know. I suppose I thought after you lost the baby there wouldn't be any more.' He gave a helpless shrug. 'I don't know much about these things, Rose. If I'd realised . . . ' He gathered her into his arms. 'Oh, my love, I'm sorry.' He passed his hand over his face. 'God, what a mess!'

She took his hand. 'Don't spoil it, Dan.'

He frowned. 'What do you mean?'

'Don't spoil it. I know there'll be awful trouble when Michael finds out. And your mother, too. But just now, let's pretend it's all right.' She put his hand on her flat stomach. 'It's our baby in there, Dan. Yours and mine. Conceived in love. Nothing can alter that. For the moment it's our secret and for a few more weeks it can stay that way. Not that I want it to be a secret. I'm so happy I want to shout it from the rooftops.'

'Rose. You don't know what you're saying,' he protested. 'You're my brother's wife, even though it's only in name now. Think of the scandal! God, what are we going to do!'

She turned up his hand and kissed the palm. 'We're not going to do anything for a few weeks. For the moment let's just be happy about our baby. Yours and mine.'

He stroked her hair with his free hand. 'Oh, Rosie, if only it was as simple as that. But it isn't you know. It isn't.'

Chapter Twenty-Five

In spite of Dan's misgivings, which she knew to be entirely justified, Rose couldn't bring herself to worry about the future. She was carrying Dan's child under her heart and she wanted this child more than anything else in the world. She was in a state of blissful euphoria. For the moment nothing else mattered to her.

'You realise you'll have to go away, soon, darling,' Dan whispered one night as he put his hand on her swelling belly under the bedclothes. 'You've been lucky so far, nobody's noticed. But soon you won't be able to hide it.'

She put her hand over his. 'But I don't want to hide it, Dan. I want everybody to know.'

'Even your husband? Oh, God, Rose. You can't know what you're saying,' he said in exasperation. 'Mike's my brother, for heaven's sake. And you're his wife. Sometimes I feel so guilty I can hardly face him, knowing what I'm doing behind his back. But I can't help myself, God help me. I love you so much.' He buried his face in her neck.

She stroked his hair. 'I've thought about it, Dan,' she said calmly. 'I've worked it all out. I'll go and stay with my mother. She'll look after me until you can find somewhere for us to be together.'

He was silent. He knew he could never leave the mill while his ageing mother and crippled brother needed him. He knew he was tied to it as surely as if it was a prison with iron bars. He knew, too, that they must never find out that Rose was carrying his child. But she would have to go further away than Crick's Farm to keep that secret from them. And she would have to go alone. But how could he say all this to her? How could he ruin her naive happiness? He stared up into the darkness. He loved Rose but what they had done was wrong and had to be paid for. He feared the price would be dear.

That night there was a storm. The rain lashed the windows with icy needles and the wind rocked the very house.

Dan got out of bed. 'I must go and check the brake on the water wheel. The tides are high because it's spring so the water will come through at a rate. If the wheel starts to turn the friction could send the whole mill up in flames.'

There was a flash of lightning followed by a thunderclap. Rose followed him. 'I must go to Eve. She's terrified of storms.'

They reached the bedroom door just as Eve's door opened and she appeared, a shawl thrown hurriedly round her shoulders.

Dan muttered something about 'just come to see that Rose was all right'.

Eve nodded. 'And now you're going to check the brake on the wheel, aren't you?' She spoke calmly but her knuckles clutching the shawl were white.

'That's right.' He escaped down the stairs, to put on oilskins over his night shirt and do battle with the storm.

'Come into my room with me,' Eve said, grabbing Rose's hand. 'You know I can't bear storms.'

Rose followed her. She wasn't sure whether Eve had been taken in by Dan's lie so she didn't quite know what to say.

'You might as well get in beside me,' Eve said, climbing back into bed. 'There's plenty of room and you don't want to take cold.'

She hesitated. 'Wouldn't you like me to make you a cup of tea?'

Eve grabbed her hand again. 'No. You mustn't leave me. You know how I hate the thunder.' She ducked her head as the room was lit by a flash of blue lightning. 'Oh, quickly, throw this shawl over the mirror before you get into bed. And light the candle, then the lightning won't seem so bright.'

Rose did as Eve asked and then climbed in beside her. The bed was warm and soft and very comfortable.

'When's the baby due?' Eve asked, cringing at yet another vicious clap of thunder.

Rose stared at her. 'I ...'

Eve smiled. 'Do you think I hadn't guessed, Rose? Do you think I didn't know Dan came to your room every night? I'm a very light sleeper, you know.'

Rose covered her face with her hands. 'Oh, God. Whatever must you think of us?'

Eve was silent for several minutes. Then she said, 'It may be wicked of me, but I can't find it in my heart to blame you for what you've done, Rose. Of course it's wrong because you're married to Michael, but to his shame he's treated you so badly ...' She shook her head, then went on, 'I know Dan loves you, in fact I guess I've known it longer than he has. It's quite plain that you're right for each other.' She sighed. 'But that doesn't alter the fact that you're in a predicament, does it? When did you say the baby was due?'

'I didn't. But it's next summer. About June, I think. Michael told me today I was getting fat.'

Eve put her hand over Rose's. 'I'll do all I can to help you. I've already thought it out. You'll have to go away, of course. We'll say you're ill and have to rest. You can have the baby and get it adopted and when you come back nobody will be any the wiser. But you and Dan will have to be much more careful in future,' she added sternly.

Rose couldn't believe her ears. Eve wasn't even shocked at what she and Dan were doing. And from her last words she wouldn't object to it continuing in the future.

'Perhaps you could go and stay with Lissa,' Eve continued. 'Just until the baby's born. She'd like that, I'm sure.'

'I don't want my baby adopted,' Rose said desperately. 'It belongs to Dan and me. I couldn't bear someone else to have it.'

Eve sighed again. 'Everything has a price, my dear. And I'm afraid this is the price you'll have to pay.'

'It's too high,' Rose moaned. 'I can't do it.'

'You have no choice, Rose. You are a married woman. Think of the scandal.' Eve's voice hardened. 'I'll support you in all you do, Rose, as long as you are discreet and there is no breath of scandal.' She leaned over and kissed her daughter-in-law.

'It's hard, I know, child, but in years to come you'll see it was all for the best. We'll start to make arrangements tomorrow. The sooner you go away the better. I shall miss you, dear.'

Rose crept back to her own bed and cried herself to sleep. Eve had been surprisingly accepting and generous but Rose wasn't sure she could accept the terms.

The next morning was clear and bright but everywhere there was evidence of the ravages of the storm. Trees had fallen and blocked the lane and the rate of the water rushing through the mill stream had blocked the wheel with all manner of detritus.

'I shall have to get down there and unblock it,' Dan said at breakfast.

'Mind you don't get swept away,' Eve said anxiously. 'I daresay the water's still going through there at a good rate.'

'I've got weights to tie on my feet. It's what I always do.' He got up from the table. 'I'd better get on with it.' He was clearly uncomfortable in his mother's presence. He hadn't returned to Rose's bed the previous night so she had had no opportunity of repeating his mother's conversation to him as yet.

After he'd gone, Rose took Michael and Silas their breakfast. The room was blue with stale tobacco smoke as usual. This was the only thing that turned her stomach now that she was pregnant and she tried to hold her breath so that she didn't gag every time she went into the room.

'I'll ask her,' Michael was saying to Silas as she walked in.

'Ask me what?' she said, speaking quickly.

'Not you, mawther. The Matriarch. I'm going to ask her to buy me a motor car.' He was gleeful and Rose suspected he had already been at the bottle. 'She'll be so glad last night's storm has gone she'll say yes to anything.'

'I wouldn't be too sure about that. Anyway, you won't be able to drive it.' She stood near the door so that she could take deep draughts of fresh air.

'Silas can learn. He'll drive me.'

'Motor cars cost a lot of money. I can't see Eve agreeing to it.'

'You don't know anything about it. Anyway, it's nothing to do with you. Go and get your breakfast. And don't eat too much. I

310

told you before. You're getting fat.' Michael roared with laughter and his laugh turned into a hacking smoker's cough.

She hurried out of the room and down the hall to the kitchen, fear fluttering in her breast. Eve and Dan were right. The baby was beginning to show. Something would have to be done. And soon.

'Is Dan back?' she asked when she got there.

'No.' Eve looked a little worried. 'Put your coat on and go and see how he's getting on, will you, Rose? Michael always used to stand by when Dan cleared the wheel. Somebody ought to be there in case anything goes wrong.'

Rose hurried across the yard, putting on her coat as she went. *Patience* was just tying up at the jetty and she gave Jim Barnes a wave.

'Rough owd night, Missus,' he called. 'But a lovely marnin'.'

When she reached the mill bridge she could see why Eve had been anxious. Even though Dan was wearing thigh boots the water reached nearly to the top of them and she knew that without the weights on his feet he would be swept away by the fast running stream. As she stared down into the swirling water the dreadful cold premonition of evil was so strong that it seemed to wrap her in a cold, clammy cloak. She glanced fearfully over her shoulder. But the mill pool was calm and peaceful. Almost, it seemed, deceptively so. She shuddered and trying to restore a sense of normality called to Dan, 'Have you nearly finished?'

'Yes. I've cleared most of the rubbish away. Oh, my Christ!' he was staring at something in the water. Suddenly he looked up, his face drained of all its colour. 'Go back to the house, Rose.'

She leaned over the hand rail. 'Why? What have you found, Dan? What is it? It looks like an old football.'

He waved her away. 'I said go away, Rose. Go back to the house.' He waded to the bank but his back was to her so she couldn't see what he was holding. He half turned. '*Go back to the house, Rose. For God's sake, do as I say!*' He waited, watching to make sure she obeyed.

Bewildered, she went back to the house. She couldn't see why he should make such a fuss over an old football.

'Did he clear the wheel?' Eve asked as she walked in.

311

'Yes. There was a lot of rubbish, including an old football. How on earth do you reckon that could have got there?' Rose said.

'There's no telling. Once they found the remains of an old armchair, you know, all the stuffing and springs and things, when they cleared the wheel. Goodness knows how that got there, either. I think people must use the mill pool as a dumping ground late at night when nobody's about.'

Dan came in at half-past twelve for his lunch but he didn't stay long. Rose realised it was because he was still wary of his mother's reaction to seeing him come out of her bedroom.

'Will you be in the mill this afternoon?' she asked, looking for an opportunity to speak to him about it.

'No, there's something else I've got to see to. Jim Barnes is going to give me a hand. You stay indoors. It's bitterly cold out there.' He went off.

'I expect it's to do with the wheel. Sometimes the paddles need attention and it's a two-handed job,' Eve said. She rubbed her hands together. 'But bitterly cold or not, I must go over to the mill and do the books this afternoon. I've neglected them rather, lately.'

'I could help you, if you like. I used to do my father's accounts,' Rose said eagerly.

Eve hesitated. 'Yes. When ... after you've ...' she hesitated, and came up with the euphemism '... been away, I should be very glad for you to take over.' She smiled. 'But not today, it's too cold. You stay here by the fire.'

Rose didn't argue. She was glad to be left by herself in case Dan came in. She washed up and then tackled the pile of ironing. She wished he would come. She wanted to ask him about what he'd found caught up in the mill wheel but even more than that she wanted to tell him what Eve's amazing reaction to their love affair had been. But he didn't come and at four o'clock she lit the lamp and began preparations for supper.

'Rose! Where are you, damn you? Rose! Come here. I want you.'

The noise of Michael's voice bellowing down the hall, breaking the silence, made her start.

She hurried along to his room, wondering what on earth could be the matter.

He was sitting impatiently in his wheelchair, banging his hands on the arms. 'I want to see the Matriarch. Take me out to the kitchen,' he said, without so much as a please or thank you.

'She isn't there. She's over at the mill.'

'Then take me over to the mill, damn you. God, how I hate this bloody chair.' He looked up at her, his face flushed with drink. 'Come on, look lively.'

'It's heavy. I don't know if I can manage it. Where's Silas?'

'Gone out. Of course you can manage it. Look out, woman! You nearly pushed me into the door.'

'Well, I'm not used to it, am I?' Carefully, she manoeuvred the chair out of the room and across the hall. 'Wait a minute. It's cold out there. I need a coat and you need a blanket round your legs.'

'Well, hurry up, then.' He drummed his fingers impatiently while he waited.

'What's your hurry?' she asked breathlessly, as she pushed the heavy wheelchair over the cobbles to the mill.

'Never you mind. Just get me over there.'

She got him through the mill door and manoeuvred him in the gloom through to the office in the far corner, where Eve had lit the oil lamp when it began to get dark.

'I don't know why the hell you don't have gas laid on,' he grumbled instead of a greeting. He jerked his thumb back at Rose. 'She nearly pushed me into a bloody beam out there because she couldn't see where she was going. And it isn't as if you can't afford it.'

'You don't know what I can and can't afford, Michael,' Eve replied without looking up. She laid down her pen and straightened some of the papers that littered the desk. 'But what brings you over here? Oh, I don't need to ask, I suppose you want something. And where's *that man*? Rose shouldn't be pushing that heavy chair,' she stopped herself in time from adding 'in her condition'.

'Silas is out. And it won't hurt her to do a bit for me now and again. She's still my wife.'

Eve leaned back in her chair and sighed. 'So what is it you want, Michael?'

'I want a motor car.'

'*You want what?*' Her voice was nearly a shriek.

'You heard. I want a motor car. Silas can drive it. I'm fed up with only being able to get as far as the marsh. In a motor car I could go all over the place. You could come too, sometimes,' he added as something of a carrot.

'You must be out of your mind.' She picked up her pen again. 'Where do you think I'm going to find the money for a motor car?'

'You've got plenty of money. You must have. You never spend any,' he replied rudely. When he saw that wasn't going to work he sighed and tried another tack. 'Don't you think I deserve it, Mother? Just think. I'll never walk again. I'm tied to this chair, a cripple. My legs are useless.' His voice had taken on a whining tone.

'I know all that. And I'm sorry, Michael, desperately sorry. You're my son. Don't you think I'd do anything in the world to have you back on your feet again? But Dr Holmes and the specialist both say there's nothing to be done so we must accept it.'

'A motor car would make my life more bearable.'

'I've told you, I can't afford . . .' the words froze on her lips as Dan burst into the office with Jim Barnes right behind him. They were both wet, dirty and dishevelled.

'I've found him. Oh, God, we've found brother George!' Dan cried.

'Oh, thank God.' Eve's face lit up and her shoulders sagged with relief. 'I knew he'd come home one day.'

Dan shook his head. 'No, Mother. I don't think you quite understand. George hasn't come back. It's his body we've found.'

She put her hand to her throat. 'His *body!*'

He nodded, his face agonised. 'It was in the mill pond, weighted down with chains.'

'But how . . . ? I don't understand.' Eve looked from Dan to Michael and back again.

'Neither do I. He's talking rubbish, if you ask me.' Michael shrugged his shoulders. 'I'm cold. I want to go back to the house. Push me back, Rose.'

'No, Michael. I think you should stay and hear what Dan

314

has to say. After all, George is ... was your brother, too.' Eve turned back to Dan. 'Explain, Daniel.'

'When I cleared the mill wheel this morning I found something ...' he closed his eyes, 'You don't want me to go into detail, do you?'

'Of course,' Eve's voice was cold.

'Very well. I found a skull. That was what was blocking the wheel. It was unrecognisable, of course, but I knew it could only have come from the mill pool so I fetched Jim from his boat and we've spent the afternoon dragging for the rest of the body. We found it, or what there was left of it, weighted down with chains.'

'That's what's been haunting the bridge! I knew something terrible was there,' Rose cried, clapping her hand to her mouth.

'But what makes you think it's George?' Michael asked, ignoring her.

'I recognised his coat. It was still fairly intact, and so were his boots. You know how he always wore those long leather boots, you couldn't mistake them. Oh, there's no doubt it's George. Anyway, the police will find out for sure.' Dan was watching Michael as he spoke and he saw the flicker of alarm that crossed his face. 'I'm going to fetch them now, but I thought I ought to tell you all first.' He turned to leave the office.

'No. Wait a minute.' It was Michael. He was frowning, trying to concentrate his drink-fuddled brain. 'Surely, there's no need to involve the police, Dan. After all, if George accidentally fell into the pool when he was drunk we don't want the whole world to know, do we?'

'Whether he was drunk or sober he'd hardly have weighted his own body down with chains before he fell in,' Dan pointed out. 'No, Mike. George didn't fall in. He was murdered. It's as plain as a pike staff. He was murdered and then thrown in the mill pool.'

'Do you think it could have anything to do with that body I saw on the marsh that night, Michael?' Rose turned to her husband. 'I know you said it wasn't a body at all, but perhaps you were mistaken. Perhaps it was George's body.' Rose clapped her hands over her mouth in horror at the very thought.

'Don't be so bloody daft. Of course it wasn't. There wasn't a body that night, it was your imagination. I told you that at the time. I even went out with Dr Holmes to look for it but of course we never found anything because there was nothing there.' There was a strange, wild gleam in Michael's eye as he spoke.

'I suppose you could have led him in the wrong direction,' Dan said carefully.

'Why should I do that?'

'If you'd killed George you'd have every reason. And it wouldn't be beyond belief. Everyone knew you hated him. You were as jealous as hell of him.'

'*Daniel!* Do you realise what you're saying?' Eve said, shocked to the core.

Michael ignored her. 'Well, it's true. He got my goat, lazy bloody drunk that he was. But I didn't wish him dead.'

'Then who did?'

Michael shrugged. 'How should I know?'

'But you think someone might have done?' Eve said quietly. 'And Rose did see a body that night?'

Michael gave another non-committal shrug.

'I think she did. And I think you disposed of it, Mike,' Dan said.

There was a long silence. All eyes were on Michael. At last he said, 'Well, I couldn't just leave it there, could I?'

'You should have called the police. You don't go around disposing of dead bodies, unless ...'

'But wait a minute. Whoever it was, that body couldn't have been George,' Rose broke in. 'Because you saw him, didn't you, Michael? The day we got engaged. Don't you remember? You ran after him and he told you he'd got married and taken a pub just outside Ipswich.'

'That's right.' Michael smiled at Rose. 'Fancy you remembering that.' He took out a handkerchief and mopped his brow. 'Whew, it's hot in here.'

Dan shook his head. 'No. I reckon that was just a pack of lies to cover your tracks, Mike. After all, nobody else saw him. And I've always thought that was a bit strange, because George wouldn't have disappeared quite so completely if he'd taken a pub. *Somebody* would have known where he was. No,

316

you killed George, didn't you, Mike? It had to be you, otherwise you'd have reported it when you found his body on the marsh. I reckon the way it happened was that you saw him walking home across the marsh after his drinking spree in Ipswich and you were so furious that you hit him.'

'As you seem to know so much about the way it was done, perhaps it was you that did it,' Michael sneered.

'I was in Ipswich, remember? Looking for George. Or, to be more precise, I'd nipped over to see Granny Dowland and was whitewashing her kitchen.' Dan shook his head. 'Maybe you didn't intend to kill George, Mike, maybe you had an argument and got into a fight with him but that's what happened. Of course you couldn't do much about disposing of the body in broad daylight but you knew it was safe where it was, nobody was likely to come along that part of the sea wall and find it. After dark you intended to go back and dispose of it properly. But then Rose appeared and ruined everything, because she'd seen the body lying in the gully. Am I right?'

Michael's eyes swivelled in turn to each of the three faces watching him. More than anything he reminded Rose of a rat she had once seen trapped in the corner of the barn while her father advanced on it with a cudgel. Finally, his gaze rested on Dan and his face crumpled.

'I didn't mean to kill him,' he whimpered. 'But when I saw him reeling back along the sea wall, knowing what a fuss of him the Matriarch would make, I went up and told him what I thought of him. He lunged out at me and that made me so bloody mad I hit him back. I didn't mean to kill him, but I was so bloody furious I couldn't stop. I was thinking, if he never comes back I'll be the eldest and I'll be the one to inherit instead of this lazy bastard.'

There was a wild glint in his eye now and a tiny fleck of foam at the corner of his mouth. 'I did it for you as well as me, Dan,' he said desperately. 'I thought of all the things we could do ... install rollers ... have gas laid on, oh, I've got great plans for when *she's* gone, Dan.' He nodded briefly in his mother's direction. 'Even now, if you keep your mouth shut you and me can really go places with this mill.'

He looked from one face to another until his eyes rested on Rose.

His lip curled. '*She's* the one who fouled things up,' he said. 'That stupid bitch. I'd got it all planned. I was just going back to dispose of his body ...'

'How?' Dan's eyes had never left his brother's face.

'I was going to take it out in my boat and dump it overboard. There's a deep hole just off the point. It's in deep water so no one would ever have found it. But then *she* came crawling along the wall, blabbering about having seen a body and I knew I didn't have time so I had to go and fetch it and throw it in the mill pond before I went for the doctor. I said I'd been a long time because I'd had a puncture ...'

'Oh, Michael.' Eve's face was anguished.

Michael didn't appear to notice. He stared at Rose, then said vindictively, 'I knew she'd seen more than was good for her. But I thought about it a bit and realised that she wasn't bad looking so probably the best thing to do under the circumstances was to marry her. I wasn't all that keen, but I thought if I married her and anything should come out about George I'd be safe because a wife can't testify against her husband.'

'My God, you are a callous sod.' Jim Barnes said under his breath. He wished he'd stayed in Ipswich and not come down with the ebb, then he wouldn't have been involved with all this. He liked a bit of gossip but this was not to his taste at all.

'I thought you meant it when you said you loved me,' Rose whispered. She felt dirty; betrayed.

'Nah. As far as I was concerned love didn't come into it,' Michael said brutally. 'I married you in case I needed to save my own skin.'

'And it was a pack of lies when you said you'd seen George and his wife that day we went to Ipswich. The day we got engaged.' She put her head in her hands. 'And to think I was so happy that day! If only I'd known ...'

'Of course it was. I simply went round the corner and had a smoke. Then I came back and spun you that yarn.' Michael looked round at his audience. His trapped look had gone now and he appeared to be enjoying his own cunning. 'Well, that's how it happened. Now you all know. You can take me back to the house now, Rose. Chuck the body back, Dan. Nobody knows about it except us and if we see Jim all right he won't say anything ...'

318

Dan stared at his brother, a look of absolute incredulity on his face. 'You're out of your mind, Mike. I'm not throwing the body back. You killed our brother and you must take the consequences.'

'But I did it for you, Dan. For us. You're near enough an accessory,' Michael pleaded.

'I'm nothing of the kind. I'm handing you over to the police.' Dan's face was granite.

'But I'm a sick man. I'm a cripple,' Michael whined.

'Then I expect they'll let you go to the gallows in a wheelchair,' Dan said grimly. 'Jim, will you go and fetch Constable Fletcher? Take my bike, I daresay you can lift it over the trees that were blown down in the night. I'll stay here and keep an eye on things.'

'I'll be as quick as I can.' Jim hurried off, glad to get away.

Dan turned to Rose. 'Rose . . . ?'

But even as he turned to her she sank to the floor in a dead faint.

'Take her into the house, Dan. The smelling salts are on the dresser,' Eve commanded briskly. 'Poor sweet, I'm not surprised it's all been too much for her.'

Dan picked Rose up in his arms, then hesitated. 'Will you be all right here, Mother?' He nodded anxiously towards Michael.

She gave a tired ghost of a smile. 'Of course I shall. He's my son. And he's not going anywhere, is he?'

Chapter Twenty-Six

Dan carried Rose over to the house and laid her gently on the settle by the fire. The cold air had begun to revive her and the smelling salts did the rest. She sat up and put her hand up to her head.

'I can't believe it, Dan. I simply can't believe it,' she murmured.

'Neither can I, my darling, but I'm afraid it's all too true. Jim Barnes has gone for the police. I hated having to do it, Mike's my brother, when all's said and done. But there was no alternative.' He sat down beside her and put his arm round her. 'Are you feeling better now?'

She nodded. 'I'm sorry. It was stupid of me to faint like that.' She got to her feet and went over and pulled the kettle forward. 'I think we could all do with a cup of tea. Where's Eve?'

'She's over at the mill with Michael. Yes, I'm sure that's what we all need. You sit down, darling, I'll ... ' he cocked his ear. 'What was that? Did you hear a noise coming from Michael's room?'

'No, I don't think so. But if there was it was probably Silas.'

'Silas is out. Wait a minute, I'll go and see.'

He hurried through to Michael's room and Rose followed more slowly.

'God, this place is a mess,' he said as he opened the door. 'And it stinks.' Then, 'What the hell do you think you're doing?'

Silas was kneeling at the chest at the foot of Michael's bed. It was open and he was stuffing notes into his pocket. He got up as they walked in. 'Well, I'll bid you good day,' he said, and made to push past them.

'Hang on a minute,' Dan caught his arm. 'What have you got there?'

'No more than my dues. I helped Mike earn the money, and a risky enough business it was, too. He never did give me my proper share, so I'm takin' it now. I don't s'pose you'll want it, seein' as it's smugglin' money. An' it won't be any good to him, where he's goin'.'

'And where do you think he's going?' Dan still hadn't let go his arm although he kept trying to shake himself free.

Silas used his free hand to mime a noose round his neck. 'I saw what you an' Jim Barnes dragged outa the mill pond and I follered you in an' listened to what was said. I ain't surprised. Mike's got a fearful temper on him an' I knew he was hidin' somethin'.'

Rose was feeling faint again. She sat down on the edge of the bed and passed her hand across her face. 'Oh, let him go, Dan,' she said wearily. 'And let him take the money. We don't want it.' She looked down into the chest. 'Oh, I see.' Her face cleared. 'I didn't realise there was a false bottom in it and that was where Michael kept his money. No wonder I couldn't find anything when I looked.' She waved her hand towards Silas. 'Oh, take it. Take it all. I don't want it. Anyway, I guess you deserve it for looking after Michael.'

Silas stuffed his pockets and sidled towards the door. 'Thankee, Ma'am.' He touched his filthy old cap. 'An' you, Sir.' The front door slammed and he was gone.

'Are you sure you've done the right thing? That money was yours by rights, Rose.' Dan said.

'I'd rather beg for bread than touch a penny of it,' she said vehemently.

They went back to the kitchen, where the kettle singing on the hob was lending a touch of normality to a nightmare situation.

'I think you should go back to your mother and brother, Dan,' she said. 'I'll make the tea and bring it over.'

'But will you be all right now?' he asked anxiously.

She nodded. 'Yes. I'm fine. I'll be over in a few minutes.'

He opened the door. 'The moon is very bright tonight,' he said. Then, 'Oh, my God! Whatever's happening?'

*

After Dan had carried Rose from the mill Michael waited a few minutes, then leaned towards his mother.

'Good. Now they've gone you'll be able to help me, Mummy,' he said, reverting to his childhood use of her name. 'This is what you must do. You must push me out on to the marsh. That's where Silas has gone. He'll help me. He'll get me into the boat and take me away to somewhere where nobody knows me.'

'I can't push that chair, Michael, it's far too heavy for me,' Eve said, shaking her head.

'Don't be ridiculous, of course you can. I can help a bit. Look, I'll push the wheels a bit with my hands ...' He tried to push the wheels round but they wouldn't move.

Eve watched him quite dispassionately. 'No,' she said and her voice was weary. 'I won't help you. You've got to be a man and take the consequences of your evil deed, Michael. You were never an easy child,' she mused. 'You were the middle of the three boys and always felt you were missing out because you were neither the eldest, with the privileges that went with it, nor the youngest, to be spoiled as the Benjamin of the family. It wasn't true, of course. Your father and I loved you all equally, even if we didn't show it ...'

'Oh, stop drivelling on, woman, and do something to help me,' he interrupted rudely. 'If you won't push me yourself, then go and find Silas. He will.' He banged his fist on the arms of the wheelchair. 'Oh, this bloody, bloody contraption. Why can't I use my legs like other men! Go and get help, woman. This is a matter of life and death.'

'I know,' she nodded.

'Well, why are you sitting there so bloody calm, then, nodding your head like some damned puppet.' He threw himself back and forth in his chair, trying to make it move. When it wouldn't he leaned over and grasped his mother by the wrist. 'For the last time, are you going to help me, or have I got to kill you, too?'

'Oh, Michael, what good do you think that would do?' she asked sadly. 'It would only mean you being hanged for two murders instead of one. And let me go, please. You're hurting my wrist.'

'I shan't let you go.' He gave her wrist a jerk that made her

322

cry out and lunged towards her, trying to reach her other arm, but all he succeeded in doing was to knock the oil lamp to the floor with a crash that shattered the glass reservoir and splashed oil over the floor that immediately ignited.

For a long second they both watched, horrified, as the flames shot up, burning the papers on the desk and snaking along a trail of oil towards the door.

Then Michael screamed. 'Put it out, you silly bitch! Why don't you put it out!' at the same time flailing his arms to try to beat out the flames, which created a draught that only fanned them and spread them further. 'Don't you realise this mill's like a bloody tinder box? We'll be burned alive. Get me out of here.'

He was throwing himself about in his chair. The oil had splashed on to the blanket covering his legs, setting it alight. The flames had also spread to the leg of the desk. In a matter of minutes the whole mill, old, dusty and highly inflammable, would be alight.

Eve glanced towards the door. There was still time to escape. Whatever evil deeds he had done Michael was still her son, and she couldn't leave him to burn to death. She struggled to push the chair across the room, then went round it in order to get the door open.

'Oh, no you don't!' Terrified she was trying to escape without him he threw himself at her, overbalancing the wheelchair in his efforts to clutch her skirt.

'Oh, you stupid boy! Don't you realise I was trying to wheel you to safety?' She looked down at him, lying helpless on the floor as the flames shot through the open door and roared up the stairs.

'You'll have to drag me.' He choked, clutching at her dress and setting light to it with the flame from his coat.

'I'll try.' She began to pull at him ineffectually, choking with the smoke as the flames took hold of her dress. 'It's no good,' she panted. 'I can't move you. I can't breathe.' She sank to the floor.

He gave her no more than a passing glance and began to haul himself towards the door by his elbows, screaming with pain as the flames from his clothing seared his back. He didn't get far.

The flames from the mill could be seen from halfway up the lane as Jim Barnes and Constable Fletcher returned. The alarm was raised, but by the time the fallen trees had been removed and the fire engine arrived on the scene it was too late. Nothing of the mill could be saved. From the position of the two charred bodies it was only too clear how they had died.

After what seemed hours the police and firemen left.

They went back into the house and Rose bound up Dan's hands, burnt when he had tried to get into the mill to save his mother and brother. Then she helped him to change out of his smoke-blackened clothes.

'I couldn't get to them,' he kept repeating, shaking his head from side to side. 'I tried, but I couldn't reach them. The flames ...'

'I know.' Rose soothed, putting cream on his face, reddened by the heat. 'The police and firemen all said you could never have got into that inferno to save them.'

He was silent for a long time, then he got wearily to his feet. 'Oh, come on, Rose. Let's get away from this place. I'll take you to your mother's.'

Chad was in the piggery when the two shocked and exhausted figures arrived. He took one look at them and hurried them indoors, where Emma sat them down in the big, untidy, homely kitchen and made them all cocoa before they were allowed to tell their terrible tale.

'Do you think Michael started the fire on purpose?' Emma said, when they had finished their story.

Dan shook his head. 'No, I'm convinced Michael would never do that. He had such plans for it.'

'But how could he have plans, my boy?' Chad pointed out. 'Since he was about to be charged with murder.'

Dan's mouth twisted. 'Oh, I'm sure my brother never ever thought he would be convicted. He thought he bore a charmed life.'

They sat in silence for a long time, then Rose said, 'Poor Eve. I feel so sorry for her, dying like that. She'd had a loveless life, that was what made her how she was. But underneath the hard shell she was really very kind, you know. I was beginning to feel I knew her quite well because she'd talked to me about her past. Lissa will be sad, too. Things were getting so much better between them.'

'Did she know about your baby?' Emma asked innocently.

Rose looked up, surprised and blushing. Of course her mother would know. She always did.

'Yes.' She turned to Dan. 'Eve knew about it, Dan, even without me telling her.'

Dan groaned. 'Oh, dear.'

She stretched out her hand and laid it on his arm. 'But the wonderful thing was, she didn't judge us, Dan. She didn't blame us at all. In fact she'd already made plans in her mind for me to go away and have the baby and then come back.'

He raised his eyebrows. 'She didn't condemn us?'

'No. In fact, all she said was that we should have to be more careful in future.' She put her hand on her stomach protectively. 'The only thing was, she wanted me to have the baby adopted. I couldn't have done that.'

'It won't be necessary now, anyway, darling. We'll be married as soon as it can be arranged. Our baby won't be born outside wedlock, I promise you that.' He reached over and took her hand.

Chad cleared his throat loudly. 'I'm afraid you're overlooking one thing, my boy,' he said, shaking his head.

Dan flushed guiltily. 'Of course. We'll be married with your permission, Sir.'

'Oh, not that.' Chad waved his hand. 'If it were that easy you could be wed tomorrow.'

'Then what, Dad?' Rose asked with a frown.

'I'm afraid it's against the law,' he said with a sigh of regret. 'A man cannot marry his dead brother's widow.'

They were all silent for a long time. Then Rose said slowly. 'I never told you this, Mum, but Dan and I were planning to go away and live together anyway, until Michael had his accident. Then of course we couldn't leave. Well, now he's dead so we can.' She lifted her chin. 'And I'll be proud to go with Dan wherever he wants to go and to live with him as his wife.'

'God knows I couldn't blame you for that, my girl. Dan's more of a husband to you than Michael ever was,' Emma murmured.

Chad nodded. 'Sometimes the law is a bit heartless.

Nevertheless it is the law.' He smiled. 'However, it is an indisputable fact that you are Mr Dowland and Mrs Dowland, so your child can legally bear Dan's name, Rose.' He waited for this to sink in, then turned to Dan. 'I suppose it's too soon for you to have made any plans, my boy, but I know I speak for my wife as well as myself when I say you will both be more than welcome to stay here at Crick's Farm for as long as you like. Until the mill is rebuilt, perhaps. If that's what you intend to do.'

Dan shook his head. 'I don't think I could afford to do that. You see, it was never insured.' His mouth twisted. 'It was ironic. My mother wouldn't insure it because the premiums were too high, it being such a fire risk.' He spread his hands. 'Anyway, I'm not sure that I'd want to rebuild it. I never really wanted to be a miller. I always wanted to work on the land.'

'But you've still got the house, Dan,' Rose reminded him. 'That will be yours now, won't it?'

'Yes, but you wouldn't want to live there, Rose, would you?' He took her hand. 'It isn't exactly full of happy memories for you, is it?'

'No.' She bit her lip. 'Yet I remember how excited I was when I first went there. I thought it was such a beautiful house and I was so thrilled to be living there. But then so many bad things happened ...' She looked nostalgically round her mother's shabby kitchen.

'It wasn't the house, it was the people in it,' Emma said sagely. 'You and Dan could make it into a happy home. If that's what you want.'

'I don't want to. I want to farm. I've always wanted to farm,' Dan said firmly. 'I think we should sell the house and buy a farm.' He gave a wry smile. 'I guess there may be quite a bit of money, too. My mother never spent a lot, did she, Rose?'

'We didn't go short of food,' Rose said loyally. 'But no, she didn't spend a lot.'

Chad was silent for several minutes. Then he said, 'You may not think this is a very good idea under the circumstances, but if you're looking for a farm, this one's for sale.'

'Chad!' Emma admonished. 'You can't ... Think of the gossip!'

But Rose was smiling. 'Do you really mean that, Dad?'

326

'Indeed I do,' Chad answered. 'It would make me very happy if you and Dan took it over, because it would mean Crick's Farm would stay in the family. All I ask for it is enough for your mother and me to buy a little cottage with sufficient room for my books—'

'And my pottery,' Emma added, momentarily forgetting the gossips.

'Your pottery, Mum? But you don't know anything about pottery,' Rose laughed.

'Of course I don't. But that doesn't mean I haven't always wanted to learn.' Emma closed her eyes and gave a contented sigh. 'And now, after all these years, God willing I'll have time.' Her eyes snapped open again. 'But we're dreaming. It would be far better for you both to go away somewhere where you're not known. Where you'll be accepted as husband and wife. Anyway, Dan may have other ideas and it's not for us to impose ours on him.'

Dan looked round the big comfortable kitchen. There was so much he could do to it to make it better. The farm, too. He had often thought of all the improvements that could be made there. He smiled at Rose and took her hand. 'At the moment I can't think of anything I'd like better than to live here, at Crick's Farm. And I reckon my shoulders are broad enough to brave any gossip. But what about you, Rose, my love? How would you feel about it?' He looked at her anxiously.

Rose smiled at him. 'I don't care what people say about us. We know we're not doing anything to be ashamed of. And if people only knew what Michael was like ...'

'They will! Make no mistake about that!' Emma said firmly. 'If the village folk don't hear it from me, they will from Grace or Babs – if they haven't already. I think you'll find you have more sympathy than condemnation from Stavely village, my girl. After all, this is where you were born and grew up. Everyone knows you. Everyone knows what you're like.' She paused and then nodded. 'And I reckon they'll respect you more for staying and being open about what you're doing than if you was to run away as if you were ashamed. Specially when they know you've both got our blessing.'

'Your mother's quite right, Rose,' Chad said. 'As she usually is,' he added with half a smile in his wife's direction.

Rose gave a deep, contented sigh. 'Then yes, please, I'd like to come home to Crick's Farm with Dan.'

Chad got to his feet. 'Nevertheless, I think we should sleep on it. We shouldn't make hasty decisions. Things might look different in the morning. Come along, Emma, it's time to ascend to the marital chamber.'

After they had gone Dan said, 'It pains me that we can't be properly married, Rose. It seems that even now Mike's got the last laugh.'

She touched his cheek. 'It doesn't matter, Dan. We know how we feel. We know we'll always be together.' She got up from her chair and went to her father's book case and came back with the prayer book. She put it down on the table and said shyly, 'But I would like us to say the marriage service together. Just the two of us. Then we'll know we've made the promises to each other, and before God, even if we can't do it in church. Can we do that, Dan? Will you say it with me?'

He took the prayer book and opened it. Then he drew her down beside him and put his arm round her.

'I will, Rose. Oh, I will.'